PRAISE FOR *A TIME FC*

"*A Time for Violence* has something for everyone. Whether you like your violence straight up or prefer savoring more complex notes and a lingering finish, you'll find it here."

— **Charles J. Rzepka,** author of *Being Cool : The Work of Elmore Leonard*

"The stories in *A Time for Violence* pack quite a punch. Ranging from tales reminiscent of the classic pulp variety to those with a more contemporary slant, they feature both good and bad guys for whom violence plays a determining role in their lives, sometimes habitually, sometimes unexpectedly. Who knew violence could be portrayed in such a variety of interesting ways."

— **David Geherin,** author of *Carl Hiaasen: Sunshine State Satirist*

"Let yourself be seduced by great, well-known authors and lesser-known – but in the story they tell us just as big – let yourself be carried away and enchanted, because the stories of these authors are very different, some, wonderful laconic, let a shiver of rapture, delight and horror run across your back, the others let you have respite before they hit us with full force..."

— **Caroline Feith,** author of *Tod eines Managers*

A TIME FOR VIOLENCE

VIOLENCE

STORIES WITH AN EDGE

An Anthology
Edited by Andy Rausch & Chris Roy

Featuring

Richard Chizmar
Richard Godwin
Mark Slade
Andy Rausch
Paul D. Brazill
Bev Vincent
C. Courtney Joyner
Stewart O'Nan
Billy Chizmar
John A. Russo
David C. Hayes
Elka Ray
Tom Vater

Tyson Blue
Wrath James White
Joe R. Lansdale
Max Allan Collins
Andrew Nette
T. Fox Dunham
Isobel Blackthorn
James H. Longmore
Tony Knighton
Stephen Spignesi
Peter Leonard
Richard Christian Matheson
Chris Roy

Close To The Bone
An imprint of Gritfiction Ltd

Edited by Andy Rausch and Chris Roy
Cover Illustration and Interior Design by Craig Douglas

First Printing, 2019

CONTENTS

ACKNOWLEDGEMENTS

Blood Brothers by Richard Chizmar first appeared as an original chapbook of the same title, Subterranean Press, 1997. Reprinted by permission of the author.

Scab by Wrath James White first appeared in *Whispers in the Night: Dark Dreams III*, Dafina, 2007. Reprinted by permission of the author.

Santa at the Cafe by Joe R. Lansdale first appeared in *Bleeding Shadows*, Subterranean Press, 2013. Reprinted by permission of the author.

Summer of '77 by Stewart O'Nan first appeared as *Endless Summer* in *The Year's Best Fantasy and Horror: Fourteenth Annual Collection*, edited by Terri Windling and Ellen Datlow, St. Martin's Griffin, 2001.

Wire by C. Courtney Joyner first appeared in *The Traditional West*, Western Fictioneers Press, 2011.

Guest Service: A Quarry Story by Max Allan Collins first appeared in *Murder Is My Business*, edited by Max Allan Collins and Mickey Spillane, Dutton Adult, 1994.

Channel 666 by John A. Russo first appeared in *Scream Queens Illustrated*, Spring 1999.

The Edge by Richard Christian Matheson first appeared in *Dystopia*, Crossroad Press, 2011.

All other stories appear here for the first time by permission of their authors, copyright 2018.

INTRODUCTION

by Andy Rausch

In the 1980s, there were suddenly short story anthologies — mostly horror — appearing on supermarket book racks on a weekly basis. This was largely the result of the paperback horror boom, which was mostly a result of author Stephen King's new and unprecedented popularity. Suddenly, anthologies like the *Night Visions* series (edited by multiple editors, including George R.R. Martin) and Charles L. Grant's *Shadows* series were all the rage, and short stories were in demand like never before. What a time it was to be a reader of short fiction! Some of these stories were predictably pedestrian, but others were fantastic, even transcendent.

Throughout the years, countless wordsmiths have produced their own story collections, but the book you are now holding is a love letter to the great anthologies of yesteryear, assembling stories by a variety of talents, packaged neatly and often connected by a singular theme.

What is the theme for this collection, you ask? Its title is *A Time for Violence*, so it should be obvious; the theme is violence, plain and simple. But why, you ask? Are we encouraging or promoting violence? Are we rejoicing and revelling in the physical harm of others? No, of course not. So, why violence then? Well, *A Time for Violence* was a cool title, which was where it began, but beyond that, it's a simple theme that inspires edgy, transgressive material. And at the end of the day, that was the real theme — edginess and transgression.

So, what genre are these stories? Does this book have a chosen genre? Yes and no. Co-editor Chris Roy and I told the writers in this hand-picked line-up we were seeking horror and crime. But what ended up within this book's covers is something that transcends that description.

For instance, there are crime stories of all shapes and sizes, some horrific, some not. Perhaps the gulf between Chris Roy's story *Waste Management* and my own story, *The Sweetest Ass in the Ozarks*, best illustrates the diversity of approach you will find in this book. They are as different as apples and oranges, or maybe, if we're being honest, the difference between apples and sledgehammers. They are not even remotely the same thing. My story is a dark, but comparatively light, tale of vengeance and empowerment. After reading it you might be tempted to shrug and say, "That story didn't feel all that light to me." But I assure you it will once you compare it to Chris' story, which is as gritty and disturbing as a story can be — material so dark and twisted it would make Jeffrey Dahmer's jaw drop. (His mouth might be filled with human flesh at the time, but his jaw would still drop.)

And to further illustrate the variety of stories that appear here, C. Courtney Joyner's *Wire* is a Western, but still a crime story nonetheless. (A damned good one, too!) What's more, there are numerous stories about hitmen, but they are all unique and different takes on what would appear on the surface to be similar. For instance, David C. Hayes' *Epiphany in the Third* and Max Allan Collins' *Guest Service: A Quarry Story* are as different as Barack Obama and Donald Trump.

But if you're looking for real diversity, you'd do well to check out Stephen Spignesi's superbly-written, powerfully dark tale *James and Sallie*. This story is neither crime nor horror by standard definitions, and yet it's the worst of both. This is as heart-wrenching a story as there ever was. This is no celebration of violence, but quite the opposite — a sickeningly realistic, yet deeply moving examination of the most wicked, vile acts humans are capable of committing.

There are cop stories here, too, which are equally as diverse. Tyson Blue's *Gunfight at the Golden Gator* and Peter Leonard's one-act story *Manner of Death: Homicide* are nothing alike. *Gunfight* is loud and boisterous, featuring a, well, gunfight, hence the title, and *Manner* is a somber look at a murder investigation.

There are stories of all types in this volume. Some are graphic in their depictions of violence, whereas in others the violence is merely implied. The writing styles of these writers are as diverse as their approaches, but still there is one unifying characteristic which binds them, and that is talent. Whether they have achieved the great heights of success some of the more well-known authors in this collection have, like John A. Russo, who co-wrote the film *Night of the Living Dead*, or Max Allan Collins, who wrote *The Road to Perdition*, or they are the up-and-comers, still obscure but making a name for themselves, each writer is supremely talented and well deserving of inclusion.

Everyone knows how discouraging it is to purchase an anthology comprised of three or four "name" authors and fifteen hacks, presumably recruited from behind laptops at the local Starbucks. But I assure you that is not the case here. *A Time for Violence: Short Stories with an Edge* is a collection of work by a plethora of masters, all brilliant, all ridiculously talented. Maybe you aren't familiar with all of them yet, but you soon will be. And for the introduction, feel free to thank us later.

BLOOD BROTHERS

by Richard Chizmar

Richard Chizmar is the editor and publisher of *Cemetery Dance* magazine. He is the author of the collections *A Long December* and *The Long Way Home*, as well as the bestselling novella *Gwendy's Button Box*, which he cowrote with Stephen King.

ONE

I GRABBED THE PHONE ON THE SECOND RING AND CLEARED MY throat, but before I could wake up my mouth enough to speak, there came a man's voice: *"Hank?"*

"Uh, huh."

"It's me…Bill."

The words hit me like a punch to the gut. I jerked upright in the bed, head dizzy, feet kicking at a tangle of blankets.

"Jesus, Billy, I didn't recog — "

"I know, I know…it's been a long time."

We both knew the harsh truth of that simple statement and we let the next thirty seconds pass in silence. Finally, I took a deep breath and said, "So I guess you're out, huh? They let you out early."

I listened as he took a deep breath of his own. Then another. When he finally spoke, he sounded scared: *"Hank, listen…I'm in some trouble. I need you to — "*

"Jesus Christ, Billy! You busted out, didn't you? You fucking-a busted out!"

My voice was louder now, almost hysterical, and Sarah lifted her head from the pillow and mumbled, "What's wrong? Who is it, honey?"

I moved the phone away from my face and whispered, "It's no one, sweetheart. Go back to sleep. I'll tell you in the morning."

She sighed in the darkness and rested her head back on the pillow.

"Hey, you still there? Dammit, Hank, don't hang up!"

"Yeah, yeah, I'm here," I said.

"I really need your help, big brother. You know I never woulda called if …"

"Where are you?"

"Close…real close."

"Jesus."

"Can you come?"

"Jesus, Billy. What am I gonna tell Sarah?"

"Tell her it's work. Tell her it's an old friend. Hell, I don't know, tell her whatever you have to."

"Where?"

"The old wooden bridge at Hanson Creek."

"When?"

"As soon as you can get there."

I looked at the glowing red numbers on the alarm clock -- 5:37.

"I can be there by six-fifteen."

The line went dead.

TWO

I SLIPPED THE PHONE BACK ONTO ITS CRADLE AND JUST SAT THERE for a couple of minutes, rubbing my temple with the palm of my hand. It was a habit I'd picked up from my father, and it was a good thing Sarah was still sleeping; she hated when I did it, said it made me look like a tired old man.

She was like that, always telling me to stay positive, to keep my chin up, not to let life beat me down so much. She was one in a million, that's for damn sure. A hundred smiles a day, and not one of them halfway or phony.

Sitting there in the darkness, thinking of her that way, I surprised myself and managed something that almost resembled a smile.

But the thought went away, and I closed my eyes, and it seemed like a very long time was passing, me just sitting there in the bed like a child afraid of the dark or the boogeyman hiding in the bottom of the closet. Suddenly — and after all this time — there I was thinking so many of the same old thoughts. Anger, frustration, guilt, fear — all of it rushing back at me in a tornado of red-hot emotion…

So I just sat there and hugged myself and felt miserable and lost and lonely and it seemed like a very long time, but when I opened my eyes and looked up at the clock, I saw that not even five minutes had passed.

I dressed quietly in the cold darkness. Back in the far corner of the bedroom. I didn't dare risk opening the dresser drawers and waking Sarah, so I slipped on a pair of wrinkled jeans and a long sleeve t-shirt from the dirty laundry hamper. The shirt smelled faintly of gasoline and sweat.

After checking on Sarah, I tiptoed down the hallway and poked my head into the girls' room for a quick peek, then went downstairs. I washed my face in the guest bathroom and did my business but didn't flush. For just a second, I thought about coffee — something to help clear my head — but decided against it. Too much hassle. Not enough time.

After several minutes of breathless searching, I found the car keys on the kitchen counter. I slipped on a jacket and headed for the garage.

Upstairs, in the bedroom, Sarah rolled over and began lightly snoring. The alarm clock read 5:49.

THREE

H E SAVED MY LIFE ONCE. A LONG TIME AGO, BACK WHEN WE were kids.

It was a hot July afternoon — ninety - six in the shade and not a breeze in sight. It happened no more than thirty yards downstream from the old Hanson Bridge, just past the cluster of big weeping willow trees. One minute I was splashing and laughing and fooling around, and the next I was clawing at the muddy creek bottom six, seven feet below the surface. It was the mother of all stomach cramps; the kind your parents always warned you about but you never really believe existed. Hell, when you're a kid, the old "stomach cramp warning" falls into the same dubious category as "never fool around with a rusty nail" and "don't play outside in the rain." To adults, these matters make perfect sense, but to a kid…well, you know what I'm talking about.

Anyway, by the time Billy pulled me to the surface and dragged me ashore, my ears had started to ring something awful; and the hell with seeing stars, I was seeing entire solar systems. So, Billy put me over his shoulder and carried me a half-mile into town, and Dad had to leave the plant three hours early on a Monday just to pick me up at the Emergency Room.

I survived the day, more embarrassed than anything, and Billy was a reluctant hero, not only in our family, but all throughout the neighborhood. Old widow Fletcher across the street even baked a chocolate cake to celebrate the occasion with Billy's name written out in bright pink icing.

I was thirteen, Billy twelve, when all this happened.

Like I said, it was a long time ago, but the whole thing makes for a pretty good story, and I've told it at least a hundred times. In fact, it's the one thing I always tell people when the inevitable moment finally arrives and they say, "Jeez, Hank, I didn't know you had a brother."

I hear those words and I just smile and shrug my shoulders as if to say, "Oh, well, sorry I never mentioned it," and then I slip right into the story.

This usually happens at social gatherings — holiday work parties, neighborhood cook-outs, that sort of thing. Someone from the old neighborhood shows up and mentions Billy's name, asks what he's been up to, and another person overhears the conversation.

And then the questions:

"What's your brother's name? Does he live around here? What's he do for a living? Why haven't you mentioned him before, Hank?"

Happens two, three times a year. And when it does I just grin my stupid grin and tell the drowning story one more time...and then I make my escape before they can ask any more questions. "Excuse me, folks, I have to use the restroom." Or "Hey, isn't that Fred Matthews over there by the pool? Fred, wait up. I've been meaning to ask you..."

It works every time.

***

Billy was just a year behind me, but you never would've guessed it growing up. He looked much younger; two, maybe even three years. He was short for his age and thin. Real thin. Dad always used to say — and at the time we could never figure out just *what the hell* he was talking about — that Billy looked like a boy made out of wire. Little guy is tough as wire, he'd always say, and give Billy a proud smile and a punch on the shoulder.

Despite his physical size, Billy was fast and strong and agile and much more athletic than me. His total lack of fear and dogged determination made him a star; my lack of coordination made me a second-stringer. But we both had fun, and we stuck together for the three years we shared in high school. We played all the same sports — football in the fall, basketball in the winter, baseball in the spring.

Baseball. Now, that's where Billy really shined. All-County second-base as a sophomore. All-County and All-State as a junior, and again as a senior.

A true-blue hometown hero by the time he was old enough to drive a car.

After graduation, I stayed in town and took business classes over at the junior college. Summer before sophomore year, I found an apartment a few miles away from home. Got a part-time job at a local video store. Played a little softball on Thursday nights, some intramural flag football on the weekends. Stopped by and saw the folks two, three times a week. Ran around with a few girlfriends, but nothing serious or lasting. For me, not too much had changed.

Then, Billy graduated and went upstate to college on a baseball scholarship and *everything* seemed to change.

First, there was the suspension. Billy and three other teammates got caught cheating on a mid-term English exam and were placed on academic probation and suspended from the team.

Then, a few months later, in the spring, he was arrested at a local rock concert for possession of marijuana. It shouldn't have been that big a deal, but at the time, he'd been carrying enough weed to warrant a charge for Intent to Distribute. Then, at the court trial, we discovered that this was his second offense and the university kindly asked him to clear out his dorm room and leave campus immediately. His scholarship was revoked.

He was lucky enough to receive a suspended sentence from the judge, but instead of moving back home and finding a job — which is what Mom and Dad hoped he would do — Billy decided to stay close to campus and continue working at a local restaurant. He claimed he wanted to make amends with his baseball coach and try to re-enrol after the next semester if the university would allow him. So, he moved in with some friends and for a time it appeared as though he'd cleaned up his act. He kept out of trouble — at least as far as we (and his probation officer) could tell — and he stopped by on a regular basis to see Mom and Dad, and he even came by my place once or twice a month (although usually only when he needed to borrow a couple of bucks).

So, anyway, things went well for a while…

Until the rainy Sunday midnight the police called and told Mom and Dad they needed to come down to Fallston General right away. Billy had been driven to the Emergency Room by one of his roommates; just an hour earlier, he'd been dumped in the street in front of his apartment — a bloody mess. Both hands broken. A couple of ribs. Nose mashed. Left ear shredded. He was lucky to be alive.

We found out the whole story then: it seemed that my baby brother had a problem with gambling. The main problem being that he wasn't very good at it. He owed some very dangerous people some very significant amounts of money. The beating had been a friendly reminder that his last instalment payment had been twelve hours late.

Billy came home from the hospital ten days later. Moved into his old room at home. This time, Mom and Dad got their way without much of an argument. A month or so later, when Billy was feeling up to it, Dad got him a job counting boxes over at the plant. Soon after, he started dating Cindy Lester, a girl from the other side of town. A very sweet girl. And pretty, too. She was just a senior over at the high school — barely eighteen years old — but she seemed to be good for Billy. She wanted to be a lawyer one day, and she spent most of her weeknights studying at the library, her weekends at the movies or the shopping mall with Billy.

One evening, sometime late October, the leaves just beginning to change their colors, Billy stopped by my apartment with a pepperoni pizza and a six-pack of Coors. We popped in an old Clint Eastwood movie and stayed up most of the night talking and laughing. There was no mention of gambling or drugs or Emergency Room visits. Instead, Billy talked about settling down, making a future with Cindy. He talked about finding a better job, maybe taking some classes over at the junior college. Accounting and business courses, just like his big brother. Jesus, it was like a dream come true. I could hardly wait until morning to call the folks and tell them all about it.

To this very day, I can remember saying my prayers that night, thanking God for giving my baby brother another chance.

That night was more than eight years ago.

I haven't seen him since.

FOUR

I DROVE SLOWLY ACROSS THE NARROW WOODEN BRIDGE. CLICKED on my high-beams.

There were no other cars in sight.

Just empty road. Dense forest. And a cold December wind.

My foot tapped the brake pedal, and I thought to myself: *Hank Foster, you've lost your mind. This is crazy. Absolutely crazy.*

I reached the far side of the bridge and pulled over to the dirt shoulder. I sat there shivering for a long couple of minutes. Looking up at the rear-view mirror. Staring out at the frozen darkness.

I turned the heater up a notch.

Turned off the headlights.

It was 6:17.

***

I looked at my watch for the tenth time. 6:21.

Jesus, this really *was* crazy. Waiting in the middle of nowhere for God knows what to happen. Hell, it was more than crazy; it was dangerous. Billy had sounded scared on the phone, maybe even desperate, and he'd said he was in trouble. Those had been his exact words: *I'm in some trouble.* Even after all this time, I knew the kind of trouble my brother was capable of. So, what in the hell was I doing out here? I had Sarah and the girls to think about now, a business to consider...

Or maybe, just maybe, he had changed. Maybe he had left the old Billy behind those iron bars and a better man had emerged. Maybe he had actually learned a thing or two —

— yeah, and maybe Elvis was still alive and catching rays down on some Mexican beach and the Cubs were gonna win the goddamn World Series.

Nice to imagine, one and all, but not real likely, huh?

I was starting to sweat now. *Really* sweat. I felt it on my neck. My face. My hands. And I felt it snaking down from my armpits, dribbling across my ribcage. Sticky. Cold and hot at the same time.

I leaned down and turned off the heat. Cracked the window. Inhaled long and deep. The sharp sting of fresh air caught me by surprise, made me dizzy for a moment, and I realized right then and there what was going on: I was scared. Probably more scared than I had ever been in my entire life.

With the window open, I could hear the wind rattling the trees and the creek moving swiftly in the darkness behind me. In the dry months of summer, Hanson Creek was slow-moving and relatively shallow, maybe eight feet at its deepest point. But in the winter, with all the snow run-off, the creek turned fast and mean and unforgiving. Sometimes, after a storm, the water rose so quickly, the police were forced to close down the bridge and detour traffic up north to Route 24. One winter, years ago, it stayed closed for the entire month of January.

The old house where we grew up — where Mom and Dad still live today — was just a short distance north from here. No more than a five minute drive. Back when we were kids, Billy and I walked down here most every morning during the summer. All the neighborhood kids came here. We brought bag lunches and bottles of pop and hid them in the bushes so no one would steal them. Then we swam all day long and held diving contests down at the rope swing. When the weather was too cool to swim, we played war in the woods and built forts made out of rocks and mud and tree branches. Other times, we fished for catfish and carp and the occasional bass or yellow perch. On *real* lucky days, when it rained hard enough to wear away the soil, we searched for (and usually found) Indian arrowheads wedged in with the tree roots that grew along the creek's steep banks. We called those rainy days *treasure hunts*, and took turns acting as "expedition leader." The creek was a pretty wonderful place.

I thought about all this and wondered if that was the reason Billy had chosen the bridge as a meeting place. Was he feeling sentimental? A little nostalgic, maybe? Probably not; as usual, I was probably giving the bastard too much credit.

***

Like I told you, I haven't seen him in more than eight years. Not since that long ago autumn night we spent together talking at my apartment. One week later, Billy just up and disappeared. No note, no message…nothing. Just an empty closet, a missing suitcase, and eighty dollars gone from Mom's purse.

And to make matters worse, Mr. Lester called the house later that evening and told us that Cindy hadn't been to school that day — was she with Billy by any chance?

The next morning, Dad called Billy's probation officer. He wasn't much help. He told us to sit tight, that maybe Billy would come to his senses. Other than that, there was really nothing we could do but wait.

And so for two weeks, we waited and heard nothing.

Then, on a Sunday afternoon, Mom and Dad sitting out on the front porch reading the newspaper, still dressed in their church clothes, there was a phone call: *I know I know it was a stupid thing to do but you see Cindy's pregnant and scared to death of her father he's a mean sonofabitch real mean and California is the place to be these days heck we already have jobs and a place to stay and there's lots of great people out here we've got some really nice friends already c'mon please don't cry Mom please don't yell Dad we're doing just fine really we are we're so much in love and we're doing just fine...*

Six months later, Cindy Lester came home. Alone. While walking back from work one night, she had been raped and beaten in a Los Angeles alley. She'd spent three days in the hospital with severe cuts and bruises. She'd lost her baby during the first night. Cindy told us that she'd begged him over and over again, but Billy had refused to come home with her. So, she'd left him.

Over the next three years, there were exactly seven more phone calls (two begging for money) and three short handwritten letters. The envelopes were postmarked from California, Arizona, and Oregon.

Then, early in the fourth year, the police called. Billy had been arrested in California for drug trafficking. This time, the heavy stuff: cocaine and heroin. Dad hired Billy a decent lawyer, and both he and Mom flew out to the trial and watched as the judge gave Billy seven years in the state penitentiary.

I never went to see him. Not even once. Not at the trial. Not when Mom and Dad went for their twice-a-year visits. And not when Billy sent the letter asking me to come. I just couldn't do it.

I didn't hate him the way Mom and Dad thought I did. Jesus, he was still my baby brother. But he was locked up back there where he belonged, and I was right here where I belonged. We each had our own lives to live.

So, no, I didn't hate him. But I couldn't forgive him, either. Not for what he had done to this family — the heartbreak of two wonderful, loving parents; the complete waste of their hard-earned retirement savings; the shame and embarrassment he brought to all of us —

— bare knuckles rapped against the windshield, and I jumped so hard I hit my head. I also screamed.

I could hear laughing from outside the car, faint in the howling wind, but clear enough to instantly recognize.

It was him, all right.

My baby brother.
Suddenly, a face bent down into view. Smiled.
And I couldn't help it — I smiled right back.

FIVE

E HUGGED FOR A LONG TIME. CAR DOOR OPEN, ENGINE still running. Both of us standing outside in the cold and the wind. Neither of us saying a word.

We hugged until I could no longer stand the smell of him.

Then, we stopped and sort of stood back and looked at each other.

"Jesus, Billy, I can't believe it," I said.

"I know, I know." He shook his head and smiled. "Neither can I."

"Now, talk to me. What's this all about? What kind of trouble are — "

He held up his hand. "In a minute, okay? Lemme just look at you a while longer."

For the next couple of minutes, we stood there facing each other, shivering in the cold. The Foster boys, together once again.

He was heavier than the last time I'd seen him; maybe fifteen, twenty pounds. And he was shaved bald, a faint shadow of dark stubble showing through. Other than that, he was still the Billy I remembered. Bright blue eyes. Big stupid smile. That rosy-cheeked baby face of his.

"Hey, you like my hair," he asked, reading my thoughts.

"Yeah," I said, "who's your barber?"

"Big black sonofabitch from Texas. Doing life for first-degree murder. Helluva nice guy, though."

He waited for my response and when I didn't say anything, he laughed. This time, it sounded harsh and a little mean.

"How's the folks?" he asked.

I shrugged my shoulders. "You know, pretty much the same. They're doing okay."

"And Sarah and the girls?"

My heart skipped a beat. An invisible hand reached up from the ground and squeezed my balls.

"Mom and Dad told me all about 'em. Sent me pictures in the mail," he said.

I opened my mouth, but couldn't speak. Couldn't breathe.

"They're twins, right? Let's see…four years old…Kacy and Katie, if I remember right."

I sucked in a deep breath. Let it out.

"I bet you didn't know I carry their picture around in my wallet. The one where they're sitting on the swings in those fancy little blue dresses — "

"Five," I said, finally finding my voice.

"Huh?"

"The girls," I said. "They just turned five. Back in October."

"Halloween babies, huh? That's kinda neat. Hey, remember how much fun we used to have trick-or-treatin'? 'Member that time we spent the night out back the old Myer's House? Camped out in Dad's old tent. Man, that was a blast."

I nodded my head. I remembered everything. The costumes we used to make. The scary movies we used to watch, huddled together on the sofa, sharing a glass of soda and a bowl of Mom's buttered popcorn. All the creepy stories we used to tell each other before bedtime.

Suddenly, I felt sorry for him — standing there in his tattered old clothes, that dumb smile refusing to leave his face, smelling for all the world like a dumpster full of food gone to spoil. I suddenly felt very sorry for him and very guilty for me.

"I didn't break out, you know," he said. "They released me two weeks ago. Early parole."

"Jesus, Billy. That's great news."

"I spent a week back in L.A. seeing some friends. Then I hitched a ride back here. Made it all the way to the state line. I walked in from there."

"I still can't goddamn believe it. Wait until Mom and Dad see you."

"That's one of the things I need to talk to you about, Hank. Why don't we take a walk and talk for a while, okay?"

"Sure, Billy," I said. "Let's do that."

So, that's exactly what we did.

SIX

I STILL MISS HIM.
It's been four months now since that morning at the bridge - and not a word.

I read the newspaper every day. Watch the news every night.

And still there's been nothing.

I think about him all the time now. Much more often than I ever used to. Once or twice a week, I take a drive down to the old bridge. I stand outside the car and watch the creek rushing by, and I think back to the time when we were kids. Back to a time when things were simple and happy.

God, I miss him.

***

He wanted money. Plain and simple, as always.

First, he tried to lie to me. Said it was for his new "family." Said he had gotten married two days after he got out of prison. Needed my help getting back on his feet.

But I didn't fall for it.

So, then he told me the truth. Or something close to it, anyway. There was this guy, an old friend from up around San Francisco. And Billy owed him some big bucks for an old drug deal gone bad. Right around thirty grand. If he didn't come up with the cash, this old friend was gonna track him down and slit his throat.

So, how about a little help, big brother?

Sorry, I told him. No can do. I'd like to help out, but I've got a family now. A mortgage. My own business barely keeping its head above water. Really sorry. Can't help you.

So, then he started crying – and begging me.

And when that didn't work, he got pissed off.

His eyes went cold and distant; his voice got louder.

He said: "Okay that's fine. I'll just hit up the old man and the old lady. They'll help me out. Damn right they will. And if they don't have enough cash, well, there are always other ways I can *persuade* you to help me, big brother. Yes, sir, I can be mighty *persuasive* when I put my mind to it…

"Let's start by talking about that store of yours, Hank — you're paid up on all your insurance, aren't you? I mean, you got fire coverage and all that stuff, right? Jeez, I'd hate to see something bad happen when you're just starting out. And how about Sarah? She still working over at that bank Mom and Dad told me about? That's a pretty dangerous job, ain't it? Working with all that money. Especially for a woman. And, oh yeah, by the way, what school do the girls go to? Evansville? Or are you busing them over to that private school, what's it called again?"

I stabbed him then.

We were standing near the middle of the bridge. Leaning against the thick wooden railing, looking down at the water.

And when he said those things, I took out the steak knife — which had been sitting on the kitchen counter right next to where I'd found my car keys — I took it out from my coat pocket, and I held it in both of my hands and brought it down hard in the back of his neck.

He cried out once — not very loud — and dropped to his knees.

And then there was only the flash of the blade as I stabbed him over and over again…

***

Last night, it finally happened. Sarah confronted me.

We were alone in the house. The girls were spending the night at their grandparents' — they do this once a month and absolutely love it.

After dinner, she took me downstairs to the den and closed the door. Sat me down on the sofa and stood right in front of me. She told me I looked a mess. I wasn't sleeping, wasn't eating. Either I tell her right now what was going on or she was leaving.

She was serious, too. I think she was convinced I was having an affair.

So, I told her.

Everything – starting with the phone call and ending with me dumping Billy's body into the creek.

When I was finished, she ran from the room crying. She made it upstairs to the bathroom, where she dropped to her knees in front of the toilet and got sick. When she was done, she asked me very calmly to go back downstairs and leave her alone for a while. I agreed. What else could I do?

An hour or so later, she came down and found me out in the backyard looking up at the moon and the stars. She ran to me and hugged me so tight I could barely breathe and then she started crying again. We hugged for a long time, until the tears finally stopped, and then she held my face in her hands and told me that she understood how difficult it had been for me, how horrible it must have felt, but that it was all over now and that I had done the right thing. No matter what, that was the important thing to remember, she kept saying — I had done the right thing.

Then we were hugging again and both of us were crying.

When we finally went inside, we called the girls and took turns saying goodnight. Then we went to bed and made love until we both fell asleep.

Later that night, the moon shining silver and bright through the bedroom window, Sarah woke from a nightmare, her skin glistening with sweat, her voice soft and frightened. She played with my hair and asked: "What if someone finds him, Hank? A fisherman? Some kids? What if someone finds him and recognizes him?"

I put a finger to her lips and *ssshed* her. Put my arms around her and held her close to me. I told her everything was going to be okay. No one would find him. And even if they did, they would never be able to identify him.

"Are you sure they won't recognize him?" she asked. "Are you sure?"

"Absolutely positive," I said, stroking her neck. "Not after all this time. Not after he's been in the water for this long."

And not after I cut up his face the way I did.

No one could recognize him after all that...not even his own brother.

GUNFIGHT AT THE GOLDEN GATOR

by *Tyson Blue*

Tyson Blue has written for numerous publications, including *The Twilight Zone, Castle Rock: The Official Stephen King Newsletter, Midnight Graffiti,* and *Cemetery Dance.* He is the author of the highly-regarded book *The Unseen King.* His short stories have appeared in numerous anthologies.

Author's Note: The events in this story take place before those in *Home Cookin',* which appears in the anthology *Rise of the Dead.* Although the time frame of that story was changed to 1968 to fit the parameters of that anthology, its original setting, like that of this one, is contemporary.

ROGER JAMES PILOTED THE LAREY COUNTY SHERIFF'S Department vehicle designated 1264 southeast on Highway 441, headed back into Shannon, the county seat, after a swing through the northwest part of the county. The clock on the radio read 3:10am. James' riding partner, Tim Foster, sat in the passenger seat, his right arm out the rolled-down passenger window as the car rolled through the warm, muggy July night. They were headed back to the Sheriff's Office after a routine patrol to grab a few winks before turning things over to the next shift at 8:00 a.m.

"I guess you heard about the latest from the Mullis brothers," James drawled.

Tim hadn't heard; he knew who the Mullis brothers were — everyone in Larey County law enforcement did. The Mullis brothers, Skeeter and Woodrow by name, were, like the *Dukes of Hazzard,* just good ole boys. But when it came to the "never meanin' no harm" part, they broke the mold. Rape, drugs, guns, prostitution — if there was a crooked dollar to be made at it, the Mullis boys were into it, along with their cadre of redneck thugs.

The southern part of the county was their kingdom, the way they saw it. They ruled the roost from the Golden Gator, a sun-faded yellow pole barn just north of the county line, which offered drinks and dancing every Friday and Saturday night, an often volatile combination that sent deputies and/or State Patrol officers down there to clean house.

The Gator had been there, under one name or another, in one form or another, since the 1920's, when the first wooden building had been thrown up on the south side of Alligator Creek, which had at that time been the county line. Legend had it that the Larey County sheriff at that time, anxious to have the club's revenue, had sent a couple of deputies to uproot the county line signs and set them up about 500 feet farther south down the road, putting the building in Larey County. A subsequent lawsuit had been decided in the sheriff's favor.

The Mullises were always there when trouble hit, speaking politely but with a sneering smirk plastered across their faces all the while. They had managed to always put a few people between themselves and a provable case, so that neither of them had ever darkened a jail cell door. Until last week, when Woodrow had been pulled over by Roger on 441 south for speeding, and had been caught with a sandwich bag full of cocaine in the passenger seat of his car.

He'd made bail — money wasn't a problem for the Mullis crew — but the case was a solid one, and Woodrow was looking at a nice stretch in prison. If, that was, there was anyone to testify against him.

"Seems ol' Woodrow done figured out that if I'm not around to testify against him in court, he'll go free," James explained. "So word is him an' ol' Skeeter's put a hit out on me."

"Well, *that* makes my heart go pit-a-pat, me sittin' here in the car with you," Tim said. "Any idea when this might happen?"

The car headed into Shannon proper, passing the Waffle House and a liquor store, then cruising past the Toyota dealership and starting the left turn into the traffic circle which ran around the Larey County Court House.

James said, "Naw, I..."

He broke off as the radio squawked to life.

"1264," said Lucius Cole, who was working the radio. "Got a call about a disturbance down at the Gator; caller says they tearin' the place up. Go ahead." 'Go ahead' sounded more like 'gyedd'.

James scooped the microphone in one beefy paw and thumbed the switch, "1264, we will respond."

He racked the mike and floored the accelerator. The police interceptor motor roared beneath the hood as the car zoomed completely around the courthouse and sped down the main drag, gathering speed as it went. Tim flicked on the lights and siren. In the middle of town, James turned the wheel sharp left, and the car skidded to follow 441 as it veered east, then slewed again as the road turned right to head south toward the county line.

There was hardly any traffic at this time of night, so James was able to open the car up. As the speed headed toward 90, the roof began to pop, so both deputies rolled up the windows.

"Is the shotgun loaded?" James asked.

"I'll see," Tim replied.

"Try not to blow the roof off," James chuckled. "Or shoot me."

Tim half-turned and pulled the gun down off the rack behind the front seat, making sure not to touch the trigger. He grabbed a shell from a box in the glove compartment and pushed it in. The magazine took two more before it was full. Tim checked to make sure the safety was on and placed it back in the rack.

The car left the city limits of Shannon and headed on into more open country, blasting over I-16 and continuing south. The car bounced lightly over bumpy places in the road. Even at speeds in excess of 120, the Gator was fifteen minutes or so away.

"Roger," Tim said. "you think this has anything to do with what we were talkin' about a few minutes ago?"

James mulled that over a moment.

"Naw," he finally said. "Prob'ly just another Friday night at the Gator."

He thought a moment more, then spoke again.

"Still, it wouldn't hurt to have some help."

He picked up and keyed the mike again.

"1264," he said.

"Gyedd," Lucius came back.

"We got any other units in the area can back us up on this call?"

"1263 is over near Treutlen County, I can send them down there."

"Let's just have 'em stand by for now. Anybody else?"

Lucius thought a moment.

"1265's on a call in Dexter right now," he said. "I can head them your way when they finish up."

"Sounds good," James said, racking the mike and putting both hands back on the wheel.

"When we get there, I'll take the shotgun and see if I can quiet the crowd down," James said. "You keep your sidearm ready just in case."

Tim loosened the strap that held his Colt Python in place. The Python, a .357 Magnum, was a big gun and, loaded as it was with hollow point rounds, could crack an engine block, and would definitely do some damage to a crowd of rednecks.

The car roared through an intersection, with a small store on one side and a house on the other. There was a concrete slab in front of the house, on which a man in a strappy T-shirt sat watching television set on a white steel table, nursing a can of beer. He glanced around as they went by, blue lights flashing, then turned back to whatever he was watching.

There was a crackle of static from the radio, then a new voice spoke.

"1264, this is GSP."

James keyed the mike and spoke to the Georgia State Patrol radio operator.

"GSP, gyedd."

"We been monitoring your traffic," the voice said, cool and authoritative. "We've got some cars down your way, wondering if you want some backup."

"It wouldn't hurt," James answered. "If nothing else, we might need the back seats to bring some folks back to the jail."

"10-4," GSP said. "I'll have them head over your way. GSP out."

"1264 out," James replied, and hung the mike up.

"Never hurts to have 'em on call," James said to Tim. He was nervous.

Tim did a quick mental inventory of his other equipment. There was a can of mace in its holster on the left-hand side of his utility belt, and the slap-jack in his right back pocket. The small, shot-filled leather cudgel could lay a man out cold with one blow if properly applied. He reached down and fingered the tonfa-style nightstick which lay on the seat beside him, the short handle projecting from its side angled toward Roger.

They were now about ten minutes away from the Gator. Tim turned to James.

"Should we wait for 1263 before we head in?"

James thought a minute, rubbing his jaw.

"Naw, let's check things out first, then see if we need to wait for anybody." Tim nodded and picked up his hat. He placed it on his head, making sure the strap was in the back, so no one could grab it and pull him off balance. The car topped a small hill, and they could see the Gator on their right across the bridge. James began slowing down as they crossed Alligator Creek and pulled into the parking lot.

By the light of the one security light on the utility pole in the dirt lot, the deputies could see a teeming mob of about thirty people milling around something that was happening in the middle of the group, about twenty feet from the door of the club. There were fists flying, but so far, no weapons could be seen.

James put the car in park and killed the siren. He left the lights on, and turned on the roof-mounted spotlights, which shed a harsh, glaring light over the scene, which both gave them a better look at what was going on and also dazzled anyone who turned to look at them. He reached behind him and grabbed the shotgun, flicking off the safety with his thumb as he went.

"Get out and get ready on your side," James muttered under his breath to Tim as he opened the door and stepped out. Holding the slide with one hand, he racked a round into the chamber with the distinctive double *clack* sound that could put a stop to a fight faster than anything either man had ever seen.

"All right, folks, break it up!" James shouted, cradling the weapon. At the same time, Tim stepped out on his side, sliding the Python from its holster.

Before either deputy could step around the open car doors to close on the crowd, the mob parted like the Red Sea to reveal Woodrow Mullis, laughing gleefully and cradling an AR-15 across his scrawny chest. His eyes glittered wildly — most likely a meth high, Tim thought.

"We-he-helllll," drawled Mullis, taking a step forward. "If it ain't my favorite deputy dawg," he laughed. "Thought you was gonna send me off to prison, did ya?"

James began to step out past the door to head toward Woodrow, but before he could, Woodrow swung the rifle around to point it at James and pulled the trigger.

"Well think again, motherfucker!" he exclaimed, although he was drowned out by the sound of his weapon. Most of his initial fusillade hit the car door, but one slug caught James in the ankle, and two more caught him in the shoulder and high up in the left side of his chest. Blood sprayed from the upper-body wounds and James staggered back, still holding the shotgun in his right hand.

Tim leaped back into the car as the burst started, grabbing James and dragging him back into the car, across the seat and beneath him to the passenger side, praying that Mullis had exhausted his first clip and that he had enough time to get the cruiser out of there before he opened up again.

Sliding himself into the driver's seat, Tim glanced over at James, who was writhing in pain. Blood flowed sluggishly from the two wounds in his chest — no arteries hit, thank goodness.

"You okay?" Tim asked, throwing the car into gear.

"No," growled James, wincing.

Tim threw the car into gear and backed up, both doors still open.

Light showed through holes in the driver's side door — James had been lucky. Tim grabbed the mike.

"This is 1264 at the Golden Gator," he said. "10-33, 10-32, 999, Deputy James has been shot!" This told radio operators that there was an emergency, that a gun was involved and that an officer was down, and that urgent help was needed.

"Shit fire!" Lucius said, then called out for all officers in the area to respond.

"Hold tight, 1264, they're coming."

"10-4," Tim replied. He turned to James.

"Can you put pressure on those wounds?" he asked.

James nodded weakly and pressed his right hand to the wound near his shoulder. Tim continued backing up toward the road. James glared over at him.

"Where are you going?" he gritted through clenched teeth.

"I'm gonna get out of range and wait for the others."

James gritted his teeth, then shook his head.

"No," he said flatly. "Larey County Deputies don't run."

Tim shook his head in disbelief.

"He's got a fuckin' machine gun!" Tim bleated. "We're not running, we're falling back to regroup and wait for reinforcements."

James just looked at him, then spoke again.

"Larey. County. Deputies. Don't. Run."

Down in the parking lot, Woodrow had slammed a new magazine into the AR. A second burst of shots took out the car's driver's side headlight and one spotlight.

"I don't fuckin' believe this," Tim said, throwing the car into drive and pressing the accelerator to the floor. Tim slumped as low in the seat as he could, and pulled James down as well. As the car roared straight at Woodrow, he continued to fire, his eyes blazing the glare of light. A bullet passed through the windshield between the two men and exited through the back window.

The crowd drew back as the car hit the low point in the parking lot, then bounced, leaving the ground just as the front end caught Woodrow at waist level and carried him along, the upper part of his body draped over the hood, his crazed eyes staring into Tim's from mere feet away.

Then the car hit the flimsy metal wall of the building, crashing into the interior of the club and severing Woodrow's body in two at the waist. The car came to a stop, and as Tim watched, the life went out of Woodrow's eyes, and his torso slid slowly off the hood and onto the club's dance floor, leaving a thin slick of blood that steamed on the hot metal. The barrel of the AR clattered on the floor.

Tim grabbed his Python in one hand and the shotgun in the other as he opened the door, which had slammed shut sometime during the journey across the parking lot and into the club. James reached out and grabbed his arm.

"Leave the shotgun," he said weakly. "I need something to defend myself."

Tim laid the gun down, and dropped a handful of shells next to his partner.

"Skeeter's probably around here somewhere," he said. "I gotta finish this. You okay here?"

"I'll be fine," James answered. "Just don't take long."

Tim got out of the car, gun at the ready, and walked around the front end of the car. It was dark in the club, with only the one spotlight giving any illumination, so Tim was spared a good look at what was left of Woodrow in shadows on the floor. The club was pretty much cleared of people after the car burst through the wall, and what few people were left were getting away.

Except, that was, for Skeeter Mullis, who suddenly strode into view from the back of the club near the stage, an AK-47 in his arms. He glared at Tim across the empty dance floor, his beady brown eyes drug-free and filled with a cold anger.

"You killed my brother," Skeeter said softly.

"He tried to kill me," Tim replied. "And my partner."

"That was business," Skeeter answered. "This is revenge."

He began to swagger slowly across the floor toward Tim, bringing the AK up. As he came, Tim squatted down, his eyes firmly fixed on Skeeter. He found what he was looking for and stood up, holstering his Python and gripping Woodrow's AR-15 in both hands. He stood squarely, the gun leveled on his opponent at waist level.

"Avenge away, asshole," said Tim. He fired a three-round burst at Skeeter, shattering a beer bottle on a nearby table as Skeeter broke and ran, retreating toward the bar near the back of the club. Reaching it, he vaulted the bar and then fired a quick, un-aimed burst from the AK, which missed Tim by several feet. As Tim advanced, Skeeter edged down the bar toward the left, where a small stage was set up for live bands to play. As Tim fired twice more, narrowly missing his target, Skeeter dodged behind the stage and headed for the wide load-out door, which bands used to bring their equipment in and out.

As Tim edged around the stage, his quarry went out the door and left the building. He looked left, then right, spotting Skeeter running down the back of the Gator toward the north end of the parking lot. If he got to a car, he could get away. As Tim headed toward him, Skeeter raised the rifle one-handed and fired a single shot. It spanged into the wall beside Tim, who returned fire with the AR-15.

Tim moved to follow Skeeter when a hand behind him grabbed the collar of his shirt and yanked him back.

"Hey, porker," snarled a burly man in a sleeveless plaid shirt, his bald head covered by a greasy MAGA cap. "What're you…?" which was all he had time to say before Tim's slapjack slammed into his temple. He hit him so hard that the stitching at the top of the jack let go and lead pellets sprayed out, clattering against the metal wall. As the MAGA cap fell to the ground, Tim turned and ran after Skeeter.

As Tim rounded the corner of the club, he swept the parking lot looking for Skeeter. He spotted him when another shot from the AK buzzed by his ear. Tim rounded the corner and headed toward Skeeter, lifting the AR to his shoulder to fire. There was a hollow click. Empty!

Tim looked down at the rifle for a moment and stepped into a slick patch of mud, lost his balance and fell to one knee, dropping the AR. He reached for it, looking down as he did so, and froze as he heard a metallic click. He looked up, and found himself staring at the barrel of a revolver pointed directly at him about three inches from the end of his nose. The tips of hollow point slugs filled all he could see of the cylinder. The finger on the trigger was turning white as pressure was applied. Without thinking, Tim reached forward and grabbed the gun, sticking his index finger in front of the hammer. He twisted sharply and wrenched the gun away from the man, and as he rose to his feet, he swung the gun around and slammed it into the would-be shooter's face. The man went down without a sound, his face already starting to swell. Tim freed the gun from his hand, picked up the AR and went after Skeeter.

A man ran up, wearing a dirty T-shirt with a paunchy Rebel soldier on it, carrying a Confederate Battle Flag and saying, 'If You Ain't From Georgia, You Ain't Shit'.

"Hey, pig, you just wait a minute."

Without breaking stride, Tim hit him square in the nose with the butt of the AR-15. His nose broke with a wet pop, and he spat of mouthful of teeth and blood before he clapped his hands over the mess, groaning inarticulately. Tim threw the useless rifle aside and ran after Skeeter, drawing the Python as he went.

Skeeter crossed the parking lot, heading toward Alligator Creek. He splashed into the water, holding the rifle at port arms to keep it from getting wet. The creek was waist-deep at its deepest, and as Tim reached the edge, he levelled the gun at Skeeter and stopped at the edge.

"Drop it, Skeeter," he commanded.

Skeeter stood there, defiantly. There was a booming grunt from the darkness behind him, but neither man paid any attention to it. For a quick moment, the two stared at each other. Then Skeeter swung the AK around to point at Tim, his mouth open wide and emitting a roar filled with mad cracker hatred.

Simultaneously, Tim fired the Python, getting off four shots as fast as he could pull the trigger. Bursts of fire a foot long shot out of the ribbed barrel, and all but one hit Skeeter Mullis in the head. The top of his skull flew off and skipped across the water of the creek like a stone. He stood there for a moment, staring at Tim from eyes which gradually lost their focus. Then, he slowly fell back into the creek, and just before he slipped beneath the surface, an alligator rose from the creek and clamped its huge jaws down on Mullis' shoulder. A second one grabbed the other shoulder, and he began to come apart between them as Tim turned his back and strode back up the bank toward the Gator and his car.

The sky was starting to lighten, and in the distance, Tim could hear the sounds of sirens approaching. Sometime during all of this, people had left the Gator in droves. Only one or two cars were left, a few people milling about. One, a young blond man in a ragged tank top, tattoos scribbled all over his arms, moved toward Tim. He raised the Python and pointed it at him, and the man immediately raised his hands, palms outward, and began back-peddling.

"No sir," he said meekly. "No sir."

Tim ignored him and stepped back into the club. He moved to the car. James was still slumped in the passenger seat, his shirt soaked in blood, but he was awake.

"You doin' okay?" Tim asked.

"I'll hold out 'til help gets here."

"Sounds like they're comin'," Tim said, climbing into the driver's seat to wait.

"Thirsty," Rogers said. He licked his dry lips. "Hungry, too, believe it or not."

Tim felt something pressing against his right hand on the car seat. He picked it up. It was a packet of cheese crackers with peanut butter sandwiched between them. He opened the package and took one out, holding it toward his partner.

"Wanna cracker?" he said.

GUNS, MIRRORS

by Richard Godwin

Richard Godwin has written more than 20 novels, including *Confessions of a Hitman, Apostle Rising,* and *Noir City.*

EVERYONE WANTS A PIECE OF THE FUCKING ACTION.
It never started as a stick up, but with the Wild West coming to Surrey in the UK.

The party began late afternoon and lasted until the evening. The drinking contest pulled in a big crowd, as Murphy Stubbs knew it would. He'd got barbecues set up across the field and ordered a thousand bottles of Wild Turkey, his favourite bourbon, all the way from Kentucky, a neat slice of Appalachia poured straight into the green belt of Surrey with its stockbrokers and tame women. Murphy would change all that. He had plans fetched from a childhood spent watching Westerns, John Wayne blasting his way through the bad guys while Murphy became so absorbed he never stirred as a small boy sitting mesmerised on the tattered sofa with its broken springs as he took it all in. That hot day, he'd got the locals round to watch the buffalos. The smell of charred meat and whisky hung in the summer air. Murphy watched as a man collapsed from too much booze, he shook his head, and put another chunk of buffalo meat on the barbecue he was attending to, a regular host with an unusual interest in livestock, whisky, rodeos and female riders, especially ones who knew how to ride a buffalo. Murphy was six foot two, well-built, and had platinum hair cropped close to his skull. It looked like ice as the sun caught it. He had dark eyebrows and heavy black stubble on his face that gave his skin the look of sandpaper. As he took in the scene, his expression was neutral. He had intense blue eyes and a face with regular features that some might have considered handsome, but there was a harshness there. He wore a pearl-white Jack Daniels shirt that he'd had made especially so the lettering looked like a cattle brand. He wore Wrangler jeans, and black cowboy boots. As he spoke, his face became suffused with an intent look.

"Nothing like a bit of buffalo and Wild Turkey," he said to a man in a denim Western-style shirt.

"Whatever you say, cowboy."

The man he spoke to was slightly shorter than him and wiry. He had the chiselled features of a film star but lacked the good looks of one,

and instead bore the expression of a man with too much hunger in his
veins. He took a burger out of Murphy's hand, and strolled away. Murphy
gazed after him, with a fleeting recognition, taking in his swagger and his
Levis that were covered with dust. He wore a cowboy hat, and he seemed
to Murphy another exile from the Virgin Land where his dreams lay
broken and his future awaiting resurrection. It seemed apt that a man like
this had come to his show, he was attracting actors from a Western, his
own movie in which he would star with his Colt 45s clenched tight in his
gnarled fists. They were his favourite gun, in the same way that the Smith
and Wesson Schofield was the favoured weapon of the other man. His
name was Lawrence Cavalry, and it was more than coincidence and less
than circumstance that he shared Murphy's obsession. Lawrence, or Larry
as he liked to be called, was a nut for all things Western, so much so he
made his four wives dress up as cowgirls on their honeymoons. He went
through them like a dose of salts and was now single, in search of the right
kind of gal, old-fashioned, obedient, and able to ride a horse bareback
while lassoing a bottle of bourbon and singing a Tammy Wynette song. In
the same way that Murphy loved the feel of a Colt 45 in his hand, Larry
loved the elegant design of the Schofield, and the fact that it was
redesigned for the cavalry. It had his name on it, he felt. He saw meaning
in things, as if they were intended for his own personal use. He would
often stare at the scroll pattern it bore, considering it a work of art. Neither
man knew each other, but they existed alongside one another in a few
weeks of a Surrey that saw burning temperatures and the bizarre events of
their Western movie unfold like a series of incongruous improbables.

As Larry walked away in search of cowgirls, Murphy shook his
head, poured a double shot of Wild Turkey into a glass tumbler and
knocked it back. Then he went to his office. It was air-conditioned and
looked out at the field in Surrey where he owned 1,000 buffalos. Murphy
had a few obsessions. In addition to buffalos, he wanted to bring America
to England, and he had a thing, as he called it, for female rodeos. As he
reached for a bottle of Wild Turkey, the phone rang. It was a neighbour
complaining about the racket and the buffalos on his land.

"This is fucking America, asshole, and don't you forget it," Murphy
said, hanging up and looking at the stars and stripes that decorated the
receiver.

He was hot and sweat had gathered in his armpits. He poured a
shot, knocked it back. He changed his clothes, putting on a pair of
Wrangler jeans, a Western shirt and cowboy hat, then his needlepoint
cowboy boots. He stared at the accumulated bills on his desk, all unpaid, all

demanding money that he didn't have. Murphy was in debt, serious debt, and he needed cash fast.

His financial problems resonated with the poverty of his childhood. The bills brought back memories of his childhood, of watching his father slaughter cattle. The abattoir smells were etched into his mind and formed his character at an early age. Murphy once saw his father screw a stable-hand. He stood behind a hay bale and saw the young woman raise her skirt as his father entered her, then he watched him butcher a cow. The two events became fused in his mind, the pleasure and the pain. Westerns were his escape.

He sat down, slung his cowboy boots up on his desk, his hands behind his head, his fingers locked together, and he thought about the farm in Kentucky where he grew up. He watched a reel of film that played out soundlessly in his head. It was a set of images of events he'd displaced from himself, and he watched them in silence. The first image was of a young woman in dust-covered denims saddling up a black steed, her buttocks clearly outlined in the faded jeans. Then there was the horse, its eyes as black as wet coals, its expression somehow savage, its gaze directed at the camera. Suddenly, the film is alive, these snapshots converted to graphic liquid. The woman mounts and turns her face to the camera, holds her gaze there before she whips the leather reins twice across the horse's neck. She is irresistibly beautiful, a classic timeless beauty set on celluloid now, a stitched up trauma settled by the movie. For it is Murphy's movie and he set the stitches on the past. He is the camera, the watcher of a sexual event he had no understanding of in its narrative present in the decadent bruise of his life. Murphy's eyes are the lens, his psyche a prism, his heart a lump of meat beating for her body, the one woman he desired. Beneath the kaleidoscope of his emotions, something rattles like tin, like a bullet loose in his skeleton reminding him of time.

The woman rides out of the barn, passing through the dust and tiny particles of hay and into the sunlight, and she is gone. Momentarily. The camera turns, swivels, focuses and zooms in on the mouth of the barn. The woman is there, walking towards the camera, a smile on her lips, a riding crop in her hand, her blouse undone, her breasts showing, but not the nipples. She continues to walk towards the camera and begins to strip.

There is another figure, an older man with huge shoulders and hands. He touches her, he does things to the rider that are part of Murphy's curious sexual education. It is never clear in the film whether the man knew Murphy was there, watching behind the hay. He enters the woman on the ground, his boiler suit thrown hastily down to his scarred ankles, his white buttocks rising and falling in a ghostly dance as the woman moans and runs her cherry red fingernails across his hard back. Her mouth looks obscene, a mockery of man, and the camera zooms in on it, a cavernous hole of female desire.

They get up and dress, like patients in a doctor's waiting room, and the man turns his back on her and walks outside into the hot day. He stands beneath an azure sky, surveying the land, the father of the tribe, the sun relentless in its heat. He walks to an old hand-operated water pump and stands there washing his hands and arms for several minutes, his face blank, as he stares at nothing or maybe the countryside, the water cool and gurgling, the pump rust-coloured. Then the entire blue landscape turns red in Murphy's movie, but it is always blue in his aching memory. Because of the sky, because of Rhonda and the things he saw in the barn. He likes it blue and hollow now, blue as indigo in his mind as he thinks of Kentucky. There is no one about on the farm. The camera zooms in on the water, erotic somehow, obscene. The man stops washing. The entire scene is a rural idyll, a piece of Kentucky beauty. But there were no idylls for Murphy growing up. There were no prairies, no matter how much Murphy wanted one. The man turns and looks at the camera. He scrapes his hand across his jaw, the sound of his bristles is like sandpaper. Then he is gone.

Murphy was fourteen years old when he watched his father mount the pretty young rodeo. Murphy had followed her home from school with a dying peony in his hand, and a bulge in his ill-fitting jeans that made the school girls titter. He never got to give her the flower and never picked another one.

In fact, to the mature Murphy Stubbs who sat staring at the wall seeing the movie, flowers were an obscenity, a pointless aesthetic that stank of moral hypocrisy. He was like a colour-blind man in a garden of roses able only to see the thorns. There were no petals in Murphy's world, no blossoms in his heart. He smelled no perfume but instead the odour of Wild Turkey and the heavily-charred meat he liked to pack into his mouth like gunpowder.

The movie of Rhonda is the map of his mind, the key to his heart. The need for the Wild West lodged inside him like a bullet. He purchased his movie with the brushed metal of a Colt 45 packed with hollow points. Murphy was as Southern as they come. That night, Murphy watched his mother peel potatoes, a tear in her blackened eye, blood dripping onto the peelings from her cracked lip. He watched his father snicker.

He began his journey across the states, in bars and fights, acquiring the muscle to be the man called Murphy Stubbs, giving more scars than he acquired. He began his trek to Surrey, landing in the UK years later with a good sense of people and an ambition to bring America there. And all the time, he hungered for his celluloid star. He searched for her in every whorehouse and bar in America.

He sometimes said her name, pushing out his lips as if he wanted to kiss it, 'Rhonda,' he'd say sometimes alone in his office, or at night when he barked his knuckles on a man's teeth in a dream and woke tasting blood, his hand reaching for the bottle of Wild Turkey that stood by his bed, like a nocturnal watchman, his dark addiction's liquid gold. Murphy thought he had his hand on the temperature gauge, wheeling up the dial to the Wild West, to the temperature of sexual delirium, bringing old Kentucky home.

Larry had his own ideas, he was living in a flea pit of a bedsit, one bedroom of peeling paint and damp. It didn't sit well with his ideas of being a Western star. But he had his guns. He needed money fast if he was going to do it, make it as a celluloid gunfighter. Both men shared the past, and it was a past of ruined promise, less an idyll than a dereliction. It had driven them there, all the way to Surrey with their wild obsessions. Two men for whom Westerns were the only way out of a town called degradation.

Larry spread his legs wide and stood before the mirror on the chipped wardrobe, a Schofield in each hand. And he recalled being beaten by his daddy in Kentucky. He imagined firing at bad guys. Larry's emerald green eyes were like two pinpoints of fury as he smelled cash rising from the handles of his guns. He couldn't afford this room that he hated. But he would find a way to get the dough. Larry always found a way, he told himself. He changed his shirt, his back to the mirror that reflected the hard scars that ran across his pale skin like angry red welts.

It was getting hotter, the sky looked like polished lapis through the dirty window that stared out at the vacant street. And it all seemed to be part of a movie set right then to the two men who were both lost in Westerns, the heat and the soaring temperatures, there for their raid on Western glories, the sky bearing a Southern look, and Surrey ready for the action. Larry stepped out into the heat as Murphy fingered the barrel of his Colt 45, the smell of cordite rising from the gun as he got ready for the action. It was a smell he hungered for like a woman's perfume, and as he inhaled its implicit violence, he knew what he would do to get the money for the movie in which he was the leading star, an administrator of old-style justice in a corrupt world.

They had planned the heist for months, those two gunslingers lost in their private delusions. And while the reasons for their Western psychoses lay in their scarred and tattered childhoods, they felt high that day of adventure. The sky seemed made of polished blue glass to Murphy as he loaded his Colt 45s with bullets. To Larry, it was all a cartoon, from the people in the street to the men he might have to shoot in order to make the Wild West happen right there in Surrey. That was how he thought of it, the reality of the robbery as abstract as a bruise on a statue's shoulder. Curiously, both men mouthed the same words as they left their derelict lodgings, 'No competition.'

They made their way there on foot, their weapons concealed under long and baggy shirts, their thoughts on the money. They hid their watchful eyes beneath the brims of their cowboy hats, the necessary accompaniment to an act fetched straight from their movie world, the sartorial means of identifying who they were and what they were there to do, their shared psychotic uniform. Murphy could hear horses as he entered the Shell station at one p.m., he could smell the odours of a barn a long time ago, and he could feel the hard scars on his shoulders rubbing against the seam of his sweat-stained shirt. Larry heard hooves thundering across prairies as he walked through the automated door and entered the chilled atmosphere of the air-conditioned station he had had his eyes on for weeks as he collected debt and desperation in equal quantities. The desperation he pushed away with his dreams, the debt just mounted. Murphy walked towards the cashier, waiting for a man in a suit to buy his sandwich and leave. No need for casualties, he thought. He put one hand inside his shirt and felt the comforting grip of his Colt 45 there nestling against his skin.

Larry walked straight past a customer to the cashier. He looked in the eyes of the young man behind the counter, and began to draw his weapon. The cashier looked back at him, not reading the event, not understanding what was about to go down. It all became as bright and detailed as a high definition movie to Larry as he took charge and showed the man his guns. The cashier looked past him, over his shoulder. Larry didn't see the customer leave nor the man behind him, but he turned out of curiosity to face Murphy standing with his two Colt 45s trained on him.

It was a scene straight from a favourite movie, he thought, but he didn't know which one. Just two cowboys standing there with their loaded guns. It didn't occur to him that they were in the wrong country. They couldn't even afford the gas this place sold. Murphy narrowed his eyes at the competition. The Beach Boys singing *Help Me Rhonda* chimed out of the gas station's sound system, like an unearthly echo in Murphy's bruised psyche. Then Murphy was back in the barn in Kentucky.

That was when he opened fire. Larry followed, and they sprayed the potato chips and soft drinks with blood. Larry advanced, Murphy countered, Larry retreated, and they staggered and reeled like two cartoon characters, all the way to the door that opened to let them out as they emptied the chambers of their weapons. The cameras were rolling all right, capturing their final moments on CCTV for no audience beside the amused cops who studied the bizarre footage and cracked jokes about the two cowboys who were dumb enough to blow one another away in a bodged robbery. But Murphy and Larry were not aware of the lens, they were immersed in the shoot-out, the act locking into place for them like a broken bone resetting itself as they starred in their movie, two old time gunslingers in the wrong town.

They were outside now by the pumps, and they finished it there, standing tall before they fell to the gas stained concrete. Overhead the sky was darkening, but beyond the clouds there was a crack that looked indigo, and it reminded Murphy of Kentucky. To Larry, it looked straight off the set for a Western movie as the sky faded. They closed their eyes as from inside the gas station The Beach Boys stopped singing and Rhonda finally faded from Murphy's mind like an eroded tattoo. Then it began to rain, the storm coming in from the South, the drops hitting Surrey like liquid bullets.

SCAB

by Wrath James White

Wrath James White is a former World Class Heavyweight kickboxer, a professional kickboxing and mixed martial arts trainer, and the author of many books, including *The Resurrectionist, Like Porno for Psychos,* and *Succulent Prey.*

THE LITHE AND SENSUOUS CINNAMON-SKINNED BLACK WOMAN whose desk lay directly across from Malik's cubicle was staring at him again. Malik could feel her eyes crawling over him like maggots on a fresh corpse. He knew what she was thinking.

"Tar-baby, mud-duck, black scab, black dog, nigger, jungle-bunny, ugly, dirty, filthy, African!"

He'd heard it all before, not from some racist rednecks but from his own people, every day of his life for as long as he could remember. He was getting tired of it. Sick and tired. As a teenager, he'd used every skin lightning crème on the shelves, and he'd done nothing more than given himself a severe case of acne and several chemical burns that had blistered and left scars.

He turned his head to catch her staring, and she smiled at him, holding his gaze. Malik turned quickly away. He knew she was just trying to fuck with him.

Malik's self-esteem had been formed in the early eighties when he was just reaching puberty, and Michael Jackson, Prince, and Ray Parker Jr. were the symbols of black male sexuality. Effete, sallow-toned, androgynous beings, whose voices lilted like castrated tenors and whose racial composition was as ambiguous as their sexuality. Malik was the very antithesis of that cultural aesthetic, being the color of liquid night, with thick African features, and a large muscular body that held no suggestion of femininity. By eighties pop-cultural standards, he was pure ugly, a *bete noire* destined for solitude and depression.

The fact that the modern aesthetic now favored his complexion and physique was not lost on him. He had been amazed when he first began to see models and actors with skin as dark as his, thick lips, wide-noses, and shaved heads. He'd been even more amazed when a black woman had come up to him and called him beautiful for the first time in his life. But more than a decade later, he still found it hard to believe them and harder still to forgive them and impossible to forget. The cruel mocking voices of his youth haunted him without relent.

"You so black that if you went to night school they'd mark you absent!"

"I bet when you step out of a car the oil light goes on."

The echoes redoubled. They ricocheted around Malik's skull building up momentum and making him feel like his skull was about to rattle apart. His chest started to feel tight. He began to hyperventilate just as he had back in Junior High School when the walls would close in and suffocate him as he watched the curly-haired, caramel-skinned crowd lord over their darker brethren, insulting them every chance they got and teaching them to hate themselves for not having more European features.

Malik looked back across the room at the beautiful office assistant and saw one of the greatest tormentors of his youth leering at him with that cruel smirk as her mind worked feverishly to concoct the next put-down. Her name was Kelly. Her cocoa brown visage swam into view transposed over the face of the office girl. A vicious sneer twisted her lips as they moved to form that vituperative storm of insults Malik had come to expect from her.

"Ewww! You so black you look like you've been dipped in shit. You could stick your finger in hot water and make coffee. Ya black scab!"

The irony was that she was just a shade or two lighter than him. Definitely not the coveted high yellow complexion favored at that time. But she was not alone. Jennifer Hart, who was the color of buttermilk, added her voice to the choir.

"He's so black that if you tossed him in a volcano for about a million years, he'd come out a diamond!"

Between the two of them, they had driven him to two suicide attempts and numerous elaborate murder/suicide schemes that he'd plotted out to the last detail but had never put into action. He still heard their thirteen- and fourteen-year-old voices in his head even though reason told him that they would be well into their thirties by now. He heard them whenever he looked at beautiful cappuccino-colored women like the one staring at him from the next cubicle. The one smiling seductively as if she might actually be interested in a black scab like him.

"She's too pretty for you, ya ugly mud duck! You think a pretty little redbone like that would touch a spook like you? She's looking for Denzel, not Darrell... or Malik."

No. He didn't think she would want him. All she would do is make fun of him and his African ancestry. She would call him a spear-chucker behind his back, when all the girls were gathered around the coffeemaker gossiping in the morning. She'd tell them how disgusting it would be to kiss his big lips. How his hair felt like Brillo. And how his thick arms and chest made him look like an ape. Then she'd laugh just like Kelly and Jennifer had. She'd laugh and laugh until Malik would have no choice but to kill her.

He caught her looking at him again, and once again she did not turn away when he looked back. She held his gaze and smiled, batting her eyelashes flirtatiously, waiting for him to say something. She twirled a pencil in her left hand and touched it to the corner of her mouth, nibbling the end of it as she tilted her head and let her eyes slide slowly down his body and then back up again. He could almost feel the heat of her smoldering stare warming him as it traveled over his flesh, turning him on despite Kelly and Jennifer's combined voices interpreting every gesture she made into a diatribe of racial slurs.

"You big black Mighty Joe Young looking ape!"

Malik winced as if he'd been slapped as the woman continued to stare at him. He was still turned on, but now he was getting angry as well.

"How dare that bitch make me feel like this? Why is she fuckin' with me? Why can't she just leave me the fuck alone?"

He whirled around in his chair turning his back on her and trying without success to go back to his work. He stared at the screen, but all the letters and numbers were running together into one indecipherable alphabet stew. He could still feel her eyes on him as intimate caresses touching him everywhere. He wanted to get up and choke the life out of her.

Malik had always made it a point to steer clear of women like the beautiful tan-skinned woman in the next cubicle. The majority of his romantic conquests had been with white women or women with skin as dark or darker than his, though even they sometimes made him uneasy. Not all of the girls who'd teased him back in high-school had been light-skinned. Even the ones with skin the same color as his had looked down on him as if his onyx complexion made him somehow subhuman. Usually when he went after Black women they were African or West Indian or even darker-skinned Cubans and Puerto Ricans. With American girls there was always the fear that some honey-complexioned gigolo with hazel eyes and wavy hair would come and take her away from him.

One of the other office girls had now joined the girl in the next cubicle. Her skin was smooth and flawless and the color of milk chocolate. Her hair was thick and wooly, though neat and well-kept the way his had been before he'd gotten tired of fussing with it and shaved it all off. Her nose was wide with nostrils flared like a wild beast scenting a fresh kill and her lips were full and thick. The very same features he'd been ashamed of all his life she wore with beauty and grace. On her that wooly afro looked stylish and trendy, that wide nose wild and exotic, those full lips sensuous and sexual. He knew that there were women out there who looked at him the same way. But they were usually not black women.

The two women were smiling and whispering, and now they were both staring at him. Malik wanted to melt into the floor. He felt as if he were in an interrogation room under bright lights. He knew everything they were saying about him. He could read their lips even with his back turned. He could hear them in his head. See them laughing and pointing at him in his mind's eye, tearing him apart piece by piece until there was barely enough left of him to flush down the toilet.

"You shit-colored black scab!"

His mother had tried to teach him to be proud of his African heritage.

"Your skin is dark because your bloodline isn't diluted. You can trace your ancestry all the way to the slave ships and even back to the motherland. You're a thoroughbred, a pedigree, the descendant of kings and queens and great warriors! You should be proud of your black skin. Those half-breed mulatto kids are just jealous because they're mutts. You just tell them, the blacker the berry, the sweeter the juice."

Malik got up and stormed away from his desk with Kelly and Jennifer screaming in his head and the two office assistance boring their eyes into his back. He had to get some fresh air.

Walking briskly past rows and rows of identical cubicles in which the other office drones toiled, Malik began to calm down. The voices in his head began to slowly abate. He hurled himself into an elevator and rode it downstairs to the lobby then dashed out onto the teeming city streets into the flow of pedestrian traffic. He leaned up against a light pole and inhaled deeply several times finding himself inexplicably wishing he had a cigarette even though he'd never smoked a day in his life. The voices were quieter now, but they were still there, whispering hateful things to him. It had been a long time since they had come on this strong and Malik knew the reason for their renewed vigor. That damned office assistant with the Halle Barry smile and complexion. Despite his anger he could not ignore the fact that he'd been immensely attracted to her, and Kelly and Jennifer had known it too. That's why they had attacked him.

"Those fucking bitches! Why can't they just leave me alone!"

Malik gnashed his teeth together, the squeaky grinding sound drowning out the sonorous echoes in his skull. He whirled suddenly and almost jumped out into the street, pin-wheeling his arms to stay on the

curb as a cab rushed towards him, his eyes fixed in horror at the beautiful
light-skinned office assistant that'd just placed her hand on his shoulder.
She reached out for him again to help him regain his footing, pulling him
back onto the sidewalk.

"I'm so sorry. I didn't mean to frighten you."

"You almost killed me!"

She continued smiling at him despite the bristling rage and hate
boiling off of him in waves. She was oblivious. "She probably expects the
world to love her," Malik thought to himself as he struggled to calm his
galloping heartbeat.

"I just wanted to introduce myself."

"Why?" Malik found himself backing away from her in horror as if
she were something dangerous that might attack him. The woman took a
step closer with every step he took in retreat until he was once again
teetering on the edge of the curb.

"What do you want?"

"My name is Danika." She held out her hand, and Malik had to
take it to keep from falling off the curb into traffic.

"I'm Malik."

"I know. The girls in the office already told me about you." She
swept her eyes down to his feet and back up to his eyes again and once
again his body tingled everywhere her gaze landed.

"What did they tell you about me?"

"They said that you only date white girls."

"What? That's stupid. I date plenty of Black girls. I date all kinds of
girls."

"Then why haven't you asked me out? How come every time I look
at you, you look like you want to run away? Do you think I'm ugly or
something, or are you just scared of me?"

"Why was she doing this?"

"I'm not afraid of you, and you know you aren't ugly."

"Then what's the problem?"

"Why would you want to go out with me?"

"Why? Look at you! You're gorgeous!"

Malik paused and looked closely at Danika's face to see if she was
serious, hunting for any sign that she was putting him on or patronizing
him.

"What, do you have some kind of bet with your friends or
something? Is that what this is about?"

"Look, I just think you're fine as hell and I'd like to get to know you. But if you're not interested, I ain't going to beg you. A sista does have her pride. If you prefer those white girls, then that's just your loss."

She turned on her heels and started walking back into the building.

"Danika?"

"Hmmm?"

"How about tonight?"

***

The date was going well. Malik was surprised by how much he and Danika had in common. Even the voices in his head were silent for once. Malik was enjoying himself. Each time Danika laughed he laughed with her. She reached out and took his hand as she told him about how her grandparents had to flee the South sixty years ago with the KKK hard at their heels because her grandmother had married a black man. She told him how much she hated being called 'high yella' or 'redbone' as if she were some other race than black and how she hated being called a mulatto most of all because it sounded so much like 'mutt' which she'd also been called on a few occasions. Malik kept his own stories to himself, listening instead, staring at her tiny brown hand in his and wondering what he'd ever been afraid of.

"What about your parents? Were they both Black?"

"My mom, like I said, was half black and half white and my dad was Puerto Rican."

"So what do you consider yourself then?"

"Well, Puerto Ricans have Black blood in them too, so I just call myself Black. It gets too complicated otherwise."

She smiled, and Malik smiled with her. The waiter brought their food, and they ate their meal of Cornish game hens stuffed with wild rice and cranberries in small bites in between conversation, sipping zinfandel and never once breaking eye contact.

When the check came, they both agreed not to let the night end. They went to a nightclub down the street and sat at the bar drinking and talking. A Marvin Gaye song came on, and they went out on the dance floor, hugging each other closely and swaying to the beat. He kissed her lightly on the lips as they danced to *Let's Get it On*, and she kissed him back deeply and passionately as the song ended.

An hour later, she nestled close to him with his arm around her shoulders and her head on his chest as he hailed a cab.

"Where to?"

They looked at each other and Danika smiled again when Malik gave the taxi-driver his home address.

"So why did you act so weird around me at the office? I've been there a week, and you never even looked at me."

"Oh, I looked at you. I just didn't know why you were always looking at me. It made me nervous."

"What? Did you think I was some kind of crazy stalker or serial killer or something?"

Malik chuckled.

"Something like that."

"I'm sorry. I didn't mean to freak you out. I just wanted to get with you, so I was trying to let you know I was interested."

"Girls like you aren't normally interested in brothas like me."

"What do you mean girls like me?"

Malik paused. He knew what he meant, but knew that it would offend her if he said it.

"Sistas as pretty as you don't normally dig me. I mean, I know a lot of white girls are into my look, but you know how they are. Once they decide they're into brothas, they ain't too choosy."

"Don't tell me you've got self-esteem issues? You? I would have never guessed that. I mean, with a body like yours, I'd think you could get any woman you want. I was worried that I didn't look good enough for you."

"You're the most beautiful woman I've ever seen."

He reached out and stroked his fingers through her thick curly brown hair, staring at her staggeringly beautiful face, amazed that she was actually attracted to him.

"Is that why you spend so much time working on this magnificent body of yours? You really don't believe you're handsome?"

She ran her tiny brown hands over his thick muscular chest as they huddled together in the back of the taxi. She slid them up over his shoulders and up his neck, cupping his face in her palms.

"I think you're the most handsome man I've ever seen."

They were still kissing when they paid the taxi and stepped out onto the sidewalk in front of Malik's house. Malik was in heaven. It almost felt as if he was falling in love, on the first date, and with a woman whose skin was the color of cinnamon pastry. The whole thing made Malik as nervous as it did happy. It had been hours since he'd heard Kelly or Jennifer's voices in his head. As much as it was a relief, it was also a source of worry. They had never gone away on their own like that, not without medication, or without Malik giving in to them and giving them what they wanted, and there was no way Malik was going to do that, and he hadn't taken his medication in weeks. Still, he hadn't heard those shrill scathing voices spilling their relentless stream of vitriol since he'd agreed to the date with Danika. Desperately he hoped that meeting her had somehow ended their hold on him, which made him panic at the thought of her leaving him now or ever.

"Come inside for a while."

"*This* is your house?"

It was a large single story with decorative stone all around the front entrance, a long driveway covered in stamped concrete that continued up the walkway to the front door. The front yard was desert-landscaped with large palm trees and big shrubs of rosemary and sage. It was over two thousand square feet squatting on a lot that was about a fifth of an acre.

"I got lucky on this one. I bought it before the market went nuts. I only paid a hundred and eighty for it six years ago."

"Wow. My house is half this size and I paid three hundred for it. I had to take an interest-only loan out and pray that the thing appreciates in five years so I can refinance. You did get lucky."

"Come on in."

He opened the door, and they stepped into the foyer. They were in each other's arms kissing passionately before the door was closed. They undressed in a hurry, desperate for each other. Malik lifted her slim delicate body into his arms and carried her to the bedroom, still kissing her passionately, their tongues duelling, lips bruising against each other. He laid her on the bed and kissed his way slowly up her thighs, pausing between them to taste her sweet musk, sending a quiver through her and stealing the breath from her lungs. He kissed his way up her stomach, kissed and sucked each nipple, flicking his tongue across them and making her moan, before returning to her lips. She was trembling all over when he finally entered her. She matched his rhythm as their flesh entwined in urgent thrusts, slowly at first and then with greater and greater urgency, building to a mutual orgasm that shook them both. They collapsed into each other's arms, catching their breath before making love once more. Their bodies complemented each other's perfectly. They made love without inhibitions, not holding anything back, exploring every inch of each other's bodies, getting to know all the spots that drove each other wild.

The night was half over when they lay spooned against each other breathing heavily with sweat and semen drying into the sheets.

"You still think I only like White women?"

Malik kissed the back of her neck gently.

"Oh, you definitely know how to appreciate a sista."

He laughed.

"I'll be right back"

Malik got up from the bed. His legs felt as if they were made of Jello. He staggered into the bathroom and closed the door behind him, grabbing onto the sink to steady himself. He was just about to turn on the lights when he heard them.

"That bitch must be crazy, fucking a big black scab like you. That nasty trifling ho! If you won't kill that bitch than we will."

Malik knew why he hadn't heard the voices in his head all day. Jennifer and Kelly weren't in his head any more. They were right there in his bathroom.

He turned his head and watched as the two small shadows crept from his shower stall, forming the tiny teenaged bodies of the two girls who'd tormented him since grade school. They hadn't changed in almost twenty years. Kelley still wore her ruffled shirts with the Izod sweater and tight Gloria Vanderbilt jeans. Her hair was permed and straightened and hung down to her hips. Jennifer was dressed almost identically except her hair was Jeri curled, and she wore a denim jacket with Prince and Michael Jackson buttons pinned all over it and one lace glove. They both were carrying knives.

"We're going to cut that disgusting bitch's heart out."

They kept fading in and out of the night. One second they were featureless silhouettes, shadows moving within the darkness, and the next their features were sharp and clear, knives glinting in the moonlight.

"You can't be here. This isn't possible!"

Malik groped for his medication, shattering the mirror on the medicine cabinet as he ripped the door open and fumbled inside for the little prescription bottle.

"Are you okay in there?"

"We're going to kill that bitch. She shouldn't have touched you. You've contaminated her now with your filthy Black African hands. You were probably just a mercy fuck anyway. She just felt sorry for you. You were her good deed for the day. A charity fuck."

"Ewwww! That's so nasty! How could she do that with you?"

"She said I was handsome."

"You're not handsome!"

"She said you were handsome? Ewwww!"

Malik found the bottle of anti-psychotics and struggled with the child proof cap. He removed the cap just as Kelley stepped forward and slashed his wrist with the knife, fading back into the night after delivering the blow. Malik screamed as Jennifer lashed out and slashed the other wrist.

"We should just kill you. You're the one always bringing these whores here and forcing them to have sex with you, making them stoop to your level."

"Malik? Are you okay in there?"

Danika knocked lightly on the bathroom door.

"No, let's kill her. She makes us look bad. She makes this filthy black nigger think he's good enough to be with us. He's so black he sweats oil."

"Yeah, let's kill that high yellow bitch!"

Jennifer reached for the doorknob and began to open it. Malik rammed into it slamming it shut, and the two girls turned on him and began slashing at him, cutting up his forearms as he struggled to defend himself. He struck at them with his fists, but his arms passed harmlessly through the darkness as the two girls faded in and out of the shadows.

On the other side of the door, Danika had heard enough. Something was wrong. Fear gripped her as she heard Malik in the bathroom arguing and fighting with someone who shouldn't be there, arguing about killing her. Just minutes ago, she had been lying in his arms, thinking to herself how easy it would be to fall in love with this man. Now she was afraid that he was some type of psycho.

Danika hit 911 on her cell phone and left the line open as she rushed to gather her clothes. Whatever was going on in the bathroom was growing more and more violent. It sounded as if Malik was in pain. She was just about to run out of the house when something in Malik's voice made her stop. Maybe someone or something was really in there with him?

"Run, Danika! Get out of here!"

"Filthy black ape, black scab. You shit-colored African jungle bunny!"

Malik was covered in cuts and slashes when he came staggering out of the bathroom carrying a knife in each hand.

Danika watched him slash at the air and then slice his own forehead. Blood rained down his face and dripped from the wounds in his neck, chest, and forearms. Danika screamed as she watched Malik's face twist and contort, morphing between rage and terror as whatever demons he was struggling with made war within him... and he was heading right towards her... swinging the knives.

Danika ran. She didn't know where she was going. The house was big and she could not find her way to the front door in the dark so she opened the first door she came to and ducked inside. It was the garage.

There were big metal canisters that looked like oil drums scattered here and there inside the garage, and Danika tried to tell herself that she had just seen too many horror films when she began to speculate on what might be inside. She felt along the wall for the switch to open the garage door, afraid to turn on the light for fear that Malik might find her again. There was no switch. She'd have to open the door manually.

"That half-white bitch shouldn't have been slummin' around with your big gorilla looking ass. Ya black spook! You so black I can't see you at night until you smile."

"He's so black he could hide in a coal bin."

The voices coming from the house were sounding less and less like Malik and more and more like someone else. Like children's voices in stereo. It sounded as if he was possessed. There were more sounds of struggle as glass shattered and something heavy fell over with a thud. She heard Malik scream again and wondered if whatever was inside his head had slashed one of those knives across his throat and ended his suffering. But then she heard the voices again.

"We know that nasty redbone bitch is still here. We're going to find her. We'll kill her and then we'll finish you off too."

"Nooooo!"

Malik screamed again and Danika stopped halfway to the garage door when she heard him sob and whimper. He was in pain. Those evil voices were torturing him.

"Leave him alone!" Danika yelled.

The garage door raised and Malik was standing there in the driveway a knife in one hand and the moonlight behind him silhouetting his form.

"I said, leave him alone."

She didn't know what she was doing. She didn't know what she was saying. All she knew was that she had to help. It might be the only way to save her own life as well as Malik's.

"You filthy slut! You'll fuck anything if you'll fuck this filthy black scab."

"He's so black that when I close my eyes I can see him better!"

The voices no longer sounded anything like Malik. His lips didn't even move when they spoke. They were the voices of spiteful children. Conceited little girls who thought it was fun to ridicule anyone that they believed to be less than them.

"You're wrong. He's beautiful."

"He's a nasty black ape!"

"He's a beautiful black man. You girls are behind the times. Black is beautiful now. Those light-skinned pretty boys are so eighties. Women want real men these days and the bigger and blacker the better."

"She's lying! Nobody wants you. You're just a big ugly black African!"

Malik was still standing there on the driveway holding the knife. His mouth still did not appear to be moving even as insults poured out of him. There were shadows hovering around him. As Danika looked, she thought she could almost make out the silhouettes of two young girls. She even imagined she could see their faces twisted into smirks of superiority.

"They're wrong. I wouldn't have come home with you tonight if that was true. I- I thought I was falling in love with you. We might have fallen in love together if these little bitches hadn't gotten in the way."

Malik turned and looked right at the two shadows standing by his side. He raised his knife to slash into them when the two police officers tackled him knocking him into the garage right into the barrels. Three of the metal canisters fell over and the lid came off of one of them. Danika screamed as a woman's torso tumbled out of the barrel followed by her head. The disembodied head spun as it tumbled across the garage floor turning towards her. Even dead, Danika could tell that the woman had been very beautiful, with long curly brown hair, light cappuccino colored skin and hazel eyes just like her own.

Danika turned to the other barrels and began knocking them over. One after another, curly-headed, tan-skinned heads tumbled out onto the garage floor. Danika looked from one face to the next as more police officers crowded into the garage.

"Are you okay, Ma'am? Jesus Christ! Are those real? We need a coroner over here. Somebody call CSU. It's a fucking bloodbath in here! We've got bodies everywhere!"

Danika pried her eyes away from the lifeless faces lying on the garage floor and back up to the garage entrance where the two shadows were still standing there, smirking in superiority, unnoticed by everyone except her and Malik. She looked back down at Malik as what looked like half a dozen cops piled on top of him, twisting his arm behind his back and handcuffing him, their fear making them use more force than necessary as they tried to restrain him. Malik stopped struggling and looked up into her eyes even as her vision slowly faded and everything began to go black.

"Why? How could you do this?"

"I'm sorry, Danika. I didn't want to hurt you. Some wounds don't heal. Some wounds never heal."

Danika fainted, thinking about scabs that continued to rip open and bleed decades after the wounds that caused them. The girls had called

Malik a black scab. In a way, they had been right.

MEAN BUSINESS

by Mark Slade

Mark Slade is a fiction writer whose novels include *Queen of the Light*, *Electric Funeral*, and *Blackout City Confidential*.

LONDON HAD NEVER BEEN FURTHER SOUTH THAN CRABTREE, Maryland, and that is so far Northeast that it crowded New Castle, Pennsylvania. There he was, though, in Limewater, Georgia, sitting in a hillbilly bar, all eyes on him and Marty Stuart on the jukebox. One particular man in an Alabama baseball cap and Roll Tide T-shirt was very interested in London. He sat at the bar nursing a glass of beer, staring a hole in the back of London's head.

London was at a table, sitting across from Julip Havers, an associate of London's boss, Peter Choaladi. How a hick like Julip Havers got in business with a Cuban crime boss was beyond London. Making money off of chop shops is nothing new for Choaladi and his cohorts.

Choaladi has been in the business since the late 70's when his brothers set up in New Jersey. Stealing cars and selling them to chop shops all over the country made the Choaladi family the darlings of the criminal world. So whenever any of his associates have problems, he lends Barry London out to take care of the problems.

"The fat one over there," Julip said. "By the jukebox talking to the blonde in the white dress."

"He knows where your brother is?" London asked, staring a hole in the large man with the long beard and body shaped like an oversized globe.

"Yep," Julip answered. "I'm pretty sure Barge Franklin. Those are his brothers, Colin, Rip, Feign, and Toss. I'm sure they helped Barge take Rook from the garage last Thursday. The mailman was watchin'."

"Who's the blonde?"

Julip shrugged. "Carla. Nobody special. Just some squeeze Barge sees sometimes.

"I guess I'll ask him a few questions," London stood.

"Wait!" Julip tugged on the sleeve of London's sports jacket. "You can't just go up to a Franklin and start asking him if he kidnapped somebody!"

"Who says I'll talk first?" London pulled away and ambled over to the fat guy in the black wife-beater way too small for his robust body.

Just as London tapped the fat man on the shoulder, Julip called out the man's name. London turned, and Julip was right behind him

"Hey, Barge," Julip sound. "Me and my friend wanna know if you got a minute to talk."

Barge grunted. His mouth worked overtime on a ball of chaw. He leaned to the side and spat out a long line of brown and black phlegm that wrapped itself around a stripper's pole.

"Fuck you want?" Barge said.

"Where's Julip's brother?" London wasn't going to waste time with niceties.

Barge or any of the other locals in the bar wasn't, either. Barge's brother's decided they wanted to hear the conversation. Feign and Rip had pool sticks. Colin retrieved a claw hammer from his toolbox. Toss still had the knife he used to gut the fish he caught this morning. All four had the same scowl that plagued Barge's ugly face. They crowded around London and Julip, screwing in their tiny eyes and breathing heavy for effect.

"He's probably face down in a ditch, drunk and stoned out of his head," Barge said, barely raising his voice above a decibel human ears can detect. "I bet Julip didn't tell you Rook is a chicken head. Somebody better tell Rook meth can rot the brain."

London gave Julip a disappointed look. Julip looked away. London knew he still had to take care of the situation or Choaladi would be disappointed in him. He returned his harsh gaze to Barge, who by now restarted his conversation with Carla. She made sure Barge looked at her tits. Everyone could see she had no bra on underneath that thin white cotton dress.

"What a man does in the privacy of his own home is his business," London told him. Barge continued to ignore him. "There's witnesses that you and your inbred brothers took Rook from their garage."

Barge continued to ignore London. The blonde ran her hand through her hair and giggled. London noticed the woman had a cleft in her chin big enough to land an airplane. Barge's brothers stayed where they were, crowding Julip and London.

"Come on, London" Julip said in his lazy, slow accent. "This is a waste of time."

Barry London laughed. He unsheathed his Glock from his breast holster and fired at the closest man to him. The bullet went through the man's left shoe. He screamed, dropped the claw hammer and fell to the wood floor. A cloud of dust followed, either from the body of Barge's brother or from the floor. The other two scattered, hands over their ears, as Julip did the same.

Barge jerked his head around. Carla yelped and trotted to a corner of the bar.

"You-you shot Colin!" Barge exerted in shock.

London put the barrel of his Glock to Barge's fat cheek and said, "I bet you'll talk to me now."

"I don't like bein' threatened!" Barge stated.

"I don't like being ignored, double stuff," London rattled off, his voice carried louder than the jukebox. "Start talking, or I'll shave some fat off of you!"

"Okay," Barge said. Anxiety took over. His barrel chest heaved sporadically. "Let's take the conversation to the back." His eyes danced back and forth between London and his other two brothers. "Feign, Toss, help Colin to the backroom." Barge turned to the blonde and said, "Carla, looks like you're goin' to have to get another bullet out of Colin. He's like a magnet for those suckers." Barge laughed at his own joke as he waddled to the office behind the bar.

***

"We were paid to take Rook," Barge confessed. He reached over and turned the radio off.

Funny, London recognized the song and the singer. *Texas Cookin'* by Guy Clark. Pop is a big fan of Outlaw Country. He has a stack of Vinyl records of Townes Van Zandt, Waylon Jennings and Willie Nelson sitting side by side with James Brown and Curtis Mayfield. Pop works with Choaladi as well, running a newspaper stand to cover up the illegal gambling operation. Pop always liked being a surrogate father to London, as well as finding any info London needed to do the job. Pop missed his own sons. He didn't say, but London figured the three of them didn't chat often except holidays and birthdays. So when London asked Pop, AKA Leon Brown — a retired bus driver from Manhattan — why he listened to country music, Pop's response was classic. "Music don't have color barriers, son," he said. "I like the way they sing, and boy, they pick those guitars!"

London reached over Barge's messy desk and turned the radio back on. Barge didn't like that.

"I like that song," London smiled. The song ended, and a commercial came on. London turned the radio off. "Who hired you?"

"Lou Stills," Barge said. "He has another chop shop in Kaye

County. Stills never got along with your family," he said to Julip.

Julip nodded. "Goes back to our grandfathers and back when they use to race."

"What? Like in Nascar?" London asked.

"Never got to that," Julip laughed. "Neither grandfather was that good. Just local stuff. Once they raced in Atlanta, but both washed out on that track. Track was dirt then. Both hit the wall, got out, and started throwin' punches right away. That was in the early sixties. Almost any rule was bent or broken. Both cars had been messed with."

London met with one of the brother's eyes. He was to trying stare London down. He must have seen something and got spooked. The man quickly looked down at his shoes.

"Where did you take Rook?" London asked Barge.

"Across the county. In Hopewell. There's an abandoned farm," Barge said nervously. "Look, man…we just did a job. That was all. I really don't dislike Julip…Rook gets on my nerves some, but I ain't out to do nothin' bad to the Havers. Me and my brothers just did it for a thousand."

London stood. Barge leaned back in his chair, his eyes as big as his belly. He drew in a frightened breath with his gaping mouth. His brothers took a few steps back. Julip was well prepared to fall on the floor and bury his face in the blood and cum-stained carpet. London took his wallet from the breast pocket of his jacket.

The stress level in the room returned to normal, except for the smell of warm urine. London smiled and wondered which one of them was afraid of him. His guess was Julip. But he should already know he wasn't going to hurt him because of ties to Choaladi. London removed several twenties from the black billfold and counted out a thousand dollars. He laid them out on the desk.

"Take me to that farm," London said. "The money is yours. Any blood spilled and you guys survive, you get another thousand."

***

The farm was three counties over and a mile from swampland. No one had farmed on that land for decades. The house had weeds and grass reaching the second floor. All the windows were busted out and the walls on the back of the house had become non-existent. The four barns had definitely been in use. Most likely for various criminal activities over those several decades; London just knew of the hidden 'hot cars' and one barn used for storing weed.

They all rode in Barge's Silverado pickup. Barge drove, and London sat in between him and Julip, with the three brothers in the bed, with their rifles and shotguns out in the open. London thought that was the dumbest thing he'd ever seen until he saw three or four other trucks on the freeway with men in the bed of a pickup with shotguns clinging to them. A cultural shock, no doubt, but a humorous education. Just like he learned that Barge could kill a twelve pack all by himself and still be a competent driver.

He nearly hit a tree once.

An elderly man in a stained STP cap and a silk blue shirt came out of the second barn. He removed a paper towel that had been tucked in the lapels of his shirt. He chewed feverishly, wiped his mouth with that paper towel, and then discarded it. Fifteen more men followed, all cradling shotguns, rifles or flashing pistols. That young blonde from the bar, this time wearing jeans and Run-DMC T-shirt.

Barge screwed down his mean eyes and uttered an expletive that women usually take offense to. From the elderly man's stance and over-confidence, London gathered the man was Lou Stills. London's eyes met with Julip's. Julip was shaking. London sighed. He was hiding something. London wasn't sure when he met with Julip, he just had a feeling.

Now he was sure.

"Get out," London ordered Julip. Julip hesitated, and opened the car door. "Hey," London pulled on Julip's pants leg, Julip sat still momentarily. "Speak to Stills and no one else. Tell him why we're here. And don't let your fucking voice tremble. Got it?"

Julip drew in a breath and strained to let it back out.

"Okay," he hiccupped, got out of the car.

Julip wasn't given a chance to say anything. A gun was fired and a single bullet pierced his forehead. Julip yelped. He kept his mouth open and as wide as his traumatized eyes. A trickle of blood ran down his face before he fell to the ground. Lou Stills had hate in his eyes. He was screaming at his men to fire.

"Go! Go! Go!" London screamed at Barge and ducked in the seat.

The truck spun around, and Barge's brothers opened fire. A barrage of bullets sharply assaulted the truck. The brothers in the bed of the truck kept the battle going, even though all three were struck. Two of Stills men were eliminated. As soon as Barge got good length between Stills and his men, the truck slammed into a barn on the far left.

Everything went black.

***

London heard someone say in a voice that sounded like it had been run through a blender, followed by laughter. He opened his eyes and saw Lou Stills hovering over the truck, his men standing behind him. At some point London must have opened the door on the passenger side and passed out again. There was massive waves of pain in his forehead. He felt blood running down his face.

London looked over at the driver's side. Barge was dead. A wooden plank fell from the ceiling of the barn when the truck slammed into the front of the makeshift building, which was built three or four decades ago and built too swiftly. The wooden plank went through the windshield and tore into Barge's face. Blood had splattered not only all over the seat and dashboard, but soaked the left side of London's jacket.

London moved his hand slowly, felt for the Glock. It was gone.

"Looking for this?" Stills showed him the gun, holding it by the muzzle. "You really think we're dumb hillbillies, huh?"

"A picture... is... worth... a thousand... words...," London managed to say. "Looks like you're selling...the image very well...No...I don't think that... I think you make dumb mistakes."

"Mister, I don't know you, you don't know me. My boys here tried to convince me to kill you without caring who you are," Stills shook his head. "I ain't like that. But you attacked us."

"No sir," London said, his senses coming back to him quicker the more he blinked his eyes. "You shot Julip Havers."

"I damn for sure shot him!" Stills screamed. "He defiled my little girl! He and his brother Rook! And when I find him..."

"Wait. You don't have Rook Havers? That was the whole reason we came here. You paid Barge and his brothers to bring Rook to you..."

"Why would he do that?" Stills spit in the opposite direction, wiped his mouth. "I have my boys for that sort of thing! Mister, I think you got took."

"I think we both did," London said. "My boss is not going to be happy about this."

"Just who in the hell are you?" Stills demanded.

"I'm Barry London. Peter Choaladi sent me to resolve this matter."

Stills thought about it. His snarl became broader, but confusion set in his eyes. "Now, why would Peter Choaladi be dippin' his toes in my waters? I'm protected by Leon Gershom."

That part London didn't know. He did know Choaladi and

Gershom are friends. Never a sore word between them and a hostile takeover of either's business concerns would never happen. Unless someone was trying to take over themselves.

"Look, I don't know you, true," London said. "I'm pretty certain Rook and Julip Havers had plans to get everyone involved killed, and both Chop shops would be theirs. I bet there was a deal with Barge and his family to kill you and your family. But I bet they had help. Can I speak to your daughter?"

Stills' eyes lit up red. His lower lip flubbed for thirty seconds, then went right back into a nasty snarl. "My daughter is dead. June killed herself last month," Stills said.

Oh shit, London thought. I just put my foot in my mouth.

"Throw him in the Arbus house," Stills commanded.

The boys exchanged glances. Nervous energy filled their bodies. There was the shuffling of feet and guns from one hand to the other. None of the boys jumped at the chance to be at their daddy's beck and call on this incident. Finally, one spoke up, "You sure about that...?"

"What did I just say?!" Stills barked. "Now you all just git! Do as I say!"

"Come on," London tried. "I didn't know anything about your daughter or what these creeps were up to..."

London caught the butt of a rifle, and it sent him to la la land.

***

London woke up. He rubbed the blurriness from his eyes, feeling a piece of hay sticking in his ear. He sat up, looked around. The whole floor of the barn was made up of hay. Old hay, from the looks of it. All of it brown, smelling sour.

London heard movement under the hay. He followed the moving strands all the way to his feet. What the hell could that be? Mouse? Rats? Bugs of some kind? He didn't know. London was a city dweller. His only contact was a hayride when he was fourteen and Mandy Von Bara sat on his lap while he copped a feel.

He heard the hissing.

Ohhhh shit, London thought. A snake is in here.

London hated snakes. Again, he was not used to the country and all of the creatures that coexist with everyone else. One bored night, London watched a program on American snakes. This would be a test of what he learned, since he watched the show two or three years ago.

The snake popped his head up. Bright orange patterns surrounded the snake's head. A corn snake, London remembered them being called. Harmless. Used to cut down rat and other pests' populations. London let out a sigh of relief when the corn snake slithered away from him toward another bale of hay.

As soon as he felt a moment of comfort, he heard other sighs. Then more slithering. Suddenly, the entire floor of hay began to move, and soon the other inhabitants showed who they were and what snake kingdom they came from. Copperhead. Pinewoods snake. Pygmy Rattler. Eastern Diamondback. Red belly snake.

The Diamondback popped up on the left side of London's face. The Diamondback's face was at his cheek, tongue slipping in and out. London stayed still. His heart was beating so fast he felt the vibrations in his toes. He fought the urge to piss himself. London kept his eyes straight ahead, no blinking. He felt the snake's dry, scaly skin crawl across his face, slither down his neck and across his belly, and to an old tractor tire.

Why the hell was there so many different kinds in here?! London panicked in his head. He didn't know if he said that out loud or just thought it.

"Because my cousin used this barn to study snakes for his Doctrine at the University Georgia State." Carla stood in the doorway. "He don't study no more. Lou shot him for smokin' the meth he was supposed to be selling."

"That's a helluva story, lady. But can you get me the fuck out of here!" London said. He tried to contain his fear and nervousness, but his voice betrayed him.

Carla laughed, snorted. "Just stand up and walk out."

"I don't want to get bit," London told her.

"I walked in, didn't I? And I'm barefoot."

Sure enough, Carla had no shoes on. Her feet were almost suntanned like the rest of her, and for some reason, paleness collided with the tan and made her pink toenails stand out.

"Just take a chance," Carla said. "Fifty-fifty you won't get bit I'll leave you here to die. Hmph! You got shoes on."

London decided to put his fears in his back pocket and decided to tempt it. He stood slowly, and paced his steps as if he didn't care what was crawling on the hay floor. Luckily, he didn't step on any snakes.

Carla stepped out of the barn door. London followed, saw one of Lou Stills' boys and pushed her to the ground. Carla fell with a whimper, rolled to the right side of the barn behind a hedge. London dropped to his belly and crawled to her. He gripped her neck and squeezed just enough.

"You scream," London whispered. "I'll break your neck. Nod if you understand."

Her blue eyes were wide and wild. She bobbed her head up and down quickly, and those blonde tresses did the same. She wasn't out of danger yet. London squeezed again to make a point. He had one more demand.

"Get me out of here. Nod your head if you understand."

Carla swallowed back loud sobs and nodded.

London removed his hand from her neck. Her chest heaved until her breathing became normal. She sat up, slowly pointed to an old beat up, grey Sierra pickup with a white shell. No one was around the vehicle. Carla stood, took a few steps to wait for London to get to his feet. She ran to the truck and opened the driver's side. She let London hop in first before slamming the door.

One of Lou Stills' boys waddled over. He was big and thick-bearded, armed with an assault rifle. Curiously, he wore a Roll Tide T-shirt and an Alabama cap. He lived in Georgia. Why didn't he represent the Bulldogs? London ducked to the floorboard, and the blonde tossed a blanket over him.

"Where you goin', Carla?" he said.

Carla turned the charm on. She stuck her tits out, smiled big, and sighed. "Lou wants some chicken," she tossed her hair out of her eyes. "Guess I'm goin' to Wendell's super store."

"Well, alright! Can you get a batch with Sriracha on it?"

"You got it, Alva," Carla fluttered her eyes.

The man's eyes fell from her face to her heaving breasts under that white cotton dress. He began to salivate. She felt a smack on her ankle. That was definitely a signal from London to drive on and quit flirting.

"Well," Carla giggled. "I'll git. Chicken and Pabst Blue Ribbon coming up!" She turned the ignition, the pickup sputtered, then roared. She moved the gear shift to Drive and hit the gas. The pickup sped off down the wooded lane, kicking up gravel behind it.

***

London and Carla ended up on a dirt road headed into a deep wooded area. Twilight was setting in. Tree frogs and cicada sang their songs loud and clear, in different sides of the speaker, one on the left, the other on the right. Bats fluttered close to the windshield, and glided away from imminent death. Neither had spoken for thirty minutes. London decided it was time he found out some things.

"Are you kin to Lou Stills?" London blurted out.

"No," Carla shook her head. "I was his daughter in law for a few months. I was married to his oldest son, Gregory. Greg wanted out. I wanted out. We were going to get out. He joined the Marines. He went to boot camp in California. I went too, San Diego. Greg was sent off to Afghanistan and got himself killed. Mortar attack. Had no real chance of getting out." She looked at London, full of hate, regret, all rolled into one glance. "Back to being country folk."

"Why?" He asked. His eyes stayed level with the road in front, never once drifting to Carla.

"Why what?"

"Why would Rook fuck with Lou Stills? Why would Julip get Choaladi mixed up in a hogtying contest between inbreeds?"

"We're not inbreeds, mister," Carla's nostrils flared. "We're country folk."

"You are not country folk. Don't bullshit me," London said. Slowly, his eyes moved over to Carla. His glare was colder than Antarctica. "You are not the cast of the Andy Griffith show. This area is not Mayberry. You deal in meth and stolen vehicles."

"There is no other industry…" Carla tried to apologize. London wasn't having it.

"I don't care what side you are on! Just don't put me on! I've been in this game for years, lady!" London screamed. "I know the stakes. I know poverty as well as you do. Don't ever try and make me believe that you, Rook, or Stills is normal!"

They were quiet now. Another couple of minutes, London started up again.

"What was the plan you, Rook, and Julip had?"

Carla sighed. "We wanted in on his meth business. Julip wanted the Chop shop. We paid Barge to take Rook. Julip called your boss, hoping Choaladi would send foot soldiers to take Lou Stills apart," she said, shrugged. "He sent you instead. Well…Julip fucked things up."

"He had sex with Still's daughter. Okay. So what? I think he over reacted…"

"She was fourteen, London. Fourteen years old," Carla said. "To make it worse, Julip put it on a website. That's how Lou found out. That's why he was scared to go with you."

London nodded. "I knew he had something to hide."

"Don't we all," Carla said.

***

In the horizon was a cabin stuck behind brush. Carla eased the pickup to the right side of the cabin, just beside a hollowed out tree bent over backwards. London heard movement from the bushes. Before he could react, the barrel of a Walther PPK was in his face. London whispered expletives to himself and heard the man laugh.

"You idjit," Alva said. "Get out. Nice and slow." Alva opened the door for him, and waved the pistol as if he was using his hand to usher London out.

Alava moved the gun up and tried to come down on London's neck. London was pistol whipped before, so he knew the move. When Alva's arm came down, London grabbed his arm. Next, he kneed Alva in the crotch and pushed him into a tree. London stripped the gun from Alva, then gave him a combination of rights and lefts to the midsection.

Out of breath, and damn tired of the whole ordeal, London shoved the pistol in Alva's face and was a half a second of pulling the trigger. He heard a shrill scream from Carla. Begging came next.

"Please…please don't! Oh God!" She sobbed, ran from the driver's side of the pickup and threw herself between Alva and the gun.

"Get the fuck out of the way!" London yelled.

Carla pushed the Walther away. "You can't kill him! Please…no, London, you can't kill Alva!"

"I said get the fuck out of the way, or I'll spread your brains all over this cabin wall, bitch!!"

"You can't kill him," she wept hard, pulling Alva's face to hers. Her voice was muffled when she said. "We're going to have a baby. We're going to have a baby…"

London sighed, looked away. "Fuck," he whispered.

"Don't tell him about the money… just…don't tell him about the money…" A thick Georgia accent cut through the noise the cicadas were making.

A very thin, bearded man with black curly hair appeared from the cabin door. He was just wearing stained biker shorts and no shirt. He looked like he hadn't bathed in days. The man had nervous energy and wild eyes.

"Shut up, Rook!" Alva screamed at the man.

"Go back in the cabin," Carla left Alva lying on the ground to help the gangly man back inside.

London cut his eyes at Alva, bright red embers burning hot.

"What money?" London asked.

Alva picked himself off the ground, shook his head. "There ain't no money," Alva smiled.

London smacked him across the face with the pistol. Alva cried out.

"What money?" London repeated the question.

Alva just shook his head. London smacked him again with the pistol, this time in the throat. Alva fell backwards on the ground, coughing. London stood over him, ready to shoot if the question was not answered.

"What fucking money?"

"We...we...we've been skimming from Stills and your boss," Alva's vocal chords strained to form the sentence.

"You morons live a dangerous lifestyle. So, if you were never caught - I highly doubt that scenario - but if you weren't, that wouldn't be enough for you? You have to take over both businesses? Fucking morons."

"Stills knows someone is doing it," Alva stood, a hand caressing his neck. He still struggled to speak in between coughs. "He knows Carla is involved with someone else from his troop. He doesn't know who."

"What about the deal with Lou Stills' daughter?" London asked.

"We didn't expect that to happen," Alva said. He coughed, and shrugged. "We didn't think she'd kill herself. Shit... we were hopin'...hopin' the shame would be too much for Stills and..."

A single gunshot shrieked across the night sky. Alva didn't finish his sentence. He and London were caught off guard, London more than him. London turned to find the sound, and Alva jumped him. The pistol fell to the ground, bounced a few times and slid under the cabin. Alva kicked London in the ribs. London fell to his knees. Alva then kicked London in the mouth. London fell on his back, and rolled toward the cabin.

London put his hands on the cabin wall and pulled himself up. Two scythes were leaning against the cabin wall. Laughing, Alva stormed London. London took hold of one of the scythes, swung at Alva the same time he dove for London. Alva fell on his face. The scythe shredded the back of his T-shirt. One long cut appeared on Alva's back, blood ran down his jeans. Alva stood quickly, took hold of the other scythe. He swung a few times, London backed up.

"Boy, you don't know what trouble you're in now!" Alva said excitedly. "I've used one of these since I was four-years old!"

Alva charged London. London swung, barely missed Alva. Alva sideswiped London, slicing through his coat sleeve. A gash appeared on his forearm and blood drained to his wrist. He had no time for the pain or to worry about the blood.

Alva swung again, and London ducked. He pulled the nub end of the scythe and poked Alva in the ribs. Alva yelped, and staggered backwards. London saw Carla's hand holding a .32 snub nose. London jerked back just in time and the gun fired. The bullet zipped past him. Without a thought to it, London swung full force.

The blade of the scythe sliced through Carla's wrist, severing the hand that still held the .32.

Carla let out a high pitched squeal, and fell to her knees. London watched without remorse. But he temporarily forgot about Alva. He turned and swung his scythe, catching nothing but air. Alva was lying on the ground, the bullet that whizzed by London had caught Alva square in the forehead, making a black, bloody dot. London averted his eyes back to Carla, who was now curled up in a fetal position. She was holding her bloody stump with her left hand, weeping hard.

"Hey!" London screamed at Carla. "Where's Rook?"

At first, Carla didn't answer and London repeated the question. "He's dead," she whined. "Dead. Dead. Deaaaaaaaad!"

Carla tried to close her eyes. London pushed her with the tip of his shoe. "Uh-uh! Open your eyes!" He pushed her again and she did what she was told. "I want you to see this!" London walked over Alva. He raised the scythe high over his head and brought the blade down hard. A large gash stretched Alva's head from his neck. A second swipe, took it completely off.

Carla cried out. The scream pierced the hot night air.

***

The pickup pulled up in the driveway of the farm and parked next to Stills' vehicles. Stills came out of the farmhouse and stood on gravel drive, rifle aimed at the pickup. His men backed him, shotguns and assault rifles targeting the same vehicle. Stills lowered his rifle slightly when he saw Carla in the rider's seat bawling, clinging her bandaged right hand to her chest. London got out on the driver's side, holding both hands up in the air, his left hand holding a pillow case. That pillow case looked like it had a soccer ball inside.

"Don't shoot!" London called out. He eased around the pickup, indicating he was not armed by showing the inside of his coat.

"The fuck do you want, city boy?" Stills said.

"I have something for you. Plus, I brought back her." London told him.

"Why in the hell would you think I want her back?"

"One thing I've learned about you Lou Stills, is you are very family oriented. I don't give a shit what you do with her. But the baby, I think you should keep it."

"Baby? She's with child?"

"Yeah…" London looked at Carla and snarled. "She's carrying Alva's child. Get out of the fucking truck!" he demanded.

Carla slowly got out, walked two paces and one of Stills' men took her and forced her into the farmhouse.

"I'll be damned," Stills spit his wad of chew out. The dark black tobacco stained the patch of grass beside him. "What do you have in the sack, city boy?"

London chuckled. He tossed the pillow case at Stills' feet. "Your problem solved!" He got in truck. He started the engine, hit the gas. The pickup roared and slid backwards. "Courtesy of Peter Choaladi!"

London put the gear in drive and the pickup sped off.

SANTA AT THE CAFÉ

by Joe R. Lansdale

Joe R. Lansdale is the author of 45 novels and 30 short story collections. He is best known as the author of the Bram Stoker Award-winning novella *Bubba Ho-Tep*, which was adapted into the Don Coscarelli film of the same title, and the "Hap and Leonard" series, adapted into the popular television series.

WHEN SANTA CAME INTO THE CAFÉ, HE HAD THE FAKE BEARD pulled off his chin and it hung down on his chest. He had his Santa hat folded and stuck through the big black belt around his waist. His hair was red, so it was a sharp contrast to the rest of his outfit.

No one took much notice of him, as the city was full of Santas this time of year, but the middle-aged man behind the counter, a big guy wearing a food-stained white shirt, lifted his hand and waved.

Santa waved back. It was their usual greeting.

Santa took a seat at a booth in the rear, sat down with a sigh and took a look around. The place was packed, as it always was this time of night, and with it being Christmas Eve, and with many eateries shutting down early tonight, it was a natural gathering spot. He felt lucky to have found an empty booth. There were still dishes left on it from the last customer.

A young woman, who looked as if she might be one cup of coffee short of her hair starting to crawl, came over and sat down across from him. She said, "Do you mind?"

He did mind. Or he would have normally, but she wasn't bad looking. She was thin-faced and nicely built with eyes that drooped slightly, as if she might drop off to sleep at any moment. She had a wide mouth full of nice teeth. She had blue jeans on, a sweater and a heavy coat. She had a huge cloth purse with a long shoulder strap.

She said, "There are only a few seats."

"Sure," he said. "Sure, go ahead."

She took off her coat and sat down.

"You work the department store?" she asked.

"Yeah. I got off a few minutes ago."

"Don't see many thin, red-headed Santas," she said.

"Well, at the store, I got this pillow, you see, and I put it under the suit. When I finish for the night, I put the pillow back. It don't belong to me, it belongs to the store. The suit, that's fine though. I do this every

Christmas. You can make pretty good money if you work it right."

"Yeah? How's that?"

"I do it for a couple weeks before Christmas, and if there are enough kids sitting on my lap, and they feel like they're bringing in some business, they like to toss a little extra my way. I mean, you can't live on what I make, but it's a nice enough slice of cheese."

While they talked, a man came over and gathered up the dishes, came back with a rag, and wiped their table, and was gone as swiftly and silently as he had come.

The waitress, wearing a striped uniform the color of a candy cane, arrived. She walked like her feet hurt and there was nothing to go home to. She wore a bright green sprig of plastic mistletoe on her blouse. For all the Christmas spirit she showed, it might as well have been poison ivy.

The young woman ordered coffee. Santa ordered steak and eggs, a side of wheat toast and a glass of milk.

When the waitress left, Santa said, "You ought to eat something, kid. You look like maybe you been holding back on that a bit."

"Just cutting calories."

He studied her for a moment.

"Okay," she said, withering under his gaze. "I'm short on money. I'm not doing so good lately."

"Let me help you out. I'll buy you something."

"I'm fine. Thanks. But, I'm fine."

"Really. Let me. No obligations."

"None?" she said.

"None," he said.

"I don't want you to think I'm trying to work you. That that's why I sat here."

"I don't think that," he said, and then he thought, you know, maybe that's exactly what she did.

But he didn't care.

Santa caught the waitress's eye and called her over.

She came with less enthusiasm than before, which wasn't something Santa thought she could do, and took the woman's order, and went away.

"What's your name?" asked Santa.

"Mary. What's yours?"

"Hell. Tonight. Just call me Santa. I'm buying you a late dinner. Or early breakfast, whatever you want to call it.

They walked a little, and Santa liked the talk. The food came, and when it did he removed the beard and folded it up and pushed it into his belt on the opposite side of his Santa hat.

While they were eating, he saw that the crowd was thinning. That's the way it was. Business hit hard, and then went away. He had taken note the last two weeks. Every night after work he'd come here to eat and watch the crowd. It was entertaining.

He and the young woman finished eating, and Santa looked up and saw a nervous young man come in. Very nervous. He had sweat beads on his forehead the size of witch warts. He sat down and shifted in his seat and touched something inside his coat. The waitress came over and the man ordered.

Santa kept his eye on him. He had seen the type before. Fact was, the nervous man made him nervous. The young woman noticed the nervous man as well.

"He don't seem right," she said.

"No. No, he doesn't."

"Place like this," she said, "it'll fool you. There's lots of money made here. For a greasy spoon it maybe makes as much as Bloomingdale's."

"I doubt that," said Santa.

"All right, that's an exaggeration, but you gotta think, way customers come and go, it does all right."

"I figure you're right."

After a while, the customers thinned. There were half a dozen people left. A few came and went, picking up coffee, but that was it. Santa looked at his watch. 2 a.m.

"You got a home to go to?" the young woman asked Santa.

"Yeah, but I been there before."

"No wife?"

"No dog. No cat. Not much of anything, but four walls and a pretty good couch to sleep on."

"No bed?"

"No bed."

"What do you want to do when you're not Santa?"

"These days, I don't do much of anything. I lost my job a while back."

"What did you do?"

"Short-order cook... Hell, look there."

"She turned to look, the nervous man was up and he pulled a gun out from under his coat just as the waitress was approaching the booth.

For no reason at all, he struck out and hit her on the side of the neck, dropped her and the coffee pot she was carrying to the floor. The pot was hard plastic and it rolled, spilling coffee all over the place. The waitress lay on the floor, not moving.

The man pointed the gun at the man behind the counter. "Give me the money. All of it."

"Hey now," said the man behind the counter, "you don't want to do this."

"Yeah," said the nervous man. "I do."

"All right, take it easy." The counter man looked at Santa, like maybe he had some magic that would help. Santa didn't move. The girl didn't move. The well-dressed man at the bar turned slightly on his stool.

The nervous man pointed his gun at the well-dressed man. "I say don't move, that means you too. You too, over there, Santa and the chick. Freeze up."

Everyone was still, except the counter-man. He started unloading the money from the register, sticking it in a to-go sack.

"Come on," said the nervous man, shaking a little. "Hurry. Don't try and hold back."

"Ain't my money," said the counter-man. "You can have it. I don't want to get shot over money."

The counter-man was stuffing the money in a big take-away sack. There was a lot of it.

When he was almost finished with the stuffing, the nervous man came closer to the counter. The well-dressed man hardly seemed to move, but move he did, and there was a gun in his hand, and he said, "Now hold up. I'm a cop."

The nervous man didn't hold up. He turned with his gun, and the cop fired his gun. The nervous man staggered and sat down on the floor, got part of the way up, then staggered and fell over one of the tables at a booth. He bled on the table and the blood ran down into the coffee the waitress had dropped.

The well-dressed man got up and leaned slightly over the counter and said, "Actually, I ain't no cop. I want the money."

"Not a cop?" said the counter-man.

"Naw, but I thought it might stop him. I didn't want to kill nobody. Just planned on the money."

The counter-man gave him the bag and the well-dressed man walked briskly out the door.

The Cops came. Santa, the young woman and the counter-man

gave their statements, told how two crooks had got into it, and how one of them was, dead and the other had walked away with about two thousand dollars in a to-go bag.

It took about an hour for the interviews, then the dead man's body was carried away, and the waitress, who had come to with a headache, told the man behind the counter she quit. She went out and got a taxi. The man behind the counter got a mop and a bucket and pushed it out to wipe up the blood and coffee.

Santa and the young woman were still there. The counter man told them they could have free coffee.

"I'm gonna close it," said the counter-man, when they had their Styrofoam cups of coffee.

Santa and the young woman went out.

"That was some night," she said.

"Yeah," Santa said. "Some night."

She caught a cab after a long wait with Santa standing beside her at the curb. Santa opened the door and watched her get in and saw the taxi drive off. Santa sighed. She was one fine looking girl. A little skinny, but fine just the same.

Santa went back to the diner and tugged on the door. It was locked. He knocked.

The counter-man came over and let him in and locked the door.

"Damn," said the counter-man. "How about that?"

"Yeah," said Santa. "How about it?"

"Makes it easier, don't it?"

"Yeah, easier."

"Come on," said the counter-man. They went back behind the counter and into a little office. The counter-man moved a bad still-life painting on the wall and there was a safe behind it.

As he turned the dial, the counter-man said, "This way, no one will be looking for you or thinking of me. It's better this way, way things worked out."

"It's one hell of a coincidence."

"I was worried. I figured you took the money at gunpoint, they might think I had something to do with it."

"You do."

The counter-man talked while he turned the dials on the safe.

"I know. But this way, you don't even have to be a fake robber. We just slit it. It works out good, man. I told the police the robber got all we had. All of it. I didn't mention the safe. Boss asks, I'll tell him it was all out.

I hadn't put it in the safe yet. Meant to, but got swamped. But I put it in all right. It was safe. All the guy got was the till. You and me, we're gonna split twenty thousand dollars tonight, and the cops, they're looking for a well-dressed man who pretended to be a cop and got away with a few thousand. They think he got it all. It's sweet."

"Yeah," Santa said, "that's sweet all right."

They split the money and the counter man put his in a take-away bag, and Santa put his inside his Santa suit. It just made him look a little fat.

They went out of the café and the counter man locked the door.

Walking around the corner, the counter man said, "You parked in the same lot?"

"No. I didn't come by car."

"No?"

"No," said Santa. And then the counter man got it. They were at a dark intersection near an alley. No one was in the alley. Santa pulled a gun from one of his big pockets and pointed it at the counter man.

"Come on, man," said the counter man. "You and me, we been friends since you was a fry cook, back over at the Junction Café."

"I knew you from there," Santa said, "But friends, not so much."

"For god's sake," the counter-man, said, "it's Christmas Eve."

"Merry Christmas, then," Santa said and shot the counter-man in the head with his little pistol. It hardly made more than a pop.

Santa picked up the dropped take-way bag and put it inside his suit. Now he really looked like Santa. He put on the beard and the hat and shoved the pistol in his pocket.

He walked smartly back toward the café. He had to pass it on his way to the subway. When he was almost there, he realized there was someone pacing him on the sidewalk across the street. It was dark back where he had been, but now as he neared the café there was light. He could see who was there. Walking on the opposite side of the street was the young woman.

He stopped and turned and looked at her as she crossed the street.

"I decided I didn't want to go home," she said. "You think maybe you could show me your place?"

"My couch?" he said.

"Sure, I can stand it if you can."

"You just been waiting on me?"

"I drove down a piece, changed my mind and walked back. I thought I might catch you."

"That was a long shot."

"Yep. But here you are."

Santa smiled. It was some night. Money, a profitable dissolution of a partnership, and now this fine looking dame. "All right," he said.

She patted his belly.

"You put on weight since I seen you last, what, thirty minutes ago?"

"I got a takeout order with me. Something for tomorrow."

"Under your coat?"

"Yeah, under my coat."

She smiled, and he smiled, and then he quit smiling. She had a gun in her hand. It came out of her big purse as smooth as a samurai drawing a sword.

"I got to say it, just got to let you know that I know your type," she said, "cause I'm the same type. I saw you watching the counter-man count that money. I could see it in your eyes, what you had planned, though I didn't know the counter man was in on it. That was something else. There I was, thinking how I can hang in there until everyone leaves, because, you see, I got plans myself. Then that nervous man came in, and the other guy, the well-dressed fellow, that was some coincidence. When all that happened, I was glad to leave. As I was driving away in the taxi, I looked back, saw you go back to the diner. I thought that was suspicious, 'cause you see, I'm the suspicious type. I had the taxi stop. I walked back and hid in the shadows. Saw the two of you come out. I followed, carefully. I'm like a cat, I want to be. I saw you shoot the counter man, take his share. Guess what, it all fell together then, what went on. Now, I'm gonna take both your shares. That's what I call a real Christmas surprise and one hell of a present for me. I mean, come on, you're Santa. You got to want me to have a good Christmas, right?"

"Now, wait a minute," Santa said, easing his hand toward his pocket for the gun.

He didn't make it. A bullet parted his beard and hit him in the neck and he went back and leaned against the diner wall.

She popped him again. This time in the hand.

Santa sat down hard. His hat fell off.

She opened up his coat and got the money. It was a lot of money. She put the gun away, stuffed the money that was loose inside his suit into her huge cloth purse. She picked up the to-go bag. Someone saw it, it could be a bag of sandwiches, a bag of doughnuts. It could be most anything.

"Merry Christmas," she said to Santa's corpse, and crossed the street and started toward the lights and the subway, and a short ride home.

THE SWEETEST ASS IN THE OZARKS

by Andy Rausch

Andy Rausch is author of *Mad World, Elvis Presley: CIA Assassin*, and *Riding Shotgun and Other American Cruelties*.

STARING AT THE SHELF FILLED WITH SNACK ITEMS, ROACH managed to stand out as a dirtbag, even here, smack dab in the middle of *Deliverance* hillbilly country. His body hadn't been washed in weeks, and his clothes — the standard-issue uniform for a mid-west meth head — were just as dirty. He wore a filthy black beanie, despite it being mid-July when the temperature was ninety almost every day. He reeked of body odor, and his remaining teeth — all eight of them — were the color of piss, complementing his breath, which smelled like something akin to that.

As he stood there mulling over which type of cupcakes to steal, he noticed a ridiculously-attractive young woman entering the convenience store. She was obviously a spoiled little rich girl, probably about 20, wearing tiny designer shorts painted on her ass that highlighted its perfection. Her face looked like that of a porcelain doll — something so flawlessly crafted that one feared it might break if you touched it. Looking at her there, oblivious to his very existence, Roach instantly assessed her as being a stuck-up bitch.

He finally settled on a pack of Ding Dongs, carefully sliding them down the front of his boxers, exposed above his sagging jeans. He turned towards the counter, waited in line for a moment, scratching his nuts, and then purchased a pack of grape cigar wraps. When he turned around, he found the girl now standing right behind him, waiting to buy a single bottle of water. He grinned, exposing his missing teeth.

"I'll bet you got the sweetest ass in the Ozarks," he said, making a point of looking her up and down. As he'd said the line, he'd felt proud of it, genuinely believing she might appreciate it and find it flattering.

She didn't.

She made a face of revulsion. Roach grinned and strode past her, exiting the store. When he got outside, he pulled out the Ding Dongs from beside his own and climbed into his dirty, rust-covered 1990-something Honda Civic. He sat behind the wheel, munching on the stolen cupcakes — the first meal he'd had in days — and watched the door of the store. The chick with the nice ass walked out, making her way to a little red

Corvette, still unaware of his presence. Roach was surprised to see that she was alone.

She got into her car, sat there for a moment, and then pulled out of the lot and onto the street leading back to the interstate ramp. Roach followed at a distance, careful not to draw her attention. He stared ahead through the dirty bug-guts-covered windshield, making sure to leave considerable distance between their vehicles. Having done this very thing on many an occasion, he was somewhat of a pro at this.

He reached down to the floorboard, littered with a couple years' worth of trash, and felt around for the pack of smokes he'd accidentally dropped earlier in the day. After feeling around amongst a moldy half-eaten Egg McMuffin, dozens of damp cigarette butts, and a few empty beer cans, he finally located the Pall Malls. He picked up the pack, fished out a cigarette, and put it to his lips, lighting it.

He stared at the Corvette, imagining the sexy little girl inside it. He remembered every single curve of her body. Her beautiful face. Her plump breasts. He started to fantasize about the many things he would do to her if he caught her alone. He planned to make sweet love to her if given the chance. Of course, society had other less savory words for the act, like rape or sexual assault, but to Roach this was lovemaking, and he had made his share of love in his day. Now driving in the opposite direction he'd originally been traveling, this little side mission would add time to his trip to visit his old cellmate Russell. But Russell would understand. Russell knew the importance of a good piece of ass, and if he could get an eyeful of this chick, he'd have fully understood Roach's motivations.

Getting bored and needing stimuli to entertain his short attention span, Roach turned on the radio. He scanned through the stations. After discovering that the local radio stations were all Christian, Country, or even worse — Christian Country — he switched the damn thing off.

Roach had followed her for about fifteen miles when he saw the Corvette's right turn signal begin to blink. He slowed a little, careful to maintain an adequate distance. She turned off onto a small blacktop road heading off into the boonies. When Roach came to the road, he turned as well, continuing to follow her. Maybe he wouldn't lose as much time as he'd thought. If he could catch her out in the middle of BFE, he could hold her down and make sweet love to her. Then he could turn back around and head for St. Louis.

A few minutes later, he saw the Corvette stop on the side of the road. He looked around, making sure there were no witnesses anywhere around. There weren't. In fact, he hadn't passed a single vehicle since they'd started down this road. Roach slowed down, idling toward her vehicle. He watched the Corvette, but the girl didn't emerge. He edged slowly towards her car, their distance shrinking rapidly. Finally, he was right behind her. He pulled over and stopped. He left the motor running, thinking this wouldn't take long. He climbed out and closed the door. He stood there for a moment, scanning the area once more to make sure they were alone. He moved slowly towards the driver's side door, creeping around the car like a cautious cop during a traffic stop.

When he came to the window, he was happy to discover it was already down. The chick looked up at him, smiling. This caught him off-guard, momentarily confusing him. Had she known he'd been following her? Had she decided she wanted to have sex with him out here in the middle of nowhere? Maybe. Anything was possible, and Roach considered himself to be a pretty good-looking dude.

He smiled, flashing that winning smile again. "Is everything okay?"

"Yeah," she said, chewing gum. "What makes you ask?"

"I thought maybe your car broke down."

"And what? You thought you would be a Good Samaritan, help me out?"

He grinned, now believing she was warm for his form. "Yeah, something like that."

She grinned a mischievous grin, really laying it on now. "Can I show you something?" she asked in a tone that was upbeat and sexy.

"What you got?"

"Something hot," she teased.

"Sure," he said. "I'd love to see anything you got that you wanna show me."

"Come over here, real close to the window."

He could feel his erection starting to writhe around in his boxers. He grinned, leaning in towards her. It was then that she raised her arm, holding out a large pistol, training it at his face.

"What the fuck?" he asked, startled and unsure how to react. He stiffened, stepping back.

"You move and I'll shoot your dick."

"Okay, I won't move."

"So, I guess this wasn't what you thought I had?" she asked.

He shook his head. "No."

"What were you gonna do out here? Were you gonna rape me? Were you gonna hurt me?"

"No," he insisted. "I swear, you got it all wrong. I was just tryin' to help."

"Be a Good Samaritan."

He nodded. "Exactly."

She extended her arm towards him, pointing the pistol for emphasis. "Open my door, fucker," she said. He nervously opened the door, and she climbed out, never once taking her eyes or the gun's aim away from his face. She stood before him now.

"Get in the car," she said. "You and me, we're going for a ride."

His mind was reeling. "Why would I want to do that?"

"Because I said so."

"But…"

That was the moment she squeezed the trigger and shot him in his right arm. The impact knocked him back, and he yelped with pain. He reached up with his left hand, grabbing the bloody wound. "God help me!" he screamed, looking up at the sky, searching for divine intervention.

"He won't help you now," she said. "That's rich, though. A minute ago you were planning to rape me, you rapist piece of shit. Now you're asking God for help."

Roach said nothing. He just stood there, holding his blood-covered arm, crying and heaving in a way no adult man should. She motioned with the pistol. "Get in the fucking car."

He stared at her, hesitant, still in shock.

"You want me to shoot your ass again?"

"No," he managed, sort of stuttering the word.

"Then get in the goddamn car."

He turned for the passenger's side, but she stopped him. "No, you're gonna drive. That way I can keep my eye on you."

Roach didn't say a word. He opened the driver's door and climbed in behind the wheel. As the woman walked around the back of the vehicle, he had the idea he should start the car and take off. The only problem was she had taken the damn keys. She climbed into the passenger's seat, the pistol still aimed at his head.

She handed him the keys. "Start her up and then turn around and head back to the interstate."

He did as he was told.

"You ever drive a Corvette before?" she asked.

"Can't say I have."

"I kind of figured. Most scumbag crank fiends don't have high-end sports cars. Most of them got trashy old beaters like you got… at least 'til they sell them for meth."

He started to feign offense at the suggestion he was a meth addict, but thought the better of it. So he kept his mouth shut and drove. Neither of them said a word except for the occasions on which she gave him directions. She was turned towards him in her seat, still looking hot as ever. Even now Roach thought about the love-making he would probably never get to do with her.

About thirty minutes later, they exited the interstate, heading into Springfield. She directed him to her house. It was a tiny little blue house, something quaint and middle class you might expect a grandma to live in. It didn't look like someplace a little rich bitch like her would live. He wondered if she had pissed off Mommy and Daddy and they had cut her off. Roach looked around, hoping some random neighbor or two might see them, but there were none in sight. She ordered him to get out of the car. He did, and she followed him up the driveway and to the front door. She handed him the keys, and he unlocked the door. He entered the house first, and she and the gun followed close behind.

She grinned. "Do you mind if I show you something?"

Recognizing the familiar question, he steeled himself for whatever might be coming.

"That didn't work out so good for you last time, did it?" she asked.

Roach said nothing. She opened a door inside the kitchen, revealing wooden stairs that led down into a darkened basement. She instructed him to walk down them. He took two steps on the rickety wooden stairs before she flipped a light switch, lighting up the place. It had the smell of every basement ever, bringing back memories of the summers he'd stayed with his cousins, Mel and Jenny, who'd had a basement that had been converted into a nice little family room. As he walked down the steps, Roach saw that this basement was very different. There was no nice little family room here.

He looked down at what was there in disbelief.

"You like that?" she asked, sounding pleased with herself.

Roach stared at the heavy chains bolted to the brick wall. There was dried blood splattered on the cement floor and on the walls. This was a goddamn torture room! What kind of girl was this?

When they reached the bottom of the stairs, he started to turn back towards her. She pointed the gun at the chains. "Go over there and put the cuffs on, you piece of shit."

He begrudgingly did what she told him to do. He put his back to the brick wall, reaching up and fastening the metal clasp around his left wrist. It locked into place with a metallic snap. With his left arm tethered there, he couldn't fasten his right wrist. Before he could say anything, she muttered, "I know, I know..."

She walked towards him, striking him hard across the face with the hard pistol, cracking and bloodying his nose. She grabbed his right arm and held it up to the hanging cuff, fastening it around his wrist. Now he was completely at her mercy, and that fact was not lost upon him.

Blood poured from his nose, running into his mouth, down onto his chin, and dripping onto his yellowed once-white Sublime shirt. The blood was thick and salty, and he knew eventually he would gag on it. "What now?" he asked weakly.

She sat the pistol on the floor.

What was this?

She started to unbuckle his belt. Roach was unsure what this meant, unsure if this was a good thing or a bad thing. Maybe this was just some kind of kinky shit she was into. Maybe all of this was part of some detailed sex game. Maybe they would still make love. She yanked his jeans and his boxers down around his ankles, exposing his flaccid penis, poking out through a dense foliage of curly hair. She chuckled, staring at his dangling manhood. "That all you got, sport?"

She turned and walked across the room to a solitary green Army foot locker sitting against the wall. She leaned down and opened it. The lid now sat open, but its contents were obscured from Roach's view. She crouched over the box for a moment before standing again. When she turned towards him, Roach saw that she was now holding a large hunting knife, the kind hunters used to skin their prey.

"No," he said. "Please don't. I'll... I'll be good."

She moved towards him, her face now completely slack, as if this was simply some mundane chore she had to do; a task that brought her no pleasure. As she approached, Roach stared at the blade, which caught a glint of light from the overhead lamp. She came to him, close enough that he could smell the gum she was chewing.

He closed his eyes, frightened, hoping it would all go away. Soon he felt the flat side of the blade caressing his testicles. She moved it slowly along them, loosely hanging skin dragging behind. When she brought the blade upwards, still torturously slow, it rubbed across the head of his penis. This contact, unwelcome as it was, nevertheless brought his dick to life. It started to stir. She rubbed the blade against it slowly.

"What do you think? Should I cut your dick off?"

"No," he said, starting to sob again.

"What were you gonna do with it?"

He said nothing.

"Where you gonna rape me with it?"

He remained silent.

She turned and walked back to the foot locker. She knelt down again, hovering there for a moment. When she finally stood, she held her arm behind her back, concealing whatever she now held. She walked towards him, and he wondered what sort of weapon she now possessed.

When she was up in his face again, she brought out her arm, revealing a giant black dildo.

Roach was instantly terrified, his mind imagining a plethora of possible scenarios, none of which were good. *"No,"* he pleaded. *"Please, no."*

"Were you gonna rape me, motherfucker?" she asked, staring past the plastic dick and into his eyes. "Is that what you wanted?" Her voice grew angrier and more venomous with every word she spat.

"What was it you said to me?" she asked.

"What?" He had no idea what she meant.

"Back at the store. What was it you said?"

"I don't know."

"I do." She smiled, pushing the dildo into his face.

He turned his head, whimpering.

She repeated the words: "I'll bet you got the sweetest ass in the Ozarks."

And Roach started to scream.

***

It was almost dark when she pulled the Corvette into the gravel driveway of the abandoned farmhouse. She drove to the end of the gravel, then pulling off into the yard. She drove slowly through the weeds and high grass, around the farmhouse to the old stone well.

As she idled the car towards it, she considered its history, wondering how old it was. Probably a hundred years or so, at least. She stopped the car and pushed the button to pop the trunk. She got out and walked to the back of the vehicle, seeing Roach's dead, naked body in the trunk, half covered by an old My Little Pony blanket. At least this guy was skinny, she thought. He would certainly be lighter than the gross old truck driver she'd picked up the previous month. Getting him into the well had been a real chore. Moving this meth-smoking dickhead wouldn't be a walk in the park, but it should be at least a little easier.

She grabbed the green backpack she kept in the trunk. She unzipped it and pulled out a pair of latex gloves, sliding them onto her hands. She then reached into the trunk and grabbed Roach under his arms. She didn't like doing this. The rancid scent of his arm pits would be on her person, even with the gloves. She shrugged to no one and then hefted the body out of the trunk, letting it fall hard to the ground, head first, Roach's neck snapping upon impact. She looked over at the well, only a few feet away.

I just have to do it and get it over with, she thought. Once she was finished, Roach would be with all the others in the bottom of the well, and she could go home and have dinner with her cat Bedelia and watch *Grey's Anatomy* before bed.

GUEST SERVICE : A QUARRY STORY

by Max Allan Collins

Max Allan Collins is best known as the author of *The Road to Perdition*, which was adapted into the hit film starring Tom Hanks. He has written many, many novels including the popular series *Nolan, Mallory, Nathan Heller, Dick Tracy, Eliot Ness,* and *Quarry,* which was adapted as a series for Cinema. He has also written many novelizations, including *Saving Private Ryan, The Mummy,* and *American Gangster.*

AN AMERICAN FLAG FLAPPED LAZILY ON ITS SILVER POLE against a sky so washed-out a blue the handful of clouds were barely discernible. The red, white and blue of it were garishly out of place against the brilliant greens and muted blues of the Minnesota landscape, pines shimmering vividly in late morning sunlight, the surface of gray-blue Sylvan Lake glistening with sun, rippling with gentle waves. The rails of the grayish brown deck beyond my quarters were like half-hearted prison bars that I peeked through, as I did my morning sit-ups on the other side of the triple glass doors of my well-appointed guest suite.

I was not a guest of Sylvan Lodge, however: I ran the place. Once upon a time I had owned a resort in Wisconsin not unlike this - not near the acreage, of course, and not near the occupancy; but I had *owned* the place, whereas here I was just the manager.

Not that I had anything to complain about. I was lucky to have the job. When I ran into Gary Petersen in Milwaukee, where he was attending a convention and I was making a one-night stopover to remove some emergency funds from several bank deposit boxes, I was at the loosest of loose ends. The name I'd lived under for over a decade was unusable; my past had caught up with me, back at the other place, and I'd lost everything in a near instant: my business yanked from under me, my wife (who'd had not a clue of my prior existence) murdered in her sleep.

Gary, however, had recognized me in the hotel bar and used a name I hadn't used since the early '7Os: my real name.

"Jack!" he said, only that wasn't the name he used. For the purposes of this narrative, however, we'll say my real name is Jack Keller.

"Gary," I said, surprised by the warmth creeping into my voice. "You son of a bitch...you're still alive."

Gary was a huge man — six six, weighing in at somewhere between three hundred pounds and a ton; his face was masked in a bristly brown beard, his skull exposed by hair loss, his dark eyes bright, his smile friendly, in a goofy, almost child-like way.

"Thanks to you, asshole," he said.

We'd been in Vietnam together.

"What the hell have you been doing all these years, Jack?"

"Mostly killing people."

He boomed a laugh. "Yeah, right!"

"Don't believe me, then." I was, incidentally, pretty drunk. I don't drink often, but I'd been through the mill lately.

"Are you crying, Jack?"

"Fuck no," I said. But I was.

Gary slipped his arm around my shoulder; it was like getting cuddled by God. "Bro - what's the deal? What shit have you been through?"

"They killed my wife," I said, and cried drunkenly into his shoulder.

"Jesus, Jack - who...?"

"Fucking assholes...fucking assholes...."

We went to his suite. He was supposed to play poker with some buddies, but he called it off.

I was very drunk and very morose, and Gary was, at one time anyway, my closest friend, and during the most desperate of days.

I told him everything. I told him how after I got back from Nam, I found my wife - my first wife - shacked up with some guy, some fucking auto mechanic, who was working under a car when I found him and kicked the jack out. The jury let me off, but I was finished in my hometown, and I drifted until the 'Broker' found me. The 'Broker', who gave me the name 'Quarry', was the conduit through whom the murder for hire contracts came, and, what? Ten years later, the 'Broker' was dead, by my hand, and I was out of the killing business and took my savings. I went to Paradise Lake in Wisconsin, where eventually I met a pleasant, attractive, not terribly bright woman. She and I were in the lodge business until the past came looking for me, and suddenly she was dead, and I was without a life or even identity. I had managed to kill the fuckers responsible for my wife's killing, but otherwise I had nothing. Nothing left but some money stashed away that I was now retrieving.

I told Gary all this through the night, in considerably more detail, though probably even less coherently, although coherently enough that when I woke up the next morning where Gary had laid me out on the extra bed, I knew I'd told him too much.

He was asleep, too. Like me, he was in the same clothes we'd worn to that bar; like me, he smelled of booze, only he also reeked of cigarette smoke. I did a little, too, but it was Gary's smoke: I never picked up the habit. Bad for you.

He looked like a big dead animal, except for his barrel - like chest heaving with breath. I looked at this man - like me, he was somewhere between forty and fifty now, not the kids we'd been before the war made us worse than just men.

I still had liquor in me, but I was sober now. Too deadly fucking sober. I studied my best – friend – of – long - ago and wondered if I had to kill him.

I was standing over him, staring down at him, mulling that over, when his eyes opened suddenly, like a timer turning on the lights in a house to fend off burglars.

He smiled a little, then it faded, then his eyes narrowed. "Morning, Jack."

"Morning, Gary."

"You've got that look."

"What look is that?"

"The cold one. The one I first saw a long time ago."

I swallowed and looked away from him. Sat on the edge of the bed across from him and rubbed my eyes with the heels of my hands.

He sat across from me with his big hands on his big knees and said, "How the hell d'you manage it?"

"What?"

"Hauling my fat ass into that Medivac."

I grunted a laugh. "The same way a little mother lifts a Buick off her baby."

"In my case, you lifted the Buick onto the baby. Let me buy you breakfast."

"Okay."

In the hotel coffee shop, he said, "Funny...what you told me last night...about the business you used to be in?"

I sipped my coffee; I didn't look at him - didn't show him my eyes. "Yeah?"

"I'm in the same game."

Now I looked at him; I winced with disbelief. "What...?"

He corrected my initial thought. "The tourist game, I mean. I run a lodge near Brainerd."

"No kidding."

"That's what this convention is. Northern Resort Owners

Association."

"I heard of it," I said, nodding. "Never bothered to join, myself."

"I'm a past president. Anyway, I run a place called Sylvan Lodge. My third and current, and I swear to God my ever-lasting wife, Ruth Ann, inherited it from her late parents, rest their hardworking souls." None of this came as a surprise to me. Grizzly bear Gary had always drawn women like a great big magnet - usually good-looking little women who wanted a father figure, Papa Bear variety. Even in Bangkok on R & R, Gary never had to pay for pussy, as we used to delicately phrase it.

"I'm happy for you. I always figured you'd manage to marry for money."

"My ass! I really love Ruth Ann. You should see the knockers on the child."

"A touching testimonial if ever I heard one. Listen...about that bullshit I was spouting last night..."

His dark eyes became slits, the smile in his brushy face disappeared. "We'll never speak of that again. Understood? Never."

He reached out and squeezed my forearm.

I sighed in relief and smiled tightly and nodded, relieved. Killing Gary would have been no fun at all.

He continued, though. "My sorry fat ass wouldn't even be on this planet, if it wasn't for you. I owe you big-time."

"Bullshit," I said, but not very convincingly.

"I've had a good life, at least the last ten years or so, since I met Ruthie. You've been swimming in Shit River long enough. Let me help you."

"Gary, I..."

"Actually, I want you to help me."

"Help *you*?"

Gary's business was such a thriving one that he had recently invested in a second lodge, one across the way from his Gull Lake resort. He couldn't run both places himself, at least not 'without running my fat ass off'. He offered me the job of managing Sylvan.

"We'll start you at $50k, with free housing. You can make a tidy buck with no overhead to speak of, and you can tap into at least one of your marketable skills, and at the same time be out of the way. Keep as low a profile as you like. You don't even have to deal with the tourists, to speak of - we have a social director for that. You just keep the boat afloat. Okay?"

"Okay," I said, and we shook hands. Goddamn I was glad I hadn't killed him.

Now, a little more than six months into the job, and a month into the first summer season, I was settled in and damn near happy. My quarters, despite the rustic trappings of the cabin-like exterior, were modern - pine panelling skirting the room with pale yellow pastel walls rising to a high pointed ceiling. It was just one room with a bath and kitchenette, but it was a big room, facing the lake which was a mere hundred yards from the deck that was my back porch. Couch, cable TV, plenty of closet space, a comfortable wall bed. I didn't need anything more.

During off - season, I could move into more spacious digs if I liked, but I didn't figure I'd bother. Just a short jog across the way was an indoor swimming pool with hot tub and sauna, plus a tennis court; a golf course, shared with Gary's other lodge, was nearby. My duties were constant, but mostly consisted of delegating authority, and the gay chef of our gourmet restaurant made sure I ate well and free, and I'd been banging Nikki, the college girl who had the social director position for the summer, so my staff relations were solid.

I took a shower after my push-ups and got into the usual gray Sylvan lodge t - shirt, black shorts and gray – and - black Reebox, to take a stroll around the grounds, and check up on the staff. I was sitting on the couch tying my tennies, with a good view of the patch of green and slice of sand below my deck, when I heard an unpleasant, gravelly male voice tearing somebody a new asshole. "Why the fuck *didn't* you rent the boat in advance, Mindy?"

"I'm sorry, Dick."

"Jesus fucking Christ, woman, you think I want to come to a goddamn lake without a goddamn boat?"

His voice carried into my living room with utter clarity, borne by the wind coming across the lake.

I looked up. He was big - not as big as my friend Gary, but big enough. He wore green and red plaid shorts and a lime - green golf shirt and a straw pork - pie hat with a wide leather band; he was as white as the underbelly of a crocodile, except for his face, which was a bloodshot red. Even at this distance I could see the white tufts of eyebrows over narrow-set eyes and a bulbous nose.

He was probably fifty, or maybe more; his wife was an attractive blonde, much younger, possibly thirty-five. She wore a denim shorts outfit that revealed an almost plump but considerably shapely figure, nicely top - heavy. Her hair was too platinum for her age, and too big for her face, a huge hair - sprayed construction with a childishly incongruous pink bow in it.

Her pretty face, even from where I sat on my couch, was tired - looking, puffy. But she'd been beautiful, once. An actress or a dancer or something. And even now, even with the too big, too platinum hair, she made a man's head turn. Except maybe for my chef. "But I thought you'd use your brother's boat..."

"He's in fucking Europe, woman!"

"I know...but you said we were going to use Jim's boat..."

"Well, that fell through! He loaned his place *and* his boat to some fucker from Duluth he wanted to impress! Putting business before his own goddamn brother..."

"But I didn't know that..."

He grabbed her arm; hard. "You should've made it your business *to* know! *You* were supposed to make the vacation arrangements. God knows you have little enough to do otherwise. I have a fucking living to make for us. You should've got off your fat ass and..."

"Let's talk to Guest Services," his wife said, desperately. "Maybe they can help us rent a boat somewhere in the area."

"Excuse me!" I called from the deck.

Still holding onto the woman's arm, the aptly named Dick scowled my way. "What do you want? Who the hell are you?"

I was leaning over the rail. "I'm the manager here. Jack Keller. Can I be of any help?"

He let go of her arm, and the plump, pretty blonde moved toward me, looking up at me with a look that strained to be pleasant. "I called both numbers your brochure lists and wasn't able to rent a boat..."

"It's a busy time," I said. "Let me look into it for you."

"We're only going to be here a week," Dick said. "I hate to waste a goddamn day!"

She touched his arm, gently. "We wanted to golf while we're here...we did bring the clubs...we could do that today...."

He brushed her hand away like it was a bug. "Probably have to call ahead for that, too."

"I'll call over for you," I said. "You are...?"

"The Waltons," he said.

"Excuse me?"

"We're the fucking Waltons! Dick and Mindy."

The Waltons. Okay....

"Dick, I'll make the call. After lunch, around one - thirty a suitable tee time?"

"Good," Dick said, pacified. "Thanks for your help."

"That's what I'm here for," I said.

"Thank you," Mindy said, and smiled at me, and looped her arm in his, and he allowed her to, as he walked her over to the restaurant.

I called over to the golf course and got the Waltons a tee time and called Gary over at Gull Lake Lodge to see about a boat.

"They should've called ahead," Gary said. "Why do you want to help these people? Friends of yours?"

"Hardly. The husband's an obnoxious cocksucker who'll browbeat his wife into a nervous breakdown if I don't bail her out."

"Oh. The Waltons."

"Addams Family is more like it. So you know them?"

"They were at Sylvan the last two seasons. Dick Walton is a real pain in the ass and an ugly drunk."

"Maybe we don't want his business."

"Trouble is, he's as rich as he is obnoxious. He's from Minneapolis - runs used car lots all over the Cities. Big fucking ego - does his own commercials. 'Big Deals with Big Dick' is his motto..."

"Catchy."

"It's been popular with Twin Cities school kids for a couple decades. He's worth several mil. And he brings his sales staff up for conferences in the off-season."

"So we cater to him."

"Yeah. Within reason. If he starts busting up the bar or something, cut him off and toss his ass out. When he starts spoiling things for our other guests, then fuck him."

"I like your attitude, Gary. But what about a boat?"

"He can use mine for the week. It's down at dock nine."

"That's generous."

"Generous my ass. Charge him double the going rate."

***

The restaurant at Sylvan's is four-star, and it's a real asset for the business, but it's the only thing Gary and I ever really disagreed about. Dinner was by reservation only, and those reservations filled up quick; and the prices were more New York than midwest.

"The goddamn restaurant's a real calling card for us," Gary would say. "Brings in people staying at other lodges and gives 'em a look at ours."

"But we're not serving our own guests," I'd say. "We're a hotel at heart, Gary, and our clientele shouldn't have to mortgage the farm to buy supper, and they shouldn't get turned away 'cause they don't have reservations."

"I appreciate your dedication to the guests, Jack. But that restaurant brings in about a third of our income, so fuckin' forget it, okay?"

But of course I didn't. We had this same argument at least twice a month.

That particular evening I was having the house specialty—pan-fried walleye-and enjoying the way the moon looked reflected on the silvery lake when I heard the gravel-edged sound of Dick Walton's voice, singing a familiar tune.

"You're a stupid cunt!" he was telling her.

They had a table in the corner, but the long, rather narrow dining room with its windows on the lake didn't allow anyone much privacy. Even approaching nine-thirty, the restaurant was full-older couples, families, a honeymooning couple, all turned their eyes to the asshole in the lime sport coat and green and white plaid pants who was verbally abusing the blonde woman in the green and white floral sundress.

She was crying. Digging a Kleenex into eyes where the mascara was already smeared. When she got up from the table to rush out, she looked like an embarrassed, haunted raccoon.

He shouted something unintelligible at her, and sneered, then returned to his big, fat, rare steak.

The restaurant manager, a guy in his late twenties who probably figured his business degree would get him a better gig than this, came over to my table and leaned in. He was thin, sandy - haired, pockmarked; he wore a pale yellow sweater over a shirt and tie.

"Mr. Keller," he said, "what should I do about Mr. Walton?"

"Leave him alone, Rick. Without his wife to yell at, I doubt he'll make much more fuss."

"Should I cut him off with the bar?"

"No."

He gave me a doubtful expression, one eyebrow arching. "Personally, I..."

"Just leave it alone. If he passes out, he won't bother his wife or anybody, and that would probably be ideal."

Rick sighed - he didn't like me much, knowing that I was lobbying to have his four - star restaurant turned into a cafeteria - but he nodded in acceptance of my ruling, and padded off.

I finished my walleye, touched a napkin to my lips and headed over to Walton's table.

"You got my message about the boat?" I asked.

His grin was tobacco-stained; the tufts of white eyebrow raised so high they might have been trying to crawl off his face. "Yeah! That was white of you, Jack! You're okay. Sit down, I'll buy you one."

I sat where his wife had been (her own walleye practically untouched on the plate before me), but said, "I had enough for tonight. I know my limit."

"So do I, buddy boy..." He pointed a steak knife at me and winked. "...it's when the fuckin' *lights* go out."

I laughed. "Say, what was the little woman riding you about? If you don't mind my asking."

His face balled up like a fist. "Bitch. Lousy little cunt. She fucked up royal this afternoon."

"Oh?"

"Yeah, fuck her. We're playing with another couple - the Goldsteins, from Des Moines. He's a dentist. Those docs are loaded, you know. Particularly the Hebrew ones."

"Up the wazoo," I affirmed.

"Anyway, Mindy is a decent little golfer...usually. Shoots a 19 handicap on the country club course back home...but this afternoon she didn't shoot for shit. I lost a hundred bucks because of her!"

"Well, hell, Dick - everybody has a bad afternoon once in a while."

His aftershave wafted across the table to tickle my nose - a grotesque parody of the pine scent that nature routinely provided us here.

"I think she did it just to *spite* me. I'd swear she muffed some of those shots just to get my fuckin' goat."

His speech was pretty slurred. '

"That sounds like a woman," I said.

He looked at me with as steady a gaze as he could muster. "Jack - I like you."

"I like you, Dick. You're a real man's man."

I offered him my water glass for him to clink his tumbler of Scotch on the rocks against.

"I'll have to sneak away from the little woman," he said, winking again, "so we can spend some *quality* time together."

"Let's do that," I said. "You going fishing tomorrow?"

He was lighting up an unfiltered cigarette; it took a lot of effort. "Yeah - me and that kike dentist. Wanna come along?"

"Got to work, Dick. Check in with me later, though. Maybe we can take in one of the casinos."

"One of the ones those injuns run?"

Gambling having been ruled legal on reservation land, casinos run by Native Americans were a big tourist draw in our neck of the woods.

"That's right, Dick. A whole tribe of Tontos looking to fleece the Lone Ranger."

"Hah! How 'bout tomorrow night?"

"We'll see. If you're getting up early tomorrow morning, Dick, to fish, maybe you ought to hit the sack."

He guzzled at his drink. "I ought to hit that fuckin' cunt I'm married to, is what I oughta hit."

"Take it easy. It's a hell of a thing, but a man can get in trouble for hitting a woman these days."

"Hell of a thing, ain't it, Jack? Hell of a thing."

I walked out with him; he shambled along, slipping an arm around me, cigarette trailing ash.

"You're a hell of a guy," he told me, almost crying. "Hell of a guy."

"So are you, Dick," I said.

Outside the real pines were almost enough to cancel the room-freshener cologne he was wearing.

Almost.

***

I was sitting in the dark in my underwear, sipping a Coke in the glow of the portable television, watching a Randolph Scott western from the 1950s. I kept the sound low, because I had the doors to the deck pushed open to enjoy the lake breeze, and I didn't want my movie-watching to disturb any of the guests who might be strolling along the beach, enjoying the night.

Something about the acoustics of the lake made her crying seem to echo, as if carried on the wind from a great distance, though she was at my feet, really-stumbling across the grass beneath my deck.

Underwear or not, I went out to check on her - because the crying sounded like more than just emotions: there was physical pain in it, too.

"Mrs. Walton," I called, recognizing her. She still wore the flowered sundress, the scoop top of it displaying the swell of her swell bosom. "Are you all right?"

She nodded, stumbling. "Just need a drink...need a drink..."

"The bar's closed. Why don't you step up here, and I'll get you a beer or something."

"No...no..." She shook her head and then I saw it: the puffiness of the left side of her face, eye swollen shut, the flesh already blackening.

I ran down the little wooden stairs; if somebody complained to the manager about the man running around in his underwear, well fuck 'em: I was the manager. I took her by the arm and walked her up onto the deck and inside, where I deposited her on the couch in front of the TV, where Randolph Scott was shooting Lee Van Cleef.

"Just let me get dressed," I said, and I returned with pants on and a beer in hand, which I held out to her. "It's all I have, I'm afraid," I said.

She took it and held it in her hands like something precious; sipped it like a child taking first communion.

I got her a wash cloth with some ice in it.

"He's hit you before, hasn't he?" I said, sitting beside her.

She nodded; tears trickled from the good eye. Her pink-bowed platinum blonde hair wasn't mussed: too heavily sprayed for that.

"How often?" I asked.

"All...all the time."

"Why don't you leave the son of a bitch?"

"He says...he says he'll kill me."

"Probably just talk. Turn him in for beating you. They go hard on guys who do that, nowadays, and then it'll be harder for him to do it again."

"No...he would kill me. Or have somebody do it. He has...the kind of connections where you can get somebody killed, if you want. And it'll just be written off as an accident. I bet you find that hard to believe, don't you?"

"Yeah." I sipped my Coke. "Sounds utterly fantastic."

"Well, it's true."

"Are you sure you're not staying 'cause of the prenup?"

She sighed, nodded slowly, the hand with the ice in the washcloth moving with her head. "There *is* a prenuptial agreement. I wouldn't get a thing. Well, ten thousand, I think."

"But you're not staying 'cause of the money."

"No! I don't care about the money...exactly. I got family I take care of. A younger sister who's going to college, mom's got heart trouble and no insurance."

"So it *is* about money."

The good eye winced. "No! No...it *was* about money. That's why I married Dick. I was...I was trash. A waitress. Topless dancer, for a while. Anything to make a buck...but never hooking. Never!"

"Where did you meet Dick?"

"In a titty-bar a friend of his used to run. I wasn't dancing, then...I was a waitress. Tips in a topless place are always incredible."

"So I hear."

"This was, I don't know...over ten years ago."

"You been taking this shit all that time?"

"No. He was sweet, at first. But he didn't drink as much in those days. The more he drank, the worse it got. He calls me stupid. He can't have kids...his sperm count is lower than he is. But he calls *me* 'barren' and hits me...says I'm fat. Do you think I'm fat?"

I'd been looking down the front of her sundress at the time, and swallowed, and said, "Uh, no. I don't like these skinny girls they're pushing on us, these days."

"Fake tits and boy's butts, all of them." Her lips were trembling; her voice sounded bitter. "He has a girlfriend...she works in a titty bar, too. A different joint - this is one that he's got money in. She's like that: skinny little thing and a plastic chest and a flat little ass."

"You should leave him. Forget his threats. Forget the money."

"I can't. I...I wish he was dead. Just fucking dead."

"Don't talk that way."

Her whole body was trembling; she hugged herself with one arm, as if very, very cold. "I need a miracle. I need a goddamn miracle."

"Well, here's a suggestion."

"Yes?"

"Say your prayers tonight. Maybe God'll straighten it all out."

"With a miracle?"

"Or something," I said.

***

"Hop in," he said.

He was behind the wheel of a red-bodied, white-topped Cadillac; his bloodshot face was split in a shit-eating grin as he leaned over to open the door on the rider's side. He was wearing a green-and-orange plaid sportcoat - it was like a Scotsman had puked on him - and orange trousers and lots of clunky gold jewelry.

I slipped inside the spacious car. "Didn't have any trouble getting away?"

"Naw! That little bitch doesn't dare give me any lip. I'd just knock some *more* sense in her! Anybody see you go?"

"No. I think we're all right."

I'd had him pick me up at the edge of the road, half a mile from the resort, in darkness; I said I was on call tonight and wasn't supposed to be away.

"You tell your wife where you were going and who with?"

"Hell no! None of her goddamn business! I tell you, Jack, I should never have married that lowlife cunt. She's got a family like something out of *Deliverance*. Poor white trash, pure and simple. No fuckin' class at all."

"Why don't you dump her, then?"

"I just might! You know what a prenuptial agreement is, don't you, Jack?"

"Got a vague idea."

"Well, my lawyer assures me I don't have to give her jack shit. She's out in the cold on her flabby ass, soon as I give the say so."

"Why don't you, then?"

"I might. I might...but it could be bad for business. I use her in some of my commercials, and she's kinda popular. Or anyway, her big ol' titties are, pardon my French."

"She helps you put up a good front."

"Hah! Yeah, that's a good one, Jack...that's a good one..." The drive to the casino was about an hour, winding through tall pines and little bump-in-the-road towns; the night was clear, the moon full again, the world bathed in an unreal, and lovely, silver. I studied the idyllic landscape, pretending to listen to Walton blather on about his accomplishments in the used-car game, cracking the window to let some fresh air cancel out his Pinesol aftershave and cigarette smoke.

It was midweek, but the casino looked busy - just a sprawling one-story prefabricated building, looking about as exotic as a mobile home, but for the huge LAKEVIEW CASINO neon; the term 'Lakeview' was cosmetic, as the nearest lake was a mile away. Some construction, some expansion, was going on, and the front parking lot was a mess.

He pulled around back, as I instructed; a couple of uniformed security guards with guns - Indians, like most of the employees here - were stationed in front. None were in back. A man and a woman, both weaving with drink, were wandering out to their car as Walton found a place to park.

"No limit here, right?" he asked.

"Right. You bring a pretty good roll?"

"Couple grand. I got unlimited cash access on my gold card, too."

The car with the couple in it pulled out, and drove unsurely around the building. Once their car lights were gone, it was as dark as the inside of cow, back here. I got out of the Cad.

"If you need a couple bucks, Jack, just ask."

He had his back to me as we walked toward the casino. When my arm slipped around him, it startled him, but he didn't have much time to react: the knife had pierced his windpipe by then.

When I withdrew the hunting knife, a scarlet geyser sprayed the night, but away from me. He fell like a pine tree, flopping forward, but the sound was just a little slap against the pavement. The knife made more noise as it clattered against the pavement; I kicked it under a nearby pick-up. He gurgled a while, but that soon stopped.

Yanking him by the ankles, I dragged him between his Caddy and the dumpster he'd parked next to; a slime trail of blood glistened in the moonlight, but otherwise he was out of sight. So was I. I bent over him, using the same flesh-colored, rubber-gloved hand that had held the knife, and stripped him of his gaudy gold jewellery and lifted his fat wallet from his hip pocket, the sucker pocket the dips call it. I removed the wad of hundreds and tossed the wallet in the dumpster.

The jewellery was a bit of a problem: if somebody stopped me to talk to me about the dead man in the parking lot, I could be found with it on me. But a thief wouldn't leave it behind, so I had to take it, stuffing it in my jacket pockets. Tomorrow I would toss it in Sylvan Lake. Right now, with my couple of thousand bucks, I walked around the front of the casino, said, "Nice night, fellas," to the Indian security guards, who grunted polite responses to the paleface.

Inside, the pinball-machine-like sound of gambling fought with piped-in country western - the redskins seemed to favor cowboy music. I found Nikki where I knew she'd be: at the nickel poker machines. The slender girl had a bright-eyed, pixie face and a cap of brown curls.

"Jack! I'm doing *fantastic*...I'm up four dollars!"

"Sounds like you're making a killing."

"How about you?"

"Same."

I had told Nikki I'd meet her here - we usually took separate cars when we went out, since the manager and his social director weren't supposed to fraternize.

She moved up to the quarter poker machines, at my urging, and ended up winning about thirty bucks. Before long, I was up two hundred bucks on blackjack. If somebody found the body while I was there, things could get interesting; I'd have to dump that jewellery somewhere.

But I didn't think anybody would be using that dumpster tonight, and I knew nobody would use the Caddy. Leaving too soon would be suspicious. So I stayed a couple hours.

"Jeez," I said, as we were heading out finally, her arm in mine, my hand on my head. "I think I drank a little too much."

"That's not like you, Jack."

"I know. But you better drive me home."

"What about your car?"

My car was back at the resort, of course, parked where Nikki wouldn't see it when she went to her own cabin.

"I'll have Gary drive me up for it tomorrow."

"Okay," she said, and she steadied me as we walked back around to the parking lot in the rear.

It was still dark back there and quiet. Very quiet. I could barely make out a dried dark streak on the pavement over by the Caddy, but nothing glistened in the moonlight, now.

First thing the next morning, the police came around to see me; Gary was with them, a pair of uniformed state patrolmen. It seemed, around sun-up, that one of our guests had been found dead in the parking lot at the Lakeview Casino. His wallet, emptied of money, had been found nearby.

"Mr. Walton wore a lot of jewellery," I said. "The gold kind?"

"Asking for trouble," said one of the cops, a kid in his mid-twenties.

Gary, wearing a gray jogging suit, wasn't saying anything; he was standing behind them like a mute grizzly, his eyes a little glazed. "That casino's probably gonna get sued," the other, slightly older cop said. "Bad lighting in the parking lot back behind there. Just asking for it."

"Both Walton *and* that casino," the young one said.

I agreed with them, said sympathetic things, and pointed them to the cabin where they could find - and inform - the new widow. Gary stayed behind.

***

"You know," he said quietly, scratching his beard, "I'm glad that bastard didn't get killed on our grounds. We might be the ones getting sued."

"Right. But that's not going to happen around here."

"Oh?"

"Don't worry, Gary." I put a hand on his shoulder; had to reach up to do it. "*We* have adequate lighting."

He looked at me kind of funny, with narrowed eyes. He seemed about to ask me something, but thought better of it, waved limply and wandered off.

***

I was doing my morning sit-ups when she walked up on my deck, looking dazed, her perfect, bullet-proof platinum hair wearing the girlish pink bow, her voluptuous body tied into a dark pink dressing gown. She stood looking through the cross-hatch of screen door, asking if she could come in.

"Of course," I said, sliding the door open, and took her to the couch where she'd sat two nights before. "You heard about Dick?" she said in small voice. She seemed numb.

"Yes. I'm sorry."

"You...you won't say anything, will you?"

"About what?"

"Those...terrible things I said about him." Her eyes got very wide; she seemed frightened, suddenly, but not of me. "You don't think...you don't think I..."

"No. I don't think you did it, Mrs. Walton."

"Or...or hired somebody...I mean, I was saying some crazy things the other night."

"Forget it."

"And if the police knew about Dick hitting me..."

"Your face looks pretty good today. I don't think they'll pursue that angle."

She swallowed; stared into nothing. "I don't know what to do."

"Why don't you just lean back and wait to inherit Dick's estate? You can do those TV commercials solo now."

She turned to look at me, and the faintest suspicion seemed etched around her eyes. "You've been...very kind, Mr. Keller."

"Make it Jack."

"Is there anything I can do to...repay your kindnesses?"

"Well...you can keep coming to Sylvan Lodge, despite the bad memories. We could sure use your business for those sales conferences and all."

She touched my hand. "I can promise you that. Maybe we could...get to know each other better. Under better circumstances."

"That would be nice."

"Could I just...sit here for a while? I don't really want to go back to the cabin. It still...still smells of Dick. That awful cologne of his."

Here all you could smell was the lake and the pines, real pines; the soothing touch of a breeze rolled over us.

"Stay as long as you like," I said. "Here at Sylvan Lodge, we strive to make our guests' stay as pleasant as possible."

BABY'S GOT A GUN

by Paul D. Brazill

Paul D. Brazill is the author of many books, including *Too Many Crooks, A Case of Noir*, and *Small Time Crimes*.

C HARLIE HARRIS SITS AT HIS USUAL TABLE IN THE COSY CAFÉ. He's sipping a mug of milky tea, and he's got a copy of today's Sunday Times spread out across the table in front of him. He's staring at the cryptic crossword like it's a magic eye picture. He's licking and biting his lips. Furrowing his brow as if he's deep in concentration. Not that Charlie understands the crossword clues, mind you. It's all gibberish to him, for sure. He's as thick as pig shit, is Charlie. But he does have a mate who always texts him the answers to the crossword so he can look clever to the café's punters, who aren't exactly the sharpest tools in the box, either. His phone buzzes, and he reads the message.

Charlie smirks.

"I think the answer to 21 down is *Remembrance Of Things Past*," he says loudly.

A couple of prune-faced old men nod approvingly, clearly impressed.

Charlie sucks the end of his betting shop biro and then carefully writes in the answer. Smirking, he sticks the biro into his earhole and cleans out a load of wax. It doesn't seem to bother him when he sucks on the pen later. He's a class act is our Charlie.

I'm sat at a table near his, but Charlie doesn't notice me, even though we've met a couple of times before. He doesn't register me at all. But, then, that's Charlie all over - he's so far up his own arse he could give himself an enema. I've just been paid quite a lot of money to kill Charlie. It's not personal, of course. Though, I really can't stand the bloke and won't exactly be riddled with guilt after I croak him. Good riddance to bad rubbish and all that.

Everyone in the cafe is listening intently to a local radio news report and tutting accordingly. Apparently, London is now riddled with bag snatchers riding scooters. The grubby tabloid I have in front of me tells pretty much the same tale of woe. From the radio report and the café's customers reactions, you'd think it's the end of days but London has survived worse: the plague, the Great Fire, the blitz, the IRA. It'll survive this, for sure. It's a city of survivors. I should know, I'm one of them.

Leonard Houseman, the café's owner, limps over and chats with Charlie. They have a laugh about something or other and Leonard pats Charlie on the back. He seems to be grinding his teeth. Leonard's a bit of a dark horse. He wears half-moon glasses and a baggy beige cardigan. He looks like a librarian or an accountant, but there's something about his manner that makes me think he's really a bit of a hard bastard. A wolf in sheep's clothing. A man with a murky past, maybe. Leonard goes back behind the counter and chats to Marta the little blonde Polish cook. She gives him the finger and Leonard laughs.

The late afternoon melts into evening, and I sit watching Charlie drink tea and eat fried food until he completes the crossword. He gets up, picks up his ever-present blue Adidas bag and leaves.

I get up, put on my Homberg and follow him down Holloway Road. Charlie's pretty easy to track since you don't see that many big fat blokes wearing bright pink t-shirts, yellow sandals, and red cargo shorts this time of the year. No matter how cold the weather, Charlie always dresses like he's on holiday in the Bahamas. He suffers from generalized hyperhidrosis which means he sweats buckets pretty much all the time. And, of course, he's clinically obese which doesn't exactly help matters a great deal.

A lime-green Vespa hurtles down the road before jumping a red light and skidding around the corner. A police car follows, sirens wailing. An old drunk waves a fist at the police car and drops his plastic carrier bag on the pavement. The bag's contents spill out, and the old man quickly scoops them back into the bag, picks it up and heads into a nearby pub.

The lead grey sky is pockmarked with rain clouds, and by the time Charlie reaches The Luscious Launderette, the rain is pouring down in sheets. I cross the road and stand in the doorway of the bakery opposite the launderette. The smell makes me hungry, and my stomach rumbles. I realise I haven't eaten since morning. I avoid the temptation to call into the bakery for a quick snack and wait for Charlie to leave the launderette. After another few minutes, I need to go for a slash. The new hypertension tablets the doctor gave me seem to be doing the trick, but they have one particularly annoying side effect: I'm always getting caught short. And at the most inopportune moments, too. Well, it's either the drugs or it's my age. I'm a kick in the arse off sixty, after all. It has to be expected. I'm debating whether to pop into a nearby pub to use the toilet and grab a bite to eat when Charlie comes out of the launderette, his arm wrapped around Baby.

Now, Charlie is a big man for sure. To be honest, most people would call him a fat bastard, although not to his face, of course. But Baby Finnigan is huge, corpulent even. She wears a yellow polka dot dress and holds a yellow, polka dot umbrella aloft. In the dim and distant past, Baby had been known as Babycham 69, a semi- professional wrestler of some repute. When she retired, she opened up the launderette with money she borrowed from Charlie, one of the city's most ruthless loan sharks. And then, more than somewhat surprisingly, Baby and Charlie had a fling which seems to have blossomed into a full blown romance.

Charlie flags down a black cab, and they both get in. I call into The Queen's Arms. I don't worry about losing Charlie and Baby, as I know exactly where they're going. He's a creature of narrow habit, is our Charlie. I manage to flag down a taxi a few minutes after I leave the pub. As the cab heads towards Romford, I spot the lime green Vespa I'd seen earlier. It has crashed into a Post Office van. People are standing around taking pictures with their smartphones as the scooter's rider staggers around trying to take his helmet off. A siren screams.

"It's a funny old world," says the taxi driver, shaking his head.

"It is that," I say.

***

Dog racing is supposed to be a dying sport, according to Wikipedia, but the Coral Romford Greyhound Stadium is absolutely packed. Reports of its death appear to be greatly exaggerated, it seems. You could say the same for me, I suppose. Certainly, my recent attempt at retirement was a failure with a capital F and now I'm back in the game. An aging hit man with nothing better to so, it seems.

I sit at a table in Laurie's Panther Bar pretending to watch the races, but I'm really watching Charlie and Baby. They're knocking back champagne like it's tap water. Charlie is holding court, as usual, and Baby is guffawing with laughter at everything he says. Which is when I realise for sure that she's playing Charlie like a Poundland violin. There's no way Baby she can find Charlie so amusing. She's many things, but Baby Finnigan is no fool.

I take out my phone and send a text to my client. I tell him what I've found out and ask him how he wants to proceed. Whether we should just let Baby fleece Charlie and let him suffer that way. A few minutes later, he texts me back telling me to keep on with the project. Baby and Charlie start canoodling, mouths and fingers everywhere. I take that as my cue to leave.

***

The next day, Charlie follows the same routine as he did the day before and I follow him again. As he approaches The Luscious Launderette, a motor scooter races past me, slowing down to pull the blue Adidas bag from Charlie's hand. However, Charlie pulls it back with force, and the scooter goes over onto the pavement, spilling its rider. The rider falls into Charlie who pulls out a cosh and hits the rider on the arm. The rider screams. There's a loud gunshot, and he falls to the ground. I look toward the launderette. Baby's stood in the doorway and she's got a gun in her hand. She fires it at the rider as he tries to stand, and he spins back into the road. An ice cream van skids to avoid him.

Baby rushes over to Charlie, who clutches his chest. People scream, sirens wail, and I head off in the opposite direction.

***

The Bistro is empty when I walk in. A radio plays a 24-hour news station in Italian, and Alessio is behind the counter cleaning the La Spaziale coffee machine. The young Italian pretty much dotes on it. In the corner, Greta is packing the vacuum cleaner away.

"Are you having a nice day, Mr Bennett?" she says when she sees me walk in.

"Yes, Greta," I say. "The weather could be better, but it could be worse."

She smiles. I've tried to get her to call me Tommy, but she always says that isn't the Lithuanian way. I am her boss and her senior, so I will always be Mr Bennett to her. Greta is just over forty, but she is much more conservative than a lot of British women of that age.

I hang up my hat and coat and take the Daily Mirror from the counter. I sit near the window and flick through the newspaper with little interest in the world's problems.

"Coffee, Mr B?" says Alessio.

"Yes, please son," I say. "And could you make it a little Irish?"

He smiles. I open the newspaper to the crossword and think of Charlie. I can't help but grin.

Alessio brings over my Irish coffee as Alice Merton's 'No Roots' kicks out. He dances back behind the counter and I take a sip. A few minutes later, Lee Hughes walks in. Lee is tall and tanned. He has recently had his teeth bleached and blond highlights put in his hair. He's wearing black leather and is carrying a Harley Davidson motorcycle helmet. Lee won the lottery a bit back and has taken to employing me for what he calls payback jobs, one of which being the long overdue death of Charlie Harris who had apparently made Lee's mum's life a misery.

Lee says something to Alessio and smiles at Greta. He puts his helmet on my table and sits opposite me. Heavy rain machine guns the window.

"Just in time," says Lee. "I don't fancy riding in that."

"I imagine riding a motorbike in London is a bit of a high risk activity these days," I say.

"A Harley Davidson is more than just a motorbike, Tommy."

I chuckle.

"If you like," I say.

Alessio brings over Lee's espresso.

"Have you heard what happened to Charlie?" says Lee.

"Yeah," I say. "I contacted a friend of mine that works at Hammersmith Police Station. Apparently, Charlie's in a coma, although I doubt a lack of brain activity is unusual for him."

"I expect Baby got herself arrested?"

"For sure. She'll probably plead self-defence or something."

"The bag snatcher?"

"He's in a bad way, it seems, but not dead, luckily for Baby."

Lee hands me an envelope.

"There you go," he says.

I pick it up.

"This feels a bit heavy to me," I say. "Considering I didn't finish the job."

Lee shrugs.

"As far as I'm concerned the job's done. You put the graft in. The leg-work. Charlie's out of action now. Maybe indefinitely. If he ever wakes up from that coma, maybe you can tidy things up then," he says, smiling.

"Well, that's something to look forward to," I say.

Lee knocks back his espresso and pats me on the shoulder.

"Later," he says, and leaves.

I gaze out of the window at the city's rain soaked streets, the Bistro's neon sign reflected in the pavement. The people rushing by oblivious to anyone else but themselves. I sigh, put the envelope in my pocket, and let the sense of resignation enfold me.

LADIES DAY AT THE OLYMPIA CAR WASH

by Andrew Nette

Andrew Nette is a pulp scholar and author. He has written two novels, *Ghost Money* and *Gunshine State*. He is also the co-editor of *Girl Gangs, Biker Boys & Real Cool Cats: Pulp Fiction and Youth Culture, 1950 to 1980*.

BUDDHA APPEARS OUT OF THE GLARE, SHUFFLES ACROSS THE cracked concrete towards me, cigarette hanging from his mouth. He sits in the plastic orange bucket seat next to mine.

I pretend to concentrate on my paperback, but I can't focus on the words with him stewing so close. I brace myself, knowing what he's going to say before the words leave his mouth.

"Man, I hate fucking Tuesdays."

I nod, not wanting to encourage him.

He grimaces, as if in deep psychic pain, swears in Greek.

Just after nine and already the temperature is in the early thirties according to the announcer on the classic hits radio station that gets piped through the speaker on the office wall.

"Going to be a hot one today," I say, trying to change the subject.

"Yeah, suppose so." Buddha drops his half-smoked nail on the ground next to the grey tray of dirty sand labelled *Please deposit cigarette butts here*. He extinguishes it under the heel of a Nike high top, lights another.

"Worst motherfucking day of the week, Tuesdays."

The muscles in my face clench in annoyance. Obvious to most people, but Buddha takes no notice, continues to cuss out Tuesday, alternating between Greek and English.

By early afternoon the sun will have obliterated the shade in front of the office, forcing us to either retreat inside, where there is only a portable fan for relief, or bake in the heat. Buddha will still be bitching, and the classic hits will be going strong.

Welcome to the hell that is my Tuesday, Ladies Day at the Olympia Car Wash.

Right now, a customer would be a blessed relief, better than rain or a cold drink, anything to relieve the monotony of having to sit and listen to Buddha. I look past the row of small Greek flags hung from a rope across the entrance, bleached almost colourless by elements, try and will one of the passing cars to pull in.

Fresh graffiti has appeared overnight on the empty billboard across the road from the car wash. *The joy of not being sold anything* it says, in large, misshapen black letters.

I'm not exactly sure what it is about the idea of a half-price car wash and polish for female customers on a Tuesday that's so offensive to my co-worker.

"Makes us look like a couple of motherfucking wankers, man," is all he'll say when pressed.

"What, unlike the rest of the time we're sitting here on our arses waiting for something to happen?"

I suspect he's mostly disappointed at not being up to his armpits in bored horny housewives, like Nick – Buddha's uncle, our boss – promised when he started working here. Most of our customers are either businessmen in a hurry or rev heads from the nearby housing estate. The few housewives we do get never leave the air-conditioned comfort of their land cruisers. Or they're so pissed by misbehaving kids, work, or whatever they fought about with their husbands that morning, they don't give Buddha and me a second glance, let alone shower us with offers of sex.

Then again, Buddha has been angry about most things ever since we first met in high school. Back then, Buddha – his real name is Lambros – was a dumpy, overweight Greek kid, pissed at the racism he was subjected to by many of our schoolmates. That was nearly twenty years ago. In the intervening period, he'd lost the weight but kept the nickname, and we'd remained friends.

"I tell you brother," Buddha gives me a sly sideways look. "We get some cash together, we could piss this place off, go into business for ourselves."

I don't reply. I know Buddha really doesn't want an answer, at least not an honest one. I know where this is leading, an argument about what happened the last time I took part in one of Buddha's moneymaking schemes.

"I can guess what you're thinking, but I'm telling you, man, it'll be different this time."

"I seriously doubt it."

"Do you have to be so negative?" Buddha pushes his aviator sunglasses onto his forehead. "I mean, fuck dude, you're dissing my idea before you're even heard it."

I return to my book, make like I don't hear him.

"Do you know what your problem is? You've got no ambition. Not just you, all of you skips, you're not prepared to risk anything."

"That so?"

"Yeah, that's exactly fucking so." He lights a cigarette as he talks, warming to his subject. "You're content to sit on your arses and let us do all the hard work."

"Who exactly is 'us'?"

"You know exactly who, us migrants, not just the Greeks, all of us."

"Buddha, you're a second generation Australian citizen, for Christ's sake…"

"My father helped build the Snowy Mountains scheme, then came to Melbourne, slaved away in a factory making machine parts."

"You're not exactly following in his footsteps," I check my temper. "And the only Greek you know is swear words."

"That's not the point, mate, I mean, I'm just saying, there's no reward if there's no risk."

"Listen, *mate*, you're hardly one to lecture me about risk." I can feel the vein in my neck start to throb and my breathing quicken. "Not after what happened last time."

"*Farken* hell, you bloody *malaka*," Buddha always tries to be more Greek when he's angry. "You always have to bring that up?"

"My fucking oath, I do. The last time we acted on one of your schemes, I ended up doing three years in Port Philip Prison. And don't you forget it."

Buddha looks away to hide the guilt on his face. When he turns back, his sunnies are covering his eyes again. "Fuck you and the horse you rode in on." He stands, walks away.

"Where you going?"

"The shithouse."

"Don't take all day," I call after him. "I don't want to be left short-handed if there's a sudden rush."

Buddha gives me the middle finger over his shoulder, disappears around the corner of the officer.

I reach down and pick up the clear plastic bottle at my feet. The working day is less than an hour old, and already the water is lukewarm. I look at the graffiti across the road. *The joy of not being sold anything.*

I smile at how much displeasure the sentiment is bound to cause our extreme capitalist boss. Making Tuesday ladies' day was Nick's idea, one of many he's come up with to try and grow the business and get some cred with old Jimmy, who owns the set up.

It's by no means Nick's worst idea. That would be the short-lived 'Hawaiian Friday', when Buddha and I had to dress in colourful shirts while a collection of sixties surf music Nick found in a local op shop was piped through the loudspeakers. Or maybe it was his idea of a free souvlaki with every wash and polish. Buddha and I had to do the cooking as well as the washing and polishing. We stank of roast meat, and the scraps attracted rats.

All Nick's ideas for improving the business are pointless, because the only thing Jimmy wants these days is a place he can wash his car, a mint condition 1977 Lincoln Continental. "Something that makes him feel he's still someone other than a washed up wog gangster," as Buddha once put it.

Nick doesn't put in much time at the car wash, but he always shows up Mondays, when Jimmy comes in to have his car cleaned and polished, looking like a child behind the wheel as he pilots the giant automobile onto the lot. Nick greets the old man like the second coming, opens his car door, lights his cigarettes, utters one or two word replies to Jimmy's rapid fire questions in Greek.

You saw Jimmy in the street, you'd think he was just another of the area's rapidly dwindling tribe of original Greek migrants. Solid build, olive skin, hair white as snow, dressed the same no matter what the weather in a fisherman's cap, old slacks and a brown cardigan over a red checked flannel shirt.

But back in the eighties and early nineties, Jimmy the Greek, as a tabloid once referred to him, was a big deal in Melbourne's northern suburbs. He controlled a couple of local councillors and several businesses, including a used car yard he appeared in the late night television ads for. I can still remember one of those, Jimmy in a shiny grey suit, hamming up his Greek accented English as he handed giant cardboard cheques to customers to symbolise the bargain they were getting.

Now all that's left of his interests is this car wash and a social club, a dingy place with cheap furniture, frequented by old men who sit around all day playing cards, bitching about their kids and how shit the Greek economy is. Most of his power base, the migrants who emigrated here in the late fifties and sixties, are either dead or have been shipped off to retirement homes in the outer suburbs by children eager to sell their parent's now obscenely overvalued homes.

Buddha returns, zipping up his fly as he walks, sits with exaggerated force, folds his arms over his chest.

"All I'm asking is you listen to my proposal. You don't like it, promise, I won't say another word."

"This proposal, is it legal?"

"Sort of."

"Sort of?"

"Not really."

I fix Buddha with a deadpan look, and wonder, not for the first time, how our friendship has survived nearly two decades.

Both of us had gone onto university, me to an arts degree I finished but didn't use, him, engineering, which he quit after two years. We didn't see each other for several years, drifted back into our friendship during the tail end of my disintegrating marriage. He helped me through the breakup, and we re-bonded anew over the shared sense of entering our thirties as complete failures.

I'd always suspected Buddha had a gambling problem. He was forever short of cash, always had to borrow a few dollars, even when he was working. But I didn't know how bad the situation was until he confided in me that he owed fourteen grand plus interest to a moneylender and asked for my help.

"It's not as though I'm particularly flush myself," I'd told him.

"Nah, I don't want your money, man. I want you to help me do something."

Our third service station robbery, the last one Buddha promised, a winter evening on the edge of the Western suburbs. The first couple had been surprisingly easy. We didn't expect number three would be any different.

We hadn't counted on the Indian behind the counter wanting to play hero and refusing to hand over the money. I kept watch while Buddha jumped the counter, jammed his pistol hard against the kid's temple and forced him to open the till.

We also didn't plan for the off duty cop filling up as we ran to our car. My bad luck, the cop rugby tackles me. It's no contest. I'm a skinny fucker. He's built like a truck. Before I know it he's got my arms pinned behind my back, and I'm chewing concrete. I remember hearing the squeal of car tyres as Buddha drove away.

I didn't blame Buddha. Faced with the same situation, I would've run, too. It didn't stop me being pissed at him, though, but more at myself for getting into the mess in the first place.

He came to see me in prison, always nervous as he entered the visiting area, like a riot would break out at any moment, his head full of too many prison movies.

And he was waiting for me when I got out. The same shit eating grin, but a new leather jacket and a tight fitting black dress shirt open to reveal the tiny silver crucifix nestling in a chest full of black curly hair.

Several hours later, we're drunk, sitting on a couch in a Kings Street strip club. He slaps me hard on the back, pulls me close.

"Don't worry about a thing, mate. I'll look after you until you get back on your feet. I've got you somewhere to stay and a job at the same place as me."

I'd nodded, knowing this was as close as I'd ever get to an apology for what happened.

"Promise me, Buddha, nothing illegal. I've fucked my life up enough already. I never want to go back to jail."

"On my mother, I swear, strictly above board."

Some days, Tuesdays in particular, prison doesn't seem so bad compared to working at the Olympia. I never had to listen to Buddha whine in prison, and I spent far less time on my arse there than I do here. The car wash business isn't exactly booming. In prison they try and keep you active, even if it's just meaningless shit, because in prison, boredom usually leads to trouble, whereas here, it just leads to Buddha and I bickering.

I'm thinking about prison, wondering if Buddha's started gambling again, whether there's any point reminding him of my pledge to go straight, when a red car pulls into the lot, sits there, engine idling. The tinted front windshield prevents me from seeing the driver.

"You want to take this one?"

Buddha shakes his head, still sulking from my refusal to hear out his latest plan. "Nah, you do it for a change."

I deliberate whether to take issue with his implication but can't be bothered. I get up and walk to the driver's side. The automatic window comes down. I lean a forearm on the car, peer into the cool interior. My narrow face is reflected in the female driver's large round sunglasses. Music, some sort of jazz, is on the sound system. Her hands rest on the steering wheel, a gold band on her left ring finger.

She pushes her glasses onto her nose with a little finger, and calm, clear blue eyes gaze up at me. She's wearing a tight-fitting grey skirt and white shirt. Her black hair is pulled into a high ponytail. Red lipstick accentuates her bone-white skin. At the point where the hem of her skirt meets her thigh, I spy part of a tattoo, the head of a bird.

"Take a picture, you'll remember it longer," she says, tugging at her skirt in an unsuccessful attempt to cover the illustration.

"Sorry." I look at her face, my cheeks flushed with embarrassment.

"So, this ladies' day gig you got going here, that a real thing or what?"

"Yes."

She nods, peers out the windscreen to Buddha sitting outside the office, smoking. "What's he for, decoration?"

I ignore the question, step back and give her car a once over. Not a scratch on the duco, hardly any trace dirt, the radial tyres similarly sparkle like new.

"Doesn't look like it needs a wash."

She flashes me a humourless smile. I notice the mistakable dark shadow of a bruise under the foundation around one eye. She pushes her sunglasses back into place.

"I'm hoping you can help me out," she says, choosing her words carefully. "This is my husband's car. He was out last night. It was dark. He hit and killed a dog on the road. He didn't want to just leave the poor animal where it had died, so he put its body in the boot, drove it back to our place and buried it."

"Very civically-minded of him."

"Yeah," she laughs nervously, "he's that kind of guy."

I nod for her to continue.

"Anyway, the dog bled all over the inside of the boot and I was wondering whether you could clean it."

"I could get some soapy water, muck it out for you."

She opens the car door, extends a well-toned leg to the ground. For some reason, I expected to see her foot clad in a stiletto. Instead she's wearing running shoes, the edges of which are caked with mud and grass.

"I was hoping you could use something a little stronger than water, something to get the stains and the smell out."

"I might be able to find some bleach."

"That'd be great."

"Anything else."

She bites her lower lip. "It would be good if you didn't do the job here."

"What do you mean?"

"Can I take the car around the back, do it there?"

"Sure."

She eases her leg back into the car, closes the door after her, drives to the rear of the lot.

I find the bleach, fill a bucket with water, collect some rags and a pair of plastic gloves, walk to the rear of her car. She pops the trunk. I open it, recoil at the smell. The woman said the dog was already dead when it had gone into the trunk. But whatever died in here had been in bad shape and taken a while to do it. There's blood everywhere and scratch marks on the inside roof of the trunk.

I take my handkerchief out, tie it around my mouth and nose and get to work. It takes half the bottle of bleach, several buckets of water and twenty minutes of scrubbing to get the boot clean. I'm drenched with sweat, but it feels good to be doing something other than just sitting around. The woman doesn't move from the car the entire time, just sits in the driver's seat staring through the front windscreen.

I'm cleaning out a hard-to-reach crevice at very back of the boot, when my rag dislodges something small and shiny. I hold it up to my eyes. It's a solid silver cufflink.

I stare at the back of the woman's head. She's oblivious to my discovery. I roll the piece of metal in the palm of my hand, watch it catch the sunlight. I think about the phone in the office, remember my pledge not to do anything illegal, pocket the cufflink, and close the boot.

I rap a knuckle gently on her window. She looks at me with a start, lowers the window.

"All done," I say.

"That's marvellous. Thank you so much."

She reaches for a black leather handbag on the passenger seat, passes me a crisp new hundred-dollar bill.

"I'll get your change."

"No, keep it."

"This is way too much."

"Don't worry about it." Her smile exposes two rows of perfect white teeth. "What's your name?"

"Richard."

"Thanks, Richard."

She cranks the stereo high. I hear a blast of rich trumpet solo before the window goes up, and she backs out of the lot. Her vehicle pauses for a moment before it merges with the traffic and disappears from view.

"What'd she want?" Buddha says as I sit next to him, reach for my drink bottle.

"Just a bit of clean."

He snorts, swears in Greek. "I tell you, we're never going make a cent stuck in this shit hole."

I draw a forearm over my brow to wipe the sweat away. "Okay mate, tell me about this idea of yours."

THE INVISIBLE MAN

by Bev Vincent

Bev Vincent is the author of the Bram Stoker Award-nominated *The Road to the Dark Tower* and *The Stephen King Illustrated Companion.* He is also the co-editor (with Stephen King) of the anthology *Flight or Fright.* His short fiction has appeared in many publications and anthologies, including *Cemetery Dance, Borderlands,* and several volumes of *Shivers.*

"**Y**OU'RE GETTING TOO OLD FOR THIS SHIT," HERB TOLD HIS reflection. He was tending to the injuries a flailing miscreant had done to his face a couple of hours earlier. His lip was split, his nose was bleeding, and his left eye was going to be colorful come morning.

That was just the visible damage, caused by a lucky blow. In addition, Herb knew from experience that his muscles would be sore for the next few days due to over-exertion. Now that he was in his mid-fifties, it was taking longer and longer to recover from these outings. The cuts and bruises healed soon enough, but the aches persisted. If only he could soak in a hot tub to soothe his aching body, but his apartment featured no such luxuries. The bathtub was so short his legs dangled over the edge, and he invariably got a crick in the neck if he reclined in it too long.

Another rough night of martial arts training, he'd tell his co-workers tomorrow morning. Over the years, he'd claimed he was studying a variety of disciplines to explain his condition when he showed up at work sporting cuts and bruises the day after a violent encounter. If he'd been married, people might have suspected he was in an abusive relationship, but Herb had been living alone for most of his adult life, and just about everyone in his small circle of acquaintances knew it. A few surmised he was gay — they referred to him with the code phrase "confirmed bachelor" — but everyone else assumed he was a nerd who'd never figured out how to ask a girl out on a date — and they wouldn't be far wrong. He wouldn't be the first IT guy without any social skills, after all.

To the extent anyone gave his personal life a second thought, his explanation of Jiu Jitsu sessions, or Taekwondo, Krav Maga — or whatever else was the current trend — was a reasonable cover story. No one had ever asked if they could come see him compete.

In truth, Herb was reasonably accomplished at self-defense tactics, although he was strictly self-taught. His greatest ability was in avoiding serious injury during his altercations. He took the occasional shot to the head or the torso — that was to be expected. Even a broken clock, and all that. But the expression "you should see the other guys" was his personal motto, even if he rarely got to utter it.

Staring in the mirror, he ran his hand through thinning blond hair that was streaked with grey. He prodded a tender spot on his cheek and winced. He had to accept the reality that his reactions were slowing down. He should have been able to duck the roundhouse that had caught him in the face. For a few seconds he'd seen stars, something he'd previously thought was only an expression. Not just stars — entire constellations. Then he'd regained his wits and wrapped up the job before retreating home to nurse his wounds.

Rather than subjecting himself to the cramped tub, Herb turned on the shower, letting it run as hot as he could stand. After being enveloped by hot water and steam for a while, he felt he might be able to sleep, although it proved fitful. Adrenaline coursed through his body on nights like these.

The next day, one person made a wry comment about his appearance, but it was nothing his colleagues hadn't seen before. The talk in the lunchroom was mostly about the three thugs who'd been rounded up and delivered to the police department the previous evening. Herb was waiting for the day when someone put two and two together, connected the times when he showed up to work looking worse for wear with the exploits of the urban hero the press had dubbed the "Invisible Man." So far, no one had. Nobody paid much attention to him, truth be told, and that was fine with Herb. Although, he had to admit, the media nickname smarted a little because it was so on-the-nose. Most days he did feel invisible.

He'd said as much to Jenny, his therapist, although he'd tried to present the observation in a constructive light. Herb didn't like talking about himself, but given the solitary life he was leading, he'd decided to give therapy a try. After the first few sessions, he felt unburdened. He came to a momentous decision — he'd decided to entrust Jenny with his secret.

She'd been skeptical, of course, trying to dig deeper to find some underlying psychosis. Over time, though, she accepted what he told her — or, at least, accepted that he sincerely believed what he told her, whether or not it was true. And why shouldn't it be? There was also a long tradition of the misfit nerd with a heroic alter ego.

This week, Herb took a new idea out for a test drive. "I'm thinking about quitting," he told her.

"Your IT job?" she asked. "Why?"

"Not my job," he said. "The…you-know…" He often struggled to find the proper words to describe what it was he did, allowing her to fill in the blanks.

"The crime fighting," she said. "I see."

"I'm not getting any younger. Well, no one is." He winced when he realized how trite that sounded.

"Did something happen?"

"I got roughed up a bit the other night." He held his face to the light so she could see the bruises and cuts. "Zigged when I should have zagged."

"My goodness," she said. "Looks like that hurt quite a bit."

He nodded. "Maybe you read about it?"

"Hmmm," she said. "I'm not sure."

"Those three guys who got arrested? The ones who've been running a protection racket on the south side, beating people up? Threatening businesses?"

She scribbled a few notes. "Sounds familiar. I guess. Are you saying that was you?"

And so it went. Therapy gave Herb the opportunity to reveal his deepest secrets, although perhaps a little circuitously, and someone else heard him, even if she didn't necessarily believe.

They discussed his feelings about getting older, and all the unpleasantness that went with that. Jenny was at least twenty years his junior, so he wondered what made her think she was an authority on the subject, but he kept that observation to himself.

As they were getting ready to wrap up for the week, she asked him again — it came up at almost every session — if he shouldn't think more about companionship. If not a girlfriend, perhaps a regular friend. Someone to go to movies or a ball game with, or play video games with or go out to a bar with. Had he ever tried karaoke? It was surprisingly liberating, she said, especially after a drink or two. "Maybe if you weren't running around trying to solve the city's problems, you'd have more time for yourself," she said. He heard the implied "air quotes" around her description of his activities.

They ended with Herb agreeing to give deeper consideration to quitting. Ultimately, he decided to stick with it a while longer. The city needed him. The people needed a hero and he was willing to make the sacrifice. He did make a few lifestyle changes, though. He improved his diet. He increased his workout regimen, including a number of exercises he found on a web site that promised to stave off some of the physical changes associated with aging.

And he got a dog — the only kind of companion he could deal with at present. It was nice to have someone there to greet him when he got home from an evening adventure. He found himself talking to the creature, which probably wasn't totally healthy. "Small steps," he told Jenny the next time he saw her. "Small steps."

Herb's injuries from his outings were never bad enough to send him to the ER, but he was a regular customer at the first aid section of the local pharmacy. During his annual physical, his doctor remarked on his overall physical condition, which was "pretty decent for a guy your age." Dr. Kemp looked too young to have a driver's license, let alone an M.D. He noted some recent insults to Herb's body, which Herb deflected with the standard excuse of an overenthusiastic workout.

"I'm glad to hear you're exercising. Blood pressure is a touch on the high side, though," Kemp said after having it checked a second time. "Are you experiencing significant stress? At work, perhaps?"

Herb admitted to a certain degree of pressure in his daily routine. "I deal with a lot of idiots," he said, although he was referring to the criminals he routinely apprehended and not the people whose computers he maintained.

"We'll make a note to keep an eye on it," Kemp said, tapping on his tablet computer. "Have you considered a vacation? They can be very relaxing."

Herb couldn't remember the last time he'd gone out of town. Or the last time he'd taken a day off from work, for that matter. He considered a beach house on the Gulf at first, but they all seemed designed for a dozen or more people, and were well out of his price range, anyway. His job paid a decent salary, but his moonlighting gig ridding the streets of troublesome individuals wasn't exactly a lucrative proposition. More of a calling.

His online research turned up a site offering five-day cruises at a deep discount. He had to get his passport renewed, plus find a place to board the dog, so it was a few weeks before he could book passage, during which time he was involved in six more after-hours incidents that left him exhausted and ready to get away from it all.

His first day at sea was everything the promotional material promised. He had no interest in the on-board casino or in any of the instructive seminars that proved to be little more than glorified sales pitches, but there was still no shortage of things to do. He swam in the pool, reclined in a *chaise longue* in a shady spot on the Lido deck, power walked around the promenade, caught a little sun in a breezy corner of the deck, joined the book club, took full advantage of the all-inclusive drinks package, dined in style, and attended a show in the theater. A man could get used to this, he told himself as he watched all the beautiful people enjoying the ship's amenities.

True to form, nobody paid him much attention other than the uniformly polite waiters, bartenders, and other ship's crew. His fellow passengers were mostly families and couples, although there was one group of golden singles, most of them at least a decade his senior, and a gaggle of women young enough to be his daughter, if he'd had one. He didn't hold out any hope of meeting someone beyond the random group of people at his assigned dinner table, who engaged him briefly in chit-chat before turning away to talk among themselves. Even if he did, by some miracle, meet someone — where could it possibly lead? Two more days and they'd each head off in their respective directions. Two ships, and all that. Better to remain invisible.

On the morning of the second day, the ship arrived in Cozumel. Herb stood on the deck and admired the slow motion ballet as the massive vessel performed a 180° turn to get into docking position, and the beehive of activity below as workers retrieved ropes as thick as a man's chest and made them fast. Then he joined the throngs of passengers who disembarked for a day in the Mexican resort.

Herb had no interest in t-shirts and other souvenirs, so he shied away from the more tourist-focused establishments near the pier. He wanted to see the real Mexico, to the extent that was possible on a tropical island. He hadn't been able to afford the Chichen Itza excursion, so he hired a cab to take him to the Mayan ruins at San Gervasio instead. He paid a little extra for the guided tours and marveled at the lizards and iguanas sunning themselves on the ruins.

On the way back to town, he used his broken Spanish to ask the driver to take him to his personal favorite restaurant for lunch. The driver smiled and released a string of words, most of which went over Herb's head. The cantina was within walking distance of the waterfront — just outside the tourist district in a residential part of town. Herb paid the man and gave him a nice tip for his service.

The meal was the best Mexican food he'd ever eaten — even if the establishment's attention to sanitary matters appeared somewhat on the lax side — and the margaritas were potent, nearly lethal. Afterward, he decided to stagger back to the ship and relax by the pool, which would be quiet with most of the other passengers away on excursions.

Outside the restaurant, he oriented himself and headed toward the main street that ran along the waterfront near the cruise terminal. A block from his destination, he encountered a group of tourists wandering aimlessly up the narrow *calle* with all the obvious indicators of people who'd consumed several margaritas and were in search of more.

A Vespa carrying two people rounded the corner and zipped past the oblivious, inebriated tourists. The scooter's passenger used the hooked end of a cane to snag a purse from the arm of the woman closest to the street. Before the others realized what was happening, the driver gunned the throttle and took off.

For half a second, Herb considered doing nothing. He was on vacation, damn it. Before he had made a conscious decision, however, his legs were carrying him down the street after the fleeing thieves.

They never saw what hit them — they never did, not even the ones who fought back.

Ten minutes later, he dumped the two crooks on the front doorstep of the tourist police headquarters. He'd used the stolen purse's straps to secure them, patting himself on the back in appreciation of the ironic gesture. Then he made good his escape, arriving back at the cruise ship out of breath but exhilarated. If anyone noticed the scrape on his cheek from an errant fist, or the bruising on his knuckles, they didn't say anything to him. That was the way it went.

At the next port of call, Herb stayed on board. He didn't want to tempt fate. If he was going to relax and lower his blood pressure, the best place for him was on a lounge chair by the pool, out of the direct sunlight, with a drink in one hand and a book in the other.

By the time he got back home, sporting his first tan in decades and greeted by his friendly canine companion, he'd come to the conclusion that any thoughts of retirement were ludicrous. He could no more stop himself from intervening in criminal activities than he could cease breathing. His other job — his day job, as he thought of it — that one he could see himself giving up someday. If only there were a way to monetize his extracurricular activities. How did his fellow crusaders manage? He wondered. Where did they turn for support? It was a lonely existence. They all toiled in secret — even the ones with larger than life personas.

He discussed this with Jenny during his first session after his vacation.

"You look good," she said. "Got some sun, I see."

He told her about his adventures south of the border, about his personal epiphany, and about his fiscal quandary. She listened as always, making the occasional note and offering observations designed to get him to explore the matter from a different perspective, but he came away without any answers.

The more he thought about it, though, the more Herb found himself wondering if this wasn't a problem somebody had already solved. He couldn't be the only crusader who needed financial — if not moral — support, could he?

So he turned to the one place that offered solutions to any problem a person might encounter — the internet. At first, it was like trying to self-diagnose an illness based on a set of symptoms. There was a lot of misinformation out there, some of it quite disturbing or misleading. His challenge was to sort the wheat from the chaff, as it were. To filter out the wannabes from the real McCoys. He explored the dark net and various other corners of the worldwide web that offered products and services that would shock the average person. After several fruitless days, during which he almost surrendered, Herb fell down a rabbit hole that got him in the right neighborhood. There was, he was surprised to discover, a secret network devoted to issues and matters pertaining to people like Herb. This was an ill-defined concept. If it applied to you, you recognized it.

On this 'super-net', there were message boards and forums galore, along with a passel of other resources that until now Herb hadn't realized he needed. Much of the information was practical and useful, but of more value was the sense of community he discovered. He wasn't alone in the world.

After a while, he no longer felt invisible. He was part of an elite group, with a purpose. They all had a common goal — the betterment of society.

The next time he went out on his evening rounds, he did so with a renewed vigor. A spring in his step. He confronted a trio of hoodlums who were harassing an old woman, threatening to take her pension check and other valuables. He looked them straight in the eye, one at a time. He made them see him and waited for them to tremble with fear when he told them to leave the woman alone or they'd live to regret it.

As a group they exchanged glances and backed away from their intended target. Then they set upon Herb and gave him a beating unlike anything he'd ever experienced. In the past, he had been able to bob and bounce and evade most intended blows, but on this particular evening he took the full brunt of every swing. Knuckles made contact with his face, torso, stomach, kidneys, skull. When he went down, they kicked him until they were exhausted.

Then someone summoned the authorities and they fled the scene. Herb was able to talk his way out of an ambulance ride and refused to file an official police report, but it was three days before he felt presentable enough to go back to work. Even then, his co-workers winced when they saw him. He retreated to his office, where he toiled in isolation, shoring up the company's fragile computer infrastructure.

"There are worse things than being invisible," he told Jenny during his next session.

DISRESPECT

by T. Fox Dunham

T. Fox Dunham has published hundreds of short stories and is the author of the novels *The Street Martyr, Mercy*, and *Destroying the Tangible Illusion of Reality; or, Searching for Andy Kaufman.*

"**T**HE BOSS DOESN'T LIKE DISRESPECT," FRANK SAID, TRYING to explain it to his cousin. "We go in, have some drinks, spread some cheer — and you keep your fucking mouth shut. And maybe, just maybe I can convince Little Nicky Scarfo not to bury your ass off the expressway."

"Scarfo sends his guys after me, and I'll slit all their fucking throats," Joey said, then snorted — probably still sucking down the blow he'd freebased at the Farley Service Stop. Frank grabbed the shoulder of his brown leather jacket.

"You blow this, and I'll be the one who does it. Fucking junkie."

"I don't know what the big deal is," he said. "I'm just talking shit, having a good time. All the guys do it."

"Yeah, but you did it in Little Nicky's restaurant while he was upstairs having dinner. He's clipping guys just for looking at him funny, and you called him a fucking phony big shot."

Frank parked the car one street over from Maple Avenue and Scarfo's family compound in Margate. Christmas lights blinked up and down the small businesses, though several were closed for the season. The lights reflected in the black puddles of melting snow, and melted snow fell and splattered onto the windshield. They wouldn't bother driving back to Philly tonight and get a room at one of the resorts. Frank checked the wave in his black hair before he stepped carefully in his Bottega Italian loafers, avoiding the gritty slosh that had melted onto the sidewalk. Being a good altar boy, he checked his silver crucifix's position along his neck and straightened out the religious idolatry. "You got the Christmas card?"

"Bullshit," Joey said and accented it with a snort. He grabbed his card off the dashboard, put out a cigarette, and lit another one before getting out.

"He's the king of Philly. We pay our tax. He lets us operate. That's the thing." Frank checked for the .22 he'd taped under the car seat. Once he found it, he got out, and they crossed the street then walked down the row of parked cars to the Margate compound. In the distance, the lights of the towers of Atlantic City blinked silver and white, a shining temple of glory and hope — the golden city on the ocean. Poor slobs had jammed the Atlantic City Expressway, coming east for a pull of the lever and a chance of wealth and power. The idea made him chuckle. Being on the inside, Frank knew casinos really functioned like a slaughterhouse. Eventually they took everything from you then tossed your bones — bones soon taken by the tide. Little Nicky and his crew fed off the lost souls, getting their hooks into them. "A gambler with a debt is a hen that keeps laying golden eggs," Frank's father used to say.

"I hate coming down here," Frank said. Thinking of his pop, he remembered these horrible pilgrimages in his youth. Frank's dad had brought him here to attend *family* social functions, usually a birthday party for some old guy wrapped in oxygen tubing he called uncle, even though both his mother and father had no brothers. By the next year his uncle would be gone, either serving their last years inside until they got backdoor parole. No one ever died surrounded by their families. That's not how this story usually ended, certainly not his father's. Pop had tried to get their family out, but a dirty cop tipped off the boss that he was a rat. Frank was never quite sure where they'd buried Pop — either in the Pine Barrens close to Exit Seven to the shore points or maybe sealed up in an oil drum and dumped in the bay. Some nights he'd lie awake next to Connie wondering.

Joey and Frank approached the compound. Plastic reindeer decorated the yard out front of the two-story building. The Scarfo family had owned the place since the 1930s, and it's where the boss held court when he wasn't up at the business office in Atlantic City or out in Philly taking care of business. Every year, he hired caterers from his restaurant in the casino to come out and fill the place up with food and liquor. He enforced attendance and sat above the party in his private apartment, working out deals and settling beefs before the New Year. You'd better be dead if you didn't make an appearance.

Before going in, Frank fixed his collar and ran a mini lint roller over his pristine wool coat, and Joey took out his silver flask from the inside pocket of his ratty leather coat, then took a drink. His bloodshot eyes bulged out their sockets, and veins swelled on his temples and down his jowls, vanishing into the scraggly brown beard that earned him the moniker of "the rat." He snorted again, then stumbled in the street. Frank slammed him against a station wagon. "You high?"

Joey looked away, unable to meet his eyes. "No, man. Well, yeah. Some. To take the edge off. But I'm cool, mother. I'm cool."

"You're not worth dying for." He let him go, and they walked over to the loud party. Friends and family danced, ate, and drank downstairs, enjoying the holiday while upstairs the boss doled out life and death like a Roman emperor overseeing gladiatorial combat. Guys climbed up those stairs but didn't come back out, and it was usually your best friend that did the thing. "So tired of cleaning up your shit."

"No one asked you to," Joey said, and they both knew that wasn't true. So many times their dads had made speeches about loyalty, sticking with your friends, never turning on the family. Now, Frank's dad was gone, and Joey's dad died in Springfield.

"Fuck this," Joey said. "We should blow."

"They're not going to whack us at their Christmas Party. Just come on. We'll have a sit down and put this behind us. I'm not saying it isn't going to cost." Joey hesitated, standing in a patch of snow that had blown out on the sidewalk. Sleet pricked Frank's face, falling among the light snow. "Hey. If they whack me, you can sleep with Connie."

"Already did last night," Joey said.

"Come on, you pussy. I hate the shore this time of year. Freezing my balls off."

Guests entered through the left door to the party after being checked by Scarfo's guys. With this thing going on in Philly with Harry Riccobene, the boss placed extra guards on the door. Ladies clomped on heels, wrapping furs around their necks and shoulders. Guys wore their best leisure suits and chains, handing the guys at the door a couple bucks and kissing each other on the cheek. The boss' apartment upstairs could be accessed either through the right door out front or up an outer staircase leading up to a door on the second floor. Frank always made note of the exits.

"Mr. Scarfo is expecting us," Frank said to Mike.

"You heavy?" Mike the Fishhead asked.

"It's a Christmas party," Frank said. They still patted him down then moved on to Joey.

"What's a matter?" Joey asked. "Your wife not putting out? Need to grab a quick feel?"

Frank laughed, trying to pass it off as a joke.

"You're the guy always breaking balls," Mike said, then smiled, chilling Frank deeper than the wind blowing off the Atlantic.

Frank clutched his partner's arm and dragged him up to the private apartment. Mike followed them up. He squinted in the light, causing his eyes to protrude from his skull — this is how he got his name.

Sinatra sang Christmas carols on a Linn Axis record player. Sparse garland and tinsel decorated the designer furniture in the pristine apartment. Framed photos of Nicodemus Scarfo shaking the hands of union leaders, politicians, and movie stars covered the pale white walls letting everyone know he was a big fucking deal. Thick smoke miasma burned Frank's eyes, and among the 'made' guys and crew, he spotted Scarfo's nephew, Phil Leonetti — Phil the Nut — chatting with some guys from his construction company. Pop music pulsed through the floor from the party below, and the peons danced while the king above decided life and death.

On the landing, Frank dropped his greeting card into a punch bowl. Joey just walked in, and Frank yanked his card out of his coat pocket and dropped it in the bowl for his partner. "Every fucking year," Joey said and dabbed his runny nose with his sleeve.

"Come on back, Frank," Mike said.

"Mr. Scarfo wanted to talk to us both."

"Just you," Mike said, and gestured to the white door in the hall next to the living room. Frank tried to get a read on them, but these guys had polished their acts to a fine performance, never given a hint of their true intentions. He'd heard the stories. They whacked guys without rage or fury, just turn him off like a switch and go back to playing cards. Anything could be waiting for him. He could walk into Scarfo's office, get a kiss on the cheek, then, one of the crew would step out of the shadows and shoot Frank at the base of his skull. At the same time, someone would stick an ice pick into Joey's back.

"Go get a drink," Frank said to his cousin, who kept looking over at the side door in that kitchen. "Don't do anything stupid."

"Too late," Mike said and chuckled.

Joey went over to the kitchen table covered in booze and poured some grappa into a plastic cup. He stayed clear of the rest of the guys. Scarfo's crew outranked him, and Joey knew his place in the thing. He was street trash, a small-time corner operator stealing cars and holding up the occasional truck or fencing shit. One day they might be invited to join the ranks of the organization. Until then, they were stuck scratching for coins and kissing the ass of the 'made' guys. He knocked on the door, and the boss told him to come in.

Nicodemus Scarfo sat in a leather recliner and sipped from a tall glass. His family and friends celebrated downstairs, and he sat in his throne up here, never relaxing, always accounting his kingdom. He stood up, just coming up to Frank's chin. Then, he grabbed his hand with his tiny fingers, shook then adjusted his designer suit jacket and fixed his Italian tie, tightening around the wide flaps of his pressed collar. Red and green Christmas lights blinked through the office window, playing colors off the grease of his perfect brushed-back hair. His tiny eyes studied Frank, and it always surprised him how kind and paternal the boss appeared, though he knew at any moment his infamous rage could split those angelic features.

"Thanks for coming to see me," Little Nicky said with his high-pitched voice. "Your wife, Christy. She stayed home?"

Frank didn't correct him. "Yeah. My mother-in-law is staying over."

Little Nicky sat upright in the chair, never relaxing, and sipped from his drink. "So that cousin of yours, Joey. Joey the Rat..." Scarfo paused, letting the sentence hang in the air, waiting for Frank to finish it. Frank had no idea what he wanted to hear. While he waited for Frank to answer, Little Nicky grabbed a green envelope from a pile on the table in front of him, tore it open then spilled several hundred dollars into a bowl already full of cash. What the hell did he want to hear? Dry heat poured into the room from a vent, and Frank couldn't breathe. Sweat soaked his arms.

"Mr. Scarfo. My cousin has always had a hot head. He talks big, but it's just talk. He meant no disrespect, truly." Frank didn't know what to say, and he was talking them both into a shallow grave among the pine trees in the barrens off the A.C. Expressway.

Little Nicky grabbed another card, ripped it open and dumped the cash. In the end, he only really cared about one thing.

"He's a good earner and always kicks up his tax. He's got pull in the union and a lot of the dealers owe him money."

He tore open another envelope, and Frank flinched.

"He's always — "

The boss put his hand up to stop Frankie, and he didn't know how to take that.

"I came up with your dad," Little Nicky said. "You remind me of him." His comment really knocked Frank out, considering that Pop had gone to the Feds to testify so he could get his family out of there and ended up buried off the Expressway. "He just got weak in the end and forgot his real loyalties to the family. The family comes before everything. Before your children. Before your wife. Sometimes you young guys forget that, too."

"My cousin and I both lost our pops growing up. It still gets in his head, but he doesn't mean anything. Everything we have, we earned together. That's why I've come to ask for your understanding."

"You be careful now who you give your loyalty to," he said. "Your fate will be theirs." That knocked the wind out of Frankie. The boss had made his decision, and he waited to feel cold metal pressed against his neck. Frank hoped they'd bury him somewhere peaceful far far away from this rotting diseased city.

"I've always had my eye on you," he continued. "We need good people. Steady people. Not like some of the jokers that came up under Bruno. I'm rebuilding things right, and I want all these beefs resolved by the New Year."

"We all have a lot of respect for you, Mr. Scarfo," Frank said, lying, hoping he could still maneuver his way out of this.

"We need a clean ship. I'm getting rid of all the garbage and making sure the engine runs right. All beefs need to be resolved at the end of the month.

"So this is good?" Frank dared to asked, still not sure he wasn't going to get whacked.

"Consider it resolved," Scarfo said. "Come here." The boss offered his cheek, and Frank leaned down and kissed his jowl like a little boy kissing his mother goodnight. He backed away, starting to relax. Then Little Nicky grabbed his lapel and pulled him in close. "As long as you give that mouthy son of a bitch cousin of yours this. . ." He mimicked a gun with his left hand then dropped his thumb, imitating the hammer. "You do that for me, and when New York opens the books, we'll straighten you out."

And there it was. God had commanded Frank to spill the blood of his family. The test had come. If he didn't follow his orders, they'd probably both share the same sandy shallow hole. Little Nicky let go.

"You know what works?" Scarfo asked. "You take over it like my nephew does. Ask that son of a bitch to get something out of the refrigerator, and when his back is turned..." Frank didn't say anything and nearly hit the wall trying to leave the office to face his cousin. Joey wasn't that smart, but he possessed an animal's sense for danger. He'd know something was up the moment he saw him. Frank shut the office door, stepped into a bathroom down the hall and vomited into the clean toilet. Then he washed his mouth out with some mint shit he found above the sink. How the hell had it come to this? Or were they always going to end up here? He wished he could reverse time and go back to the streets when they were kids. Those were good times. Frank washed the cold sweat off the back of his neck and stepped out of the bathroom. Joey waited for him, sipping from a plastic cup.

"What did that greasy fuck want?" Joey asked, sipping on his drink.

Frank heard him, but really didn't hear the words, just his high-pitched obnoxious voice and a snort.

"He cut your ears off, Frank?" Joey leaned against a wall. The other guys hovered about in the kitchen in dining room, sipping on mixed drinks and looking over at the two of them. Could he really do it? He'd never whacked anyone before. He'd been there when guys got shot in fights or over deals gone bad. That was South Philly. But now he'd been commanded by the king to execute a living man with a soul under the eyes of God. Did he have it in him? Frank knew that he'd been granted a test before passing onto a better position, one where he'd start to make real money and get his mom out of Philly. Did he really have any choice? "I said what did that — ?" Frank knew he couldn't spook his cousin. Joey acted like a punk, but he'd seen his cousin when he was messed up — especially when he was messed up. He'd probably kill two of the guys, and they'd both end up in the trunk of his car. "Yeah, it's good. Stop being a *stronzino*. He's taxing us, and it's coming out of your side."

Joey sighed, even looked relieved. "How much?"

Frank had to come up with an outrageous number. "Ten."

"That old man can kiss my ass."

"Not here. Not now. They'll do us both. Don't you give a shit? I go in there and put my balls into a wood chipper trying to save your ass — "

"You're not my fucking mother."

"No. But I promised your mother I'd watch you when the cancer was eating her up. Look. Just relax. It's all fixed. He asked us to mix the crew up some more drinks. Show that we can be good boys."

"Fuck him," Joey said.

"Maybe he'll take some money off the tax. And you did bartend."

"Let's do it and go play some poker." Frankie knew that he really meant find someone's apartment in A.C. and get stoned until he woke up with vomit down his leather jacket. He grabbed his sleeve and dragged him over to the kitchen. Scarfo's guys stopped chatting and parted ways, giving them plenty of space.

"Why don't you get some ice?" Frank said, watching his voice, trying to keep it cool. Joey squinted, getting a read on him.

"Ice." Joey said.

"Yeah. It's in the freezer."

"Not in the sauna?" Joey said.

"I need to get the gin. There' a case in the bedroom."

"In the bedroom?" Joe snorted.

"Yeah. A crate for the party downstairs. You get the ice. I'll do the heavy lifting." Joey just stared at him, and Frank didn't twitch. Sinatra played through the floor. Laughter roared from the party downstairs. Someone yelled the word cheese. A couple of the crew whispered to each other, watching the theater. "Do I have to hold your hand? I need a drink."

"I'm not your fucking butler," Joey said, but walked over to the open kitchenette. Once he turned his back, Frank started to shake. His legs melted under him, and he had to lean against the windowsill to stay standing. He took in a deep breath and held it, gagging on the rank miasma of cigarette smoke filling the condo. Joey went to the freezer.

"Hey, Frank," Mike the Fishhead said. "The ice sticks together. Better give him this." Mike the Fishhead handed him the thin piece of metal, sharp on the edge, heavy in the hand. He gave him a look, and Frank couldn't figure out whether it was a glance of confidence or a warning of consequences. The crew looked so sick — waxy skin, sunken eyes — like corpses in coffins dressed in their best suits. Their hair fell out, thinning at the tops of their skulls, and they stank of expensive cologne and stagnant smoke.

"Joey, you should get the number for their tailor," Frank said, trying to keep him from figuring out the situation. "Stop dressing like a street punk."

He stepped closer behind his friend, trying to get the right angle but doing it slowly so Joey didn't feel crowded.

"It was good enough for your mother last night," Joey said, not missing a beat. "There's no fucking ice in here." He rummaged through the freezer.

Frank looked back at the crew then at his friend. He couldn't do this. They had too much history. And how did he know they wouldn't do it to him right after he whacked Joey? Scarfo's crew knew nothing of loyalty, not with the way he was offing his people — loyal people that had served Bruno for years.

"Joey. Remember what you said about my wife earlier?" He said it with a vindictive tone, angry, like he was getting the final word in before stabbing him in the neck. He just hoped Joey would pick up on the signal. The crew didn't catch it. Mike even chuckled, watching over by the sink with a sadistic twinkle in his eye.

If he hadn't been *coked* up, it would only have taken him a moment to get it. Instead, it took him a few — the longest fucking seconds of Frank's life. Once he picked up on the hint, his cousin grabbed a metal serving tray off the counter and swung it at Mike. Old chips, dip and plates flew into the air. The tray connected with Mike's head, knocking him off his feet and into the wall. Frank heard his jaw crack — a sound he'd never forget. Frank used the commotion to drop the ice pick and give his partner time to get out. Two of the faceless crew reached, and Mike yelled from the floor: "Put it away!" Then Joey pushed his way out of the kitchen, kicked open the side door and fled the condo.

"Jesus Christ," he said.

The door to Scarfo's office opened, and the boss emerged from the dark. "You fucked up."

"I'll finish this," Frank said, pushing through the startled crew and following his partner. He wasn't sure where Joey would run. Margate was a peaceful shore town, a satellite of Atlantic City where the clean people stayed — not his cousin's environment. He'd stand out, and it wouldn't take long for the crew to hunt him down. Frank just had to find him first, then they'd find cover somewhere and figure this shit out. He chased his partner out of the condo, following him down the staircase attached to the outside. He hit the metal steps too fast and slid, banging his back then landing in the yard. His left shoulder throbbed, and he pulled himself up, bearing it. Pain shot from his ribs through his chest, and he spit blood from a slashed lip. He walked off, trying not to slip on the icy sidewalk. The snow turned to sleet, and cars drove slowly through the neighborhood, trying not to slide on the nascent ice. He hated coming down here in the winter. Frank got to his car, collapsed into the front seat, shaking from a mix of chill and soreness. He grabbed the piece taped under the seat, turned the ignition, then scanned the street with his headlights on. He had to find him fast. Scarfo's crew wouldn't be too far behind, and they only had one shot to get out, though he had no fucking idea where to go. They couldn't go back to Philly after this. For a moment, he wondered if he'd ever see Connie again or their apartment or all the familiar places of his childhood. In a second, it all changed, and he cringed, wondering if Joey was worth losing all of this.

He pulled out, and the wheels spun on black ice. Joey would be running towards A.C., to the grounds he knew. He wouldn't be able to trust anyone, especially not his junkie friends or the degenerate gamblers that lived in the city. Scarfo owned this town. He even owned the cops — or at least paid for information. Everyone had their seat in the orchestra.

This was the real America.

Frank drove until he spotted a hunched over figure running up a side street. He spun the wheel, trying to cut him off, then pumped the breaks, trying to keep control of the car. He threw open the passenger door. "Joey." His partner stopped running, but stood his ground, keeping a distance between them. Frank showed him the gun, then set it on the dashboard. "They're going to whack us both out in a minute." Headlights appeared in the darkness behind them, riding slowly up through Margate. Joe looked up at the spurious stars glowing and winking north from the casinos and hotels — promising hope, security, an end to pain, to uncertainty. The city lied to them, and they lied to themselves. Shaking in the cold, his cousin climbed in and slammed the door.

"What happened to your lip?"

Frank pulled out and sped on the icy roads. No one was out, and Scarfo's crew would find them. "We get across the river to Philly. Steal a car. Head west."

"I've always wanted to go west," Joey said. "Vegas. City's made of money."

Frank sighed and kept turning his head, watching for cars coming up behind him. He caught twin beams from headlights turning onto Albany Boulevard as he crossed the bridge out of Margate and into Atlantic City. The twinkling lights promised to those near and afar, across the land and the sea riches granted by deity and prayer with one pull of the lever! He clutched the driving wheel until his knuckles bleached to bone. Joey lit up a cigarette, and the acrid vapors burned Frank's eyes.

"I can't see shit in this already."

"You drive like my fucking grandmother."

"Do you even get this? Scarfo controls all of this. Everyone in his kingdom either owes or wants something, and right now, the guys back at the compound are calling everyone from the mayor to the gambling junkies."

Before turning left to head up to the Atlantic City Expressway and freedom, he looked behind one more time and swore he saw a sleek Cadillac gaining on them through the haze. Sleet banged on the windshield, and Joey blew smoke in his face. Frank never saw the traffic light change, and he pulled out into the major intersection, veering left to the expressway and their only chance of making it out of New Jersey alive.

"Fuck. Frank — "

A tourist bus slammed into the back of their car, pushing them to the far side of the intersection. The car spun on the ice until they faced the opposite way, and the force knocked Frank's head against the window, cracking one of his molars. Air bags blew inflated, slapping his face. He blacked out for the next few seconds until the distant pierce of sirens woke him. He pushed down the airbag and got his seatbelt off. Moving his head shot needles through his neck and his back. Joey shook it off, threw open the door, and slithered out of the vehicle. He held his arm and ran towards the temple of lights. "Joey! Motherfucker." Frank struggled with the handle, but the door jammed. Police lights glowed in the distance. If it was one of Little Nicky's guys, they'd shoot on sight. Frank pushed the revolver into his jacket pocket then maneuvered across the front seat, dragging his bruised body through passenger side door and collapsed onto the slushy road. He looked up to see the bus driver standing trying to calm a herd of seniors.

"Dude, take it easy," the pudgy driver said. "An ambulance is on its way. What the hell was that? You guys have too much rummy nog?" Frank pushed himself up on his car. His heart rammed into his ribs, and suddenly, the pain just washed out him. He tasted copper in his mouth, and he got to his feet, then ran after Joey. They couldn't go east now, not down miles of empty highways and closed motels. Their only chance lay in the lair of the beast, west to Atlantic City to hide in hell from the devil. He spotted Joey up ahead at a crossroads, two blocks up from the boardwalk. The helpless child paced back and forth, shaking his hands in the air.

"What the fuck is rummy nog?" Frank asked.

"I need to clear my head," Joe said. "I know a place above a bowling alley. It'll be cool. Steve's a friend. He'll hide us."

Frank smacked the back of his head. "You don't ever put your life in a junkie's hands."

"Then what the fuck do we do?" Two more AC cruisers pulled up to the accident scene. The cops hadn't seen them yet, but that would change.

"We get off the streets," Frank said. "I did some work on Lion's Pride. It's closed. Huge." He yanked on Joey's jacket, and he followed. His cousin shook — not from cold, but need.

"I need my medicine," Joey said. "I need to clear my head."

"You need to shut your mouth."

A police cruiser raced down the avenue, flashing its lights through the crippled and rotten heart of the city. Beyond the walls of the casino castles the tide washed in and out. Behind the walls, apartment buildings decayed and few jobs existed that paid a liveable wage. The casinos provided the means of the life for the mostly black and Russian people mucking out an eager living in the filth below the great and glittering towers. Graffiti decorated the stucco and brick walls. Shopping carts and old furniture littered the alleys, and winos sipped malt liquor at the corners, warming themselves by fires lit in coffee tins, burning punched playing cards discarded by the casinos. Dealers sold relief in packets and vials, sitting outside check cashing centers that gave the dealers extra percentage. If a dealer or casino worker fell behind too far this month, or say a gambler got too far into the hole, they could always find a friend ready to help them out with a loan, though often charging two points on the vig. Pretty soon you paid just to keep the debt floating. When these guys, mostly 'made' guys under Little Nicky, got their hooks into you, you were theirs forever. They fed off this desolate and hopeless world that dwelled below the high towers of luck and chance, sucking on the sour milk that leaked from a dead cow's teat. And junkies existed even deeper below, more depraved and disgusting than the whores and psychics, the dealers and shylocks in this modern inferno of Dante. If a member or associate of the family got caught selling drugs, they'd get it, but an associate could rob a dealer or charge them tax for dealing. Frank knew how to survive, but his cousin dealt, and it was probably one of the reasons this happened.

They got through the alleys, avoiding the pay-parking lots. The two cousins took shelter from the sleet and snow below the boardwalk, kicking through sticky mud and evicted nests of rats from their trash and yellow grass. The slush and sand had ruined Frank's Bottega loafers — a gift from Connie. He'd make his cousin pay for them if they found their way out of Atlantic City.

"Where the fuck is this place?" Joey asked.

Frank struggled to keep walking, limping through the shifting dunes and nearly falling several times. Blood oozed from his lip and he wiped the crimson on his white sleeves below his soaked jacket. Ahead, he noticed construction equipment stored below the boardwalk and a fence protecting the site. He knew the guards never bothered locking the gates and just hung a sign for show. They made up a ladder into the infrastructure of the Lion's Pride Casino and onto the main floor. Plastic whipped about, compelled by the wind. They made their way through the torn structure, passing the rows of silent slot machines. Insulation spilled out from the tall ceiling, the reek of paint burned Frank's throat. They'd turned off the heat, and Frank lost feeling in his hands and feet. He couldn't hold a piece this way, and they needed to warm up a bit. He wondered if it was safe, but they had no choice. They made it into what used to be the dealer's room of the Lion's Pride Casino. Frank tripped through plastic tarp and trashed blackjack tables, trying to see by the low light shed by the city lights. Roulette wheels painted on the walls reminded Frank of happier times in their youths when a night in A.C. ended well no matter the money lost. Now, here they were on the run from the whole of the city with little chance of escaping. Not more than few days ago, they were riding high on the street, making big scores and now in this room of wild chance, they'd be hunted down like animals — though Little Nicky's crew was only looking for Joey. Maybe they didn't know yet. Maybe he still had time.

Joey took out a plastic lighter and provided a sparse illumination, but enough so they didn't break their necks. He kept clawing at his scalp, scratching all over his skin. "Look. I'll be back. I need to piss."

"You can piss right here," Frank said. He grabbed a metal drum and dragged it closer. The adrenalin waned, and soreness spread through his ribs and neck, stiffening his shoulder. He looked for some busted-up wood, anything to get warm. He didn't want to risk a fire but knew he had to get warm or go deeper into shock.

"I can't do that in front of you," Joe said. "I'm not some fucking animal."

"Yeah," Frank said. He reached into the drum, looking for kindling and plucked out a playing card from a pile of punched decks. He turned it over. Fuck. Ace of spades.

"I'm hurting here," Joey said. "I'm just going to go down the boardwalk over to the Psychic Rose. Those Slavs don't even know who I am."

Frank ignited several of the cards and some newspaper. He mixed in the wood and stirred it to keep it going, making sure the fire didn't burn too bright. Most of the smoke dispersed into the large vault and probably wouldn't be noticed among the fog blowing off the Atlantic. He warmed his limbs, and in the light noticed blood soaking through his jacket. His own reckless driving might have done the job for Scarfo's crew.

"You stay put, Joe. I'm serious. You can't trust anyone here."

"Fucking bullshit," Joe yelled, raking claws against his scalp. His eyes faded to yellow in the sallow firelight — empty eyes, dead eyes in a corpse. It wouldn't be much longer before his clock ran out. Why was Frank risking everything for this trash? Nostalgia? "I can't think like this."

"We have to figure out a plan. They're coming for us right now, working everyone in town. They're going to be here soon. It's the only safe place we could go."

"You said we'd go down to A.C., work it out. Then you're coming at me with an ice pick. You're going to turn me over to those goombahs to save your own ass. You think I don't know?" Joey snorted like a wild boar, grunting in his pain. Sweat poured down his head, soaking his hair.

"Do you know what I gave up for you, tonight? Did you ever think about Connie? My home? The money I could have made. All I had to do was stab you in the fucking neck, and I'd be a king."

"A pussy like you?" Joey screeched with obnoxious laughter. "I'd be the fucking king. The fucking lion." He headed for the beach, walking towards the front of the building.

Flashlights caught Frank's eye from the side, and he caught the scent of the obnoxious cologne. Of course it hadn't taken the crew long. Where else could the two have gone?

"Joey," Frank said. He pulled out his piece. "Forgive me." Frank shot through his cousin's back. Joey twisted his body in surprise, then fell into a row of dead slot machines. He grabbed one of the metal arms, turning the three wheels. Frank fired again, hitting him in the lower back. His cousin dropped onto a pile of card shoes, smearing blood on the felt of a broken poker table.

"Good boy, Frank," Mike the Fishhead said, putting away his piece. They probably knew the truth of what had happened but didn't care. He'd passed the test.

"I knew he'd come here looking for a hit," Frank lied, wishing he'd done it sooner, years sooner. His lack of remorse surprised him. The events of the night had hollowed him out, but he was tired of it, tired of struggling, just getting by. He wanted more. He deserved more.

"The boss will approve," Mike said, helping him walk.

Frank figured they'd take care of the wild events of the night, pay off the right people. The car accident would be a hit-and-run never solved. They'd find his cousin's body in the trunk tomorrow morning down on S Knight Avenue. "You did the right thing," Mike said. "Nicodemus Scarfo doesn't like disrespect."

WIRE

by C. Courtney Joyner

C. Courtney Joyner is the screenwriter of many films, including *From a Whisper to a Scream*, *Doctor Mordrid*, and *Lurking Fear*. He is also the author of the popular Shotgun Western series and the novel *Nemo Rising*.

MY HANDS ARE SHAKING, BUT I FEEL I CAN STILL GET OFF A good shot if need be.

I am Jonas Terill, Jr., son of Jonas and Sara, and I will be fifteen years tomorrow. I was hoping for lemon pie and a baseball, but will likely be hanged instead. Whoever you are, you think my ending was deserved, as I have bloodied people in the past and this latest kill is my undoing.

Things wasn't supposed to go in this way.

The body lying by the wire moved a little when I rode up, but that was after the kill shot, and I've seen that before. There was a little sound, like a baby's voice, and then nothing. I have pushed the hair out of the eyes and adjusted the hat, but blood is everywhere. The face is like a red Halloween mask.

There has been gun-fire, I'd judge, a few miles away. I think this was a signal. I fired back, but I am expecting riders to see what's happened, so I will put down my confessing.

I was born in a dugout outside Rawlins, where Pa was holed up with two other men and my mother. One of the men was a lay minister who married my parents while Ma was birthing me. I wouldn't have known this, except that after my father was shot, I found a letter recounting this among his things Ma had kept dear.

We was hiding at the farm of a dead man when my father told me that if you want to make it in the world, you have to be willing to go all the way. Do what the other fellow won't. It was near Christmas when he advised me and was showing how to chop wood. He wanted me to swing a double-blade ax, when my hands could barely get around the handle. He held the blade off my shoulder and guided it down against a frozen rail, but it bounced off. I cried and he laughed from the belly and cut the rail with less than four strokes, clean through.

This was the same ax he used to kill one of the deputies who came to take him for robbing a mail hack near Jackson Hole. They said they was with Joe LeFors. That was Christmas Eve when they rode in, not letting my family alone. We never had any peace that I recall.

The deputies fired into the house, and one bullet nicked the top of my ear. Pa screamed and grabbed the shotgun from behind the stove and fired out the door, killing a horse. To me it looked like summer lightning. One of the deputies ran for the house, and Pa put the ax in his chest before the others started shooting, while my Mother curled herself around me, and used her nightgown to soak the blood. This is why I only have half an ear on my left side.

That was the last time I saw Pa, and I might have dreamed some of the things he said, but they seem real to me at this moment.

I am hearing something like shouting bouncing off the far hills, but I haven't seen riders. I could ride out, but my legs feel like they are tied to the ground. Or maybe the hands of the dead are holding me. That is what my mother would call my fanciful thinking. For everything my Pa told me about what it meant to deal with the other fellow before he deals with you, my mother's ways seem to have more value now. I wish I could go back and follow them better.

Pa had been outlawed for a year when he met my mother. She knew what he was, but understood who he was inside, and had faith that he would mend his ways. She became his woman, and then his wife and talked about this freely, without a hint of shame. She believed in my father's soul because we all have a past, but she knew that when he fell in with a bad lot, he would follow their trail rather than cut one of his own. It was his failing. She called him, 'The weakest man-of-strength God ever made.'

Like many things she said, she made me write them down and read them back, to check my writing and spelling. She couldn't read numbers, but could add any sum in her head and I have the same talent. When I have gone to school at different times, the teachers always said I had had some fine education, and I thank my Ma for that.

It was three years ago that we rode to the prison at Rawlins, and I waited while Ma signed a paper for Pa's body. He had been shot while fighting with another prisoner, and buried in the common yard. We went to see the grave, but left him with the other plain crosses.

She died six months later in the backroom of the boarding house where she was cooking. She told me she was happy to see I had grown into my Pa's face, but not to follow that path. She left me with a ring and forty dollars.

I confess now that I lost the forty dollars playing faro, and the ring was the cause of my killing a man.

There has been a shot. I can see something moving, a group of riders, in the far distance. The sea of grass makes it hard to focus beyond it, but they are there and coming for me. If they are men like me, I know what will happen. Somehow, I am writing with a steadier hand.

I am hours away from being fifteen, but I know what it is to ride beyond the law. After the undertaker and I buried Ma, I rode alone from town to farm, looking for work. Some folks were generous, others were not. I stopped by a schoolhouse and asked the Master about chores, hoping I could stay on. Ma would embrace that. He refused me nastily, so I stole his grey mare and sold her to a n'er-do-well. I am not proud of this, but sometimes we do things we don't expect.

The night I got the money for the horse, I slept in a rooming house, and a man claiming to be a trail boss took exception to Ma's ring that I wore on my smallest finger. You can't explain anything to a drunk, so he was deaf to my words and swung a whiskey a bottle.

I reacted the way Pa would have wanted me to, and the gun was in my hand, but I didn't feel it. The sound was louder than anything, and he flew back down the stairs. Because I was thirteen, and there were people in the house, I was let go. The law was also a drunkard and didn't wish to be bothered with this killing.

Now I had my father's name and a reputation following it. I didn't know what I wanted, but it wasn't this, although work now seemed to come a little easier from cowboys who had heard the story. And a few strangers bought me meals if I would re-tell it.

That's how I came to this war.

I was leaving a dogtrot when a man named Caleb rode in with some cowboys, but he wasn't covered in mud and hair. He had a new shave and a gold watch fob. We talked and he told me about The Newbridge Cattle Co. and if I wanted to be a Range Protector. I wouldn't get my hands dirty and I'd draw more pay than the cowboys, if I could handle a gun and was willing to use it. He heard the tale about me, and thought I'd be a good one. I had less than a dollar in my jeans, and had to listen.

I can hear voices and shouts. The riders are closer now, and I can't make out any of them, but in a war, you don't know the guy who's going to take your life. An enemy is an enemy. That's what Mr. Newbridge told me when I signed on for the job. It was his range and his wire, and I was one of his soldiers. He shook my hand, telling me what a pleasure it was I was riding for him.

Ma and Pa would have been proud of that, because I was drawing real pay. I was loaned a Winchester, and practiced with it when I wasn't riding the fences. Truth be told, I stood back while the other boys beat the homesteaders who were cutting through our range. No one challenged us, they were just folks, and my finger never came close to the trigger. Caleb shot an old man through the eye who'd swung at him with an ax just like my Pa did, only now I was one of those deputies.

If Caleb reads this, he will think me a coward, but I was sick after this incident. I should have ridden out of Wyoming and never looked back. I didn't have what my Pa had. I have been a thief, and a killer by chance, but not for wages. This wasn't how things were supposed to go, not the way Ma had wanted. I don't know why, but I needed to prove myself to the men I was riding with. That's my failing.

This morning all I was thinking of was my birthday and lemon pie. If I did a good job today, then Caleb and the others might celebrate me, and I could move on without shame. That is what was in my mind when I was riding along the miles of Mr. Newbridge's barbed wire.

That is what was in my mind when I saw the fence cutter. There was nothing for miles except someone in hat and coat, bending by the wire with a cutting tool. That's a concealed weapon, and if you shoot, then you're defending yourself. I dropped to the ground and fired the Winchester once, trying for a wing. But my aim was poor, and I struck the cutter in the head.

When I rode up and saw the cutter, I thought I screamed, but I became light in the head and fell from my saddle. I woke up lying by the wire, the cutter next to me. Her face was covered with blood, but she was pretty with yellow hair and blue eyes, and close to me in years. I imagine she was helping her folks, who wanted to come through our range. She didn't have a gun, and her horse had bolted.

I have tried to be gentle with her, and started to put down my thoughts so people will know that it was just chance that this happened, like anything else in this life. She made the choice to cut, and I chose to shoot. I wish we had done neither. Instead, we might have met in town, and want to think of what that might have been like.

The riders are not far off, and their curses and screams are quite clear. I think the one in front is her Pa. I don't know if this letter will give them any peace, but it has helped me. One rider has pulled up, and is taking aim.

I am not going to move. I can't. I can only pray to God that I…

***

Despite my years, I have bloodied others in my life, and this is my confessing.

It would be best if you are educated in more ways than me, as certain thoughts that I would like to be known will be hard to put into words. Mrs. Willougby of the _____ school once said that I had a facility, and there can be meaning beyond what is written down, and so I am praying that is so in my case. I will not surrender these pages while alive, as that would not do my mortal soul any good at all.

I'm looking at the girl lying next to me, with half of her face covered in red like a mask for Halloween, and I am lost, thinking about the kind of man who would do something like this. Who would fire the gun? It was my hand and my choice, but what brought me to this place?

Mother's fate.

My mother's look and her character. Big hands. Cried when she saw father talking to me and when he was arrested by Joe LeFors. She saw him hang, and I rode out on my own, leaving a note and money from a friend that I took.

LACQUER

by Isobel Blackthorn

Isobel Blackthorn is the author of many novels, including *Twerk*, *The Drago Tree*, and *Asylum*. She is also the author of the short story collection *All Because of You*.

T HE PUNK LEFT THE SMELL OF HIS ASS ON THE SEAT, SHARP with meaty undertones. Not knowing where the stench came from, Marcia screwed up her nose as she took up his place, the vinyl still warm.

"Hitting the high notes real fine tonight, Marcia." Her rendition of *Misty* was near perfect, as far as I could tell. She was no Sarah Vaughan and she knew it, but she was good enough, more than good enough for the Fillmore.

"Why thank you kindly, sir," she replied, putting on a cheesy Southern drawl.

She ordered a drink. Over on the dais her trio was leaning towards each other across their instruments. It was a good night, the venue full, patrons planning on staying till stumps.

"I should be going."

"You gonna stagger all the way home?"

"Stagger? Come on, Marcia, I'm not trashed."

"Sure you're not."

She observed me in that mocking, shrewd-eyed way of hers. I hated that she was right.

The club slid to the right as I stood. I gripped the bar until the woozy feeling settled then headed for the door, squinting as my feet hit the sidewalk. Friday, midnight, late August, and Fillmore Street was lively, revellers garbed in the glitzy and the outrageous spilling out of clubs and bars on their way to others, but even in my inebriated state I saw through the razzmatazz to the iniquity beneath; the punks, the pimps, the crack dealers, and the homeless shambling or cowering in doorways.

The smell of frying onions from the burger joint across the street and my guts heaved. I stumbled down the alleyway beside Dizzy's and leaned a hand against the wall as the contents of my stomach — bourbon, more bourbon, and whatever was left of the tuna hash I ate earlier — gushed from my mouth with the force of a geyser. Void, I straightened, wiped my chin, spat away the acridity, the half-digested gobbets.

I made to walk away, but my shoe had caught on something. Fabric, maybe. I pulled the toe to the side. Felt like a sleeve. I squinted at my foot, but the alley was too dark to see. I fumbled around in the pockets of my coat. The torch was down there somewhere, buried deep in loose change and old receipts, the usual detritus. I found it, wrapped my hand around the shaft, flicked on the switch. The batteries were still good. The thin beam picked out the spread of my vomit, the way it pooled in the folds of a coat.

Shining the light at my feet I stepped back, leaving behind a bloody footprint that disappeared as I watched, obliterated by the blood flowing from beneath the coat cuff. This was all too recent, the blood no doubt still warm. I pulled back some more, scuffed the toes of my shoe in the dust. Would it sink in through the shoe leather, the sock, my skin, my flesh, to mingle with my own through a nick or a cut?

Paranoia.

The prick of a syringe, the needle sinking deep into my vein, and I awaken to myself knowing it was already too late. You can't catch the cancer twice.

The body was prone. Female, judging by the curves, the hair. She was thin, average in height. The legs were out straight, missing the feet.

Giving the body a wide berth, I walked around to see the face.

There was no face. Shock, a single current, sliced through me, sobering.

What might have been the forehead, the cheeks, the mouth, was a tangle of skin flaps and mangled flesh. No nose. The mouth split in four. The teeth were missing, the gums ragged. Even her ears had been hacked. All that was left of normal were her eyes. Eyes staring ahead in terror. Was she alive when he did this?

Fascination drew me. There was artistry in the mutilation, a certain symmetry, as though every cut, every fold or bulge of skin and bone and flesh had been considered. This was no frenzied attack of an impulsive killer in a rage. She'd been flayed, her skin peeled back like so many petals of a flower.

I shone the light over the body. The coat had most of her covered. I had to be grateful for that. But where were her hands? Gone the same way as the feet. Whoever did this didn't want her identified. I walked around, shining the torch at the ground looking for clues. There was nothing. Not even a footprint. I pointed the light back at the body.

I was planning on heading back into Dizzy's to call the cops when the side door opened and a figure stepped outside. It was Marcia. My liquor-fuelled brain was slow to register I still had the torch shining down at the carnage before me. The scream that came out of Marcia's mouth was curdling. She had a direct line of sight to the face.

The cops took an age. By the time I heard the siren wail and the tires screech to a halt, I was lucid. Marcia had gone back inside.

I tried not to breathe on the cop with the notepad, but he came up too close and I had my back to the wall.

"And you are?"

"Jim Morrison."

He did a double take, then laughed. "Next, you're going to tell me you're a singer, right?"

"Yeah, and she didn't light my fire so I killed her."

That time, he didn't laugh. Not sure he got the joke. I fished out my ID. "Jim Morrison of Morrison's Detective Agency."

He paused, absorbing the information, his lips curling.

"And that belongs to you?" He pointed at the pool of sludge soaking into the coat.

I couldn't deny it.

"Business that bad, huh?"

I didn't answer. I had to hang around while they called in the detectives. Give a statement. Yes, I'm a PI. No, I didn't know her. I was drinking at the club, felt bilious, came down the alley. It was dark.

It was still dark, even with all the extra torchlight.

No one wanted to touch her. Even the medic did a double take. Eventually, inches from my acrid deposit, a cop slid his hand in a side pocket and extracted a bus ticket. "Hunters Point," he read.

"That explains it," said the detective standing by my side.

"Explains what?"

"She's from a project. Whoever did this will be related to her. Boyfriend, maybe. Brother."

"Brother!"

"You'd be amazed." He looked me up and down. "Then again, maybe not."

"You're saying it's a domestic?"

"I'm saying it's none of your goddam business." He swung around to the others. "Get her out of here. We're done for the night."

"You call that an investigation?" I muttered under my breath, loud enough for only him to hear.

"You fancy driving out to Hunters Point at this hour? Forget it."

A bus ticket to Hunters Point, and the investigation was closed by the sound of it. Just another black woman murdered by her own people. Nothing the cops should be troubled with. That about summed up the San Francisco police attitude in my mind. Yet, rankled as I was, I couldn't get involved. For once the cases were piling up and I had no spare time. Besides, who would be paying me? No one.

I went in to check on Marcia. She was a blubbering mess at the bar. Most of the audience had gone home and her band was keeping her company. I put an arm around her shoulder, felt her tremble. Her body rose as she took a breath.

"It'll pass."

She wiped her eyes, got a grip. She was tough.

"What?"

"The shock."

"I can see her, right in here." Marcia pointed at her skull. "Ain't nothing gonna shift what I saw."

"I'm sorry."

"What are you sorry for? You didn't kill her."

Yeah, but my torch...

She shuddered and the trembling started up again.

"Go home, Marcia. Get some distance."

I looked at the others. No one knew where to put their gaze. Delroy the pianist was studying his shoes. Clinton was gripping the neck of his guitar case, and Lloyd was using the bar as a snare. "Can one of you take her?"

Lloyd made a move.

Leaving them to deal with their distraught singer, I lumbered up Fillmore to Haight Street, opening the shop door to a rundown Victorian with 'Jim Morrison Agency' lettered on the glass and private investigator beneath. The signage was not that visible to passers-by thanks to a row of small trees, but the obscurity lent an air of discretion. Besides, few came knocking. The companies and government departments I worked for preferred the telephone. My apartment was on the floor above.

I slaked a roaring thirst before falling into bed, vowing to ease up on the booze. I had vomited in Dizzy's alley one too many times. It had to stop.

When I woke, it was lunchtime. I had a belter of a headache. It took me a while to cotton on to the phone ringing downstairs.

Marcia yelled at me on my hello.

"Jim, what took you so long? I've been ringing and ringing."

"There is a small thing called sleep, Marcia."

"Yeah, but there is also a large thing called a dead body."

"What about it?"

"You gotta do something, Jim. You gotta find out who she was."

"Let the cops deal."

"They ain't gonna deal. You know that. You know they'll write her off as some washed up bit of trash or hooker not worth the ground she walked on. You can find out who she is. I know you can."

I told her I would look into it.

"You will?"

"I just said, Marcia."

I sighed inwardly as I hung up. There was nothing I wanted to do less than search for the identity of that butchered Jane Doe. The blood got to me. Since the car accident, I hadn't wanted anything to do with anyone else's blood. Yet there would be no refusing Marcia. Besides, I owed her, or rather, I owed her mother.

Sheree had been a civil rights activist back in my pre-PI days, until her efforts were silenced in a brutal police attack during an Ad Hoc march. The crazed dude pierced her skull with her own placard thanks to the three-inch nails I had hammered into it. Marcia was four at the time, and me a cocky nineteen. Sheree died of her injuries. She never got to be a Panther. The cop was to blame, but I was at fault, and I never erased the if-only guilt.

I had inherited the business from my father. Not a square of the scuffed and stained surface of his desk was visible beneath the piles of folders, notebooks, and letters. A string of insurance cases and a local government department wanting me to take their side in a race discrimination case. A gun for hire, that was me, proving the claimants were alleging falsehoods. I got to take the side of power against the little guy. Not something that sat easy with me, but I had to earn cash somehow and I was never going back to security. Mostly the claims were substantial — car theft, suspicious break in, stolen jewelry — and the little guys not so little, but last week I was asked to spy on a woman from Oakland who claimed she had her bicycle stolen in Tenderloin. Tight-assed company didn't want to pay out on a freaking bicycle. My fee was probably costing more than the claim.

Then there were the missing. Missing wives, missing boyfriends, missing daughters, and missing sons. Most didn't want to be found. Or they washed up somewhere, in an alley like Jane Doe.

Any one of those old files might be her, except... I found myself collating into racial types, and then skin color. Jane had ebony skin. I was left with three folders, two hookers with desperate mothers and a manicurist. I took out the photos and scrutinized each in turn. Could any of them be her? There was no way of telling. Besides, what were the chances? Jane could be any ebony-skinned woman in San Francisco and beyond. A tourist, someone from interstate. With a bus ticket to Hunters Point? Maybe she was visiting family. Then again, mutilated and murdered, in whichever order, and left for dead in Dizzy's alley — the victim was most likely from the Fillmore.

I chose to walk to clear my head. The southern end of Fillmore Street on a hot August afternoon was no stroll in the park. Boarded up shop fronts and derelict Victorian terraces shaded into wasteland zoned for redevelopment. Didn't look set to happen any time soon. Urban clearance gave way to the brand-new Fillmore Centre that the locals couldn't afford to live in. Geary Boulevard marked the point of transition to the thriving northern end of the Fillmore, renamed by realtors Lower Pacific Heights. A microcosm of gentrification, the wealthy displacing the poor and the Black and the Hispanic residents in their tens of thousands. Only, the underbelly was right there, in the projects left tucked away down the back streets on the south side, and the people who remained scuffed their boot leather on a weekday, angry and hurting. That cop was right. The Fillmore was violent, drug-fueled mostly, and Jane Doe had no doubt fallen foul of her boyfriend.

The alley beside Dizzy's reeked of piss, human piss, recent. Odd I hadn't noticed that last night, but then again, I was canned thanks to my own stupidity, and I had other smells to contend with.

Some effort had been made to remove the blood. I walked along the wall, keeping a sharp eye on the ground, passing Dizzy's side door and on to the end where sheets of iron blocked access to whatever was beyond. Take a pole-vaulter to get over that. A search along by the clapboard of the building next door yielded nothing. Not even a cigarette end. Odd, it was as though the alley had been swept clean. Even the trash can outside Dizzy's door was empty.

Back at the office, I called Marcia, told her I had not a chance in hell of finding who our Jane Doe was because someone had swept clean the crime scene. I tried, I told her I tried, I told her I had gone through my files, but with no evidence and nothing to identify the body, what chance did I have?

"You call yourself a private investigator, Jim Morrison, and that's the best you can manage?"

"There's nothing I can do. I'm sorry."

"Sorry ain't good enough. Sorry ain't gonna get that poor woman's face outta my head. I can't sleep. I can't even close my eyes without seeing her. I'm begging you, do something."

"Marcia, please, you've got to understand, I…"

She slammed down the phone on my next word.

I sifted through the case files one more time without any idea what I was looking for. I thought back, picturing the scene, the cops, re-living it. Was I missing something? There was that bus ticket, but a bus ticket to Hunters Point wasn't going to take me far. Then I remembered Jane Doe had been wearing a coat. From memory, it was brown and thick. Odd for a summer night. *Her* coat? The killer's? It was not much to go on, but it was all I had.

Of the three cases, I had my doubts about the hookers. Those trails were ice cold, and I was facing telling the parents I could do no more for them. The manicurist had worked in Macy's Hair, a high-class salon down past Geary Boulevard, on the upmarket side of the Fillmore. The second walk of the day, and I pushed open the door on the hairspray, gave the women seated before giant mirrors a passing glance, and went through to where the owner, Bertrice, was putting the finishing touches on a bubble cut. She glanced my way. Hope and anxiety widened her eyes.

"Hey, Jim. What're you doing here? Got news?"

She was a big-boned matriarch with a heart to match. Last time we spoke, I told her there was little to no chance of finding her girlfriend. The trail had dried up months ago. Bertrice had begged me to keep looking, but without leads, what's a guy to do? Although, just then, I was starting to appear to myself a useless, washed up barfly, incapable of solving a single case.

She led me through to her office, more a windowless storeroom with a desk, and I waited for her to close the door before I spoke.

"A body's turned up in the alley by Dizzy's."

Her face crumpled, a hand reached to cover her mouth. "And you think?" she said between her fingers.

I steered my gaze away. "Not sure. Can't tell, and don't ask. Did Gemma own a brown coat?"

She hesitated. "Not that I know of. I didn't pay much attention to her coats."

"Can you have a think? Maybe ask around?"

"Sure. I'll do what I can."

"The chances are, it's not her, Bertrice. Don't worry."

"I'll try."

On my way home, I called in at Joe's grocer and grabbed some supplies and a bottle of bourbon to erase the memory of that mutilated face. The rest of the day was a blur.

Sunday, I closed the bicycle case by driving out to Oakland in the old Ford Fiat to find the claimant out on the very bicycle she alleged was stolen in Tenderloin. I had to revise my assumptions as I took a few photos. There must have been something in her claim to make the company suspicious, and they were right to investigate. Some bicycle, too. Classy.

That afternoon, I attended to my shoe, the one I had dipped in Jane Doe's blood. I would have thrown the pair out, but they were leather, made to last. I had to hold my breath as, with the aid of warm water and a cloth, the blood released its odor into the room.

By five, hunger drove me to Hamburger Mary's down on 12th Street, a welcome change of atmosphere and one of Bertrice and Gemma's favorite haunts. The place was half empty when I arrived. I ordered the usual burger and fries and sat at my favored seat, right at the back near the kitchen, the better to observe the others.

The regulars were in, too many of them too thin. Ghosts. the scourge of The Castro decimating the community. No renewal, just anguish and loss. What was once a thriving locale, vibrant, now hollowed out and haunted by a disease bent on punishing promiscuity, impulsive lust, freedom. They were not alone.

Gay men shared the cancer with intravenous drug users, with straight folk, with hemophiliacs, with accident victims in need of a blood transfusion, with me. Seeing those living corpses reminded me of my own future. I tested positive, but so far, the disease was sleeping, and I downed my food with the appetite of a bear.

On the bite of the last fry, Simple Minds' 'Waterfront' came on. Stifling a belch, I listened to the simple bass, the push and pull of the melody, the lyrics. The band was singing about the demise of their shipyards. They could have been singing about shipyards the world over. Or right here fifty years before, on Bloody Thursday. And there I was, thinking about blood and death again. There was no escaping it. Jane Doe's face flashed into my mind. Picturing Bertrice and Gemma, canoodling, I recalled Gemma's vibrant, multi-colored outfits, and I knew Jane Doe couldn't be her because I couldn't see Gemma in that brown coat. She wouldn't be seen ... No, I wouldn't let myself finish that thought.

Marcia didn't call me that night, which surprised me. I figured she had decided to leave me to it for a while. Although I knew it wouldn't be too long before she was on my back again.

Monday, I tackled the race discrimination case. I had been putting off closing my inquiries, not relishing cultivating the claimant's work colleague to shore up their justifiable grounds for dismissal. I read through the case file. The department accused Miss Dana Smith of slow productivity. She was a typist unable to make the mandatory fifty words a minute without errors. She was lazy, they said, misfiled important documents, turned up late for her shifts and one time senior management caught her with her feet on the desk reading a magazine. Why, with all that stacked against her, would she claim she was unfairly dismissed? Sounded to me like she was incompetent, but then again, they had failed to issue her with the appropriate number of warnings and her team leader had, according to Dana, berated her with a string of racial slurs in the staff canteen the day she was fired.

I arranged to meet her closest colleague, Rosie, after her shift.

I had an aversion to the skyscrapers of the financial district. Something about all that metal and glass smacked of the kind of corruption that really mattered. While I sifted the back alleys, the gutters, the drains, my slick-suited associates were busy taking the big guys to task over fraud, kickbacks, sweeteners. I figured I would look no good in a suit. I liked to be out in the street. Not behind a desk shuffling paper. Didn't make me feel any better.

Rosie hovered on the concourse between large concrete pillars. She was a smart young woman with big hair and batwing sleeves, her gathered skirt cinched at the waist with a wide leather belt.

"You still friends with Dana?" I asked when we were seated in a café nearby.

"Not so much," she said cautiously.

I picked up on the hesitation. This one might talk. Not wasting the moment, I asked what she could tell me about Dana.

"That she deserved to get fired."

"You really mean that?"

She glanced down at her lap. "I don't know if everything management is saying is true, and her team leader definitely yelled at her in the staff canteen. I was there. But the fact is she wasn't that good at her job."

"Why was that?"

"Well, she isn't that smart, know what I'm saying? And she didn't care. You got to watch your back. She didn't read the signs."

I straightened in my seat, holding back an impulse to lean forward.

I didn't want to scare her into silence. I smiled when I asked, "There was a build up to her dismissal?"

"Sure was."

"When did that start?"

"To begin with, she was doing okay. Then she started to get a thing about her nails. She went and got false ones. Bright orange, they were. She couldn't stand to get them chipped, and she was always worried they'd come off. She typed funny to compensate. Her nails got in the way of the keys and slowed her down. If she hadn't been obsessed with her nails, she would still have a job."

That was a maybe, and it didn't make up for the technicalities of Dana's case, which was strong enough to attract the attention of a pro bono lawyer. The department wanted dirt, and now I had it. Rosie's divulgence made Dana appear to put her appearance above her responsibilities. It might be enough, and at least it was something. I pictured the photo of her in my file, all showy with her cleavage protruding from a low-cut top, her makeup immaculate, her hair styled. She belonged in a cabaret or on The Strip, not in a typing pool in a government department. I imagined management would have wanted her gone and were waiting to find a way to fire her. Yet she still had grounds, the racial slurs a proven fact, and part of me couldn't help taking her side despite her obsession with her nails.

Marcia walked into my office that afternoon. She sat down heavily in the one visitor's chair. I asked her how she was. Big mistake. The quivering started, followed by the tears.

"I can't sleep," she wailed. "I'm having flashbacks. All I can see day and night is her mangled face. It's like she's haunting me."

She was not alone. Unsure for how long she planned sitting there spilling her trauma, I said, "I'm following some leads, Marcia. Don't worry. I'll find out who she was."

My fake reassurances seemed to work. A mug of hot sweet tea with a splash of bourbon and a bit of chit chat about how Sarah Vaughan was better than Billy Holliday, and Marcia calmed down and took off home. I was left with Jane Doe's brutalized face, her blood plastered like a hideous backdrop in my mind, a backdrop only liquor would erase.

There was nothing about the murder in the newspapers. As the sun streaked across Fillmore Street, lighting my office through whitewashed panes, I phoned Yvonne, my contact at the local cop station. There was no need to explain. "I heard it was you," she said with a chuckle. She said she would ask around. About an hour later she called back saying, no, no ID on the girl and no leads. They weren't planning to take it far. I wasn't surprised. All I had was the matter of the brown coat, which nagged at me as the stand out clue, if only because no one wore a thick winter coat on a hot August night. As for the missing extremities, where would a killer dispose of dismembered hands and feet? In the bay? A storm-water drain? Stuffed in a freezer? Fed to a dog?

Bertrice called. Said she had been through all her old photos and I should swing by. I told her I would be right over.

I took the car, parking in the lane beside the salon. She had the shots spread all over her desk. Gemma was in every one. I tried to impose the gruesome visage on her pretty face, but I couldn't. Not because I lacked the ability, but because I could not bear to peel away the skin, rip out the teeth, the nose, leave what was left looking like a grisly Picasso. In none of them was Gemma wearing that brown coat.

Most of the photos were spread so I could see the whole shot, some were tucked beneath others with just the portion of Gemma's face showing. In one, she was hugging someone. I pulled the photo out from beneath the one above and there was the brown coat, on the woman she was embracing. It was unmistakable.

I showed Bertrice.

"Who is this?"

She peered and frowned.

"No idea. It was taken at a party to celebrate the salon's fifth anniversary. We invited our regulars. I don't recall her though."

She was facing away from the camera, slim, of average height. I couldn't say I was convinced it was Jane Doe, but at least it was something.

"Can I take this?"

"Go right ahead. Bring it back though. It's a nice one of Gemma."

It was. Her face beamed right at the camera lens.

I slipped the photo into my breast pocket.

A hunch took me over Geary Boulevard. It was seven, and Homeless Steve would be hanging around the hamburger joint across from Dizzy's, hustling spare change and cigarettes. He had been living on the streets for years, and it showed in his ragbag clothing, in his dreadlocked blond hair and full beard, in the blackheads that peppered his nose and in the filth congregating in his cuticles. All that, and he stank of the streets, odors more putrid than the reek of frying onions and charring meat wafting out the burger bar.

I slipped him a few bucks and showed him the photo.

"Nah, never seen her," he said, handing it back.

I kept my hands in my pockets. "Take a closer look. What about the woman in the coat? Did you see anyone resembling her last Friday night?"

"Can't tell. She ain't facing the camera." He paused as he handed back the photo. "Who wears a coat in August?"

"That's what I thought."

"If she had been around last Friday, I'd have spotted her."

I crossed the street and went into Dizzy's. The place was near empty. The club never did much trade on a Monday. I sat at the bar, ordered a bourbon and dry and showed the photo to the bar staff and a few of the regulars, but no one had seen a woman in that coat on Friday night or in fact ever. All anyone said was she would have been cooking in it.

I pocketed the photo and slugged my drink. Told myself I was going through the motions. That it was the cops who should be doing the asking, not me. Besides, I was at the end of the trail. Unless something turned up, I could do no more. I wanted done with the whole macabre situation. But Marcia was right to want the identity of that woman. Maybe then the cops would take the case seriously. At least someone could be notified. She could be buried with a name.

Another bourbon sent me on my way.

Tuesday, I flicked through the race discrimination case, compiling my report and preparing my invoice. As I leafed through the paperwork, I came across a second photo of Dana Smith, pinned to the back of the original letter requesting my services. It was a headshot, and there she was, staring defiantly at the camera through sultry eyes. It was then I saw the coat, or at least, its collar. The color was brown. A chill went through me. What were the chances? But it was her. Had to be. Jane Doe. Only not Jane Doe, now I had a name. Dana Smith.

I pulled off the paper clip and slipped the photo in my pocket. I phoned Marcia and arranged to meet her at Dizzy's. After that, I would hand over my evidence to the cops.

As I pulled up, I saw the punk with the stinking ass hovering outside. Seeing him in daylight I took in his pronounced under-bite that made him look like a bulldog. Something in the way he was standing made me suspicious. He took off, heading north. I followed, keeping my distance. He crossed over Geary Boulevard. I hung back, too exposed, picking up the pace where trees lined the sidewalks. He crossed Sutter Street, as did I. He slowed as he neared Macy's Hair, turning down the lane by the salon. I stopped at the corner and peered round.

There he was taking a piss against the wall by Bertrice's side door. An animal, marking its territory. She would be livid having that stink right outside her workspace. As he walked away he fished something out of his jacket, opened her trash can and dumped it in. He glanced back, eyeballed me and grinned.

I waited for him to disappear before entering the lane. The stench of his urine matched the stench of his ass.

I opened the can. Inside, resting atop hamburger wrappers, Coke bottles, empty aerosols and hair-dye packaging was a plastic bag. A plastic bag meant for me.

There was something messed up about this murder. Domestic, that cop had said. No, not domestic, but intimate, staged. While my logical brain had been sifting through the facts, buried deep in my unconscious a hound sniffed a trail from one stench to another. The killer knew me too well, knew I would throw up my guts in the alley, knew I would trawl through my old case files. And then there was Marcia, complicit. The killer must know her too, know how she would nag. He was playing with me. Jane Doe wasn't the target, I was. That poor woman had been used like a pawn. Reaching in to pick up the bag, it was as though he had me by the neck, ready to thrust my face in more gore, rubbing my nose in the sickly bloody mess like punishment.

The bag felt heavy, whatever was inside, slippery. I replaced the trash-can lid, rested the bag on top and opened it. The metallic smell hit me straight away. Fresh. Must have been stored in a cooler. I didn't need to look to know what was in there.

It was evidence that generated more questions than it answered, not least how did the mystery woman come to be wearing Dana's brown coat? For the fingernails in that bag were not the orange I had anticipated. They were lurid pink.

I held the bag, twisted it around on itself a few times to seal in the dismembered appendages, recoiling as I tucked the bag inside my jacket, feeling the firmness of her dead flesh against my ribs.

The gory package safely hidden, I went into the salon. Bertrice was at the front desk taking a call. When she hung up, she looked at me strangely.

"I need the phone."

"Use the one out the back."

I followed her. Once in her office, she turned to me and said, "You know something." But she didn't pursue it. I waited for her to leave the room before I made the call. The cops said they would be straight over.

Not fast enough, I thought, sitting there nursing that bag with its butchered flesh beneath my jacket, the owner's flayed face imprinted on my mind, a grisly bloom.

Before they arrived, Bertrice poked her head round the door. It was an impulse, curiosity maybe, that had me ask the color of Gemma's nail lacquer.

"Pink," Bertrice said with a short laugh, as if it had been a source of amusement between them. "Always pink."

SUMMER OF '77

by Stewart O'Nan

Stewart O'Nan is the author of several novels, including *Snow Angels*, which was adapted to film by David Gordon Green. He has co-written two projects with author Stephen King, the nonfiction book *Faithful* and the novella *A Face in the Crowd*.

T HEY SAW ME AT THE LAKE, WHEN I HAD THE CAST ON, THE one I made in the basement. They saw me messing with the trailer hitch. They came over.

"Hey," they said, "need a hand with that?"

Guys and girls both, the young ones. That's who went there.

They had long earrings like chandeliers. They had long blonde hair parted in the middle, their bright combs poking out of their cut-offs. They had muscle shirts and puka beads, they had shaved legs and baby oil for the sun.

"How'd you do that?" they said.

"How do you sail with one hand?" they said.

"Let me help you," they said.

When there were two of them, I let them fix it so the taillights worked, then I thanked them and left.

They were all leaving; that's why they were in the parking lot. I could leave and come back and they'd be gone.

"How much can a Bug tow?" they said. "Nothing heavy, I bet."

They saw me from across the lot, putting away their blankets, their wet towels around their waists. Suits still wet and smelling of the lake. They walked out into the shallows and stood there sipping beers. The garbage was full of cans, every one of them worth a nickel. I almost wanted to stop and fill a bag.

"Thanks," I said. "It's hard with this on."

"No problem," they said.

"No sweat."

"My dad has one like this," they said.

They had wallets, licenses, credit cards. They had keys I had to throw in the river. Rolling papers, little stone bowls. They had bubble gum. They had Lifesavers.

"How does it go together?" they asked.

"How did it come apart?"

They knelt down in front of me to see what they were doing. They had freckles from coming to the lake; they had sunburnt shoulders, and their hair was lighter than in the winter. The ends, and around the top. They smelled like lotion, they smelled hot. They wore flip flops so you could see their toes, the hard skin of their heels.

They liked my car. They asked how old it was, if I might sell it, how much I'd ask.

"How do you shift with that?" they asked.

They lifted the two ends of the connectors. They didn't see the other set electrical-taped under the tongue. They didn't know they couldn't put it together, that it was impossible. They tried to do it the regular way, like you would.

"Here's your trouble," they said.

They turned to say it, to show it was two male ends.

The parking lot was empty, everyone down at the beach. Kites in the sky. Hot dogs on the free barbecues the county put in. Charcoal smoke.

They smiled as they turned, like I didn't know. Like I was an idiot or something, so dumb I'd busted my arm. Pathetic. A little weak thing.

The lot was empty, kites in the sky.

I had the cast over my head and brought it down hard.

"Oh," they said, the bigger ones.

Or "uh."

Nothing really interesting.

They fell across the hitch, and the first thing I did was grab them by the hair and pull them up. I could use the hand. It looked like I couldn't, but I could all along.

So stupid.

I grabbed them by the hair and the back of the waistband and spun them into the car. Because I already had the door open. They saw me like that first, with the door open. Helpless. They came over to see what they could do.

Most the same age. The older ones I let go. They were young, with good skin. I liked them best that way. Blonde, tall. The boys had muscles. They were everywhere that summer, like a song on the radio you can't get away from. You start to sing it anyway.

They came from the city, or just outside of it. They lived with their parents, or with friends over the G.C. Murphy's, or they were at school for summer semester. They had I.D.s for work, they had chips for free drinks. They had bottle caps in their pockets. Heineken and Lowenbrau, Bud and Bud Light.

LOVE, LOVE WILL KEEP US TOGETHER.

They lay back in the seat when I folded it down and put a towel over them. They were breathing, they were making breathing sounds.

The lot was full, windshields all glinting in the sun. You could hear the little sound of the lake.

"Oh God," they said.

"Please," they said.

They had freckles on their chests. They had bright white tan lines. They had the red marks their suits made around their waists. Their hair was still wet from the lake, and smelled like it. They had sand there.

They got up to see what was happening and I hit them with the cast again, backhand. Bam, straight-out. I didn't even have to look.

"Oh," they said again. "Uh."

The highway was empty, the fields, the barns. All of it hot. A mile away from the lake, you couldn't tell it was there. Just hills.

They didn't see the dust in the mirror, didn't hear the rocks clunking in the wheel-wells.

"What year is it?" they asked.

I laughed then. Me, pathetic. Weak.

"An accident," I said. "Nothing major."

"I really appreciate it," I said, and already I wanted to hit them and never stop. Right there in the lot. But I waited.

They smelled like pot, like wine, like the cheap beer from the concession stand. Old Milwaukee. Sometimes I didn't even kiss them after.

They stayed that way until I got them down to the rec room. They woke up when I opened the vinegar under their noses. I already had them tied up, their ankles to their wrists and then their necks. You could raise and lower them over the beam to make them shut up.

I didn't really need the mask; it was more for them.

"Please," they said. "Oh my God please."

They were all lying there in the sun with the waves coming in. That summer, it seemed it was always a beautiful day. The outlook for the weekend was good. They heard it in the morning, waking up to the clock-radio, drinking coffee, thinking of taking Friday off. Hard to find a parking spot. They circled the lot, signaled to stake their claim.

They drove little pick-up trucks and Camaros with pinstriping. They drove their mother's old Volare with the peeling woodgrain decal. Their keychain had the name of their insurance company on it. Their keychain had a picture of their niece.

THINK OF ME, BABE, WHENEVER . . .

They prayed. They closed their eyes and they prayed.

They had a favorite sweater around their necks, in case it got cold later. They had a dab of mustard above their upper lip. They had a bump where the cast hit them. They had a tattoo of a moon, its eye winking just below where their tan stopped. They had gold chains that broke if you pulled on them too hard, and blue eye shadow you couldn't rub off.

"What happened to you?" they asked, like it was funny.

"You do that sailing?"

They screamed when they saw the knife.

They said, "Oh my God."

They said, "No."

The lot. The lake. A beautiful day, highs in the mid-eighties.

SOME SWEET-TALKING GIRL COMES ALONG . . .

They screamed.

"Be quiet," I said.

The windows were boarded over, with cinder blocks piled against them, but they didn't know that.

I lifted them up. Now I was doing all the talking.

"Shhh," I said.

"Please," I said, and they looked like all of them by then. They looked like they knew how it felt to be me, and for a second even I was sorry for them. For a second, we were together there, me and them. We knew.

How I wanted to be honest then. You don't know.

I reached over and touched their hair, the two of us quiet in the still air of the basement.

"It's all right," I said. "I'm not going to hurt you."

THE PROBLEM WITH MICE

by James H. Longmore

James H. Longmore is the author of several novels and novellas, including *Pede, And Then You Die,* and *Flanagan.* He has also written the short story collection *Blood and Kisses.*

I T WAS KIND OF A THING I DID, A PERSONAL CHALLENGE, IF YOU will, and I had the whole routine down to a fine art.

Coming home from work, I would swing my beloved ten-year-old Mustang onto the driveway and thumb the button on the garage door remote – and as the door swung upwards on rusty, complaining hinges, the countdown began...

I could park up the car, grab my wallet, cell phone and keys, get to my beer fridge at the far end of the garage, make my beverage selection, pop the cap, and be at the door that led into the house just as the garage door opener lights clicked off and plunged the place into total darkness.

Of course, it would be easy enough to hit the switch on the actual lights before deciding upon which beer was to take the edge off, but that would have made the challenge *too* damn easy. Besides, those light switches were way over by the door – it had been abject laziness that had created my nightly challenge in the first place; the trick was to have my hand on the door handle just as the garage went black with that resounding *click*.

Childish, I know, but every guy has to have his Indiana Jones moment, even if it is a brief flirtation with the not so dangerous darkness within his own garage. I had actually been caught short several times, even barked my shin against the workbench the ex-wife had presented me with as a tenth anniversary gift less than a couple of months before she ran off with her Zumba instructor.

I saw the first mouse a month ago; the thing all but ran across my shoe as I opened up the fridge, its gray fur illuminated with the yellowish tinge from the interior light.

"Shit!" I jumped, my heart racing a little with the suddenness of the creature's appearance. I then felt rather foolish; it was only a mouse, after all, albeit a large one. The absence of a fat, scaly tail put my mind at rest that it wasn't a rat, and I quietly wished the little guy well as he scurried on his way and squeezed his chubby body into a small hole in the drywall.

I tucked my wallet and phone into my jacket pocket and picked out a nice, fruity beer from my collection, this one from a select brewery I'd discovered on my way back from New Orleans one balmy, summer's eve; it had a picture of an alligator on the label – of course – along with a crudely drawn voodoo doll. I took that first, welcome swig of the chilled, amber liquid as I made my way over to the door that led into the air-conditioned sanctuary of my house, stepping over a scattered trail of tiny mouse droppings, and I could have sworn that I heard a barely perceptible rustling, along with what I imagined to be miniscule chuckles and whispers.

My hand was upon the faux-brass doorknob at the precise second the garage light clicked off, and the entirety of the stifling, humid room was plunged into pitch blackness.

The mice became ever more daring after that night, as if once their presence had been revealed, they had no cause to hide themselves away in the dank, narrow spaces behind the drywall. I'd often see them scurrying about the rough, concrete floor of my garage when I left for work, and they were there when I returned, like tiny puppies eager to welcome their master home. They would pause to study me from atop my workbench, the pile of boxes packed with Liz's stuff that she'd not yet collected, or sometimes from the floor by my feet, their tiny, ink-black eyes glinting in the glow of the garage lights, their whiskers bristling and cute, pink noses twitching.

"Evening, fellas," I'd greet them as I completed my beer/light challenge, "hope y'all had a better day than me." And the mice would sit there cleaning their whiskers, and I knew that, without a doubt, they had.

Now, I'm not much of a whiz when it comes to vehicle maintenance, I'm that guy who calls out triple-A for a flat on his own driveway, but I do pride myself on knowing how to top up the oil and refill the screen wash – although if Triple-A offered that level of service, I'd most likely call them.

My oil light had flashed on during my drive home the night before, and so I'd decided to add a little 10W40 all by myself; it wasn't as if I had a whole lot going on at the weekends any more, that used to be the time Liz and I would set aside to spend together and to work on those kids she so desperately wanted.

But not even Triple-A could have prepared me for what greeted me when I popped the Mustang's hood.

"*Sweet mother of god...*" I groaned as I surveyed what looked to me to be hundreds of dollars' worth of damage.

It's not often that words fail me, but what I found myself staring with bewilderment at on that Saturday morning had me completely and utterly tongue-tied.

The mice had eaten the wiring.

To be more accurate, the damned rodents had chewed their way through the outer insulation of the wiring looms that snaked around and through the Mustang's engine compartment like grimy nerve bundles. They'd even made a start on the inner, once-brightly colored coating of the individual wires; there were a handful of places in which bare, bright copper shone through. My car was less than a skip and a jump away from grinding to a complete halt – or worse still, catching fire.

"You fuckers," I growled, nice and loud so the mice could hear me. I knew they'd be listening, just as I knew they were keeping their distance. I'd not seen a single one all morning – they freakin' well *knew* what they'd done. "You absolute *fuckers*," I reiterated, just in case any of them hadn't heard me the first time. And then, a thought altogether alien drifted across my conscious.

They're trying to kill me.

Irrational, I know. I am not a man prone to fits of paranoia, but why else would mice munch their way through wiring like that? Surely there's no nutritional value in the plastic insulation? Nope, in my mind there was only one rational explanation, that this was a rodent assassination attempt.

Up until them, I had considered the mice in my garage as cute, maybe even as pets, certainly insomuch as they were there to greet me every morning and welcome me home of an evening. But this – there was no doubt at all in my mind that this was a declaration of war!

So, I dared a trip out in my death-trap car to purchase insulating tape, and close to a hundred dollars' worth of poison *(irresistible to mice and rats!)*, some neck-breaking, spring loaded snap-traps that are so popular in kid's cartoons – which I baited with peanut butter, I'd read somewhere that mice just couldn't resist the great taste of *Skippy* – and a whole bunch of those sticky glue traps – rat-sized – that held the promise of a slow, lingering death by starvation.

I certainly wasn't leaving anything to chance.

Upon returning home, I patched up the Mustang the best I could – I'd sent a snap of the damage to my mechanic, and his estimate came back in quadruple figures – and laid my traps.

I dotted the cubes of green poison around the garage; a block in every corner, nook and cranny, and wherever I found little groupings of hard-dried mouse turds, and I stuck the snap-traps under and around the piles of Liz's boxes with *Bitch* written in drunken scrawl with a thick, blue, chisel-tipped Sharpie.

The glue traps, I placed carefully around my car — two on the engine block, I left the hood up so that I didn't forget them and drive off with them *in situ* — and several beneath my steel workbench.

"Eat my fucking engine now, you little bastards," I snarled into the stagnant, sweating air that clung to the inside of my garage, all too aware of the sour stink of my own perspiration — I'd been hard at it in there for near-on three hours in hundred degree Texas heat. I felt proud of my accomplishment; not only had I patched up my car, I had also launched a retaliatory attack on the murderous rodents.

In all, a day's work well done.

I declared the remainder of the day to be one of rest and much-needed relaxation, picked out the first couple of the afternoon's specialty beers and retreated to celebrate with beverages, leftover takeout pizza, and the ballgame.

A sudden, sharp *snap!* brought me back from the brink of my beer and pizza induced slumber, and I'd swear I caught the sound of a high-pitched, surprised squeak tragically cut short.

I heaved my weary carcass out of my armchair and made my way over to the garage, kicking over the handful of small, brown bottles that clinked noisily around my expensive rug. I looked down, and I can honestly say that I couldn't remember having downed more than the first two.

The sight that greeted me in the garage had my stomach churning and the acidic tang of bile rising up along the back of my throat — I'd never really been one for the sight of blood. One of my spring-loaded peanut butter-laden traps had succeeded in its nefarious task, but which one? I hunted around, shifting boxes, kicking aside the jumbled clutter of work tools, not one hundred percent sure where I'd left each one of the cheap death-dealers I'd booby-trapped my garage with.

And then I found it.

Somewhat fittingly, it was behind one of the stacks of Liz-stuff, there were tiny spatters of fresh blood across the bottom-most box — the one with *slutty lingerie* scrawled on its dusty side.

Fighting the nausea that skulked around the pit of my belly, I peered down at what remained of the mouse that had so been taken by surprise by the little wooden trap.

The business end of the trap had come down — hard — as the unfortunate rodent had been helping itself to the blob of peanut butter I'd so carefully applied. Part of the spring-loaded wire had smashed the mouse's head, shattering its skull and squashing its little snout into a kind of a deflated balloon shape. The other part had slammed into the creature's torso, bursting open the creature's tiny body and its diminutive array of pink, slippery entrails had splattered out across the warm concrete of my garage floor.

The mouse's eyes were wide open with that still, glassy stare of dead things, glaring up at me accusingly. I glowered back at the mess and figured it would be easier to clean up whilst warm and fresh.

And clean up I did, pleased with myself at having dispatched one of the perpetrators of the desecration of my Mustang; my very first victim. I did actually consider decapitating the mouse and mounting its little head on a cocktail stick next to my vehicle's engine block as a warning to the others – but quickly realized as I scooped up the critter's blood and guts from the concrete that I really didn't have the stomach for that.

***

It was Monday morning before I made my next kill, unless of course the furry bastards had been busy away at the irresistible blocks of poison I'd scattered about the garage – I figured those victims would skulk away to die within the wall space just so they could stink the place out with their little rotting corpses.

It was the incessant squeaking that alerted me to the success of the glue trap, resounding loudly the moment I stepped into the garage from the house. It was early – somewhere around five-thirty – and my brain was still fuzzy as my morning caffeine fix hadn't kicked in yet. I scoped out the garage, giving a paranoid glance at the Mustang's engine, and soon spotted the struggling movements of the fat, gray mouse that was adhered to the glue in one of the shallow plastic trays.

The critter lay on its side, its tiny flank heaving with the exertion of attempting to free itself. And, the more it struggled, the more of its fur, along with three of its legs, had become ensnared by that wicked adhesive. The mouse's only free leg – a front one – flailed helplessly in the air above its head, and it looked like it was waving me over, as an over-friendly neighbor might, across a shared fence.

There was a big part of me that would have quite merrily left the thing there to die whilst I was out at work, but there was another part of me – that stubborn grain of humanity that my ex-wife hadn't managed to strip away – that just couldn't do that. I'd had my victory, it was time to do the decent thing and deliver the *coup de grace*.

So, I put down my coffee and briefcase on the workbench, grabbed a blue, five-gallon bucket from the shelf and returned to the house, the shrill cries of the poor mouse ringing in my ears.

I filled the bucket with cold water and, being the absolute pussy that I am, I donned a pair of Liz's old gardening gloves, even though they were a size too small for me. Still, I persevered, wriggling them each one over my fingers like some modern-day OJ Simpson. Then, once my hands were suitably covered, I gingerly plucked the glue trap from the floor by its edges, and was surprised at just how heavy a full-grown mouse could be.

The rodent watched me with an intense glimmer in its bulging, beady black eye, and did its best to twitch its nose in my direction, even with its entire snout glued down. Its little paw waved frantically in the air and it let out a strident series of squeaks that burrowed into the deepest, darkest recesses of my brain.

"Sorry, little fella," I whispered as I lowered the trap into the bucket.

The mouse wriggled and gasped, its tiny mouth agape, its eye bulging with abject terror – I knew then that the creature knew it was about to die.

I looked on with morbid fascination as the mouse slid beneath the surface of the cool water, its body convulsing, paw clawing in vain at the enveloping liquid, mouth agape to catch that final breath that simply wasn't coming.

And then it was over.

The mouse had struggled and shat and screamed its silent screams for a lot longer than I'd anticipated, but somehow I felt that I *needed* to be there with it at the end, that it wouldn't have wanted to be left alone in its final moments.

Mentally ticking off *Number Two* in my War Against Rodents, I gathered up my coffee and briefcase, slammed down the Mustang's hood – yes, I did remember to remove the trap I'd left in there – and climbed aboard. There was that split second of wondering if the engine would fire up or not – it did, thankfully – then I hit the garage door remote, and I was on my way.

I took one final glance at the sinister bucket of death that sat in front of my beer fridge – I could make out the top edge of the trap and the mouse's limp tail – I would deal with it upon my return; I was already running a good half hour late.

***

It was dark when I pulled back into my driveway, and all I wanted to do was kick off my shoes, grab a handful of beers and watch TV in my underwear.

Of course, the first thing that greeted me as I swung the Mustang into the garage was that confounded bucket. I'd forgotten about the unpleasant job I'd left for myself that morning, and mentally kicked my own ass for having not gotten the whole unpleasant business over and done with – kinda like how Mom would rip off a Band-Aid in one swift action.

I clambered from the car, the garage door closing behind me, dropped my wallet and cell onto the workbench, and walked across to the bucket with that sick feeling lurking around the edges of my stomach. Fighting every instinct I had to leave the damn thing 'til the morning – I still had time to grab my beer, get to the house and beat the automatic lights – I peered into the water that filled the bucket almost to its brim.

It was gone.

Oh, the bucket was there alright, the glue trap too – but the mouse was nowhere to be seen.

Forgoing Liz's gloves, I fished the trap out of the water, and bent over to study the bottom of the bucket, in case the water had loosened the glue's hold on the creature and it had sunk to the bottom. But no, the bucket was entirely empty, save for the copious amount of crap the critter had expelled during its dying moments, and little clumps of gray fur.

I could make out the vague outline of the mouse that had been held fast in the sticky prison that morning, along with tufts of soggy fur and yet more tiny, black turds, and my eyes were drawn to what appeared to be tiny imprints in the sodden glue – they looked like miniature shoeprints.

I dropped the trap into the trash and made a mental note to Google just how long it takes a mouse to drown in a bucket, along with the effects of water upon glue trap glue.

"*Shit!*" I spat as I remembered the lights – it looked like I was going to have to forgo my beer, since that was the reward for beating my evening challenge.

I grabbed my wallet and cell from the work bench and dashed to the door. I grabbed at the handle, and just as the garage lights clicked off, I glanced down.

There, on the Hessian door mat lay a carefully arranged collection of mouse droppings.

MURDERER!

All went very black indeed, but the sight of those intricately organized turds remained etched into my mind's eye, and I imagined I felt something very small, yet persistent tugging at the hem of my pants.

I scrabbled around in the dark for the light switch – to hell with the challenge. My trembling fingers located the warm, hard plastic and I flicked the thing on.

The garage was bathed in the comforting white glow of the energy-saving LED lights Liz had had me install during one of her save the planet phases. I looked down by my feet, dreading what I knew awaited me.

All I saw was a random jumble of mouse poop.

No sinister message, no nefarious pattern.

Just mouse shit.

I let out the breath I hadn't realized I'd been holding. It gushed from my aching lungs in a long, loud *whoosh*, and along with it I felt a huge wave of relief; it had been a hellish long day, and I was no doubt carrying at least a soupcon of guilt at having drowned the mouse that morning and my mind was having a little fun with me.

I needed a beer.

The beer/light challenge could go hang just this once; I really, *really* needed that beer.

***

I think I fell asleep in front of the TV again. I'd managed to down the pair of cold ones I'd liberated from the beer fridge, and I'd struggled to stay awake through an old *CSI* rerun. I'd not even bothered to change out of my suit, nor fix myself something to eat – I'd had a Subway lunch and couldn't be bothered to even call out for the Chinese I'd been craving all afternoon.

I awoke to faint sounds coming from the garage, my mind taking a moment or two to latch on to the scuffling, pitter-patter noises that crept beneath the door at the opposite end of my living room.

"Fuckers," I growled beneath my breath, my mouth dry, my tongue stuck to the roof of my mouth – much as the mouse had been adhered to my trap. I hauled my weary self out of the chair and made my way over to the door, surprised by my eagerness to confront the mice that I could hear partying down in there; perhaps by catching them out in the open, I would frighten the critters enough to leave and go eat somebody else's goddamned car.

I flung the door open, and in one deft movement, reached around and flicked on the light. "Aha!" I shouted, determined as ever to strike the fear of God into the marauding rodents.

Nothing.

No hurried movement of small, furry bodies scurrying away. Not a sign of one single, solitary tail disappearing behind my ex-wife's boxed up life. Not one of the erstwhile fearless mice stood their ground with mean, soulless eyes and accusatory, twitching whiskers.

I could still hear them, of course. Secreted away in their hidey holes, hidden beneath the protective steel of my workbench, peeping out from dark, shadowy holes they'd gnawed in the drywall. Their tiny voices chirruped away, their agile paws scampering around and above me, and in my fatigued state, it sounded like they were whispering amongst themselves, no doubt plotting some malicious retribution in honor of their two fallen comrades.

I made a mental one to check the Mustang's wiring before I slipped the key in the ignition the following morning – in my hurry earlier, I'd neglected to pop the hood – and I decided that what I really needed right then was a beer.

***

That night was a restless one. I tossed and turned and sweated, my mind replaying the image of that mouse-turd message I *thought* I'd seen, and fooling me into believing I could hear the cautious whisperings of barely perceptible voices, all of them conspiratorial – even though my rational brain was silently screaming at me that mice just simply don't talk like that.

It's not often that the dour tone of my alarm is a welcome relief, but when morning came, I was delighted to clamber from my bed. My head felt fuzzy, all thanks to the four beers I'd downed the night before, my mind still spinning with thoughts of evil mice and the cold, cruel murderer they had turned me into.

I dressed, fixed myself a double-shot coffee, and made to leave, keen to be on the road, happier than usual to be away from the house and a couple hundred miles away from murmuring mice and their neatly arranged, tiny poops.

LEAVE THE MICE ALONE!

The message on the mat screamed up at me the instant I hit the switch by the garage door.

Spelled out in neatly arranged mouse droppings, each letter burned into my mind like some sick, nefarious fever. I stopped dead in my tracks at the threshold, the handle of the open door cold in my sweat-slicked hand, my coffee mug – *World's Best Husband*, no less – slipped from my hand and shattered loudly on the garage floor. The wash of hot, fresh coffee sprayed out, soaking the lower half of my pants to my knee and painting the gray floor with a dark brown splash pattern as it swilled away the mouse turds.

By the time I'd gathered my wits enough to step over the mat, I'd all but convinced myself that what I *thought I'd seen* spelled out had been nothing more than a hallucination brought on by a God-awful night's sleep and guilt.

I glanced around at the traps I'd left visible, and felt a wave of relief that not one of them had been successful, although I did note that several of the little green blocks had been nibbled upon, and I shuddered at the thought of the poor creatures huddled up in a dark, filthy corner to die a prolonged and painful death.

Along the shelf just to the right of my head, I could see the miniscule prints in the thick layer of dust, running to and from the poisoned cubes, I heard shuffling sounds over to my left, and from somewhere in the gloom, the faintest whisperings – I'd swear on the Bible that I heard them saying my name.

It was at that point that I decided that I needed a beer.

Stepping through the shattered remains of my mug, and the turds that had now swollen to three times their desiccated size with my desperately needed caffeine fix, I plucked a chilled bottle from the fridge, popped the cap, and chugged down a good half of it as I walked over to the car. I belched out the excess gas I'd taken in, the resounding baritone of which made me smile a little. Balancing the bottle on the Mustang's roof, I leaned in through the open window and popped the hood.

All was well with my hastily repaired wiring; either the mice had taken my hint that they really ought to quit eating my looms, or the tape I'd wrapped around the denuded wires was simply not suited to their delicate palates. Either way, my car was safe – for now.

And so, I made my way out, reversing carefully out of the garage, eyes scanning the empty space my retreating vehicle made on the floor, and hoping to high heaven that there wouldn't be small, furry corpses squashed flat by my wheels.

Thankfully, there were not.

I breathed a huge sigh of relief and thumbed the remote. I watched as the garage door slid down on its creaky old runners and thought I saw movement in the encroaching shadows within. I squinted through my windshield, straining to see the mice that were no doubt coming out to play now that the master of the house was leaving. I saw nothing, save small, nebulous shapes in my peripheral vision, some of which seemed to me to be a tad too big to be rodents.

The door clattered down. I gulped down the remainder of my beer, the cold liquid sliding down my throat all too easily, and already I was enjoying the light buzz that it provided; today was going to be tolerable, I just knew it.

***

It was late when I returned home. I eased the Mustang towards the garage, thumbing the remote at the very last second, determined to procrastinate. The garage door squealed and shuddered its way open, light illuminating the interior.

"Oh, sweet mercy," I gasped as the ascending door revealed the carnage within, "what have I done?"

I drove my car slowly forwards, nudging its nose into the tepid, musky air of the garage, cringing at the almost imperceptible crunching sounds as my wheels crushed mouse corpses.

There were *dozens* of them, all dead. There were mice in every trap, heads smashed by sprung wire, blood and pinky-white brains spattered asunder; diminutive bodies held fast and suffocated by insidious glue, and scattered tiny, poisoned corpses, the toxins they'd ingested dissolving their way through the thin, white-furred skin of their bloated bellies. Some of the wretched creatures had crawled to the top of the Liz pile to die, the excrement they'd expelled in their final, agonized death throes soaked through the cardboard, their beady little eyes bulging and glazed.

The garage door clattered down behind me – funny, I didn't remember hitting the remote button – and I killed the Mustang's engine.

It was then that I heard the whispering.

Louder than before, it seemed to come from everywhere, yet *nowhere*; inside the walls, the ceiling, beneath the car, behind the boxes and scattered work tools. I shook my head, as if that would dislodge the husky tinnitus that echoed inside.

I grabbed my wallet and cell and got out of the car, doing my level best to ignore the rancid smell that assaulted my nostrils and clawed at my throat.

"Dammit!" I yelped as my foot slid from under me. I caught myself against the car's roof and looked down to see that I had a glue trap stuck to the bottom of my shoe.

I slammed my wallet and phone down on the workbench, and as I stepped backwards to lift up my foot to extricate the glue trap, my right foot came down on another – that hadn't been there a moment ago, had it?

"Oh, come on!" I stared down in my disbelief at the traps that clung so resolutely to my shoes, trying to count a blessing or two that neither contained a mouse cadaver, and that was when my time was up.

The lights went out.

I composed myself the best I could in the dark, scrabbling around on the workbench for my phone; no way was I going to attempt to traverse the garage without a light source, the way my luck was going, I was likely to trip and break my damned neck.

Trapped there by the darkness, I imagined the nefarious whisperings to be that much louder, the scurrying sounds more akin to tiny footsteps.

Cringing as my fingers brushed against the stiff, cool bodies of the mice I'd poisoned with irresistible treats, I located my cell phone. I pressed my thumb against the fingerprint reader and the thing glowed to life. With a sigh of relief, I switched on the flashlight function and pointed the harsh beam down at my feet.

"Oh my –" I cried out as my cell's light reflected from the shiny glue, and in my panic, the phone slipped from my hand. It hit the floor with a resonant *crack* and the light snapped out. Once again I was plunged into complete darkness.

In my mind's eye, burned there with laser-like clarity, I could see the small, fleeing shape that had darted away from my cell's inquisitive beam, a shape that was unquestionably human-like, albeit on an improbably minute scale, its tiny face pinched and accusatory.

And in the glue trap, one tiny, brown shoe only a fraction bigger than the mouse turds that lay scattered across the entirety of my garage.

***

I can feel them tugging at my pants, tiny hands clawing at the thin material, tearing to get at the soft flesh beneath, the nails on their little hands like miniscule razors, ripping, shredding, drawing blood from my damp skin.

I'm done screaming now; my throat is raw, my voice all but gone. I can't move, I *daren't*, for I have no way of telling how many of them there are, or indeed, *what* they are; all I know is that they are not mice, nor are they human — despite their outward appearance, anything even remotely human wouldn't make noises like that.

They chatter, chitter and chirrup in high-pitched tones more akin to the bats that flitter above my pool to take their fill of the evening mosquitoes, their voices bolder now, and louder than the subliminal whispers they tormented me with before.

And, as I feel their scrabbling, shredding hands making their way higher up my legs — they must be clambering on top of one another — I think I hear them laughing…

SEASONS DON'T FEAR THE REAPER

by Billy Chizmar

Billy Chizmar is the co-author of *Widow's Point* (with Richard Chizmar). In addition, he has many short stories published in short story anthologies and is the director of the film *Trapped*, written by Stephen King and his father, Richard Chizmar.

I
T STARTED AS A NORMAL MONDAY MORNING FOR Detective Ira Paul Ripley. He woke at six o'clock sharp and was out of bed within fifteen seconds of his alarm sounding. Dressed in a fresh from the dry cleaners suit, he kissed his sleeping wife's forehead, grabbed his keys, and walked out the door. He climbed into his white Ford pick-up and drove the speed limit to the Dunkin' Donuts on Bel Air road. He ordered his usual breakfast: two sausage-egg-and-cheese sandwiches, a Boston Cream donut, and a bottle of Dasani water. He paid for his meal with a Visa card set to expire in the not-too-distant future, which he then slid back into the folds of his wallet, just behind a photo of his only child, Walter.

He pulled into the station parking lot at 6:25 a.m. and walked through the heavy wooden lobby doors precisely at 6:30 a.m. As usual, Ripley was second to arrive on the morning shift, behind the beloved department secretary, Mary Webster. Mary smiled at him from behind her desk and took a sip from her coffee mug. Ripley greeted her with a wave, congratulated her on the excellent sermon her son had delivered the past Sunday at mass, and then proceeded to his own office.

Ripley's small corner office was neat and austere in decoration. The pale drywall was decorated only with a large, scenic photograph of the Chesapeake Bay and a single framed *Baltimore Sun* clipping. The newspaper was dated September 13, 1997, just over a year before Walter was born. A grainy, black and white photo of an unsmiling Ripley was centered below a bold headline:

LOCAL OFFICER TAKES DOWN THE BUTCHER OF BEL AIR.

Ripley hadn't framed the clipping himself. It'd been given to him as a 'welcome back' present after he returned from his thirty-three day stay in the hospital recovering from machete wounds.

Ripley sat at his desk and glanced up at the article. He often had the urge to take it down and tuck it away in one of his desk drawers — to him, it fell right on the line of bragging — but he never did. He told himself his reluctance was due to the newspaper clipping being a gift and not wanting to be rude, but there was something else, too: a part of Ripley enjoyed the daily reminder offered by his own youthful thirty-year-old face staring back at him from the wall. Those days had been simpler times when all that seemed to matter was being a good cop.

Ripley's eyes drifted away from the framed memento and focused on the photograph of his son on the right-hand corner of his desk. Walter had been ten years old the day the picture had been taken. Shirtless and wearing a baseball cap and holding up a small white perch he had just caught off the boat dock at Mariner Park in Joppatowne. It had been his tenth birthday party — a 'fishing extravaganza' he'd called it with that big goofy smile of his — and all he'd wanted was for Ripley to teach all of his friends how to fish. Ripley smiled, remembering their shared astonishment when they'd discovered that none of the other boys' fathers had showed them the proper way to bait a hook. Walter had gotten a brand new Ugly Stick fishing rod that day, the same kind his father used. Ripley had never seen the boy happier.

A telephone buzzed in the outer office, snapping Detective Ripley back to the present. He sighed and pulled out a stack of paperwork from the top drawer of his desk. The next few hours passed in a blur of scribbled notes and signatures.

Just outside his office, uniformed officers arrived on time for morning roll call, with the sole exception of Officer Rode, who too often allowed himself a few extra minutes of sleep. A few calls came in, nothing urgent. A fender bender here, a lost dog there, nothing out of the ordinary. All was quiet for the moment in the small town of Jericho, Maryland.

***

Mary Katherine Webster had worked for the Jericho Police Department for forty-some years, from the eve of her eighteenth birthday when she'd picked up a part-time job cleaning patrol cars to help out her struggling single mother to when she'd become full-time secretary of the precinct at just twenty-and-a-half years old on account of Marietta Baker's cancer finally waking up from its benign slumber all the way up to today where she was still doing the same job she'd been doing for forty-some years — and that was okay. Sure, times had changed — boy, had they — and there were computers now and iPhones and God *forbid* that magical Cloud in which all things lie, but Mary found that embracing those changes was a whole lot easier than fighting them, and besides today's technology was a whole lot more efficient than being surrounded by a dozen stuffed-to-the-brim filing cabinets and a dial up telephone. And of course, the faces changed, officers and sheriffs came and went (one sheriff died and another cheated on his wife and got divorced and moved out of town), but the old family names mostly stuck around — that was Jericho for you, and that was all that Mary knew, and so that too was okay.

A lot can come through a door over the span of forty years, and the broad, blackened wooden beasts that presided over the lobby of the Jericho Police Station were no exception. Junkies, drug dealers, litterers, pot farmers, rapists, tax launderers, abusers, jaywalkers, drunks, racists (some small town Maryland farmers had no troubling calling Mary a nigger, many of them right to her face), mentally disturbed, the rowdy and the beaters and the brash and the criminal — and sometimes the just plain stupid. Yes, Mary felt that from her ivory tower, the grand oak desk that stood raised up from the hardwood flooring, surrounded by cabinets and drawers and files and two computers and The Cloud, nothing that Jericho could throw at her, nothing that walked, staggered, dragged itself through those doors, nothing that could wrap a writhing claw around the varnished oxidation of the heft handles could surprise her.

But the squat man in the thick winter coat and plain white ball cap did not come from Jericho, Maryland, U. S. of A. And had Mary been attending to the front door instead of searching a lower desk drawer for leftover Reese's peanut butter-filled pumpkin-shaped chocolates from the Halloween office party, she may have noticed that the tall stranger did not so much as lay a holy hand on the blackened wood of the monolithic doors, but had instead *flown* in through somewhere else that would have *certainly* surprised dear Mrs. Webster.

And so the sixty-something-year-old woman dressed in a stitched cream sweater she'd picked up on sale at Target at last found her chocolate-buttery prize in the back of the desk drawer and turned her head of blonde resilience upward only to be greeted by the stranger, whose eyes sprinkled with a delightful warmth from underneath his plain white cap. Had he been a man of stature or grimace, Mary might've found herself startled at his sudden appearance — but the visitor was just the opposite of intimidating. She couldn't help but think that if the man had been wearing a pair of thick circular glasses, he wouldn't look too different from *Seinfeld*'s George Costanza in his puffy Goretex jacket. The thought fell just short of exerting a giggle and instead resulted in a warm smile that said: *Hello!*

Welcome to Jericho — where did your car break down? But the man hadn't come to speak about a car problem. In a voice that made him sound all too much like an overly sincere insurance salesman, the portly stranger in the winter jacket asked, "Would you mind telling me where I can find Ira Ripley?"

***

Ripley wasn't in his office. He was out to lunch with the station's accountant at Box Hill Pizzeria. The name of the restaurant always exerted a sliver of ironic pleasure from Ripley; the food was absolutely delicious, but Ripley had never seen anyone eating a pizza. The family-run establishment was famous for its Maryland crab cakes and cream of crab soup, both best served with a heaping of Old Bay seasoning. Ripley ordered the crab cake platter with a side of fries and coleslaw — the exact same order he'd always placed since he was a teenager.

The accountant, a local man by the name of Steve Sines, brought good news for a change: budgets were up and expenses were down. A sprinkling of new businesses and robust suburban development over the past few years had brought the county more surplus cash than ever before, and the Jericho Police Department would benefit.

Ripley nodded and smiled as the accountant filled him in on the numbers, but couldn't stop a glimmer of sadness from creeping into his eyes. He saw the same twinge of melancholy nostalgia in Steve's face, too. With more new houses and paved streets and shopping malls and money came more people, *new* people. Chances are they wouldn't be the blue-collar folks Ripley had grown up around; they wouldn't preach hard work and grit and loyalty the way the adults in Ripley's childhood had done. Most of the new folks would be inbred from two wealthy parents and the result would be a soft-skinned mutation, bearing an annoying sense of entitlement. These people would come from nearby Baltimore County and its many suburbs, and would spread their privileged roots outward. When he'd served as a county cop, just nine years ago, he'd to deal with these outsiders on a daily basis. The one thing he'd noticed, above everything else, was an almost universal failure to take responsibility for their actions. It was *never* their fault.

Ripley felt his fingernails digging into the palm of his left hand and snapped out of his trance. He stuffed his hands into his pockets and looked up at Steve, neither of them smiling anymore. The table was silent, but the two Jericho locals understood one another loud and clear. Ripley glanced past the accountant and out the window, staring at nothing in particular. One day, this quaint restaurant and the town of Jericho would be swallowed by the shambling sloth of Suburbia.

For the rest of lunch, the two men talked about fishing and the Orioles and their pitching woes. Then they paid their separate bills in cash and made their way through afternoon traffic and construction delays back to their respective offices.

***

"I'm sorry, sir, but Detective Ripley is out of the office at the moment," Mary Webster said to the squat gentleman in the heavy jacket. "He should be back shortly, though, if you'd like to wait for him. May I ask what this is in regards to?"

The stranger from out of town with an accent that Mary could not quite place sighed in disappointment. "Could you please ask him to hurry? I'd like to confess to the murders of six people."

The older woman's eyes narrowed. "Is this some kind of practical joke? I don't got no time for — "

"I assure you, madam, this is not a joke."

And despite these words, a hint of a smirk on the man's face.

***

Fifteen minutes later, after receiving a panicked phone call from Mary Webster, Ripley found himself in the station's holding room, sitting across a table from the stranger who claimed to have murdered six people. Riley studied the man in his heavy winter jacket and thought he looked more like an accountant or a computer nerd than a killer. *How in the world had this guy put such a scare into Mary?*

The man sat there, his cuffed hands resting in his lap, his spotless white ball cap now placed on the table beside him, revealing a modestly messy scruff of brown curls atop his head. The subtle smirk had yet to retreat.

Ripley stared in the silence, observing, waiting. He preferred to let the man speak first, so as to offer him the illusion of control, but the stranger appeared surprisingly relaxed and content to just sit there, staring back at him. And that stupid little smile — Ripley wanted to smack it right off his chubby face.

The detective was a large man, standing just over six feet and two inches tall, creased face and muscular arms tan from working outside in the sun, and although Ripley was well known across town for his patience (he'd once waited forty-five minutes for a table at Bob Evans without a peep of complaint), it was also well known that Ripley's temper, once triggered, could evaporate any sense of composure the detective possessed. In this case, it was something in the childish blue eyes and the curl of thin lips of the man sitting across the table that taunted him into action.

Ripley finally broke the silence.

"My name is Detective Ripley. I'll be handling your case."

"Oh, I know," the stranger said, far too pleasant for Ripley's liking.

"It's my understanding that you're here to confess to six murders. Is that correct?"

The man nodded. "Indeed it is."

"And Officer Rode read you your Miranda Rights before I got here?"

"Yes, sir, and a fine job he did at that."

Ripley leaned forward in his chair. "Start at the beginning. Tell me everything."

The stranger craned his head toward the holding room door, which was standing ajar. Mary Webster and Officer Alex Rode were standing in the hallway, peeking inside. Ripley gave a stern nod of his own, and Officer Rode retreated and Mary closed the door.

"Now," the stranger said in that pleasant voice of his. "Could I trouble you for pen and paper?"

***

Five names.

That's all Ripley had been able to get from the weasel in the holding room. Scrawled in surprisingly dainty handwriting. Five names.

- Jonathan Constantine
- Ashlyn Thomas
- Eric Santiago
- Alexandra Walsh
- Roman Slater

Ripley hunched over his desk and went through the list of names again. They meant nothing to him, he was sure of it (though for a brief moment he'd thought Alexandra Walsh had been in his junior year calculus class, but then he'd realized the girl he was thinking of had been Sherry Walsh). Mary had already searched each of the six names in the local database and came up blank. Now she was busy with the State and National databases, but the detective knew from experience that could take all damn afternoon.

Ripley tossed the sheet of paper onto the desk and opened his MacBook. He tapped the keyboard and called up Google.

The first name, Jonathan Constantine, yielded no specific results. Dozens of Facebook profiles appeared, along with Twitter and Instagram accounts and all sorts of other sites that Ripley had far too little patience to sift through. He sat there for a moment, staring at the name on the computer screen. Then his hands began to type once more: Jonathan Constantine, missing. Ripley pressed enter.

The first listing to come up was for a recent weekend edition of *The Oregonian*. Ripley clicked on the link. The headline read:

MISSING MEDFORD MAN OUSTED AS PEDOPHILE, INVESTIGATION UNDERWAY.

Indeed, the missing man was Jonathan Constantine, who was first reported as missing one hundred and ninety days ago, and whose computer's hard drive was anonymously mailed to the Medford Police Department's office one hundred and ninety-one days ago. An unnamed source in the article claimed there were explicit photographs of Constantine with children stored on the hard drive. Seventeen different children.

"Jesus," Ripley whispered, reaching for the bottle of water on his desk. His arm brushed against the sheet of paper, knocking it to the floor. He took a drink and then leaned down and picked it up and was stunned to see there was a sixth name written in that same dainty handwriting, but much smaller, on the bottom of the backside of the paper.

- Daniel Jones

***

Detective Ripley slammed a fist down on the table.

"I have the *God-given right* to know," he shouted, spit flying from the corners of his mouth, "Now tell me about *this* name!" he said, pointing to the back of the paper.

"I want to confess to the murders of Jonathan Constantine, Ashley

Thomas, Eric Santiago, Alexandra Walsh, and Roman Slater," the stranger said, never once breaking eye contact with the detective. The smirk remained on his face.

His fury fading, Ripley slumped back in his chair and glanced up at the video camera attached to the ceiling in the corner of the holding room. Two words echoed in Ripley's mind: *Jones. Murder. Jones. Murder. Jones. Murder.*

"Jonathan Constantine, the first person I killed on the list, liked children. He liked them in a way that was unnatural. They haven't found his body yet. It's buried in a field in Bangor, Maine behind a restaurant called Nicky's Diner. I cut off his limbs and severed his tongue. He spent three weeks staring at his sinful penis, unable to act on his lust. He finally died when I stopped feeding him." The smirk grew into a smile. "Do you see the irony there? The poetic justice? I thought it was rather clever." The stranger leaned his head back and yawned.

Ripley scribbled away in his notepad, his eyes darting back and forth between his notes and the man sitting across from him.

"And then there was Ashlyn Thomas, a talented young Olympic caliber runner. She had the world at her fingertips, but there was a younger, more talented runner that threatened to take her top spot on Team USA, so Miss Lewis poisoned her out of sheer envy — spiked her Gatorade with some active ingredients from rat poison during a practice session." The stranger snorted in amusement. "I dragged her body behind her own Mercedes for almost twenty miles. I left her body, or what was left of it, in a ditch alongside Highway 80. In Nevada, I think, or maybe California, out west they all blend together. It's all that sand and big sky, you know?"

Ripley remembered the story from the news. Someone had caught her spiking the Gatorade on film. It was all over ESPN for a week — and then she disappeared. Ripley had thought she'd fled the country to avoid charges.

"Eric Santiago was a drug addict with a glutinous desire for heroin. He murdered eleven innocent people on the streets of Baltimore, tourists mostly, raiding their corpses for money and valuables. By the time the police received my tip, he had eleven needles stuck in him, some containing heroin, some containing a much more painful way to die — the same stuff that we dropped over in 'Nam.

Ripley tried to speak, but his mouth was as dry as cotton, his skin pricked with goose bumps. He still couldn't believe this was happening. A serial killer waltzing into a small town police station confessing to unspeakable crimes. *But why?*

And what about the sixth name?

"Alexandra Walsh inherited a *huge* fortune. Her father founded one of the very first solar panel companies. Guy was loaded. Before he died of lung cancer in his eighties, all he asked of his only daughter was for her to continue using a modest percentage of the family's wealth to fund a inner city charity he'd established some two decades earlier."

The stranger scratched his head, searching his memory for more details. "Anyway, suffice to say, she blew it all. Drugs, parties, trips, clothes, cars — exactly what you might expect to happen if a high school sophomore suddenly came into millions of dollars...only this woman was in her late twenties. The charity went neglected. Her family fortune dwindled to almost nothing. Even then, she sat on her ass like a sloth and let everything her father had worked for waste away. So I threw her in a well behind some an old abandoned farmhouse. Not sure how long she lasted without food," he mused.

Ripley looked up from his notepad. His patience was waning. He wanted to know about the sixth name on the list: Daniel Jones. He *needed* to know.

"You're an angry guy, aren't you, Detective Ripley?"

Ripley clenched his jaw. "Tell me about Daniel Jones."

The stranger's eyes widened, as did the irritating smirk. "Better yet, why don't *you* tell *me* about Daniel Jones?" he said.

The detective felt icy fingers caress his spine. The man sitting across from him no longer looked like an accountant or a computer nerd. His features had changed somehow, his skin now as pale as the surface of the moon. Ripley couldn't tell whether the stranger was seventeen or seventy. He appeared ageless.

***

The detective picked up the remote from the table in front of him and turned off the video recorder.

It had been the third of August 2008, ten long years ago. The birthday party was over, and the Ripleys, exhausted but giddy with happiness, were just leaving. Ira was driving, and while sitting at a traffic light, he glanced into the back seat and saw his son admiring his new fishing rod.

"It really is just like yours, Dad!" Walter said. Ripley could still remember his smile, so wide below his bright blue eyes.

And then the light had turned green, and Ira Ripley had pressed the gas pedal —

— and eighteen-year-old high school senior Danny Jones had drunkenly barreled through the intersection at sixty-five miles an hour. The brand new Mustang convertible, bought by Danny's parents, had run the red light and t-boned the right side of the used Audi that Ira Ripley had recently bought his wife as a surprise after saving up money for months.

Walter Ripley had been killed on impact.

***

When Ripley arrived home later that night, his wife noticed he was kind of quiet and distracted, but it didn't set off any alarm bells for her. Sometimes, after all these years, there just wasn't much left to say. Other nights they could talk for hours until one of them fell asleep in mid-thought. The key to a happy marriage, she believed, was to go with the flow.

Ripley had forgone much of his usual small talk during dinner and had even given up on watching the Capitals game and gone upstairs early for a shower. His wife, reading the final chapters of a mystery paperback in the den, didn't notice until almost an hour later that the shower was no longer running and Ira hadn't returned. She'd been so absorbed in her novel that she'd hadn't heard her husband sneak out the side door and start the engine of her Honda, much quieter than his own Ford truck, and pull out of the driveway.

***

Officer Rode walked into the station house at just after eight-thirty. The phones were silent, and the only other two officers present were busy doing paperwork at their desks. Rode's final patrol of the night had been uneventful, and he was grateful for that. He was exhausted; he'd had enough action for one day. *How often did you get to arrest a genuine serial killer?*

He filled up a Styrofoam cup at the water cooler and poked his head into the hallway leading to the holding cells. His breath caught in his throat.

The door to the main cell was standing wide open, and the stranger was nowhere in sight.

***

New York City was a three-and-a-half hour drive from the Jericho Police

Station — without the use of lights and sirens that is. Ripley and the stranger made the journey north on I-95 in much better time, just less than three hours. They slipped into the 63 Wall Street luxury apartment complex by means of a key produced from the zippered pocket of the stranger's puffy winter coat. Once inside, they entered a private elevator and made their way up to Apartment 305 and entered by means of another key produced from another pocket. Ripley left the stranger in the apartment foyer while he stormed into the dark bedroom, ripped the sleeping man out of bed, and knocked him unconscious with a hard elbow to the side of his head.

Ripley gripped the limp man under his arms and shuffled him into the kitchen where the stranger was waiting beside an empty chair. The detective roughly hoisted the body onto the chair and took the roll of duct tape from his jacket pocket. Breathing heavy, he wrapped the entirety of the roll around the unconscious man's body. He stepped back and examined his work — and then he reached out and slapped the man across his face, again and again, the sound loud in the silent kitchen.

The man gasped and opened his eyes, squinting in the bright light. His nose was gushing blood.

Ripley hit him again, this time with a fist to the stomach. The man groaned and struggled against the duct tape. "Pl-please. I have money..." He closed his eyes and started whimpering.

"Look at me," Ripley hissed. He grabbed the man's chin and jerked his head upward. Rivulets of blood streamed between the detective's fingers.

The man looked up at him, and his eyes went even wider with terror.

"You remember me from court, don't you?" Ripley asked.

The man opened his mouth, but no sound came out.

"You smiled when they dragged me out of there after the judge declared you not guilty. You fucking smiled."

Daniel Jones furiously shook his head, blood and tears spattering to the floor below. "No...I didn't...I wouldn't."

"You know why I'm here," Ripley said.

And then he waded in, letting his mouth go still and instead speaking in single syllable jabs, stringing together sentences of solid strikes to whatever body part they connected with, culminating in paragraphs of punishment long overdue, building and soaring with a crescendo into an essay — a thesis statement: *you killed my son, and now I'm going to kill you.*

When teeth started to get knocked out, Ira stepped back, catching his breath, and used the sole of his boot to snap off a leg from one of the other kitchen chairs. The wooden spoke was light but solid, like an old-fashioned police baton. Ira approached Danny Jones, patting his palm with it, before swinging for the fences beyond the man's kneecaps. The first attempt was disappointing — a graze of a foul ball in which the only sound was a muffled scream of pain, but on the next swing, Ira made solid contact and heard a loud *POP* — and he smiled and wondered in that instant how many times he had actually daydreamed about this very miracle.

Still grinning, he dropped the chair leg and went back to work with his hands.

It wasn't until Ripley's fists started bleeding that he stopped and pulled the hunting knife from his discarded jacket's pocket.

It wasn't until Danny saw the knife that he mustered the strength to ask a question he already knew the answer to.

"Why...?" he managed through ballooned and split lips and remnants of shattered teeth turned into kettle corn.

Ripley stepped closer but remained silent.

"It...was an accident," Danny pleaded. "I was just a stupid kid." (Although it sounded more akin to *"eh wah jus ah ahhipent id"*). "I didn't mean to hurt anyone. The judge said no one was to blame — "

"The judge your father played golf with twice a month at the country club," Ripley said. "The judge your father bought and paid for."

The detective realized the son-of-a-bitch wasn't going to admit his guilt. He wasn't going to apologize. Even now. He was too arrogant, too prideful, too blind.

Ripley roared like a primal beast in the middle of fevered sex and drove the point of the knife deep into the femur of Daniel Jones's leg with so much force that when he tried to wedge it out, the blade broke clean off and remained embedded in flesh and bone.

Ripley hadn't planned on killing Daniel Jones when he'd first entered the apartment. But that had all changed the moment he'd laid eyes on the man's smug face. Now, as if the stranger could read his mind, he felt the man's hand on his shoulder and heard his silent urging: *It's okay, detective. I'm right here with you. You can kill him. The list, Ripley, he's on my list too.*

Ripley reared back and swung a roundhouse right with every ounce of energy and anger left inside his body. His meaty fist struck Daniel Jones in the middle of his forehead, whiplashing him backward, instantly fracturing his neck.

Ripley watched the man as his eyes filled with blood. He twitched several times and made a gagging sound, and then his bowels let loose, and he went still and silent.

Ripley no longer felt the hand on his shoulder. He turned and the stranger was sitting with his legs crossed at the kitchen table, sipping a mug of steaming coffee he had gotten from God knows which pocket. The man pursed his lips and made a *tsking* sound. "After all these years, he still wouldn't take responsibility for his actions. What a miserable, prideful man he was. Oh well, good riddance, I say." He reached over and patted the empty chair beside him. "Why don't you have a seat? You have to be exhausted."

Ripley staggered to the table and slumped into the chair. He could smell the rich scent of strong coffee.

"That's a difficult thing to do, you know? Killing someone in such a violent manner. You're an angry guy. Forgiveness isn't your thing, is it?"

"He killed my son," Ripley said. "I don't give a damn abou…"

"Don't give a damn about forgiveness? Don't much care for it?" the stranger asked, leaning forward like a dog eyeing an overdue meal through a caged door. "Where I come from we have a word for that sort of thing — it's called wrath." He leaned back and crossed his arms. "And for that, Mr. Ripley, I'm afraid that you're going to have to die, too."

The detective raised his eyebrows in curious fear. "But you…you wanted me to kill him. You showed me where he lived." His voice grew louder. "He was on your list. Like the others."

The others

"Well, the others…"

lust

"…were all dead, and he was going to…"

envy

"…die too. Although, to be perfectly honest, I was hoping I'd…"

gluttony

"…have a chance to do it myself. To…"

sloth

"…kill him myself. But you and that temper of…"

greed

"…yours stole him away from me and stripped me the opportunity."

pride

Ripley inched his chair away from the table, his eyes darting around the room, searching for an escape route.

"You see…you don't get to play jury and executioner." The stranger was smiling wide now, his yawning mouth boasting more teeth and sharper, whiter teeth than any man should have. "That's *my* God-given right."

Ripley bolted up from the table, but before he could make it halfway across the kitchen, he felt invisible hands take hold of him. And begin to squeeze.

He turned back and just as he felt his consciousness slipping away, he asked, "Who are you?"

But even as the words left his mouth, he realized that he already knew what had come for him.

It was retribution.

wrath

The dark angel sitting at the table chuckled. "That's right. My name's Azrael. And you, Ira Paul Ripley, are going to die for the indulgence of the seventh deadly sin."

BOY'S CLUB

by Tony Knighton

Tony Knighton is the author of the novels *Three Hours Past Midnight* and *Happy Hour: And Other Philadelphia Cruelties.*

WHEN THE DOOR LOCKED BEHIND ME, I REALIZED I'D LEFT my key ring on the coffee table. It wouldn't have been worth the trouble to get it. They were only house keys, and there was a spare in the yard at home. I went down the stairs and outside.

I looked down at myself and scooped up some of the gray slush along the pavement to wash my hands. I scoured them until they were so cold they stung. I didn't dry them on my overcoat but did the best I could, shaking them in the frigid air and rubbing them together. I got the coat buttoned and figured I looked okay, and felt inside the pockets for my pills and remembered that I'd left my gloves in Joan's apartment, too. Again, I considered going back, but even if I could get inside, there was too much — too many things. I checked my face in a parked car's side mirror and glanced over at the huge Victorian across the street; it was still occupied, most recently as a woman's rehab, but it was too chilly for any of the smokers to be out on the porch. I dry-swallowed the last two pills in the vial and shoved my hands deep into my coat pockets. The cold air helped. I'd seen a few doctors about the headaches. Each had suggested that I cut out caffeine and alcohol.

I crossed at the light on the corner and slogged up the hill. Along the breadth of the train station, the sidewalk had been cleared, but the pavement in front of St. Madeline's was still covered with grimy snow. I supposed the Archdiocese had already lost so much in lawsuits that they weren't too concerned about the random slip and fall case anymore. I marveled at the stonework that bordered its leaded-glass rose window. The last I'd been inside was for Pete Hilferty's funeral, a few years before all this had begun to catch up with me. I'd sat in the back with Jimmy Bissell. Jimmy kept up a running commentary, under his breath, about the widow, "She'd dime you out for talking in the cloak room," and the mourners, "Look at that one, what's her name? Oh, yeah, that's Marianna DeCicco." He nodded in the direction of a woman our age who genuflected and blessed herself before taking a seat in a pew near the altar. "Her old man owned the dry cleaning place on the avenue, around the corner from the

Boy's Club, remember?" I nodded. Jimmy continued, "I fucked her in the back room, there, on the steam press, one time after school when we were in tenth grade." Jimmy talked about himself, too; he'd been one of those kids the nuns would take over to the convent at lunchtime. "Baloney sandwiches, but it was the *good* baloney, you know." I'd remembered that the nice nun would try to do this quietly, beckoning with her fingers at waist level, so not to embarrass those kids or the rest of us.

Past the church, the rise was less steep. No one was on the porch of the old-folks home. Only a few cars went by. It was early, not rush hour yet. I could still get home and inside with the spare key and take a shower before Coleen got home. I'd chew some raw onion, too. She'd know I was drunk, but I didn't want to rub her nose in it.

The next block was given over to homes – twins, most of them, with neat, terraced front yards. I checked my phone for the time, but the battery was dead. I felt bad about Joan. The sky was gray and sunless. I guessed it was sometime past three o'clock. I felt bad, but oddly relieved, like when I'd lost my license. Nothing was likely to happen today, and beyond that, I wouldn't be the only guy they'd talk to; Joan was easy. I'd wanted to be more patient with her, but when she was angry, her voice was an ice pick. Instant headache. There's no reasoning with someone like that.

We'd started up when I came home the first time. She'd been going to the noon meeting at the Unitarian church, and caught me staring at her while some guy told his story. When we stood for the Serenity Prayer, she came across the room and took my hand. It ended, and she said, "You're new, aren't you?"

I admitted that I was.

"It's kind of weird at first, but it's okay. Want to get a cup of coffee somewhere?"

A couple weeks later, she'd given me keys to her apartment. She waited tables at night and was home during the day. I'd go there when I was tired of pretending to look for work. The only thing she wouldn't do is let me keep a bar of my soap there. She'd seen it on the edge of the tub and thrown it out the window. "If you're that frightened of her, don't come here anymore." I explained that it wasn't fear, it was simple decency, but she wouldn't hear it. She folded her arms and walked away to get another beer.

A car splashed me. I squished the rest of the way to our street – really just an alley, too narrow to plow. Home was an old carriage house, converted to living quarters before the crash, when real estate was at a premium and I still had a job. I tried the front door. It was locked, as I'd expected, and I walked toward the back. Through the side window, I could see Rollo, asleep in his spot on the couch.

The key wasn't there. I looked around the patio, brushing away snow with my hands, but there was only the one spot that we kept it. I couldn't remember if I'd used it before and failed to put it back. It didn't matter. It wasn't where it should be, and I wouldn't find it in the snow. My hands were numb and red with cold. I blew into them.

I tried the back door and the windows, all the way around, without any luck. Rollo woke and started barking. I climbed the trellis. My shoe caught in the dry, lifeless wisteria, and I almost fell when one of the horizontal rails came loose in my hand. I held on and clamored over the eave, and then pulled myself up onto the pole gutter, snagging a cuff on the drip edge. I knelt across the icy slates and tried the dormer window. Rollo was barking all the while. The sash was tight, but went up. "It's all right, boy. It's just me." He kept it up as I climbed into the crawl space and then pushed down the folding staircase. Its springs made that rattling, sproinging sound. Rollo was running back and forth in the hallway, barking. I went downstairs and quieted him. "You're a good boy. Yes, you are." I left puddles of slush on the floor. My head was killing me. I'd only wanted something, some way to feel better, and it had fallen to shit, like everything else.

It was quarter past four. I needed more meds, and then to get my clothes in the wash and take a shower, but first something to take the chill off. The Scotch was kicked. In the refrigerator was an open quart bottle of Chablis that someone had given us for Christmas. I wrenched out the cork and took a pull as the front door opened. Coleen came inside and said, "What the hell are you doing?"

I hadn't heard her car – the street was impassable. She would have parked around the corner. "You're disgusting, you know that?" We stood there looking at each other for a few moments, and then she said, "Get out. I don't want you here. Go back to your whore." She took her gloves off and set them on the mail table. "I mean it. Get out. Now."

I tried to say something, and she began to scream. Rollo started back up, too. I couldn't focus on anything she said; the pain was right behind my eye. She came closer, louder, and when I put my hands up I still held the bottle. It wasn't going to work. It was just like it had been with Joan – I had to make her stop.

CHANNEL 666

by John A. Russo

John A. Russo is best known as the co-writer of the classic horror films *Night of the Living Dead* and *The Return of the Living Dead*. The multi-talented Russo has written, produced, and directed many films, and has also written his fair share of novels.

THANKS TO THE STRANGE-LOOKING CONVERTER BOX HE GOT by mugging and robbing a strange-looking man in an alley behind a video arcade, Spenser Katz's TV was bringing in programs that nobody else could get.

The box was wireless; no cables connected it to Spenser's TV. It sat on top, glowing softly, pulling in fabulous shows. Spenser figured the shows must be beamed in by satellite from somewhere.

Funny thing, but all these great shows were hosted by the same creepy guy, a guy named Nasta. He opened each show with a chuckle, saying, "Welcome to Doc Nasta's Wacky Far-Out Medicine Show!"

Nasta certainly looked like a snake-oil salesman. He also bore a weird resemblance to the old man Spenser had mugged to get the converter box. But uglier. Much uglier. His face was bruised and burned, oozing yellowish fluids, the skin stretched tight, exposing teeth that grinned perpetually as if in rictus under his black, heavily-waxed mustache.

On one of his shows, Nasta has said he was a serial killer who had died in the electric chair thirty years ago. Which couldn't be true, because there he was on TV, live, not pre-recorded. They certainly didn't have these cool, far-out programs thirty years ago — all they had was square, boring pap like *American Bandstand*.

Last Saturday, Spenser had brought his friends, Gary Parsons and Elena Holmes, into his bedroom to show them some of the great stuff he'd been watching lately. But all he could get was static. The converter box perversely decided to go on the blink at exactly the wrong time, just to make him look like a fool or a liar. He blushed and stammered furiously in front of Elena because he had a mad crush on her even though she belonged to Gary: they were engaged.

Spenser had trouble getting dates. He was gawky and shy in most situations. But underneath his shyness lurked a nasty, violent temper that he turned loose in dark alleys when he was mugging people like the old man with the converter box.

Because of the anger locked inside him, Spenser was addicted to MTV and its weird, angry, erotic imagery. He envied the rock stars, the rap stars, and pictured them in a constant orgiastic swirl with the voluptuous groupies who permeated the music videos with their red, sneering lips and pulsating perfect hips, breasts, and thighs.

Spenser's favorite rock group starred on Doc Nasta's Medicine Show, a group called Triple Six with a dynamite song called *The Devil Made Me Do It to Ya*. Spenser tried to tape Triple Six but got nothing but static. He hunted for their stuff in music stores and video stores. He asked about the group, but nobody seemed to have heard of them.

He got mad at Gary and Elena when they told him there wasn't any such group, maybe he dreamed it all up, including Doc Nasta and the Medicine Show. But Spenser knew he wasn't going crazy. This shit was *real*, goddamn it, even if he couldn't figure out why he could only tune in to the stuff that really turned him on when he was in his room all by himself.

One day Nasta read some of his fan mail out loud. Spenser didn't know how people could be writing in, since he had never seen the station's logo or address onscreen. The fan letters asked Nasta to satisfy various whims, urges, and desires. Some wanted exotic vacations, some wanted expensive cars, others wanted jewelry or furs or love or sex.

Nasta gave out 'prescriptions'. He told the people exactly what they must do in order to satisfy their wildest whims and urges. He prescribed sins for them to commit. Sometimes the sins were venial: little white lies or tiny acts of malice or spite. Other times they were mortal: rape, robbery, murder, or worse. These sins had to be 'taken' like doses of medicine.

Spenser figured it was all a gag. Nobody really wrote in. Doc Nasta just had a weird and maybe slightly evil sense of humor — because of whatever kind of accident that had caused his disfigurement. It certainly wasn't an electric chair, or he'd be dead. Maybe he got burnt by a hot wire in his own basement. He was so ugly it was easy to see why he couldn't get a job hosting a regular network show.

With a chuckle, Nasta announced that one of his fans had sent a homemade videotape to prove that she had 'followed doctor's orders'. The taped looked amazingly real, but Spenser figured it was a fake. No way could anybody get away with showing such a thing on TV, even on a cable channel. Some fat guy in loud pyjamas was being stabbed over and over by some skinny gray-haired old woman. The fat guy was groaning and screaming, blood flying all over the place, splashing the walls and soaking the mattress.

Triple Six started singing *The Devil Made Me Do It to Ya*, as the images got wilder, crazier, sexier. Spenser was riveted to the TV, horrified yet enthralled. Not only the band members but everybody in the music video began copulating with each other — right on the air!

Then Elena appeared on the screen, wearing something flimsily transparent. She smiled seductively, undulating to the beat of the music.

Spenser cried out her name, "Elena...Elena!"

She beckoned to him. He got to his feet.

He found himself in the TV screen. Suddenly, unaccountably, he was part of the music video...the beat wilder, crazier...people copulating all around him.

They fell into each other's arms, kissing passionately, their bodies writhing hotly together.

She pulled away. She kissed her fingertips and touched them to his lips.

Then Nasta's voice intruded. "Spenser Katz?"

Spenser sat up in bed startled. He still had his clothes on. His forehead was beaded with sweat. He gawked and stared — Nasta had come into his room. Behind him, the Triple Six video still blasted on the TV screen, its denizens continuing their orgy.

Nasta said, "Spenser Katz, you have just had a brief trip into my world, a special treat reserved for my disciples."

"But I'm not one of them," Spenser blurted.

"Not quite yet, for you have not fulfilled your initiation. But soon you shall do so. That is why I have allowed you to sample the delights that await you once you join my Medicine Show."

"You're kidding!? This can't be happening!"

"It can be, and it is. And now I have a prescription for you."

"What...sort of...prescription?"

Nasta emitted a sly chuckle, his waxed mustache twitching, his face wounds oozing. "You want her badly, don't you? Well, take my prescription, and she shall be yours."

"Elena?" Spenser murmured incredulously.

"None other."

"What do I have to do?"

"Kill her."

"Never!"

"Oh, but you see," Doc Nasta said soothingly, "in giving her the gift of death, you both shall become more alive. Both of you will join my show. Eternally you will feel and understand a level of ecstasy that is unknown to mortals."

"Who *are* you?" Spenser cried.

"Never mind," said Nasta, and his oily laugh reverberated as he dematerialized onto the TV screen, and the screen rapidly dissolved into static.

The very next day, Spenser got Elena to come to his room by telling her he had gotten the box working.

It turned out to be true! The box *was* working!

Elena sat on the edge of the bed next to Spenser, her short skirt hiked up, her creamy thighs showing. He didn't say, "See, I told ya, Doc Nasta is real," he just smiled and smiled, watching her take it all in.

Nasta said, "A new disciple will join us today, along with his lady love. I have given him a prescription that he is bound to follow."

Spenser got goose-bumps, partly from fear of what he was about to do, and partly from the thrill of being mentioned on television.

Triple Six blasted into the first chords of *The Devil Made Me Do It to Ya.*

Soon the orgy started.

Elena jumped up, covering her eyes, yelling, "Turn it off! Turn it *off!*"

Spenser pounced, seizing her throat and squeezing hard. She barely made a gurgle, but she pounded and scratched at him, her eyes bulging. He choked her harder. Her tongue came out between her perfect white teeth, oozing spittle and turning purple.

He kept choking even after she went totally limp and sagged at the ends of his achingly weary arms. Then at last, he let her sink onto the bed, half on and half off, till she thudded to the floor.

He looked at the screen. Triple Six was blasting. The orgy was in full sway.

He looked at Elena's dead body, shuddered, and closed his eyes.

Suddenly the music was surrounding them both, and they were *in* the TV. He was more alive than he had ever felt. And Elena was alive, too — gorgeously and nakedly alive in his arms — and he revelled in an orgasm that overcame him, sweeping him to a pinnacle of erotic delight...

But something was wrong.

Elena's skin was burnt and oozing like Nasta's, peeling away from her face.

He felt his own face, which suddenly felt as if it was on fire, and a huge gob of burning, oozing flesh stuck to his hand. He stared at the gob, then frantically tried to paste it back where it belonged and pat it into place.

Elena laughed. Her breasts were flat and rotted, her abdomen split wide open, stinking of decay.

Nasta chuckled. Standing over Spenser, he said, "Welcome to the Medicine Show!"

He wished he would wake up. But he didn't. And now he knew where the show was broadcast from. And he understood who Nasta really was.

JAMES AND SALLIE

by Stephen Spignesi

Stephen Spignesi is the author of more than 80 books, including *The Complete Stephen King Encyclopedia*, *The Official Gone with the Wind Companion*, and *The 100 Best Beatles Songs: A Passionate Fan's Guide*. He was credited with "reinventing the psychological thriller" with his debut novel *Dialogues*.

Author's Note: This is based on a true story, and thus it includes the vile language of the era.

EITHER OF JAMES'S INFRACTIONS WOULD HAVE WARRANTED severe punishment from the master, but the two combined doomed him.

First, he had been caught looking at a book, trying to suss out the letters and the meanings of the words. Slaves were forbidden to read or write, and most masters looked upon infractions of this rule as a very serious offense meriting harsh punishment, usually by flogging.

No slave was safe.

One wench the master particularly favored (he summoned her to his bed on a fairly regular basis) was a light-skinned slave named Sallie, who, like James, had been won by the master in a poker game. One day, Sallie was caught looking at a discarded half-sheet. She couldn't read, of course, but she was looking at the illustrations and the way the words and sentences and columns all lined up neatly on the page. She was immediately dragged to the big tree on the south forty, stripped naked, and tied into position with her arms and legs spread wide, hugging the tree. The overseer had then whipped her viciously with his rawhide lash thirty-nine times. He had then pressed her head against the tree, secured her left ear to the trunk by hammering a nail through the soft flesh, and then hacked off the ear with his knife. By the time he completely severed the ear from her head and tossed it to the dogs, Sallie was unconscious. She had later awakened in excruciating agony on the floor of one of the slave's cabins, still naked, and stuck to the rough wooden boards by the dried blood on her back and the side of her face. For the rest of her brief life, Sallie never again even glanced at a written word.

James had stolen a book from one of the master's children. He had heard the book being read to the child over and over by the boy's nanny and when he had it in his possession, he tried to associate his memories of the spoken story with the words in the book. It was difficult to make sense of the odd shapes that made up the many letters and words, but James tried.

The overseer had come upon James hiding with the stolen book behind a bale of hay in the loft of the barn. The master's 12-year-old son Tim was with the overseer and, when he saw his beloved book in James's hand, he became furious, grabbed the book, and punched the slave in the face.

And that was when James — a grown man a good twenty years older than the boy — committed the gravest of offenses: he struck back at the master's son. After reeling from the blow to his face, James rushed the boy and knocked him down. Before the overseer could act, James had sat down hard on the boy's chest and punched him several times in the face and chest. He ended up breaking the boy's nose and two of his teeth. The overseer had then grabbed a hoe and swung it at James as hard as he could, connecting with his head and immediately knocking him unconscious.

When James awakened, he knew his time on God's green earth was short. During his years of servitude, James had learned things about the master and his sons. Master Bill Hawkins and his three older sons, Hubert, Dwayne, and Tom, were feared throughout the area — by both blacks and whites alike. James had heard stories of night time excursions by the boys, terrible revels during which they would grab the first female slave they saw, drag her into the woods, strip her naked, rape her, and then whip her until the ground was muddy with blood. This horrific torture and assault wasn't enough for the Hawkins boys, though, and so, before they left her to die, they would gleefully pour handfuls of salt onto the girl's open wounds.

The Hawkins boys weren't picky, nor were they all that smart, and sometimes the slave girl they would use for pleasure and then toss away would belong to one of their father's neighbors. Nothing was ever said, however, although everyone in the vicinity knew the truth. They all not only knew that it was the Hawkins boys carrying out such vile acts; everyone also knew that Bill Hawkins and his boys were all quick with a rifle, or a knife, and that charging a Hawkins with anything would likely earn the accuser an early journey to the grave.

The first thing James saw upon opening his eyes were the faces of Hubert, Dwayne, and Tom staring down at him. He was lying on his back in the barn, spread-eagled and naked, his arms and legs secured to wooden posts with chains. His head was pounding with pain and it hurt terribly to move his neck or take a deep breath.

Hubert squatted down, leaned in closer and squinted. "You 'wake, nigger?"

James looked up at the three men and saw his fate in their eyes.

Behind Hubert, Dwayne and Tom stood silently. Dwayne held a thick coil of iron chain; Tom held a grappling hook with a menacingly sharp point on its curved end.

Hubert reared back and kicked James in the side. James involuntarily moaned in agony. "You hear me, nigger?"

James nodded and Hubert then stood upright – James heard his knees pop as he rose – and looked down at the shackled slave. "You done a bad thing, boy. How fuckin' *dare you* raise a hand to mah little bruther? Mah daddy always lahked you, but I never saw what was so fuckin' great 'boutcha. But daddy done warshed his hans 'a you now, boy. He done give you over to us to take care 'a ya." Hubert then turned and looked at his brothers. "Ain't that right, boys?" Neither Tom nor Dwayne said anything, but Tom reared back and spit a quantity of phlegm onto James's chest.

Hubert chuckled and said, "Cain't have niggers hittin' white boys, now can we?"

As if on cue, Dwayne and Tom put down their chain and hook and quickly moved to undo the ropes shackling James and then pull him to his feet. Tom then roughly pulled James's hands behind his back and tied his wrists together with a piece of rawhide. Tom then took a longer piece of rope and tied it around James's neck, leaving the end long enough to use as a leash.

When the battered slave was securely tied and leashed, Hubert stepped up close to him and looked him in the eyes. He was so close James could smell his stink. "We gonna give evabudy a show now, nigger. We gonna walk you lahk the dog you is, nekkid as you are, until we bring you to our fav'rit fuckin' tree." James tried to turn away from his vile gaze, but Hubert was having none of it. He roughly grabbed James by the chin and wrenched his head back to facing front. "Where you lookin' boy? Ain't no purty sky to look at ... ain't no purty nigger wenches walkin' by wid a pile 'a warsh ... you look where ah say you look. Unnerstan'?"

Hubert squeezed James's chin as hard as he could, and unhidden tears from the pain appeared in the slave's eyes. He nodded, and Hubert released his grip.

He then glanced at his two brothers and said, "Let's go. Let's go string us up a nigger."

***

The procession was the most heart-wrenching thing many of the slaves had ever seen. Hubert led the way, holding on to James's leash, while Tom and Dwayne followed behind the stumbling African, a whip in Dwayne's hand, which he used to lash out at the slave's back or legs repeatedly. The two brothers shrieked with glee every time the rawhide tore open James's flesh. Sometimes Tom would kick James in the back of the knee, causing him to fall face first into the dirt. Without his hands to break the fall, his face would take the brunt of the impact. Hubert would continue to walk, dragging the slave by the neck until James managed to scramble to his feet. The slaves in the yard knew better than to stare outright at what was going on, but they did manage to sneak glances, and many of them were in tears. James was beloved to them.

The three brothers walked James to the plantation's favored punishment tree, a tall elm in the south forty. James fell to his knees, exhausted and ablaze with pain, while Tom quickly climbed the tree and shimmied out onto a thick, low-hanging branch. Dwayne then tossed up to him the end of the chain he had brought. He attached the grappling hook to the hanging end. Tom withdrew a small hammer and an iron spike and hammered a link of the chain into the thick branch. He pulled up and similarly secured enough of the chain so that the hook hung suspended about seven or eight feet off the ground. Then he jumped out of the tree and stood quietly next to Dwayne, panting slightly. The next part of the task belonged to Hubert.

Hubert crouched down next to James. "You know mah bruther ain't gonna have no front teets now, cuz 'a you? Maybe Daddy can get that dentist feller in town to make him some fake ones, but they don't never seem to fit right ... and Tim's still a growin' boy. So he gonna have a space in his smile, nigger. Cuz 'a you. And he done had a nice smile. 'Cuz his teets ain't start'd t' rot yet."

James stared at the ground, breathing heavily. When Hubert saw that he wasn't looking at him, he slapped him in the face and said, "You look at me when I'm talkin' to you, boy."

James raised his head and stared into Hubert's face. He knew he was going to the Lord. That much was clear. And so, he knew he had absolutely nothing to lose. And that was why he smiled and said softly, "'S all right, massa. I soon gon' be wid de lawd. When yo' day come, you gon' meet Lucifa' hissef. An' ah gon' be smilin' down atcha from de right han' a' Jesus. Lawd ha' mercy."

Hubert's eyes widened, and his face turned bright red ... a crimson color, James thought, that he ain't never seen on a white man's face before. Hubert's mouth worked, and James saw spittle form on his lips, but no words came. His two brothers were similarly stunned into silence. Hubert suddenly stood up and pulled a sharp knife out of a scabbard tied to his right pant leg, and then he spoke. "You two. Get over here to lift him up," he said to his brothers without taking his eyes off James. He shot out his leg and kicked James in the chest so that he fell backwards and ended up lying on his back in the dirt. Hubert then knelt down and ran his hand up and down James's left side. When he found the right spot, he stuck his knife into James's side and made a shallow cut. He made a second cut next to the first and then sawed off the connecting strip of flesh. He then reached inside the gash, hooked his fingers around James's two lower left ribs, and then used the knife to cut around them, leaving them exposed. The white bones stood out in stark contrast to the dark flesh and blood.

During this horrible butchery, James screamed in unbearable agony, but the Hawkins boys ignored him. When the bottom of his rib cage was completely bared, Hubert stood up and nodded to his brothers. Dwayne and Tom picked up James by his head and feet and positioned him beneath the dangling hook.

Hubert grabbed the hook and, gesturing for his brothers to lift James up higher, he slid the sharp hook between James's rib's, being careful to hook at least two or three so they'd support his weight.

"Let 'im go," Hubert finally said. "Slow now."

Dwayne and Tom slowly removed their hands from James's body until his entire weight was supported by his ribs. The three Hawkins boys then stood back and admired their handiwork. James's naked body swung slowly back and forth, the pull on his ribs sending piercing stabs of unimaginable pain throughout his entire body. His position, gutted and hung as he was, also made it difficult to breathe.

Hubert circled the slave, making sure the hook had a good grip, a grip that would outlast James. He then walked to the front and looked into James's face. "Nutha' nigga from down Black'burg way lasted two days lahk this." He then spit a glob of tobacco on the ground. "Wunda how long you gon' last, boy?"

James gasped for air as the chain put pressure on his diaphragm. He looked at the white man standing before him and was struck with a storm of confusion of epic proportions. *Why he do this to me? Ain't we the same? I got kids ... he got kids ... he know mah blood is red lahk his ... why he do this to me?*

Hubert looked at James one last time, smirked, and said, "Have a good time, nigger," spit on his chest, and then nodded at his two brothers. They turned their back on the impaled slave and began walking away, heading toward the main house.

***

Later that night, around two hours before sunrise, James died. His daughter Sallie was a few yards away from him when she heard his death rattle in the night. She ran to him, but it was too late. She was barely tall enough to reach him, but she stood on tiptoes and managed to touch her father's face. She made contact with just her fingertips, only for a second or two, and then she crumpled to the ground, sobbing. She ignored the ceaseless, burning agony of her partially healed back. She remained on the ground beneath her father until the first rays of the morning sun began brightening the field. She knew she had broken the rules by leaving the slave quarters during the night without the overseer's permission. And she also knew that if she got caught committing a second offense, she'd be whipped again, only this time it would be at least a hundred strokes instead of thirty-nine.

When the sun was high enough for her to see clear across the field, she rose, gave her father one last loving look, and began walking slowly toward the main house. She didn't care who saw her.

***

Sallie died after the sixty-third blow of the overseer's lash, but he continued whipping her body until he reached the proscribed amount of one hundred strokes.

Later, James and Sallie were both buried in the patch of ground behind the slave quarters that the Master had granted the slaves use of as a cemetery. Father and daughter were buried next to each other, but no one, not even the other slaves, could take comfort in the two slaves remaining together in death.

No one had ever been told they were kin.

EPIPHANY IN THE THIRD

by David C. Hayes

David C. Hayes is the author of the novels *Cherub* and *M-Company in the Axis of Evil*, as well as a screenwriter and the creator of the graphic novel *Rottentail*.

"**A**M I DIGGING THIS GODDAMNED HOLE MYSELF?" LOUIE Scalia, semi-professional hitman, asked politely. His counterpart, Mikey Rindazzo (aka College Boy), who leaned his bulky frame against the side of the duo's 2001 Crown Vic, hunched over an iPhone, didn't respond. Mikey grunted, then shifted, trying to cover the little screen with shade. The blazing desert sun filled every nook and cranny even as it slunk toward the horizon. Mikey's back and pits were soaked. Louie, doing the brunt of the labor, was even wetter.

"Seriously, College Boy! What the hell are you doing?" To punctuate his point, Louis tossed the shovel down, narrowly missing the vaguely human-shaped object wrapped in a bed sheet.

Mikey raised a single finger, indicating that Louie needed to wait. A beat. Another. A swipe of the screen. Just as Louie was about to speak again, Mikey threw his arms in the air and cheered.

"Yes, yes, yes!" He elated. Louie watched his partner dance… all three hundred pounds of him, "I got it, I got it!"

"You better have won the fucking lottery or some test came back negative. I've been bustin' my ass in that hole for over an hour…"

"It's worth it, man, so worth it! I won it on eBay!"

Mikey turned the phone around and showed Louie the picture of a comic book. Not just any comic, though. It was an Action #292, in Very Fine condition, from September of 1962. The cover showed our hero, Superman, defending his arch enemy, Lex Luthor, against a jury of robots. That wasn't the important part, though. This comic was even more special than that.

"This comic has the first appearance of Comet in a Supergirl story, man!"

"Seriously with this shit? Supergirl I heard of. Comet's like a goddamned reindeer or something."

Mikey pulled the iPhone away like he had been pinched. "For your information, Comet was Superman's horse, all right?"

Louie, for the first time in his life, was speechless.

"I know, cool, right?" Mikey smiled a broad, toothy grin.

"Superman had a fucking horse? With, like, super powers?"

"Hell yeah! He used to be a centaur in Ancient Greece that wanted to be human. The witch, Circe, fucked up and made him a full horse so, to pay him back, she gave him super strength, super speed, immortality and telepathic thought."

Louie pondered that for a moment and picked up the shovel.

"That witch is cruel, man." Louie finally said.

"How do you mean?"

"All he wanted was to be human, right?"

"Yep."

"She made him a full horse... he probably hated that."

"Yeah, probably."

"And now he has to live forever, wanting to be human. What a bitch."

Mikey looked at his friend, the gleam in his eyes dulled a bit. "I never thought of it that way."

"See what college'll get 'ya? You start votin' with the libs and getting behind witches that make you suffer forever."

Mikey jumped into the hole, hand extended. Louie, smiling, gave the big man the shovel, and Mikey got to work. Louie took Mikey's spot at the car, leaning his bulk against it and lighting a smoke. He inhaled deeply, and stared at the pinpoints of starlight.

"You got any dreams, College Boy?"

"Like finishing this hole and getting out of here?"

"Naw, that's more of a wish. Goals. Dreams."

"I wanna own a comic book store."

"No shit?"

"No shit. I've been thinking about that recently. I love the things, man, always have. I've been saving my money and doing these jobs... it may be time."

"You'd give up the life?"

"In a heartbeat," Mikey threw the shovel over the side, landing it next to the bed sheet-wrapped object. He pulled his large frame out of the hole and regarded the bed sheet. "I just don't know how many more times I can do this."

Mikey leaned over and unwrapped the top portion of the bed sheet to reveal a man in his mid-fifties. The gray hair nearly exploded from the top of his head in tangles. His eyes were closed which highlighted the deep, black bruises that covered both of them. Mikey shook his head.

"Damn, I hate this part. Get me the pliers, hunh?"

Louie laughed and sauntered around the hole and over to Mikey and his dilemma.

"You seriously still do the pliers thing?"

"How else you gonna get the teeth out?" Mikey asked, "Someone finds this putz and IDs him, the Boss is toast."

Louie stooped and snatched up the shovel. He positioned the flat end of the shovel just below the bed sheet man's nose and lifted his foot.

"Watch and learn, College Boy," Louie smiled like a hyena as he spoke, rarely did he get to put one over on Mikey, "Just like planting a tree."

Louie jammed down with his foot. The metal shovel connected with the top row of bed sheet man's teeth with an abrupt clang and followed immediately by a snap. Bone snapping, cracking like celery, gave way to the wet, cleaver in pot roast, sound of the shovel biting into the man's face and burying itself part of the way into his spine. And then the terrible part happened.

The bed sheet man's eyes shot open. He sat up and screamed around the shovel. His arms stretched out in front, opening and closing. The anguished cry was horrible to hear. Mikey had lived near a pig farm as a very small child and could remember the screaming of the slaughtered pigs. It was a high-pitched wail that only communicated fear and pain... nothing more. The bed sheet man, complete with shovel protruding from his face, turned to Louie (who had stumbled backward, eyes as wide as the bed sheet man's) and continued to open and close his outstretched hand.

It felt like forever, but only lasted a few seconds. Mikey managed to wrap his mind around the situation, pulled his sidearm, and double-tapped the bed sheet man, putting two slugs into his brain. As quickly as it started, it stopped, and the bed sheet man slumped to the side, officially dead.

The silence lasted longer than the event. Mikey finally broke it.

"Yep. That was it. I'm done," he finally said, stashing his weapon. Louie turned to his partner, still shook up.

"I thought he was dead," Louie finally said.

"Get in line."

Mikey and Louie both leaned against the side of the Crown Vic, staring out into the desert. The light was fading fast. Louie offered Mikey a smoke and, even though he quit over a year ago, Mikey accepted. Lights around, and both of the men sucked in the smoke and nicotine, hoping it would soothe their jangled nerves.

"What'd this guy do?" Mikey asked.

"Owed the Boss some major cash. He liked to play the ponies."

Mikey laughed, "It's like an omen."

"Whaddya mean?"

"All these signs. It's telling me it's time to get out and start a comic book store. I gotta change horses," Mikey punctuated the statement with even more laughter. Louie, a little slower on the uptake, just stared at his partner.

"I don't get it."

"How'd this start, man? He played the ponies. I won the super horse auction… you think that doesn't mean anything. Shit. Where'd you pick this guy up?"

Louie took a drag, he was almost afraid to answer, "The track."

Mikey smiled. His mind was making itself up the more he talked, "Did the guy beg? They always beg. Probably had a horse he was betting."

"He kept saying, shit… this is creepy."

"What did he keep saying?"

"He kept asking me to wait. He had a bet on a horse in the third race…" Louie trailed off, he was spooking himself.

"What was the name of the horse?"

"Lois Lane's Boyfriend."

Mikey clapped his hands and pumped his fist into the air. He turned toward Louie, "Come with me, man. We can do this together!"

"Awww," Louie shook his head, "I don't know nothin' about comic books…"

"Did Lois Lane's Boyfriend win the race?"

Louie just shrugged his shoulders, "I didn't stick around to find out."

Smiling, Mikey pulled the iPhone around and accessed the internet. He waited a moment, the 4G allowing him to plan the rest of his life in the middle of the desert. The screen blinked and Mikey smiled.

"Did Lois Lane's Boyfriend win?" Louie asked.

"Nope."

Louie's shoulders drooped as if he was expecting something different, "Who did?"

Mikey smiled and turned the phone toward Louie so he could read the winner of the third race. It read 'Epiphany.' Louie looked up at Mikey, who was wearing a grin that didn't seem to have a beginning or an end.

"What does that mean?" Louie asked. He already knew the answer.

"It means that we're gonna be business partners, my friend."

They both stood there, silent, watching more pinpoints of light blink to life in the night sky.

"What was the name of the super horse?" Louie finally broke the silence.

"Comet."

"Wonder if there were any more animals like that?"

"Hell yeah, there was a dog and a monkey, too."

"No shit?"

"No shit. They were the Legion of Super Pets."

Louie took the information in and nodded, "Super Pets. I can live with that."

They were silent again. The gravity of the situation was sinking in. They were about to leave the life and that wasn't something that anybody in their business took lightly... but it felt right.

"You think we should call the store The Legion of Super Pets?" Louie asked.

"Seriously? For this job, follow my lead, ok?"

"Yeah, yeah, Mikey. Sure... so?"

"What?"

"The name."

Mikey grinned, and this time it felt genuine. "Aww, man. Epiphany. Gotta be."

Manner Of Death : Homicide

by Peter Leonard

Peter Leonard is the author of the novels *Voices of the Dead, Quiver,* and *Trust Me,* among others. He has also taken over his father Elmore Leonard's reins, continuing the Raylan series with *Raylan Goes to Detroit.*

Author's Note: Based on characters from the novel *Eyes Closed Tight.*

O' CLAIR GOT UP, PUT ON A PAIR OF SHORTS AND A TEE SHIRT, glanced at Virginia's cute face and naked shoulder sticking out from under the covers and went outside. It was seven twenty-five, big orange sun coming up over the ocean, clear sky, looked like another perfect day. O'Clair had moved to Florida from Detroit three months earlier, bought an eighteen unit motel on the beach called Pirate's Cove, a friendly pirate on the sign surrounded by neon lights.

The motel was at the corner of Briny Avenue and South East Fifth Street in Pompano Beach. Four-story condo to the North and public beach access immediately south, and next to that, a massive empty lot that a developer was going to build a twenty-five story apartment building on.

The idea of living through two years of heavy construction had O'Clair concerned, but what could he could do about it?! He'd brought a paper grocery bag with him and walked around the pool, picking up empties, a dozen or so Lite Beer cans left by a group of kids from Boston University, who'd been staying at the motel the past three days. There were nine of them, three girls and six guys. They'd caravanned down from snowy Massachusetts a week after Christmas.

He fished a few more beer cans out of the pool with the skimmer, picked up cigarette butts that had been stamped out on the concrete patio, threw them in the bag with the empties. O'Clair straightened the lounge chairs in even rows, adjusted the back rests so they were all at the same angle, and noticed one of the chairs was missing. He scanned the pool area, didn't see it, glanced over the short brick wall that separated the motel from the beach and there it was, twenty yards from where he was standing.

O'Clair kicked off his sandals, opened the gate and walked down three steps to the beach. As he got closer, he could see a girl asleep, stretched out on the lounge chair, one leg straight, the other slightly bent at the knee, arms at her sides. She was a knockout, long blond hair, thin and busty in denim Capris and a white tee-shirt, early twenties. He didn't recognize her, but figured she was with the group from Boston. She looked so peaceful, he didn't want to wake her. "You should go to your room." O'Clair said, looking down at her.

The girl didn't respond. He touched her shoulder, shook her gently. Either she was a heavy sleeper or something was wrong. He touched her neck, felt for a pulse, and there wasn't one. Her skin was cold, body starting to stiffen, definitely in the early stages of rigor. He looked at the sand around the lounge chair, surprised it was smooth, no footprints. Glanced toward the water at the joggers and walkers moving by. O'Clair went back up to the patio, wiped the sand off his feet, and slipped his sandals on.

Virginia was standing behind the registration counter, yawning, eyes not quite open all the way, holding a mug of coffee.

"What do you want for breakfast?"

"There's a dead girl on the beach." O'Clair said, picking up the phone and dialing 911.

Virginia's face went from a half smile, thinking he was kidding, to deadpan, seeing he wasn't. "What happened?"

The cruiser was white with gold and green stripes that ran along the side, light-bar flashing. O'Clair watched it pull up in front, taking up three parking spaces. Two young-looking cops in tan uniforms got out and squared the caps on their heads. O'Clair went outside, met them and introduced himself.

"You the one found the body?" Officer Diaz, the dark-skinned cop said.

O'Clair nodded.

"You know her?" Diaz pulled the brim lower over his eyes to block the morning sun, the top of a crisp white tee-shirt visible under the uniform.

"At first I thought she was with the group from BU. Now I don't think so."

"What's BU?" The big pale one, officer Bush said, showing his weightlifter's arms, uniform shirt bulging over his gut.

"Boston University. Nine kids staying with us, units 17 and 18." O'Clair didn't know the sleeping arrangements and didn't care. They were paying $720 a night for two rooms, staying for five days.

An EMS van pulled up and parked facing the police cruiser. Two paramedics got out, opened the rear door, slid the gurney out, and O'Clair led them through the breezeway, past the pool to the beach. The paramedics set the gurney next to the lounge chair, examined the girl, and pronounced her dead.

Officer Bush said, "What time did you find her?"

"Around twenty to eight."

"How can you be sure?"

"I looked at my watch," O'Clair said, like it was a big mystery.

Diaz grinned, showing straight white teeth, reminding O'Clair of Erik Estrada, tan polyester uniform glinting in the morning sun. "Did you touch the body?"

"Her neck, felt for a pulse." O'Clair saw Virginia wander down, standing at the seawall with her cup of coffee, watching them. Officer Bush went back to the cruiser and got stakes and tape, set up a perimeter around the dead girl, protecting the crime scene. The paramedics picked up the gurney and left, leaving the body for the evidence tech.

Diaz took a spiral-bound notebook out of his shirt pocket, wrote something and looked up at O'Clair. "Ever see her before? Maybe laying in the sun, walking the beach?"

"I don't think so," O'Clair said. "Someone like that I would remember."

Diaz said, "You see anyone else?"

"College kids out by the pool." He almost said drinking beer, but caught himself, doubted they were twenty-one and didn't want to get them in trouble.

"What time was that?"

"Around 11:00."

"Then what happened?"

"I went to bed."

Diaz said, "Anything else you remember? Any noises?"

"No."

"The evidence tech arrived carrying a tool box, set it on the sand a few feet from the lounge chair, opened it, took out a camera, and shot the crime scene from various angles. Diaz searched the surrounding area for evidence, and Bush questioned the morning joggers and walkers wandering up toward the scene. O'Clair watched from the patio, leaning against the sea wall. Virginia had gone back to the office in case somebody decided to check in.

A guy in a tan lightweight suit walked by O'Clair and went down the steps to the beach. He had to be with homicide. The evidence tech, wearing white rubber gloves, was swabbing the dead girl's fingernails. He glanced at the guy in the suit.

"What do you got?"

"Fatal."

"I figured that unless you were doing her nails."

"Not much here," the evidence tech said, "couple hairs, maybe a latent, and something you're not going to believe." He whispered something to the suit O'Clair couldn't hear.

"Jesus, I've seen a lot, but I haven't seen that." The homicide investigator shook his head. "Where's the blood?"

"That's what I want to know."

"How'd she die?"

"You want a guess? That's about all I can give you right now. She was asphyxiated, been gone about four hours."

"Who found her?"

The evidence tech turned and pointed at O'Clair above them on the patio. The detective came up the steps and stood facing him.

"I'm Holland, Pompano Beach Homicide." He had a goatee and a crooked nose, early thirties. "What's your name, sir?"

"O'Clair."

"I understand you found her."

"That's right."

"You down here for a vacation, or what?"

"I own the place, bought it three months ago."

"Where you from, Cleveland, Buffalo, someplace like that?"

"Detroit," O'Clair said.

"Even worse," Holland said, breaking into a grin. "Just kidding. I got nothing against the Motor City."

"Well, that's a relief," O'Clair said.

Holland wore his shield on his belt and a holstered Glock on his right hip.

"You married?"

"Living with a girl named Virginia, helps me run the place."

"The hot number in the office?"

O'Clair fixed a hard stare on him.

"How'd you arrange that?"

"I must have some hidden talents."

"You must," Holland said. "Tell me what you saw this morning."

"Same thing you did-dead girl on a lounge chair," O'Clair said.

"Know who she is?"

"No ID. No idea. Have to check with missing persons. Was the chair left on the beach?"

"It shouldn't have been. The lounge chairs are supposed to be kept in the pool enclosure. It's one of our rules here at Pirate's Cove."

"Your guests break the rules very often?"

"Oh, you know how it is. Get in the Jacuzzi with a beer, without taking a shower and you've broken three right there." O'Clair paused, playing it straight. "The rules are from the previous owner, guy named Moran. I keep them posted 'cause I think they're funny. Someone sat down and wrote them in all seriousness."

"What do you think happened? This girl was walking by, and got tired, saw your place, went up got a lounge chair, brought it to the beach, laid down and died in her sleep?"

"I'd ask the medical examiner."

The evidence tech was taking off the rubber gloves, closing the top of the tool box.

Holland said, "What else did you see?"

"You're asking the wrong question," O'Clair said. "It's not what I saw, it's what I didn't see."

"OK. What didn't you see?"

"There were no footprints in the sand. Like she was beamed there."

"So the wind erased them," Holland said.

"You really believe that?"

"It's the only plausible explanation I can think of."

"What else didn't you see?"

"No obvious cause of death. No evidence of a struggle. In fact, no evidence at all." O'Clair looked at Holland, caught something in his expression.

"You sound like you know the trade," Holland said. "What'd you do before you became an innkeeper."

"Worked homicide in Detroit."

Holland grinned. "I had a feeling. Then you must've seen her eyes were missing, right? Bulbs removed, empty sockets."

"But no blood," O'Clair said. "So it was done somewhere else. Find the primary crime scene, you'll find the evidence."

"You weren't going to say anything?"

"It's not my case," O'Clair said. "I figured somebody was going to notice sooner or later. It wasn't you or the evidence tech it would've been the ME."

"Why do you think the girl ended up here?"

"I have no idea. Why don't you roll her over, maybe you'll find something." Occasionally there was a crucial piece of evidence under the body, a lead. It could've been a round that would be tested for ballistics comparison against other homicides. It could've been money or drugs, suggesting a possible motive, or it could've been a cell phone that led to the possible killer or killers. There was nothing under the dead girl. No ID. No cell phone. Her body was bagged and the remains taken to the Broward County Medical Examiner's office. They took O'Clair's lounge chair too.

"It's evidence," Holland said. "You'll get it back eventually."

O'Clair doubted it. He knew what happened to evidence.

Bush and Diaz went upstairs and woke the BU students, and brought them down to the pool, nine kids looking hung over, yawning. Eight-twenty in the morning was the middle of the night for them. O'Clair had noticed they usually didn't get up till after noon. Holland questioned them, one by one, showed photos of the dead girl, took statements, and sent them back to their rooms. No one knew or had ever seen the girl before. No one had seen anything suspicious or heard anything during the night.

The MacGuidwins from Mt. Pearl, Newfoundland in Unit 2, who had complained about the students making too much noise, were questioned next by Holland. O'Clair watched the fair-skinned, red-haired couple shaking their heads.

As it got hotter, Holland commandeered Unit 7, his makeshift interrogation room and brought the other renters in two-by-two for questioning. There were the Burns, Susan and Randy, from Troy, Michigan, the Mitchells, Joe and Jean from San Antonio, Texas, the Belmonts, John and Shannon from Chicago, Illinois, and the Mayers, Steve and Julie from Syracuse, New York. Steve Mayer woke up with four alarm heartburn at 3:30 a.m., got up, took a Nexium, walked out by the pool, and remembered seeing the lounge chair on the beach, but didn't think anything of it. None of the other renters saw or heard anything.

O'Clair walked Holland out to his car at eleven twenty, glad to finally get rid of him.

"Miss the life?" Holland said.

"Are you kidding?"

"Some things about it, I'll bet." He handed O'Clair a card. "Call me if you think of something."

***

He was cleaning the pool the next morning when Holland called.

"Girl's name is Gloria McMillen. Cause of death was determined to be asphyxiation. Manner of death was ruled to be homicide. The killer had skill. Her eyes were surgically removed with some kind of scalpel."

"Find out if it was an X-Acto knife," O'Clair said.

"Why do you say that?"

"Was she sexually assaulted?"

"With a metal rod," Holland said. "Why would he do that?"

"Maybe he doesn't like women. Maybe he wasn't breast fed or his mother wasn't nice to him."

"How do you know it's a him?"

"You have to be strong to carry a one-hundred-twenty-pound girl from the street to the beach. It's got to be seventy yards."

"How do you know so much about this?"

"I had a case like it a few years ago, although the cause of death was way different."

"You think the murders are related?"

"I'm not saying that." O'Clair paused, but he was thinking it. "Guy named Alvin Monroe killed two prostitutes, shot them once in the head, cut their eyeballs out with an X-Acto blade, and raped them with a metal rod. Alvin was convicted of first-degree murder and given consecutive life sentences without the possibility of parole."

"A copycat," Holland said.

Holland was watching too many cop shows. "Details of the murders were never disclosed in the newspapers."

"Maybe somebody came to trial, heard the evidence in the courtroom."

"Anything's possible," O'Clair said. "Why wait six years to come after me? Let me think about it, talk to my former partner." O'Clair paused.

"Tell me more about the girl."

"Gloria's mother called two days ago, said her daughter was missing, e-mailed a photo. Came and identified the body. Gloria McMillen was twenty. She was attending classes at Broward College, and worked as a cashier at Publix."

"Gloria have a boyfriend?"

"Her high school sweetheart, a kid named Joey Van Antwerp," Holland said. "But they broke up six months ago."

"Why?"

"The mother doesn't know."

"I hope he's on your list. Any evidence? Any other suspects?"

"Nothing yet. Not much to go on. Unless we get lucky."

"You've got to work the case," O'Clair said. "Make your own luck. How long you been doing this?"

"Eighteen months."

"How many homicides you worked, you were primary?"

"Six, not counting this one." Holland sounded like he was apologizing. "How about you?"

"Fifteen hundred or so."

"I'm going to Gloria's place, look around. Want to come?"

O'Clair did feel a sense of responsibility. Maybe Holland was right - someone was trying to tell him something.

Holland picked him up twenty minutes later. O'Clair got in the car and said, "What's the crime like down here?"

Holland glanced at him. "You talking homicide?"

"Yeah. How many murders did you have in Pompano last year?"

"Eight, and that's high for a town with a population of just over a hundred thousand. Way above the national average." Holland took a right on North East Fifth Street.

"What kind of situations?"

"Everything you can think of. Two were domestic, husbands killed their wives. Both arrested and prosecuted." Holland paused. "One, a teen from Iowa arrived in town by bus, gave birth, and threw the kid down a trash chute. The girl confessed and posted a photo of herself on Facebook with a caption that said: *People you will see in hell.*"

O'Clair had investigated his share of dead babies: beaten to death by the mother's boyfriend or the mother herself 'cause the baby was crying too much. It was something you never got used to.

"Had another one," Holland said, "guy named Ricardo Arzate, killed his friend at a birthday party, shot him twice, and disappeared. You see a Puerto Rican with a tat of the Virgin Mary on his right pec, give me a call."

"Good luck," O'Clair said. "You know how many Puerto Ricans have the Blessed Virgin tattooed on their chest?"

Holland pulled into the parking lot of the Harbor Cove condominiums less than a mile from his motel. They got out and walked up the winding staircase to the fourth floor. Holland had a key, unlocked the door, and they went in. It was a two bedroom condo on the intracoastal, beautifully furnished. "How's someone who works at a grocery store afford a place like this? Did her parents buy it for her?"

"The mother said Gloria saved up."

"I'd find out who's financing it and how much she put down."

They went in the bedroom that had a queen-size bed. O'Clair checked the dressing room that was big and organized, shoes on one side, lined up on floor-to-ceiling shelves, thirty-six pairs. Her clothes were on the other side. He wasn't an expert but everything looked expensive.

O'Clair went in the adjoining bathroom. The counter was cluttered with make-up containers, smudges of color on the white Formica countertop, towels on the tile floor, shampoo, conditioner, bath oils, and candles lining the flat side of the tub.

The second bedroom was used as an office. O'Clair sat behind the sleek desk in a high-backed swivel office chair, going through the drawers, taking out things of interest: Gloria McMillen's checkbook, pay stubs, phone bills, bank statements, lining them up on the desktop next to her MacBook.

Holland came in the room and stood next to him. "What do you have?"

"What do you want to know? She put $40,000 down on the condo, has a fifteen-year mortgage, pays $2,200 a month. Drives a Mercedes EClass. Her lease with Mercedes-Benz Credit is $738 a month, and she has seventy-five grand in a savings account.

"How would she have that kind of money making $10 an hour as a cashier at Publix?"

"She didn't. Looks like she quit that job six months ago, didn't tell her mother. Gloria's been getting a weekly check from XYZ Company. Different amounts, but adds up to almost one hundred and thirty-thousand since July."

Holland said, "Is there an address?"

"A post office box in Coral Gables."

Holland made a U-shape with his right hand, rubbed his jaw.

"What's XYZ do, they're paying a twenty-year-old girl two hundred and sixty grand a year?"

"It's a shell company for an escort service," O'Clair handed him a stack of eight and a half by eleven pages Gloria must've printed from the escort web site.

Holland started reading.

"Everything you want to know about *Glamor Girls*," O'Clair said. "It's all there: rates, reservations customer rewards, FAQs. Spend fifty-thousand a year, you're a platinum member."

"What's that get you?"

"Complementary limo service, discounts at hotels."

"How much do they charge?"

"Depends where you're at," O'Clair said. "You've got the rate sheet."

Holland shuffled through a couple pages, found what he was looking for. "In Boca, it's eight hundred to a thousand an hour, two hour minimum."

"How about Pompano?"

"Doesn't say, but Lauderdale is only seven hundred to nine hundred," Holland said. "What a deal, huh? They take Visa, MasterCard, American Express, and Discover. Listen to this: *Someone once said, "The best things in life are free." Our classy ladies would love to hang out with you for nothing, but the reality is, hair, nails, makeup, and designer outfits are expensive.*"

O'Clair booted up the MacBook, brought up Safari, typed in the web site, and the *Glamor Girls* home page appeared. Rows of color shots of hot-looking girls wearing high heels, posing in bikinis and lingerie. Girls with names like Francesca and Desiree, Isabella and Darcey, Alix, Chandler and Bayley. O'Clair had never met girls with any of those names. He scrolled down and saw Gloria McMillen in casual pose facing the camera, sultry expression, leaning against an ornate banister, one leg straight, the other bent at the knee, heel hooked on the metalwork of the banister. The name under the photograph was Ashley. "So they don't know she's dead."

"They suspect something's wrong. Come in and listen to her messages," Holland said, walking out of the room.

O'Clair followed him into the kitchen. There was a Panasonic answering machine on the brown granite counter over a built-in wine cooler.

"She was killed around 4:00 a.m.," Holland said. "These came in later that morning. I think you're right, the escort people don't know she's dead or they'd get rid of her picture, wouldn't they?" Holland pressed the message button.

"Glor, it's Pam, tried your cell, no answer. A gentleman named Rick is asking for you this evening, call for the particulars. Oh, and how was your date?"

"Pause it," O'Clair said. "What time did that call come in?"

"Yesterday. ten thirty in the morning."

"Sounds like she was with someone the night she was killed. Which may or may not be the perp. But it's a place to start."

ONE HIT WONDER

by Elka Ray

Elka Ray is the author of the novels *Hanoi Jane* and *Saigon Dark*. In addition, she is the author of the short story collection *What You Don't Know: Tales of Obsession, Mystery & Murder*.

MY WIFE, TIPI, IS OFF TO SEE HER MUM, WHO'S BEEN POORLY. She lives in Surin province, four-hundred miles from us, in eastern Thailand. I went last year, before we married, for the Thai New Year. Never again. Mud everywhere. And no wifi. It's in the middle of nowhere.

Tipi's in the bedroom packing, and I'm on the verandah lifting weights. Keeping the old body fit. It seems to be working. I had a full physical five days back, and the doc was flabergasted - said I had the insides of a man half my age. Wish you could say the same about the outside, but a few wrinkles aren't stopping me. I'm seventy-two and married to a twenty-nine-year-old. Coming to Thailand was the best thing that could've happened to me. You wouldn't find a girl like Tipi back in Brighton.

Tapping high heels and the rumble of wheels signal her approach. Dragging her wheelie-bag, she's wearing tight jeans, a tight pink top, and a leather jacket, despite the heat. After the wedding, she bleached her hair orange. I prefer it black. But even bald, she'd be stunning.

Tipi pushes her case onto the verandah, the screen door clicking behind her. A gust of hot, dusty wind lifts the fake flower in her hair.

I set down the barbell I was hoisting and wipe my hands on a towel. "You off then?"

Tipi pouts. "Yes." The way she's standing - one hip thrust out, arms crossed - makes her look sexy but cross. She's been pouty of late, maybe worrying about her mum. I hope this moodiness won't last. She was never like that before we married, never stopped smiling. And the sex - like in a naughty film. She couldn't get enough of it.

I'm enjoying a pornographic trip down Memory Lane when Tipi's phone rings. "Gotta go. Driver's here," she says, pushing the phone back into her purse.

"You got everything, then?" I say and Tipi gives me a tight nod. Is she pissed I'm not taking her to the train station? But that can't be it. Her regular motorbike taxi driver lives next door. He drives her everywhere. Is it because I'm not coming to see her mum? Or should I offer some extra cash for the trip? "You have enough money?" I ask.

"I'm fine."

I fight back a sigh. In my experience of women, 'fine' tends to mean the opposite.

Still looking pouty, Tipi offers a pink cheek to be kissed. I pull her into a hug and kiss her on the lips, but Tipi wriggles free. "My lipstick."

"You're pretty with or without lipstick," I tell her, then slap her butt as she turns to go.

Tipi clucks and sidesteps. Her wheelie-bag bumps down the front stairs.

"I love you," I call out after her.

She stops to look back, cracks a smile when I blow a kiss.

"I'll miss you," I say.

Tipi's smile widens. "Me too."

At the sight of her smile, I feel giddy inside, like a teenager again. She's got the smile of a film star.

***

With Tipi gone, after dinner I head to the Big Easy, a bar popular with expats in Hua Hin. It's a Tuesday, so quiet. Even when they're retired or on holiday people tend to stick to a workweek schedule, saving their big nights out for the weekend. We're all creatures of habit.

I've had two beers and am ready to quit when someone calls my name. "Ron? Ronnie Ostler?"

The hairs on my nape prickle, that voice - high-pitched, with a wheeze - taking me back fifty years. Smoky clubs. Shrieking girls and guitars. Tight suits. Cameras flashing.

Turning to see him, I'm suddenly unsure. The light's dim. And like me, he's put on weight, especially around the middle. His hair's grey, as is mine, but still longish in the back, bringing to mind Phil Collins. I squint: "Barry?"

He seems uncertain, too, but then he smiles, and there's no mistaking him - still the same bad shark's teeth. I'm surprised he hasn't fixed them.

"Ron? What are you doing here?" asks Barry.

"Barry Golds," I say, shaking my head in wonder. "I live here. How are you?"

It's been at least forty-five years since I last saw him, outside some club in London. We had a bit of a row, if I remember right, Barry blind drunk, telling me I owed him, which was bollocks. We grew up on the same street, used to jam together, even played a few gigs, earning peanuts. Then I got my big break, and we lost touch, not that we were ever that close. Yet it's odd. You know someone long enough, even if they aren't, they start to feel important.

"It's been a long time," says Barry. He slides onto the stool beside mine and looks around, signals the barman for a beer. When he lights a cigarette, I feel both envious and smug. Gave up three years ago, doctor's orders.

Two jets of blue smoke exit Barry's nostrils. "How'd you end up living here then?"

I explain about my wife, Pornthip, whom I'd met in a bar in Bangkok.

"Pornthip?" Barry giggles. "A looker, is she?"

"Yeah." I nod, but don't like his leer. I don't like Barry, never did, now I think about it. Even as a small boy, he was shifty, dented my new bike and refused to fix it.

Still, he buys me a beer and we drink it, start reminiscing about old times. Clubs we played. Musicians we knew. Girls we dated or tried to. He doesn't mention the song, and neither do I, but I can hear it in the back of my head, stuck there, a blessing and a curse. For fifty years now, that song's haunted me and paid the bills. "Wild Child" by Ron Ostler. I still hear it on the radio and in elevators, in the goddammed supermarket. About a decade ago, Britney Spears covered it. I quite liked her video - and the extra cash came in handy. Wild Child. My sole claim to fame. My one hit wonder.

Oooh wild child
Let's take a ride
Wind in your hair
Hot double dare
Luck's by my side
C'mon wild child

I figure Barry's here on holiday, but he tells me he's 'investing'. He and his brother-in-law have put some money into a local club. It's a great opportunity. I only half-listen. Barry's always been a schemer.

Since getting married, I've cut back on the booze. But with Tipi away and my recent clean bill of health, when Barry switches to whiskey, I follow. With each glass, my nostalgia grows. We had some good times, me and Barry, back as youngsters. The Beatles and the Stones were just getting big. Even Brighton had a burgeoning music scene. The Imperial Hotel. West Street. The Belvedere. Oh, to be young again. The Swinging Sixties.

I'm surprised when the barman announces last call, although it is a Tuesday. Looking around, I see we're the only customers. Barry tries to argue, gets a bit stroppy because that's how he is. He and the barman get into a shoving match, and the barman's mates come over to help. Barry gets roughed up a bit.

I try to stay well clear of it. The Big Easy's my local. The last thing I want is Barry's stupidity to get me barred from the place. "Sorry mate," I tell the bartender after Barry's been dragged outside and left sitting on the curb. "I barely know the guy."

"Just shut him up," says the barman, because Barry's still yelling out in the empty street.

I leave the bartender with his mates and head out to Barry, crouching down. "Barry," I say. "Shut the fuck up. You're being a nuisance."

"Those bastards hit me," says Barry, voice squeaky with indignation. He keeps trying - and failing - to light a cigarette.

I glance over my shoulder. The barman and his friends are now standing outside the door, arms crossed like bouncers. For Thais, they're big, solid lads, with jaws like cardboard boxes.

"Shut up, or they'll do it again," I tell Barry. "Now get up."

He lets me haul him to his feet. While those guys pushed him around a bit, he's unhurt. "This way," I say and drag Barry towards the closest intersection.

Out of sight of the Big Easy, we stop to catch our breath. It's a hot night, the air reeking of gutters. "Must be someplace open," says Barry, peering at the boarded-up shopfronts. He sways on his feet. "For a nightcap."

"You've had enough," I say, grimly.

"Have not," says Barry. "That guy was a wanker. Lazy shit, closing early." He checks his watch. "It's not even -"

"It's past two," I say, surprised by how fast the night's gone. I'm suddenly so tired and drunk I could almost sleep here on the filthy sidewalk.

"You live around here?" asks Barry.

I don't want him over but feel too spent to protest. Taking him home seems the easiest option. There's plenty of spare rooms. The thought of falling into bed makes my knees weak. All I want is the feel of cold, clean sheets and a soft pillow.

It takes twenty minutes to stumble home. Neither of us can walk straight.

"Nice place," says Barry with a whistle, when I finally get the front gate unlocked. I nod. Lit by floodlights, the house looks grand. For the same amount, you couldn't buy a closet in London. I bought the place three months ago, or rather Tipi did. Foreigners can't own land yet, only apartments. With five bedrooms, it's far too big for us, but Tipi loves it. She's been redecorating - bit frilly for my taste but it makes her happy.

"You can sleep in there," I say, pointing Barry to a back room. "And if you want to smoke, go outside." Tipi hates smoke.

"Aw, c'mon, one more drink," he wheedles. "I'm parched after that walk."

"There's cold water in the fridge," I say. "G'night Barry."

I'm retreating down the hall when he starts to sing. Wild Child. In his high, wheezy voice it annoys me even more than usual.

I turn and glare at him. "Go to bed, Barry."

"What? I can't even sing the song I wrote?"

I feel suddenly, dismally sober. "You didn't write it, Barry."

"Sure I did." He shrugs. "Well, we wrote it together."

He tried this before, back in the day, and I told him the same thing I tell him now. "That's a crock of shit and you know it. I wrote Wild Child in one night, by the seafront. By myself." I'd just gotten dumped by red-headed Angela Cuthbert and was strung between relief and dismay. I remember it clear as day.

"Did not," says Barry. He sounds about ten. I recall how, at about that age, I'd punched him hard in the jaw for calling my brother a faggot. Course David was a faggot, I just didn't realize it yet.

Since there's no reasoning with Barry, I leave him in the hall and go off to bed. I lock my bedroom door. Despite being exhausted, I lie in bed thinking about the old days. Me and Barry. The music. Me and David. These days, being gay doesn't seem so bad. Every other celebrity's flaming. But back then, David really copped it. Would he have killed himself if he'd been straight? I don't think so. I fall asleep missing him in a way I haven't in years, throat aching, like I've been bawling.

It's still dark when I wake, covered in sweat and gasping. A bad dream: I was up on stage, flashbulbs popping, singing that damn song when blood started gushing from my mouth.

I sit up, blinking the image away. My breathing's too fast, like I've been running. The aircon hums overhead, and my mouth tastes foul. While I don't have a headache yet, one's brewing. It's been a long time since I was this drunk, the bed spinning beneath me. Come morning, I'll be suffering.

Luckily, I don't dream after falling back to sleep.

The neighbor's rooster wakes me, crowing on and on, like one of those idiotic ringtones. Lying still, brain pressed hard against my skull, I imagine wringing its bloody neck. Maybe Tipi can talk to the neighbor, buy the noisy thing off him.

When it's clear further sleep's impossible, I get up and shuffle to the john. The house is dead silent, as it should be, with Tipi away. But then I remember, and my stomach drops. Barry's here. I can't face him with this headache.

Ten-twenty-two a.m. It's later than I thought. The kitchen lies empty and quiet. Maybe Barry woke early and buggered off. I feel somewhat better.

If Tipi were here, she'd make breakfast. I settle for cornflakes and strong coffee. I'm on my third cup when the neighbor's dog starts to bark. Jesus. That neighbor. It's always something. When the guy's roosters or dogs aren't making a racket, he's revving those damned motorbikes. He's a young punk, fond of leather vests and jean shorts. Along with his motorbike-taxi business, he runs a bike-repair shop.

The dog's still barking. With this hangover it sounds louder than usual. Has it gotten into my yard? I stumble to the front door, cursing.

Stepping onto the porch, the heat hits me, my back wet with sweat before I've reached the edge of the terrace. I trip over something soft but catch myself. Christ. One of Barry's flip flops. My heart sinks. He must not have left, after all.

Leaning out over the railing, I squint towards the neighbor's shack, which rises, like a canker, from his junk yard. Old bikes and piles of scrap metal. A rusty truck on blocks. A broken wardrobe. What an eyesore. Luckily, property prices are skyrocketing. Sooner or later, he'll sell up to some nice holidaymakers.

I shade my eyes. While the dog's still barking, I can't see it, nothing moving but ripples of heat, radiating off the cement. So much for sea air. With no hint of a breeze, it's like being in a giant vacuum.

Each time the dog barks, my insides clench up. I might just kill it.

"Shut your dog up!" I bellow, and for a second, the mutt shuts up. Then it starts again with renewed vigor.

Teeth gritted, I'm heading indoors when something pale catches my eye, down below, between the fence and my terrace. I lean over the rail. It's a pack of cigarettes... and... no, it can't be. Except it is - a foot, the heel dirty and callused.

Breath held tight, I lean further out, my vision strobe-lighting, the images disjointed. The foot is attached to a bare leg. Pale, stripey boxer shorts. Another leg and a much-too-pale back. Arms spread wide, hugging the earth. Someone's face-planted in my flower-bed.

I blink, the air shimmying like in a low-budget sci fi flick, some portal opening behind the hibiscus. Soon, little green men will run out. I blink again. Heat haze. But no, that's not heat but flies...

When I start to scream, the dog stops barking.

Down the steps in a quivering daze, coffee and cornflakes puked into a planter. With the dog stunned into silence, all is quiet as I wobble closer and bend low, a shaking hand seeking a pulse. "C'mon mate," I say. "Wake up now."

Nothing.

That's when I see the back of his head, like a slice of black pudding under his thin hair. Gagging on bile, back away. Barry. That fucker has gone and died in my front garden.

If Tipi were here, she'd deal with the police. She'd know just what to say. As it is, they're stuck trying to get some sense out of me. While the head investigator, Detective Wutthisak, speaks good English, I'm not sure how much is getting through. We sit at my kitchen table, across from each other, him upright as a school marm and me hunched over, head in hands. He keeps asking the same questions, over and over.

How did I know Barry? What was he doing here? When did I last see him?

I try not to get impatient. The cops can't seem to fathom that I barely knew Barry and have no idea where he was staying or who to contact.

"What time did you go to bed?" asks Detective Wutthisak.

I shrug. My memory of last night is hazy, especially after leaving the bar. It was past two when we set off for home. I know that much. Ten-minute walk, then straight to bed. "Two-thirty at the latest," I tell the detective, then catch sight of two dirty glasses and a bottle of whiskey on the counter, like we drank a little more before calling it a night. I swallow hard. It bothers me, not remembering that. Is there anything else I can't remember?

While the cops poke around, I retire to the den. I try to watch TV but can't concentrate. Barry Gold. Dead. He could be a little shit, but we did grow up together. Another of the old gang gone. First my brother to suicide, and then Dan Moore, who O.D.'d. Little Ralphie, who lived just around the corner, dead in a car crash on his twenty-first, and Suzie Miller, the first girl I ever felt up, lost to breast cancer five years ago. And now Barry. Murdered. In my own front yard. It hardly seems possible.

My head throbs. Who the hell could have killed him? Who even knew he was here?

"Excuse me, sir?"

I look up to see Detective Wutthisak leaning around the door, timidly, like he fears he's bothering me. He's a skinny guy, with wire-rimmed specs and a tight shirt buttoned up to his prominent Adam's apple. Looks like an accountant.

Sitting up, I turn down the sound. It's some nature show, about gibbons. "Yes?"

He heads for the peach velvet armchair and takes a seat, gingerly, like he doesn't quite trust it. "Did you and Mr. Gold have a fight?" he says, looking apologetic.

"Ummm." I think back. We did argue a little, at the bar, when he wouldn't stop singing that damn song. Have the cops spoken to the bartender? Did he mention that? "I got a bit annoyed with him," I admit. "At the Big Easy. He was really drunk. Belligerent." A thought occurs to me. The bartender and his buddies, could they have followed us home? Maybe Barry went back outside, and they pounced. He did mouth them off. Barry had a talent for getting people riled up.

I mention this to Detective Wutthisak, and he nods. "We will speak to them." He removes his glasses to clean them. "Back at your house," he says. "Did you argue back here?"

I hesitate. Not that I recall. "No. We went straight to bed."

"I see..." He looks even more regretful. "Would you follow me, please?"

Heart pounding, I click off the TV. If only Tipi were here to handle this.

Detective Wutthisak leads me down the hall and into the sitting room, where he clears his throat. "How did this happen?"

Peering over his shoulder, I see a bright pink vase - recently bought by Tipi - now in pieces on the tiled floor.

"No idea," I say, frowning. If we had a cat, I'd blame it. But we don't.

"I see." The detective clears his throat again, obviously waiting for me to elaborate.

"Maybe Barry knocked it over after I went to bed."

"But you didn't hear anything?"

I shake my head. I heard nothing last night.

"Wait," I say, because something's come back to me. "Barry said he was here investing. In a club." The detective cocks his head. "D'you think the deal went sour?" Barry was dodgy as fuck. Look at him, trying to shake me down for "Wild Child" - a song he couldn't even sing, let alone write. The bars and clubs hereabouts are all mafia-run. He might have upset the wrong person.

Detective Wutthisak looks confused. "Sour?" he says.

"A bad business deal," I explain. "Barry could be..." I shrug. "This is years ago, mind. Back in England. He could be a touch... dishonest."

"Ah," says Detective Wutthisak. "Did he try to cheat you?"

I shake my head, uncomfortable with the gleam in his dark eyes. "No, nothing like that."

"Thank you," he says, and ushers me back towards the den again.

No matter which way I lie, I can't get comfortable. There's nothing on TV, and I can't stop thinking about Barry and that awful dream: me, choking on blood while trying to sing "Wild Child". Did it mean something? A premonition of what happened to Barry or my subconscious telling me to wake up? Maybe I heard something, after all. Or maybe it was my guilty conscience talking.

This last thought slips in, the way you shimmy into a train just as the doors are sliding shut. I rub my aching eyes. My hands feel clammy. What do I have to feel guilty about? It wasn't me who hurt Barry. Was it?

Now the thought's here, I can't get rid of it. It's ludicrous. Absurd. And yet... Am I sure we went straight to bed? Am I sure we didn't argue?

Out in the kitchen, people are moving around. The cops and crime techs. Detective Wutthisak.

My head throbs something awful, and my stomach rumbles. Having puked up all the cornflakes, it's dead empty. I should eat something, but just the thought turns my stomach.

Eyes squeezed shut, I struggle to remember. Me and Barry in the Big Easy. Him arguing with the bartender and his tough-looking mates. Me dragging him away, telling him to shut his stupid trap. Our long, wavering walk home. He was impressed by my house, I remember that. And he wanted to keep drinking. Did we?

Behind my closed eyelids, a figure takes shape: Barry, red-faced and drunk, blinking in my bright kitchen. I can see his bloodshot eyes and the broken capillaries around his sharp nose, see him swaying, beside the counter. Hear his reedy voice singing that damn song, after I told him to zip it. My heart quickens. Surely, that's not enough to have made me bash him.

I press the heels of my hands into my sore eyes. Barry comes back into focus.

"You hear what happened to Lionel?"

"Lionel Levin?" I said, slurring.

"Yeah. He got done for lewd behaviour. Dogging in a public toilet. Just like George Michael." He shakes his grey head and sniggers. "Damn fags. They're disgusting, they are. Remember that guy at school, the one who wrote that poem about blow jo-"

He broke off mid word, giggle turned into a hiccup, having just remembered he's talking about my twin brother.

Davey wrote a poem, the silly sod, in his Social Studies binder. Barry stole it, passed it around - a source of howling-hyena amusement. I can still remember one line, not word for word, but the gist of it, Davey comparing the feel of someone's cock to a friendly dog, nuzzling up against your palm.

My chest feels tight. Is that why I did it? Because of Davey? The permanent hurt in his big brown eyes, the way his shoulders grew more and more hunched, his steps quicker and more furtive. The doctors. The medication. Trying to cut his wrists in the tub. My mother's face when the police came to say he'd jumped from Beachy Head, his face - my face - unrecognizable after the fall.

Again, adrenaline spikes through me. Barry was one of the worst to Davey. I almost hope I did kill him.

Deep breaths. I'd better eat something soon. I'm feeling dizzy.

Shaking, I sit up. Surely I'd remember if I'd killed him. It must have been messy. I raise my hands to my face, half expecting to see blood splatter. Did I shower? For the life of me, I can't remember.

"Sir?" Detective Wutthisak is back. "We're finished for now." He clears his throat. "Please stay in town. We will need to speak with you again."

I nod, my throat so dry I can barely talk. "Ok. Where are you taking Barry?"

"To the police morgue," says the detective. "There will be an autopsy."

Just the thought turns my stomach.

I see the police out, then sink back onto the sofa.

My hangover's getting worse, instead of better, so bad I wonder if

I've caught some bug. It's like some big angry animal's trapped in my skull, kicking and clawing to break out. Sleep might help, but I can't nod off. Each time I'm close, that damn dog starts to bark. Finally, I can't take it anymore. I roll off the couch and stagger to the front door. I need a word with the neighbor.

If anything, the heat's more intense, like running up against an invisible bouncy castle and being pushed back, flailing. It takes all my strength to shoulder through it. Even my kneecaps feel sweaty.

My gate, shiny gold, solid. His gate, flimsy wire mesh, rusty.

The dog's on a short chain, cowering in the shade of the broken-down truck. It's brown, with a deep bark for its size. At my approach it barks harder, then stops when I get too close. I bare my teeth at it. Coward.

I drag myself up the shack's sagging steps and knock. Nothing. Now that the dog's shut up, I can hear something else: a TV in a back room.

Panting with the effort, I descend the steps and walk around the side of the small house. The dog has started to bark again. It's a wonder it still has a voice. It's a wonder I haven't killed it yet.

At a small window, I stop, the TV louder now. I'm about to rap on the glass when something catches my eye through a gap in the lace curtains. A woman's slim, naked back, long gingery hair. She turns to grab the remote, her red-nailed thumb jabbing at the buttons.

My stomach is a sack of sinking rocks. It's Tipi.

A blind stumble along the house, my head a fairground ride, tilting and whirling. Tipi. My Tipi. How could she? With that rough loser of a neighbor?

Just as I come around the front of the house, his door opens again. He steps onto his porch, looks around, wearing only white briefs. Seeing each other, we both freeze. His eyes bulge and his mouth forms a kid's wobbly O. He looks like he's seen a ghost.

Behind him, the door opens.

Her shapely frame wrapped in a pink sarong, Tipi steps behind him. One red-nailed hand finds his dark, muscled chest. She says something in Thai, her voice like warm honey, and leans up against him, eyes half-shut, until, spying me, they pop open.

A look of pure horror. She jumps back, eyes flying from me to him, a torrent of sharp words shooting from her mouth. A jabbing finger.

While my Thai's basic, at best, the meaning's loud and clear: What is he doing here?

A wave of cold realization crashes down on me, threatening to pull me under. My chest heaves, gasping.

Then we're all running, me for my life, Tipi and her lover, to do the job right, this time. All three of us are screaming.

I exit their gate and swing into my own, slam it shut but can't find the padlock. A mad scramble up the stairs, clumsy with panic, the pair of them closing in when a man's voice booms, first in Thai, then in English: "Stop! Police! Put your hands up!"

I'm too scared to stop, fingers clawing at the doorknob, slipping in, slamming the door, heart and lock clicking shut.

Crying now, I sink to my knees, then crawl away from the door.

Outside, men are yelling. I hear Tipi screaming. She sounds livid.

There's not a peep from the dog next door. I don't blame it.

"Mr. Ostler?" It's Detective Wutthisak.

I'm back in the TV room, on the peach sofa, a cup of tea clutched in one shaking hand.

"Are you alright, Sir? You are very white." The detective looks worried.

Am I alright? The question seems to float through my head, which, like my chest, feels awfully hollow. Am I alright? My old childhood playmate, Barry Gold, was killed in own my front garden, murdered by my scheming wife's lover, who mistook him for me, in the dark. Am I alright? No, not really.

"You are very lucky," says Detective Wutthisak.

I consider this, then nod. He's right. Just like Barry was unlucky. Wrong place, wrong time. So much of life depends on timing. Take Davey, if he'd been born later things might have turned out OK. He might have gotten married. Been proud to march in Gay Day parades. It's nice to picture - Davey, all decked out, flaming, instead of hiding away, feeling shameful.

"You need to see a doctor?" asks the detective.

I turn my head so he won't see the tears in my eyes. "Naw, I'll be fine, just need a good rest."

He nods. "I'll be in touch," he says. "We'll need you to make a full statement."

After he's gone, I stay where I am, on Tipi's peach sofa, trying to sleep. Still, I can't settle. I listen hard: where's the dog? It hasn't barked in at least an hour. Who'll look after it, now the neighbor's in jail?

Back outside, it's cooler now, everything bathed in that early-evening glow that rekindles your love for the tropics. My neighbor's shoddy gate is still unlocked, his dog still chained to that rusted truck. At my approach, its tail wags hopefully, pink tongue flopping.

"Hi Buddy." I crouch to untie it, its nose pushing against my hand, warm and insistent. "It's okay," I tell it. "You're coming home with me."

After feeding it a can of sardines I head back to the couch, the dog turning and turning before it settles by my feet. What will I name it? I nod off, smelling its fishy breath.

I haven't slept for long when the dream starts up again, me on stage, flashbulbs popping. The familiar music. Wild Child.

This time, instead of blood, shiny bubbles pour from my mouth - all rainbow-colored and floaty, loads of them, spreading out over the crowd, everyone dancing.

When I wake up, the dog's snoring at my feet. I feel strangely refreshed, and peaceful.

THE EDGE

by Richard Christian Matheson

Richard Christian Matheson is a screenwriter and author whose work has appeared in more than 150 anthologies. He is the author of the short story collections *Scars and Other Distinguishing Marks, Dystopia,* and *Zoopraxis,* as well as the novel *Created By.*

PETER YAWNED.

How long had it been? How many hours since he hadn't been bored out of his mind? He listened to the music squirting through the armrest, up the rubber tube, into his head. Stared out the window. Thought about his life. How it had all started.

The turbulence was fading and he sighed; too bad.

Clouds tumbled by and he drifted backwards.

Thirty-five years...

The doctor had ensnared his doughy head in forceps, and told Peter's mother to breathe rapidly; bear down. The struggle of Peter, slithering from between his mother's thighs, continued for hours. Then, inexplicably, stopped.

The doctor said he'd never seen anything like it. He told her Peter had suddenly stopped fighting expulsion into the world, and cooperated with the rhythmic kneading of his mother's womb, for 'no reason'.

Peter watched lights on the big, steel wing blink.

"No reason."

Absurd.

He knew better. Though decades ago, he could remember the precise second of his birth when he'd decided to stop fighting. It was no mystery to him. The whole thing had simply become predictable.

Infant years were no improvement. His mother and father would hold him in their arms and coo, but Peter could remember the sense of well-being lasting only a short while. After that, it became drab and he responded to keep his parents from feeling bad.

But it had been the same story: it just wasn't fun after a while. It was dull. Rewards were over in a moment; their capture hopeless.

As a boy, the tendency eased somewhat. Peter was popular and, after school, always had a swarm of children trailing behind, wanting to play.

But he only went along with it.

Things didn't hold his attention for any length of time. He didn't really understand it. It wasn't as if he were overly intelligent or preoccupied. It was something more fundamental. He just got bored a lot.

His mother and father became briefly concerned when he took unusual interest in the misfortunes of others. For Peter, it was the only thing that seemed to secretly reverse his descendants into the inert.

When his parents would take him to the movies, he would sit transfixed during the violent parts, eyes recording every blast and bloodstain. He would stop eating his popcorn at every scream. It hypnotized him.

Ultimately, his parents passed it off as a meaningless phase.

"After all," his father was prone to say, in Peter's defense, "Violence is part of being human."

Peter's mother would nod in agreement, though Peter didn't feel one way or the other. He just knew he liked watching pain: the only thing that seemed to lift him from feelings of ennui.

By the time he was in high school, he was on constant look-out for anything physically abusing. He was in attendance at every football game and sat as close to the front line as possible; the best view of the violence. He could hear as flesh collided, helmets and bodies battling. He could see players, when they lay on the torn ground, holding broken bodies, faces in agony.

He loved every second, and stared expectantly with each hike of the pigskin, watching for injured players. He would look intently at their hands, which would tighten in pain and clench ruined flesh.

Blood would soak grass, making it look wounded, and Peter would watch, rapt. The sufferers were carried to the side-lines or rushed into ambulances, and once they were removed, Peter always wanted to leave. The game, without injuries, was of no interest.

On his sixteenth birthday, he became concerned for himself and confessed his aberrant perspective to his father. He told him everything bored him except violence and pain.

His father laughed, saying pain was America's national pastime. He told Peter not to worry, and Peter went to the pool outside his parents' condominium, did a few laps, and tanned on the hot cement. He felt lucky, and watched in fascination when a man slipped on the decking and fell into the water.

Blood ribboned from the man's head, and he thrashed for air as Peter dashed to the pool edge to help. But instead, he just watched. The man struggled, in a pinkish swirl and gulped down water. As he looked up at Peter, eyes pleading, Peter perched, stared back. As much as Peter tried to fight it, he was consumed by excitement; pulse racing, shivers bugling through him.

As others pumped water from the man's lungs, Peter licked his bottom lip, transfixed. There was no denying it: much as good taste dictated against such obsessions, watching things brutal, violent and painful was his favorite activity.

But in time, feelings of boredom erupted more frequently. The passage of time rendered even live violence dull. His problem was getting worse.

He visited a psychiatrist and was told mental release, through vicarious imaginings was healthy. The doctor asked Peter if he'd ever done anything violent. Peter said no. The doctor said, in that case, he was just experiencing repressed anger. Peter saw him twice more, never went back.

The psychiatrist didn't understand.

No one did.

Peter knew it wasn't just imagination. It was something else; something bad. But he couldn't trace it to anything. He'd had a nice upbringing. And it happened when he'd first exited the birth canal. He knew that wasn't normal; new born babies don't get bored.

The malaise was inescapable and, indeed, even as he thought about the condition, he became bored. He tried to think about people starving to death in India, but it didn't help.

He felt lost.

By his twenty-fifth birthday, even human bloodshed no longer helped. He'd hoped something stronger might aid his outlook and headed one weekend to Mexico.

In a crowded bullring, he watched a huge, black bull, with lances buried in its shoulder, struggle against horrid pain for an hour. It helped a little. But it was feeding hunger with a bite-full.

Then, on the drive home, stuck in border traffic, it *happened*.

A VW had smashed into a Greyhound filled with commuters, and exploded into flames.

As screaming passengers watched the VW driver burning to death, Peter watched with pleased relief. He opened his window and leaned out to see the driver's flesh browning in gasoline flames, and listen to his dying screams.

Peter watched as a patrol car pulled up, and police tried to pry the driver from the tiny car. He watched as people yelled at each other to do something. He watched Spanish and English-speaking adults cover the susceptible eyes of children, close to the nightmare. He heard yelling and screaming, and watched it all with undivided attention.

For Peter, it was spectacular.

He was thrilled and found his emotions honestly moved.

Before him was life's fragility. Existence at its most extreme. He know, at that moment, what life was about.

The *edge.*

He knew from then on, if it wasn't the real thing, it was no good. Organized sports, movies, and memorized horrors wouldn't satisfy. He needed the real article. And if he got enough of it, he knew he'd never have to be bored again. Life was filled with war, misery, mutilation, disfiguring accidents, and other catastrophes ideally suited to his needs.

He'd finally found the reason to go on.

Within a week, he'd seen his fourth car accident. At night, he'd drive onto freeways and busy stretches of road, going back and forth for hours.

Looking; hunting for horror.

One night, he saw a good one.

A family of four was trying to escape an overturned station wagon. Their wretched screams were breath taking and Peter had watched as emergency workers used blowtorches, crowbars and metal-cutting saws. They worked furiously, as the family convulsed and pleaded.

It interested him for a while. But he eventually grew sluggish and drove away. Car accidents were becoming passé; the listlessness of life was engulfing him again.

On the drive home, the only way he could rescue himself from apathy was to envision a campus murder he'd read about in the paper. As he imagined a knife slicing a coed's face and torso, he perked up and enjoyed the ride home.

But it was too good to be true, and soon over.

By the weekend, nothing interested him. He'd decided to take a trip, thinking it would slow the sense of his insides sinking. He began to realize true boredom was slow death. Probably worse.

Peter was stirred from thoughts by the stewardess serving dinner.

As the 747 bounced through mountains of cloud, hungry passengers gobbled chicken and lasagne, though Peter ate without interest. The stewardess gathered the trays, and he looked out his little window, watching the sun slowly flatten; a tired eye.

A film began and he watched credits roll.

It was a comedy and he yawned.

Laughter rose.

He felt torpid; uninvolved. Nothing compelled him. Stagnation stabbed every cell. He tried to stir himself, remembering an account he'd read of an old woman who'd swallowed Drano. But it was useless.

Then, it happened.

A roar. Ripping sheet metal. A sharp tilt of the carrier's angle. An engine had failed; exploded.

Horror-stricken passengers yanked their headsets off as the jet plunged through blackness.

As it fell, flames dragged behind, and hands clutched desperately. Screams lurched like guttural beings. Faces twisted.

The jet dropped faster, and as the ground neared, passengers embraced in terror.

Peter remained in his seat, peering out the window at the burning wing and onrush community below.

He smiled.

This was going to be good.

To Kill An Arab

by Tom Vater

Tom Vater is the co-owner of Crime Wave Press, as well as the author of the novels *The Devil's Road to Kathmandu*, *The Cambodian Book of the Dead*, and *The Man With the Golden Mind*.

The Driver

IN THE SILENT AFTERNOON HEAT, AHMED HEARD THE CAR before he saw it fly across the hot asphalt that ran south along the DRÂA VALLEY, past his family property, towards to the Algerian border. The 2CV, painted black and yellow, was moving at an unlikely speed towards the crumbling but splendid Dar Hafsa, swaying across the two lane blacktop like an anxiety-ridden wasp, its modest engine crying for help.

There was nothing else to see. The stone desert stretched to the west of the road into a golden haze. To the east, Hollywood sand dunes undulated towards the low rim of a mountain range, brown and red and everything in between, shimmering on the horizon like the gateway to a promised land. The tents of the camel herders at the foot of the dunes looked deserted. The animals tethered next to the tents looked listless as only camels would.

Ahmed brushed his long hair from his face and relit his pipe for the twentieth time, trying not to singe his beard. The rich smell of hashish wafted across the rooftop of the sprawling riad, a forbidding fortress with thick ramparts and squat watch towers encapsulating a quiet courtyard ringed by open rooms.

Home.

He enjoyed his moments of 360 degree solitude. They were part of his daily rituals. On a cool day, when the desert didn't shimmer like a time portal, he could see as far as Tamegroute, the nearest town to the north. Sometimes he could hear the call to prayer wafting across the emptiness from the town's masjid. Today the desert carried no sound but that of the distressed 2CV. Nor was it a cool day.

But Ahmed was reluctant to retreat downwards into the deep shadows of the building. The car was trouble. Tourists often picked up luridly painted rentals in Marrakesh or Ouarzazate, hundreds of kilometres to the north, but they didn't drive as if trying to get away from a bank robbery. And tourists didn't rob banks in Morocco.

Now, the usually deserted road served as the race track in a scene from a vintage comedy. But neither the moment nor the fun was made to last. The car approached the building, veered off the road as if pushed by the hand of God, bouncing across the stony ravine towards the structure's rust-colored walls.

There was a sign down there, telling weary travellers that Timbuktu was fifty-two days away if one travelled by camel. That should have been clear enough.

The driver was a woman, her hijab slipped off her jet black hair, her face twisted in terror as she twisted the steering wheel of the unresponsive vehicle. Her companion, a young man with a short beard and spectacles, was as pale as a ghost. Just as the car shot out of sight, he turned his head towards the woman, his open mouth a silent scream.

The crash shook Dar Hafsa to its foundations. Ahmed dropped his pipe as he hit the floor. He felt flatter than a loaf of khobz, but his voluminous afro-style hair cushioned the impact as his head connected with the family property. A little dazed, he got up and staggered to the far side of the building which the car or its driver had chosen as its target. As he craned his neck across the riad's mud ramparts, an immense bolt of heat shot into his face. The 2CV, no longer a flying insect, exploded, throwing Ahmed onto the rooftop a second time.

A black plume of smoke rose from the side of the house into the clear blue sky. Unsure on his feet, Ahmed made his way downstairs, cursing his bad luck. All he'd wanted to do was to play guitar and get baked. Learn a new song, maybe. He wasn't living in the middle of nowhere to be attacked by flying cars.

Ahmed stepped out of the riad's central courtyard and across the sand-ridden drive and followed the building's high wall that ran parallel to the road before turning another corner.

The woman driver stood right in front of him, her face covered in blood, which slowly welled from a cut on her forehead.

She didn't say anything. She just stood and stared, sweating, crying, bleeding.

Her companion still sat in what was left of the car. The vehicle's nose had crumpled and the charred body of the passenger had had his head thrown forward through what had been the windscreen into the building's fortified wall to which it now seemed irrevocably attached. The man was definitely on his way to Jannah. The wall had withstood the assault.

She sat in silence on his makeshift bed, an unattractive collection of straw-filled mattresses, in the coolest corridor the building's inner courtyard had to offer. Ahmed let her be and retreated into the shadows, occasionally relighting his pipe. She made no attempt to leave. Time passed in silence. Ahmed was a man of few words and fewer friends. He valued his solitude. It was taking him a while to get used to her presence. In the afternoon, she started to speak.

"My name is Souhaila. My friend in the car was Mansura. We're political activists from Casa."

The girl, she wasn't more than twenty-five, hadn't bothered to pull her hijab up, which in any case, was half-burnt. She shook a little, and her eyes were not quite there.

Ahmed didn't quite know what to do. She didn't look like she needed a hospital. He concentrated on his propane cooker, trying to make tea. Tea was always good. Best in a crisis. This was a crisis.

"They've already taken my sister. Anyone protesting against the secret service making people disappear to keep the Americans happy is being kidnapped. We've heard of disappearances in Tangier and Fez. The newspapers won't run stories on political kidnappings. Mansura got hold of this list, of all the people they are arresting. Most of our friends in Tangier and Fez are on it. Every liberal activist in Morocco is on it. They want to shut us down because we fight for the law to be upheld. We are patriots. And still, they hunt us down like animals. We need to publish the list."

Ahmed handed her a glass of mint tea, loaded with sugar.

"Why did you come down here?"

She didn't answer him directly, her eyes far away on the family chameleon that hung high on the wall, nailed to a wooden board, one of his mother's creations. She'd been a great artist once.

"They took my sister. They killed Mansura. I have the list. They will kill me too if they find me here."

"You drove the car into my wall."

"They tampered with the steering and the breaks."

Ahmed was a little incredulous, but he kept his counsel.

"Someone in Tamegroute will notice the smoke. The cops will be down here. I don't have a car. I don't have a phone. There's nothing and no one else around here except for the camel herders by the dunes, waiting for tourists. They're too slow to get away from the cops."

"Are you online?"

He shook his head.

Souhaila looked haunted.

"Then all is lost."

"Where is this list?"

This time, she looked him straight in the eye.

"On a flash drive. In my ass."

Ahmed looked away, embarrassed, and grabbed his stash box.

"Do you smoke?"

She shook her head.

"Will you help me?"

Her tone broke his heart.

He poured the rest of the tea into her cup and went upstairs.

The evening was rolling in from the east. Darkness came quickly in the desert. Ahmed filled his clay pipe and lit up. He was barely through his first puff when he saw the blue lights bearing down from the north. The cops were on their way.

Souhaila was agitated.

"You will give me up."

He shook his head and waved her out of the courtyard towards the back of the building. A long row of rooms sat squat against the desert and formed a barrier against the shifting sands. He led the girl into the nearest room and pushed her through a second, smaller door into the open. The riad's pool, long dry and half-filled with desert, loomed ahead. A sun awning had once stood along its far side to protect bathers. It had tumbled into the pool and now formed a tiny tent-like structure on the sand.

"Hide under there. Hopefully they will just go away."

Ahmed left her and walked to the front of the building. The car stank of burnt flesh and gasoline. He walked around the vehicle. Mansura was charred but in one piece. Bits of black cloth stuck to his burnt skin and made tiny noises in the hot breeze. The flies were starting to move in. Ahmed hesitated for a second. Then he pulled the dead man across the seat behind the steering wheel and walked back into the building to wash his hands. A couple of predatory birds had started to turn wide circles above Dar Hafsa.

The Cop

Jamil Rizkou was the first to cross the threshold onto the property. Ahmed knew most of the officers of the Sûreté Nationale in Zagora. He knew Capitaine Rizkou best. The capitaine was sweating profusely and he was nervous. 50, overweight, drooping hair growth between nose and upper lip. He'd been handsome once. Now he looked shattered. The years could do that. The sun. The heat. The monotonous brutality of a working life in the Morrocan police force. But in Rizkou's case it was quite another reason.

"As-salāmu ʿalaykum, Ahmed. How is your mother?"

"Wa ʿalaykumu s-salām, Capitaine. I expect she is fine. She is in Casa and I am here."

Rizkou stood at a loss. Ahmed didn't move. The police chief motioned his men to move into the property. The men did so with reluctance. Orders were orders. Fear was fear.

"I don't know how you can live here, Ahmed. After what happened. This place is haunted."

"I am alone here. The way I like it. I cannot be alone in Casa. I cannot look into my mother's eyes every day."

Rizkou tried to step past Ahmed towards the building, but he couldn't quite find the courage.

"The car that crashed into your wall earlier..."

"I don't have a phone. I would have called otherwise."

"Where is the driver?"

Ahmed shrugged, "When I checked, he was sitting behind the steering wheel, burnt to a briouat. He wasn't going anywhere."

"That's not the driver. The driver was a woman."

Ahmed shrugged, wondering whether he should bother to lie, and walked into the building.

"I haven't seen a woman. There are no women here today."

The police officers had searched the obvious places and were heading back to the property's entrance. They had no urge to linger. But Rizkou blocked their way and waved at them to follow Ahmed into the courtyard. The policeman hadn't been in the house for many years and looked around with a sour expression.

"I need to find this woman. If I don't, I'll be in trouble and so will you. This woman is a terrorist. She stole a list of names of subversives, people who mean harm to our country. That list must never be published."

"She is ISIS?"

Rizkou shook his head.

"Not Islamist. Just political. Bloody leftist."

"You know I'm not political."

Rizkou couldn't take the inanity.

"Ahmed, your family has always been in politics. Bloody artists.

Ahmed fell back onto his makeshift bed.

The police man continued, "That's why what happened here happened all those years ago."

"You know that's bullshit."

Angry, Ahmed hurled the empty tea kettle at Rizkou. The metal pot bounced off the capitaine's head to the floor. Total silence pressed down on the courtyard. One of the younger cops, an out of towner, pulled his gun.

"No!" his colleagues shouted in unison.

Rizkou quickly recovered his composure, if not his respect. The capitaine usually had no compunction beating a prisoner to a pulp, but at Dar Hafsa, his powers were weak. Local people, especially the cops stayed away. Dar Hafsa had bad history.

"You're locked away in your old crumbling house, but out there the world is becoming a little more unholy every day. The past won't protect you forever. I will die one day. These men will retire. People forget. They will forget what happened at Dar Hafsa thirty years ago. I need that list. And the woman."

"I don't have them."

"She was here. I can smell her burnt clothes in here."

Ahmed was sure Rizkou was bluffing. The capitaine looked exasperated.

"The only reason why you're not on that list is because we don't report you. But the US Embassy knows who you are and that you host parties for western tourists here. The Americans know you smoke hashish with your visitors."

Ahmed laughed drily, "Yes, I had the ambassador's niece here a couple of weeks ago. Completely wasted."

"They want to shut you down. And now this. This is too big. Why did these terrorists drive their car into Dar Hafsa, the only building for miles and miles?"

Ahmed remained silent. He wasn't yet quite sure of that himself.

"We will look at the rest of the property."

A wave of tangible relief ran through Rizkou's officers who left the courtyard as quickly as possible. The entire posse circumnavigated the building like a funeral procession, with Ahmed and Rizkou forming the rear. Mansura was still behind the wheel.

They reached the pool in near darkness. A couple of officers had brought torches. One of them climbed down into the tiled rectangular space. Ahmed held his breath, but the man gave the all clear.

Souhaila had gone.

The American

Ahmed woke at dawn and found himself staring at the dead chameleon.

He'd been looking at his mother's masterpiece every morning since he'd moved back into Dar Hafsa. Its head had moved.

He grabbed his pipe and climbed the stairs to the roof. The road was clear. The heat hadn't descended yet. The sky was featureless and the dunes to the west rose movie perfect from the stony desert floor as if they'd been brushed by angels. Half-way between the dunes and the house, the silhouette of the girl stumbled forward like a black shadow uncertain of its right to exist. Souhaila half ran, half fell in his direction. But she wasn't going to reach the building. Two of Rizkou's cops had stayed behind the building overnight and now rushed to head her off.

Ahmed ran downstairs, two steps at a time and jumped up to the chameleon, smacking the board the dried up creature was nailed to. The flash drive fell from the reptile's mouth and bounced across the mud floor. Ahmed picked it up, put it in his pocket and went outside.

The two cops had Souhaila hand-cuffed. All three were leaning against the section of the outer wall that remained in the shade. Rizkou was less than thirty minutes away.

"Let her go. She's just a girl from the city. Not a terrorist. You know that."

One of the cops, Chadi, pulled a cigarette from his breast pocket and lit up. Ahmed knew him, he'd been a no-good loafer when he was younger. Much like himself.

"Still smoking hashish all day, Ahmed?"

"Only when you're not around, Chadi. Let her go."

"We'd be... I don't actually know what would happen to us if we let her go and Rizkou found out. We've got an American in Zagora. CIA we're thinking. He doesn't say, but he shouts a lot, he sweats a lot and no one likes him. All are scared. Bad times, brother."

Souhaila shivered into the wall but her eyes were resolute and boring into Ahmed. He nodded as if to himself and she relaxed. Chadi smoked. Everyone else stared across the road into the featureless void.

The cavalry from Zagora appeared on the horizon.

Getting out of the first car, Capitaine Rizkou was sweating into a freshly pressed uniform. He'd had a shave as well, not a good sign. More officers poured from three vehicles onto the roadside. The entire Zagora Sûreté Nationale was paying a visit.

Rizkou led Souhaila away from his men and started berating her. She remained mute, looked back at Ahmed once and shook her head. Rizkou shrugged into his wet shirt and walked her back.

"She won't give up the list. She's as good as dead if she doesn't."

A roar shattered the silence of the desert. A helicopter hovered above them, looking for a landing spot, turning the world into a dust storm. The cops waved towards the road. The small aircraft touched down on the tarmac. As the rotors slowed, a white man in a dark suit, accompanied by a Moroccan in plain clothes, crossed the road to meet them.

"Keep your mouth shut. Let us handle this," Rizkou snapped at Ahmed.

"Morning, gents. You found the woman, the list?"

Rizkou stepped up towards the man and shook his head.

"There's no sign of the list. She must have hidden it somewhere if she ever had it. Her companion is dead."

The American looked around disdainfully before focusing on Rizkou again.

"What's your name, son?"

Rizkou, who was roughly the same age as the American, replied politely in halting English.

"You know my name. We have met before."

The American shrugged, "Never mind the past, Rizkou. This is the future now, better be ready for it," and turned to his companion, "are we going to get full cooperation from these local sand niggers or do we have to burn this place down with everyone inside to get answers?"

The plainclothes, perhaps embarrassed, didn't answer immediately.

Ahmed understood every word the man said. He stepped into the fray.

"And what's your name?"

The American stepped forward, his chest puffed out.

"My name's T. Johnson. And the T stands for trouble. Attached to the US embassy in Rabat. And you're Ahmed, the subversive. There's a file a mile deep on you. You, your mother, your whole family. Two generations of trouble."

Ahmed spat on the ground, slowly and deliberately.

Johnson pulled his gun from his shoulder holster and pushed it into Ahmed's chest. A ripple of unease spread through the men. This was a foreigner holding gun on a local. And not just any local.

"We have a war going on, in case you piece of hippie shit haven't been watching the TV. Islamists are threatening us, are killing us. They're flying planes into our buildings. Did you know that, you ignorant fuck? And guess where these Islamists come from? They come from shitholes like this one. And if that wasn't bad enough, liberals like you are obstructing your Sûreté Nationale routing out the bad guys. So we're fighting on two fronts here. And tonight, I am closing down one of those fronts. I will shoot you dead, you piece of shit."

The American was repulsive. He smelled like a rich Rabat prostitute, but he didn't have her grace or patience. Ahmed was beginning to spin out.

Rizkou stepped in, decisively, but apparently despite himself. His right hand on his gun, he lifted his left in a calming manner. He looked almost elegant by the side of the road.

"You can't shoot this boy. Everyone here in the community knows him. Has always known him. He's never harmed anyone. You shoot him and Zagora will hate America till the end of time."

Johnson stood perfectly still for a moment, his finger itchy on the trigger. Then he lowered his gun and laughed at no one in particular.

"Hey, we're all on the same side here. We just got different methods. And we got a different urgency compared to you guys. So we'll just shoot this bitch and get moving."

Johnson winked at Ahmed. "Don't call us, we'll come and collect you if need be."

The American nodded to his Arab companion who'd unholstered his gun and now stood contemplating Souhaila. The two cops who'd been guarding her stepped away from the wall.

"You're not shooting this woman. Not on my property. Not anywhere. This isn't Texas."

"Try and stop me, Sonny, and your immunity will be gone in an instant."

Johnson raised his gun and pushed the boy out of the way.

Ahmed could smell the oil on the weapon. But he stood his ground.

"If you don't move, you'll be deaf for a week."

Rizkou stepped in again, pushed the American's arm down and calmly intoned, "Not here. Not now. It's not good."

"And why the fuck not? You guys are supposed to be cooperating. You're supposed to be the ruthless bad guys in this game. Am I getting something wrong here?"

Ahmed looked the American straight in the eye and said, in Arabic, "If you shoot me or the woman on this property, everyone here will be cursed into eternity. Your teeth will fall out and your balls will rot and you will die. Our Prophet Muhammad tells us that the evil eye, borne by jealousy or envy, is real and capable of causing great harm. The evil eye has been in this house before. Don't tempt it back."

Johnson turned to his companion. The plainclothes man had gone pale. The Zagora cops had backed off and murmured among themselves. The air between the men was special, rarefied by the crushing weight Ahmed's words carried.

The plainclothes man nodded at no one in particular, "I think it's best we leave."

"You're kidding, right? I only caught about half of that, but I got the drift."

The American raised his shoulders in mock defeat, "I thought Muslims weren't into supernatural mumbo-jumbo? You guys are as backward as you were twenty years back."

"This is my country. I decide who lives and who dies. Not you, Johnson."

"That's what you think. But times are changing. We are in accord with the highest levels of your government. And if you become an obstacle, I swear, I will shoot you dead and get another one of you in a second. Are you with the program?"

The plainclothes man took a step back and calmly eyed the foreigner.

Rizkou signalled his men to take Souhaila. She struggled against her cuffs, desperate to keep eye contact with Ahmed. As she was pushed into one of the cars, he felt as if a light had been extinguished. Johnson grinned back at Ahmed as he dropped into Rizkou's vehicle, "See you somewhere else, Sonny."

The convoy backed up, turned and was gone.

Dar Hafsa had fallen silent.

The Murder

Absorbed in a haphazard search, Ahmed eventually found the laptop he'd promised himself never to touch again, buried under dirty clothes, the testament of his life in Rabat, his failed writing career, his family.

The machine started at the press of a button. He connected Souhaila's flash drive. There was only one file on the device. He pressed Open, then sat there, absolutely still, staring at the screen, for a very long time.

Eventually he got up, unpacked his father's gun, pocketed the flash drive and headed for the road. The afternoon would bring a little traffic heading north. He'd hitch a ride. He'd done it before. Though never with as much conviction.

"If you don't let me see Souhaila, I will call every single newspaper in Rabat about Americans making Moroccans disappear in their own country."

Rizkou looked nervous.

"Keep it down, Ahmed. Do you realize I am protecting you? Stop asking about the woman. It's no use. This is bigger than us."

They sat facing each other in Rizkou's office, cups of half-drunk tea getting cold between them. The air-con and the neon strips gave the capitaine an unusually harried look.

"Us?" Ahmed intoned.

Rizkou was about to answer when Johnson walked into his office.

"What does the hippie want?"

"He wants to see the woman."

Johnson puffed up and shrugged theatrically, "So what's the problem? Show him the woman."

Rizkou deflated visibly and said to Ahmed, "I was afraid he would say that."

He got up, walked around his table, out of his office, grabbing a set of keys off a board by the stairway and headed down to the basement. To the morgue.

Ahmed had only ever seen two women naked and they'd both been foreigners. Souhaila was not just naked, laid out on a metal table. She'd been dismembered.

He turned to Johnson.

"I hope you found what you were looking for."

The huge American looked sour in the metallic light of the ceiling strips.

"Hold that thought, hippie. And get this. This is what happens when you fuck with the USA. Everyone on the list, and everyone who has the list will be killed."

Ahmed played with the flash drive in his trouser pocket, careful not to feel superior to this man. Or to vomit on the floor.

"Why did they send you here?"

Johnson grinned, "Because I was here before. During the latter period of what you call the Years of Lead. As a consultant attached to the embassy. I started your file, Sonny. And your mother's file. And your father's, that communist son of a bitch."

Ahmed started spinning out again. "What exactly are you saying, Trouble Johnson?"

"I was in your house before, Sonny. With Rizkou here who was a smaller version of himself then. I was there when your father died. I was there to kill an Arab. That's why they sent me back here, after the list. Because I know how to find subversives. Because I can close the second front in Morocco. I just need to have that list safe in my pocket."

Ahmed pulled his gun.

"Don't shoot him. Don't. It will be the end of all of us," Rizkou muttered on the far side of Souhaila's corpse.

Johnson was defiant, "Come on, hippie, shoot. You will not believe what will happen to your family if you do. My government will arrange for a show trial. Your women will be dishonoured. You will be executed. Your family name will become infamous."

Ahmed leaned into the American's taunts. He had everything under control, so far.

"I don't mind about my family name. You will tell me now what happened the night my father died."

Johnson laughed and pointed at Rizkou. "Ask him, he was there. That's why he is protecting you. But it won't last. The capitaine might be all powerful in the DRÂA VALLEY, but in the big ole world out there, he's nothing. Not even fly shit on an olive. Nothing. Just like you. And your mother."

Ahmed raised the gun in mock anger, "You're making it too easy."

Rizkou moved between them. "Don't, Ahmed, no bloodbath, please. I am trying to keep you alive."

"Why? What did you do the night my father died? What did you see? No one gets out of here alive until I know."

Rizkou took a step back, bumping into the American.

"I am your father, Ahmed."

Ahmed pulled the trigger a second before the American had time to raise the gun that had appeared in his hand. The smell of cordite filled the office.

Johnson fell back against the office wall and slid downwards. "Now you're fucked," he whispered before he passed out.

Ahmed spent the night with hands and feet shackled, alone in an air-conditioned cell. It was cold as ice. The police station murmured around him and eventually fell silent.

At dawn, Rizkou appeared in front of the cell like a tired apparition.

"The US Embassy people will be here in an hour. They are pissed. And they know we've got you. Why did you shoot him? I can't help you with this."

"What happened to my father? You're not my father."

"One of the Americans who was in on that raid on Dar Hafsa before you were born, shot your father dead. Johnson was there that night. I'm not sure whether it was him. It was a big cover-up. They were here to sell us tanks. They did some show drives near Zagora. When they heard about the raid on a communist cell in the desert, they asked to come along. We lost control of the situation. We were told by the highest office to take the blame for the killing."

"You raped my mother?"

"I tried to save her."

"By raping her?"

"The Americans wanted her dead. Taking her away from them to make her suffer, for real...it was the only way to save her life. They wouldn't let up and I couldn't fake it."

Ahmed stepped up to the steel bars separating him from his father.

"Perhaps my papa slept with my mother around the same time you dishonoured her and I am his son."

Rizkou answered, "Perhaps."

"I will kill you."

The capitaine looked away.

"I am already dead. I am a dog."

"My mother is on the list."

Rizkou started pacing.

"There's no time. If you want to save her, you have to let me go."

Rizkou swallowed hard, pulled a bunch of keys from his pocket and opened the cell.

"Go, and do what you have to. We will meet later."

Ahmed pushed past him.

"For your sake, I hope we won't."

No one stopped him on his way out. He passed Chadi who merely nodded. Outside the heat hit him with infernal strength. He walked a couple of blocks to the city's only Internet café.

He opened his email account for the first time in years and connected Souhaila's flash drive, copied the text he had written at Dar Hafsa in the morning, attached the file and addressed it to all his former colleagues. Some would have moved on by now, but many would still be manning news desks around the world or sitting in editorial meetings, sifting through emails like his one.

For a second his finger hovered over the mouse. He pressed Send.

His fate, his mother's fate, his family's fate was no longer in his hands.

The Shifting Sands

Ahmed caught a ride back to Dar Hafsa with a couple of German tourists in a beat-up Seat. He didn't invite them in. He wasn't feeling sociable. There were things that needed doing.

He recognised the car, plainclothes but black with tinted windows, hardly inauspicious, that was parked half stuck in the sand on his drive.

Rizkou was sitting in the shadow side of the courtyard, comfortable on an iron chair, his gun on his lap, hammer cocked. He wasn't in uniform. He was wearing a silk jabador, the kind grooms wore on their wedding day. On top he'd draped an equally fine djellaba.

"Have you spoken to your mother?"

"No, I don't have a phone."

"You should call her, tell her about the list. Perhaps tell her to leave the country."

"That will make her look like a terrorist to these Americans. They want their revenge for the planes flying into their tower."

Rizkou sounded frail, "They will kill her."

"Perhaps not. Do you have a phone?"

Rizkou nodded and pulled a giant smart phone from his djellaba.

"Check the news, CNN, BBC."

Rizkou didn't have to search very long.

"Moroccon heir to dissident family publishes bombshell list of democracy activists targeted by security forces under the guidance of US 'consultants'.

The capitaine leaned back into his chair and picked up his gun.

"Well done, Ahmed. In my heart I believe you are your father's son. But in a way I wish you were mine."

Rizkou picked up the gun, wedged it under his chin and pulled the trigger. His head flipped back and bits sprayed across the dead chameleon, his mother's favourite creation. The evil eye was back in the house.

Ahmed picked up his stash box and the guns of his two fathers and headed upstairs. The evening was drawing close as he packed his pipe with his best double zero. Top quality hashish from the Rif. Far in the distance, rolling down from Zagora, he could make out a convoy of flashing blue lights, moving in his direction.

WASTE MANAGEMENT

by Chris Roy

Chris Roy is the author of *Shocking Circumstances, Sharp as a Razor,* and *Her Name Is Mercie.*

H IS GRIP RELAXED THEN CLAMPED, *SNATCHED,* PUSHING WITH the other hand. A leg torqued from an uncooked chicken crackled an image in his mind, the woman's face replaced by hair in a blink.

Shoulders rolled up in soiled coveralls lingered a tense moment, heavy breathing mixed with a deep moan steaming to a sigh out of the corpse. His gloves moved, squeezed. The weight of the woman, alive, the change to a lifeless load - the *speed* of it - was a pleasantry internalized.

Lips drawn in, his thick tongue passed over them, nostrils puffing.

Mold permeated the concrete wall where it joined the pavement, service drive flooded with continuous drainage from the restaurant. The woman's body splashed onto the pavement. Ass, then hands. Legs splayed. Back to the wall. Hair where her face should be. The man watched the spot between her legs. The water darkened, spread toward his boots. His nose puffed faster.

Dishes rang from just inside the doorway. Loose rocks popped, boots coated in sludge rotated him, hard leather stretching. Solid-still as a wide cliff, bolder shifting atop, his large frame froze, head turned toward the restaurant's kitchen. He watched the light on the floor.

More dishes, tap shutting off. His nostrils ceased puffing.

Scissors tall as the building shot into motion, arms and legs swinging inky shades on the brick walls, black to gray. Heavy steel toes tread out of the dank alley, fists encased in an unknown animal hide pumped forward. Unchanging pace resounding the mass of the man that stopped in front of the truck, opened the door, stepped, swung into the driver's seat in one fluid move. Shut it.

Detonation shook the pavement, diesel engine knock-roaring to a steady thrum. The man's head appeared in the side mirror, block of pitch black with a slash of orange Illuminating his narrowed stare. The truck reversed, rumbled past the open kitchen exit, tires throwing water.

The concrete wall amplified a halting, sharp screech. The corpse at its base vanished beneath a cloud, pink exhaust thrusting through the red flash of brakes.

Setting the brake, he climbed out and grabbed the woman, strain absent from the lift. Trying not to focus on her cooling vitality, he held to the moment, the sudden charge of her life's heat, death sensed... then snuffed. An exotic battery sucked dry in a wink of plasma.

Her pants waist stretched, ass soft on knuckles, uniform collar tearing, as he hefted, tossed her into the back. The refuse compressed, enveloping her with a welcome, soft hiss.

The big diesel revved. Clutch engaged. The truck freight trained back down the alley. 'Waste Management' caught the lights towering in the plaza, the service truck accelerating into the turn. His nose puffed above the steering wheel. Gloves gripped wide. The engine cycled pings that deafened pedestrians, cab bumbling with a pulse unstoppable.

The grime on the windshield absorbed yellow-white glares cascading down at precise intervals, failed attempts to penetrate the interior. Slits of amber sitting high in the darkness inside studied the road. The direction of the next job was the man's only thought.

***

Experiences with profusions of emotion were more deeply rooted, the factual basis less reactive to changing plasticity...

Life with Mother was a single Memory. An experience continuum, with no clear divisions in time. The Memory changed from adolescence to adulthood, he knew. His days were not spent at school, on playgrounds or exploring the backyard with friends. TV was a treat limited to a single cartoon show. His days were the same Day. With the same *person*. Mother was the only person he knew, or was allowed to know.

His Day was a training schedule, learning tools and pipes and tubes and safety. Mother taught him everything he needed to be a pipe fitter.

Self-employed as a plumber, Mother could take him on jobs without his age being a hindrance. It was certain tools - the weight or oversized handles - that his ten year old hands struggled to master and kept him in the house.

"You keep saying you're ready, but you're not," she told him. "Brazing and soldering you do well enough... for the crooks at DK Flush! You'll improve your welds with the MIG on the stainless drains, too, before you ever wear one of *my* tool belts..."

His hands were hardened, burnished from the endless practice. Every morning the shop area, cleaned the day before, became littered with jigs, tube benders, and piles of scrap metal. Copper, aluminum, stainless steel and PVC intertwined with welding leads and hoses for argon/helium shielding gas.

Dog-eared service manuals took up an entire wall, floor to ceiling, on shelves fabricated with 4130 steel tubing. From these he would study diagrams and procedures until lunch. The manuals were used for his evening lessons, also, when Mother constructed jobs for him to diagnose and repair. He hated having to recite the terms for each part and tool. But it was in this way he learned to read and write.

Mother had an independent nature she was adamant about passing on to him. A work ethic disciplined with her personal philosophy.

"No wasted movements, no wasted material, no wasted time on activities that are counterproductive to providing for home or business!" they said together at breakfast, a pledge of allegiance.

His shoulders lifted, relaxed, gnawing pushed down again. It was years before he figured it out. The root of Mother's philosophy-of-family progress. The meaning for it.

It was, in reality, a psychopathy, spawn from anti-establishment principles. A cruel present from Society. Wrapped by his father with a careless bow.

And opened by his sister.

***

"Three years of battling cancer, your sister did," Mother said. "While I warred against hospitals, insurance companies, banks and the good for nothing *government...*"

She would take off her sweatband and rub her face with it, he recalled, her next words hinting at a vendetta satiated.

"Know what your father did all that time?"

His lips moved, "What did he do, Mother?"

"Made a satisfying echo. Then slowly deteriorated."

"Really? Can I do that? Like Father did?"

"No, my little Fitter. I plan better for you. He was infected, you see. And there is only one fix for that. You'll learn better, or be washed away like him and the rest."

Abandoned, in debt, Mother lost her house, and had to sell her trucks and tools to afford rent on a much smaller one... But was able to bring her daughter home, alive and free of disease.

He was only a baby then. This part of the Memory was Mother's.

Though he could envision it and feel it as his own. She retold the experience to him in different ways, a new lesson in each. Life was cruel-type lessons.

"Your sister was given a small blow up pool to swim in for her welcome home party," Mother said. "I left her to play, made sandwiches for us and a bottle for you. I stomped back to the yard and called out, 'Teresa! Let's eat, you little fish'. You know, she didn't answer."

"Why not, Mother? Was she still in the pool?" He never had a pool. Once he asked if he had to get cancer to get one. And was slapped.

"The bread floated and the bottle sank", she told him. "It was a day that life ran in reverse. So I just watched the bread float over her face and told her, 'Welcome home, little fish'."

Welcome home...

***

Government agencies. Educational and hospice systems. Social institutions... swarming with infection spewed from media outlets. Everyone with their own agenda!

Standards that put family first, make company loyalty a source of pride and community service a tradition everyone sacrifices for...

Targets of the disease on Society.

***

"Do you think the infection will come here, Mother?"
She nodded. "It will get worse."

The Memory's task wasn't fully upon him yet. Recently abated, he was able to stand and listen to the empty house, the hallway and rooms catching hollow wines from a breeze testing the integrity of termite ridden walls. Bereft of his mother's furnishings, the house bespoke a frailty, with an atmosphere of doom.

A fast food bag in the hallway crumpled. A bulbous gray rat emerged from it, nose twitching. The man's nostrils flared, eyes tracking the scavenger, then moved to the bathroom door. The stench of two decades of vagabonds penetrated everything in the tiny enclosure. Like a being of the marsh it cycled forth in lazy waves, threatening any organism that required O_2 for survival.

Mother's bedroom was the door past the bathroom. The door had been dark green once. It was missing now. The toe of his boot turned, bits of sheetrock grinding to powder.

An open nest for the soiled, infected discards of community, relegated to condemned slums for shelter...

Yet the door-less entry captured his mind, the core of the Memory, and made him enter a space where his body had never been. His toe turned, grinding. The familiar gnawing began in his stomach.

Two isn't enough, Fitter. Mother called out from the doorway, arm curled around her stomach. Voice a faint whisper never heard in the Memory, it crawled all over his skin. Throbbed in his veins.

He nodded. Straightened his back.

You will catch a late shift to pay it off, he felt her say.

Sharp teeth rendered burger wrappers underneath Mother's spectral legs. The crinkles and pops carved into the stink, rebounded, lending her substance. Determination bolstered a quavering stance. Her voice ripped at his arm hair.

Forcing his fingers closed the man kept hold of his bedroom doorway as the Memory surged, boring deeper into his innards. Demanding. Reminding.

Weeks of sickness kept her from working, from cooking and cleaning. *My entire world dismantled,* went the Memory.

The stove that boiled and sizzled Mother's meals my whole life shared no warmth. Helping her clean tools in the morning before she walked out, then again at night when she came home, routines that were my favorite...

The smell of her coveralls. The tool belt, and how she would smile every time I wiped her rolling toolbox to a shine...

If Mother goes away like Father or Teresa, there is no one, no one in the whole outside world I can work for.

And the infection will get me.

***

The man's grasp on the doorway made the sections open with wooden yawns. Excitement must have been what he felt then. A sensation that made his eyes widen, his words a stupid squeal. He had danced around in front of Mother. She had laughed.

Every day he experienced the Memory. Every day he tried to recall this particular part of it, the feeling of childish delight. And every day he failed.

All he could recall was the smell of the pizza, and that he was very happy. Then terrified.

***

He slipped out of bed, ran to the door. Looked at a notch cut high on the door frame. One he hoped to reach one day. Father's. It was the only thing he remembered about him. A game they played: Get Tall As Father. He played it every morning, determined to win.

Squinting, he studied the rough cut wood, lowering himself from toes to heels, stopping at a notch Mother cut on Easter. It marked his last growth measurement. Below it were notches that ran a foot down, darkening, stopping at the very first one over five years ago. He hated that first notch.

No way was he ever that small!

His narrow shoulders lifted, hands and teeth clenched. His frustrated expulsion zigzagged through the silent hallway. He knew he was past the Easter notch by now. He just had to be.

Carefully, he placed a wooden ruler over the crown of his head, pushing down hair. He kept his toes and heels even though tried like hell to stretch his legs, back and neck.

His hand wobbled, he pressed hard into the frame. Turned and looked. The Easter notch was bright under the end of the ruler.

He won!

Twirling the ruler above his head, he spread his feet, feeling a rush. *"Cowabunga, dude!"*

The cabinet in the bathroom clapped shut. He bit the side of his cheek, spinning, ruler hitting the corner wall above his bed behind him. He ran to his dresser and put on some shorts and a shirt. He hoped Mother didn't see him in the doorway playing Get Tall As Father in his underwear. His butt hoped so, too.

He went back to his dresser for an extra pair of shorts, just in case.

Crossing the hall he walked toward the bathroom. The door was open, Mother was looking under the sink. Her head came from underneath it, skin pale with dark pink blemishes, cheeks gaunt, accentuating eyes razor sharp with intelligence. Swiping stringy brown hair over an ear, she closed the doors back and moved over to inspect the toilet.

Lysol and iodine filled his nose, wrinkles spreading from it. He padded off the carpet onto the tile and paused, hand touching the doorknob, pulling away.

Hand on the sink, the other on the toilet lid, Mother peered around the back of the toilet. Her hand went to her chin, thumb and finger rubbing it, staring hard at the drain on the back of the toilet. Standing she put hands on waist and looked into the bowl, flushed it.

Light reflected in curious, dark brown eyes that widened, the boy turning to run back to his doorway, bathroom clicking dark on his back. Mother shut the door and forced herself to stand straight, hand pushing deep into her stomach.

He was wearing the clothes Mother wanted him to, but he still jumped back into the doorway, on the side, just in time. It was their game. She knew he was there. He knew she knew.

She knows I know that she knows... I know she I know know?

He shook his head.

Looking at her back, coveralls rustling into the living room, he crept out again to follow her into the kitchen. The doors under the sink opened. He watched her. She lowered herself, then grabbed the countertop with both hands, hard, like she was falling. But she wasn't. A moment later she sat on her boot heels looking at the plumbing. Words he wasn't allowed to say yet breathed into the cedar cabinet.

I replaced the cold water valve... a couple weeks ago? He rubbed his thumb and finger on his chin. *Did I mess up? Will that be the lesson tonight? Are we gonna do the hot water next?* He knew it worked fine, but sometimes she would take something apart just to show him how it worked or to teach him how to use a new tool.

Not the snake again... He looked at the ceiling. *Please not the snake again.*

She stuck her head in neck deep, turned up to study the drains. She nodded.

Shoot!

Mother moved to the stove, which at this time of day should be hot and busy with her cooking. He licked his lips, ran a toe up and down his calve, leaning against the wall under a framed schematic of the city's sewage and drainage systems.

Mother had been in pain for a long time, walking around holding her stomach and talking funny. She looked worse today for some reason. Always bent over. She had missed work two days in a row - he couldn't remember her ever missing a single day - so he knew she was very very sick. But too sick to cook? How would he become a man, Get As Tall As Father, if he didn't eat her cooking?

"Your father would be home and already washed, sitting at the table," she told him at least once a week, chin up and lips pursed. "That man was a Man because of my cooking. And you will be, too." He loved it when she said that.

It had been a strange morning. Not just because Mother was not herself. The entire house felt weird. His toes slid off his leg, bumped the floor.

The kitchen… there's nothing cooking! He smacked a palm on his forehead.

The stove was bare, empty of meat and vegetables that sizzled and held his attention, every day, while he waited on his TV show to come on. He went to Mother, intending to ask if she was okay.

She looked up from her seat at the kitchen table, noticed his expression and put on a smile. "Don't worry, my little Fitter. I know you're hungry. There's food coming. I ordered take out. Pizza. Can you believe it?"

Her words tapered to a slight wheeze that froze. Bottom lip in her mouth, her head hovered above the table top. The surface fogged below her nose. A hand moved from her side to tap the chair next to hers. The back of it was taller than the other three chairs.

The legs skid over the floor, he stepped on the brace under the seat and plopped into Father's chair. He tried hard not to twist around and look at the back of the chair, at the top of the backrest he knew was far above his head.

"You've never had pizza." She looked at him, chin resting on her arm. "You will be able to join the Mutant Ninja Turtles now."

"They are *Teenage* Mutant Ninja Turtles, Mother. I'm only ten." His hair brushed the back of the chair, sliding in the wide seat. His glower traced the tall backrest, mouth thinning, opening. Facing her, he said, "I mean, Michelangelo might be okay with me joining. You know? Because of the pizza, you know? I…"

"It's okay, Fitter. I want you to enjoy the pizza and not worry about me. I'm not feeling well. But I'll get better. This may be the only time we order take out. You know I don't like people coming to our home."

"Yes, Mother. I know."

He could remember only one other person coming to their house. A friend of hers, she said. A woman that stayed in Mother's room all night. He determined she left out of the window; she had to know he was awake and waiting to look at her again. Mother won their game that night.

Take out! PIZZA!

And someone will have to come here and bring it to the door, just like on the Ninja Turtles…

They both looked out the window next to the table. Thick trees flanking a large yard absorbed the delivery car's downshifts, growling Dodge Charger turning into the driveway. Shifted forward with an abrupt stop. Behind the tinted windshield the driver sat, hands on wheel. His face turned, looking around the yard, at the side of the house. The seat appeared to move left, right, his enormous shoulders sliding into view, head and arms still inside. He bumped the door all the way open and stood, pulled on a red and white hat.

It was the biggest man the boy had ever seen. He was even bigger than Shredder, when Shredder got mad fighting Master Splinter. The man saw them watching him and smiled. Lifted a big flat box, red and white like his hat, one hand holding it.

A pizza box! With PIZZA in it!

The boy couldn't believe it. He forgot about his mother being sick. Ran to open the door.

"Hey little buddy. Your mom here?" The man said, dark eyes darting over him.

"Mother is here. Father doesn't live here anymore. Mother said he washed away after my sister died. You are very tall. How tall are you? I'll win Get Tall As Father one day. But maybe not get as tall as you."

"Just you and Mom, right?"

The smell of the pizza made him forget what he was saying. He swallowed. Held his hands up for the box. "Yes. Mother is in the kitchen. Her stomach hurts."

The man put a hand on his head, held the box out of reach and pushed by him into the house.

A tall man.

Pizza...

A very tall man.

Holding a pizza!

The enticing smell began to play with his sense of taste, forming promises, wrecking reason. Tongue bouncing from one corner of his mouth to the other, he experienced a new kind of confidence: the certainty that a single bite of pizza would make him grow enough to win several notches.

Mother was right...

He could join the Ninja Turtles!

With a glassy stare he stumbled over the door step. Looked up at the very tall man. A quick smile stretched his gape. He balanced on a line in the tiles, toes placed precisely in front of the other, spinning his *nunchaku*. A ninja warrior on the edge of a roof - street far below packed with people and cars - following the wisp of pizza smell that led him home after another day of fighting the Foot.

"You just hang on to that, Bunny."

The very tall man's voice was very loud. The boy stopped by the stove and watched his mother push at the man's arm. He leaned over and grabbed her under the arms. Her boots skid on the floor. He hugged her tight. "Hop for me, bunny. I'm not going to hurt you much." He laughed. "You might just hurt *me* - you're breaking my heart right presently."

She yanked her arm from under his and waved behind his back. He didn't know what she wanted, but knew from her face she was very scared.

The boy had expected to taste the joys of pizza for the first time. A sickness ripped the dream away, burrowing into his guts. Spread all through him. Shaking, he experienced terror for the first time. Saliva gushed into his mouth. He swallowed and gagged on the strong taste of salt. His shaking became visible.

His mother flapped her hand again. He ran down the hallway to his room. Jumped onto the bed. Slipped off, ran back and shut his door.

***

He listened to them fighting. Mother's boots knocked into the table. Service manuals scattered across the linoleum, one banging into the stove. Anger burst from the man, a contained shout that deepened.

He launched out of bed, another explosion of fright splaying fingers, the horrid gurgle from Mother pushing him up on his toes. The man kept saying, "Come on, bunny. Come on…"

His eyes went to his toy bins, to the darkness under his bed. It hurt to breathe. Wooden legs barked over the floor, wall booming, stopping the table. The gurgle peaked to a squeal that broke with the cheap wood.

Instinct encouraged his legs. He ran back to the end of the hall, stopped at the corner. Mother was under the man. Smashed table under him. The man pinned her arms over her head, pressed to the floor. Eyes squeezed tight, her mouth was working, though he couldn't hear her over the man.

"Come on, bunny. Come on…"

The Memory's voices filled his head with such volume his vision blurred. The front of his body felt as if an air compressor had burst onto him, inches away, high pressure hose lashing.

The top of her coveralls tore out from under the man, monstrous arm snatching straight out. The man released the top and shoved his hand back under and down.

Fingers locked apart, lip disappearing into his mouth, he watched Mother's head rock back. Tendons standing up from a thin neck. Her bare upper chest rippled. The underside of her arms, overdeveloped from her profession, corded strained deformities.

"Come on, bunny. Come on," the man insisted. *"Hop!"*

The table crumpled another level down, wide black denim scrubbed across her blue legs. Breathing labored, his drum shaped torso rolled to the side. Hand sliding out. His eyes widened behind it. Blood ran down its length.

Mother's face relaxed, the man standing. He looked down at her, dark rivulets dripping. Her breasts moved up and down, fast, her cheeks sucked in, blew out. Wiping hands on his pants, the man pulled on the front of his crotch and fled out the front door.

***

The pressure stabbing, burning, in the middle of his chest finally stopped. Hand pressed to his ribs, his eyes roved the wrecked kitchen. Confoundment replaced indecision as he tracked the blood from his mother's privates into the hallway.

She came out of her room with something in her hands. She wore a flannel shirt. Light from his open bedroom cut across her arms, hips. She was leaning over though he could still see a dark spot on the front of her ruined coveralls.

"I want you to come in here and help me." She held up a white box, their first aid kit. Looked up from under her brows behind it. He nodded and ran to her, followed into the bathroom.

Mother turned the light on and knelt in front of the sink. She stared at the toilet. The plastic box ticked on the shiny tiles, snapped open. He squatted close to her side. He remembered feeling a feverish heat as his leg touched hers, and her coveralls were drenched in acidic sweat.

Her face was a dream now, features lost in a blurry past. He possessed no photographs to refresh her loving eyes and smile. The only clear image of Mother's face was when she opened the first aid kit. A profile of her setting her jaw, faint lines budding from compressed eyes. It was an expression he knew well; she wore it every time she had a tool in hand.

His countenance changed with the reliving. He stared at the dark hole in the hallway...

Blink, looking at him, she held the lid open. As he got older he saw the first aid kit less. Mother, only twice; he held gauze while she tapped gashes on her legs. He expected the same task. The rolls, bottles, tubes and packets where not what came into view when she opened the lid completely.

It was pink. He thought it was a ham. Like Mother would have on the kitchen counter before putting it in the stove.

Then its legs kicked out.

He had never seen a baby. Flinching, he glanced at her then stepped close, head and shoulders blocking light. Its mouth opened, and he knew, then, it was a tiny person. His eyes swept over it, finding hands, small as his thumbs. He wanted to know... so many things.

Mother turned over a long knife next to the kit, veins standing up from her grip. Chrome shimmered, the long serrated steel sliding under an arm. The point stabbed into plastic. Tiny hand hidden behind a thumb and finger, pinched, the smell of the little arm sliced - *plop* shooting over Mother's knee - remained more vivid than the spasms that ripped through the little pink form.

"He said he wouldn't try that again." She tossed the arm into the toilet. He jumped away, water splashing. She sawed into the other arm. "But he's a liar, just like your father. I knew it. Made the decision. Know how I knew?" She didn't look up. Threw the other arm in.

He stared into the bowl. Tendrils of red followed the arms down into the drain, staining the water. "No. Mother? How did you know? That that very tall man was a liar?"

"He was infected. So is this." Her chin pointed. "Flush that."

"Yes, Mother."

***

She refused to open her mouth.

The man's head tilted, nostrils puffing. He shook an aerosol can, squinting. Rocks popped under boots darkened and creased with use, threads stretching. He sprang into a turn, legs like columns of stone thudding oversized Red Wings across the service drive to the Waste Management truck.

The utility box opened, gloved hand slipped in and retrieved an item. The compartment clicked shut. He returned to the girl.

Fright - pure and intense - pushed out her stare as he approached. He stopped close enough that she felt his breath, a foul, hot gas shrouding the cold tears on her cheeks. He held up a red straw and inserted it into the can without error. In a blink his leather palm rammed into her forehead, immobilizing her face. Vision swimming, she could no longer see him. She held her breath as the pressure of his increased, eyelids squeezed tight. She felt the straw enter, slide into her throat.

He pulled it out.

Her scream was muffled by industrial grade adhesive, dull yellow bubbles of foam glue roiling from lips working to eject it.

The man stood back. Slipped the can in a pocket of his coveralls. Light gathered on his irises, wicked pulse matching his puffing nose. He caressed her throat, thumb rubbing over the spiking carotids.

Her back rose sharply, locking into a stiff arch. Eyes stuck wide. The moment passed with his nostrils flared. A tremble passed over his skin. He squeezed, hard.

Blink.

His hand relaxed. The other clenched into a fist. A single blow to her chest made her pulse return. Her eyes closed.

He tore her loose and dropped her on the pavement next to a storm drain. The backs of her hands stuck to the service exit, foam blooming from pink skin like an exotic display at a high end art gallery.

From a sheath strapped to his leg he pulled a long pry bar. Opened the storm drain and looked in. The walls of the new office complex took on a hollow rush of water. He tapped the pry bar on the thick iron lid next to his boot. Straightened, pivoted to assess the infected target.

The girl folded her arms, violent shaking commandeering the muscles in her jaw, shoulders and legs. Hair plastered to one cheek, it matched the tones in the foam mounded on her lips, now hardened.

He struck her. The pry bar bit deep into her pelvis, shattering it. Her eyes shot open. The alley hummed with anguish, her throat swelling. He dropped the tool. The steel rang inches from her ear. Core consumed by fire of mortal trauma, her obscured awareness turned completely black. The man loomed, a mountain of darkness, boots creaking on the sides of her ruined hips.

Mucus sprayed as he sat down, can of adhesive once more in hand. He inspected the straw. Slid it deep into her nose and sprayed. His nostrils puffed in sync with the arteries in her neck, bulging under his thumb.

The violent shaking in her limbs became thrashing, spine jerking side to side. Her hands, dwarfed by his gloved grip, pushed at the can. Limited edition peep toes dug for purchase on the wet pavement behind him, heels grinding down.

Pry bar in hand, standing, he tossed the can into the drain. Then struck her again. Like a boxer finishing a punch drill, fists thundering into a heavy bag, the man battered her hips. Before she suffocated, her heart failed again. The rain of steel continued, eating away the joints.

His eyes moved to her shoulders. His arms adjusted, freakish mass swinging the tool hard. The roof above turned a deep violet, dusk passing into night.

The pace of the strikes never slowed. Slight turn of his boots, and he pounded away at her neck. He stopped as if completing a precise count. Sheathed his tool and stomped down on her chest. Gloved hands wound through her long hair and pulled up. Skin elongated. *Snatch,* cartilage, vertebrae crackling. Tossed it into the drain. Grabbed an arm.

Limbs washed away, he kicked the torso. Log rolled it over to the runoff of Spring rain. Picked it up, squishing, her bloody clothes rubbing on him, adding to the spatter layered up and down his old coveralls. Turning her vertical, he dropped the corpse into the drain.

***

From the wall next to the service exit, another girl watched. The tips of her fingers picked at the hard glue that bound her to the faux granite. Her lips wrinkled and spasmed, instinct fighting the poisonous invasion adhering to the soft tissue of her mouth and throat.

She kept looking to her right. A glob of hard foam mounted her head to the wall, though if she strained she could glimpse the door knob; she knew, any moment now, the manager would step out for a smoke and...

Save me! Oh my motherfuck, save me! Sasha... what just happened to Sasha? Oh my fucking Jesus!

Her eyes darted left. Rolled back as searing pain ripped up her arms, down her back. The man sacked her over a shoulder and looked around. He blurred into a fast walk.

The girl's legs flopped against him, urine running off her heels, squiggly patterns darkening the pavement behind the truck.

Printed in Great Britain
by Amazon

36349382R00151